W. L. Barrie started writing seriously in her late forties. She has worked and lived in Scotland all her life.

This is her debut novel.

CASSIE

W.L. Barrie

CASSIE

AUSTIN & MACAULEY

A CIP catalogue record for this title is
available from the British Library.

ISBN 978 1 905609 48 2

www.austinmacauley.com

First Published (2009)
Austin & Macauley Publishers Ltd.
25 Canada Square
Canary Wharf
London
E14 5LB

Printed & Bound in Great Britain

DEDICATION

To my mother with love and thanks for her certainty that "one" day this book would be published.

ACKNOWLEDGEMENTS

I would like to thank all those in Austin and Macauley for their help and guidance throughout the production of this book, namely Annette Longman, David Calvert, Cheryl Lidster, Frances Moldaschl and Tara Nicholls.

My deepest gratitude to the following for all their encouragement - the Barrie family, Peter, Rowena, James and Fiona, the late Sheila Moulton, Barbara Todd and Carol and Keith Weaver.

My very special thanks go to Jenny Dunlap for her unstinting enthusiasm and belief in this book. I hope she will now realise how much I appreciated it. I am also eternally grateful to her for her unwavering encouragement, massive support, suggestions and for all her hard work and time she gave to reading the drafts as they came hot off the printer. I am indebted to her.

Finally to my brother Peter, many thanks for apparently taking on the role of my publicist. I truly appreciate it.

Chapter 1

It was only when her hand was completely cold that Charles reluctantly let it go. The nurse helped him to his feet and said gently that he could return later if he wished. He didn't. Lizzie wasn't there any more, so why stay.

Turning abruptly, he left the room, but after only a few steps, stopped and stared out of the long casement window, his mind a blank, registering nothing. Through the mist of grief engulfing him, the sight of the beautifully manicured lawns of Westpark Hospital angered him. He struggled for control as realisation dawned. Only a few hours ago he had been happier than he had ever known and now, now his life was in tatters. All this was beyond his comprehension. Women didn't die in childbirth any more, or so he had thought. Why Lizzie?

He tried to focus on something. If he had believed in God or any omnipotence, he would have had something to rail against, but all he had was emptiness.

A harassed young doctor careered around the corner and upon seeing Charles stopped to offer his condolences on the death of – his daughter, then quickly corrected himself and said wife. *An easy mistake*, thought Charles graciously for he was nearly twenty-five years older than Lizzie but it did slightly hurt him upon hearing it said out loud. The doctor quickly proceeded to inform him how his daughter was. Charles was trying to assimilate all the facts and failing miserably. His wife of only months was dead and he was now a father for the first time at forty-eight. It was a ridiculous age to become a father.

"Adoption," said Charles not looking away from the window.

"I beg your pardon."

"I can't look after a baby. She would be better off with someone who wants her. I certainly don't," said Charles and started to walk away.

The nurse glanced at the doctor, indicating not to pursue this but he was oblivious to the nurse's glare and caught up with Charles. "No, you don't mean that. Would you not like to see your daughter first before you decide? She is remarkable, a little fighter."

Charles continued walking. "A death certificate," he uttered. "Surely I require one?"

The doctor nodded. "Yes, yes of course, but…" Charles stopped and turning, glowered at the doctor.

The doctor gave a nervous swallow. "I'll get it straight away."

The nurse ushered Charles into the office and offered him the obligatory cup of tea. He declined. Pacing the room, he felt lost and alone and at that moment wished he could join Lizzie.

"Lord Emerson, I think you should go home and decide about your daughter then," said the nurse kindly. "We can keep her here and look after her until you get sorted out."

Charles, seemingly unaware of her, didn't reply.

The doctor entered the room and handed him the death certificate.

"I'm so terribly sorry. Is there anything I can do just now, perhaps telephone someone for you, anything at all?" There was no response from Charles who continued staring blankly ahead. "You will see on the certificate the condition is called *pre-eclampsia*. At the moment we are still unclear as to what triggers the condition. I will try my best to explain to you what is known so far, but if you care to, we can leave discussion of that nature for a time you feel would be more appropriate."

Charles nodded and after shaking hands with them both, left the stifling atmosphere of the room.

Chapter 2

The next few weeks went by in a blur for Charles. Life had no purpose now. His sister, Lydia Maitland, a wealthy widow of a successful Q.C. in London, who was five years older, had insisted upon staying with him.

"Charles, you really are going to have to do something about your daughter. What on earth would Lizzie think you were doing not having her here? It's ridiculous behaviour," said Lydia.

Charles felt his hackles rise. "Firstly, it is none of your business and she is not neglected; the nurses are there. Secondly, Lizzie would have known I was right in wanting the child to be adopted by people who would care for her," retorted Charles.

"Poppy-cock, Charles. She belongs here. This is her home," persisted Lydia. "And surely." She hesitated. "Surely by now you have a name for your daughter."

Charles glared at Lydia and with mounting anger shouted, "God damn it I will not tolerate your interference any longer. Why don't you go back to your own home and leave me alone!" With that he stormed out of the house.

He had no idea where he was going and bellowing at his sister was certainly not his usual behaviour, but she was being so persistent. Of course, deep down he knew she was right, but why could she not leave well alone? Surely she knew he hadn't the first clue about children, let alone babies. However, she had said something that struck a cord when she had asked if Lizzie would have wanted this. He had to make a decision and make it soon.

His walking took him to the lake. He was sorely tempted to continue walking until it completely covered him and all his worries would then end, but out of the corner of his eye he saw someone.

"What the devil do you think you are doing? This is private land," Charles shouted.

"I'm terribly sorry," said a young woman struggling to her feet while trying to gather up her bits and pieces. "Oh, it's you Lord Emerson, I'm sorry, I didn't realise I wasn't allowed here."

Charles reached her. "Kate? Kate Brewster?"

"Yes," answered Kate.

"I'm so very sorry," said Charles. "I shouldn't have spoken to you in that way, I was just a little startled at seeing someone. I'm sorry, very sorry," he repeated.

"Not at all," said Kate as she flicked her long dark hair away from her eyes and began to sort out her belongings. Her jeans, which appeared to have been sprayed onto her lithe frame, were all paint splattered and her T-shirt had a tear in it. Kate knew she was looking a mess but felt that Lord Emerson wasn't really seeing her or at least, that is what she hoped!

Feeling slightly embarrassed she said, "I know I shouldn't be here, but it's such a lovely place to paint so I do come here very occasionally. You did say I could, but I won't again, I promise." Charles was suddenly aware of Kate and realised she had been speaking to him. "Sorry, what did you say?"

"I won't come here again."

"No, no, absolutely come here whenever you like, it was just me," Charles said, apologetically.

He glanced down at her easel. Lizzie had also painted. How long ago that all seemed. She had been so talented and loved painting the surrounding landscape especially excelling at capturing the different colours and moods of the sky. In the deep recesses of his mind Charles seemed to remember that Lizzie had encouraged Kate.

"You're good, Kate, really very good. Is this something you are hoping to do when you leave school, take up art?" enquired Charles.

"I've actually been away from school for two years," smiled Kate.

"Ah," said Charles. "I'm a little out of touch."

"My dream is to go to London but at the moment I can't afford to go to Art College so this is just for pleasure. I'm building up a portfolio in the hope that one day I will get there and I will, I know I will," said Kate, with the confidence of youth. "I work at Wilsons in the village. It's boring and awful and I hate it but Mum needs the money so what's left over pays for my paints and things, and for saving for London."

"I see," said Charles, who had only been listening in a slightly distracted way.

"By the way, I was really sorry about Lizz…" Kate stopped and corrected herself, "…about Lady Emerson. We all were, all in the village I mean." Kate felt she was *'rabbiting on'* as she would say, but couldn't stop herself.

The villagers liked and respected Lord Emerson and considered him a good landlord. His father had been very different, disliked by most who knew him and especially those who had worked for him or had the misfortune to stay on his land. He was a bully and a tyrant but things changed when Charles inherited the estate. He had been appalled at what he saw of his father's legacy and immediately set about improving living conditions in the farm cottages and houses.

Kate continued. "I thought I would see you with your baby, wheeling her about, showing her the estate."

Charles continued staring into space. "Sorry, Kate, you were saying?"

"I was just wondering when we would get to see your daughter. We don't even know her name."

"Her name," repeated Charles, realising he had never called his daughter by name. "Oh…" he hesitated. "Her name, her name is Cassandra. Don't know why, but Lizzie wanted it."

"What a gorgeous name," enthused Kate. "Who does she look like, you or Lady Emerson?

To his enormous shame Charles felt tears prick his eyes and he quickly turned away.

"Oh, Lord Emerson, I'm sorry, I didn't mean to remind you of everything that's happened. I'm sorry, truly I am," said Kate apologetically.

"I haven't seen her Kate. I don't know who she looks like," he answered gruffly staring out to the lake.

Blinking, he turned and looked at Kate. "I've no idea what to do." He bent down and touched the grass. It was dry so he sat down. "I know what you're thinking. What kind of man hasn't even seen his daughter?" Kate knelt beside him, saying nothing. He sighed. "I feel exhausted and the truth is I don't think I want her, but I'm tormented by what to do."

Absentmindedly, he ran his hands through his wavy hair. "I haven't gone to see her because... because, oh perhaps because I'm terrified that she looks like Lizzie; or that I'll hate her."

"Why would you hate her or not want her?" asked Kate in amazement.

"Because she killed her mother. The only woman I've loved." He rested his head in his hand, not saying anything for some moments. He looked up at Kate. "If she hadn't been born then Lizzie would still be here. We'd grow old together. I'm scared I'll hate my daughter for the rest of my life because she denied me that happiness." Sighing, he said, "I can't believe I've just said that. I really can't."

Kate contemplated what she'd heard. "May I say something?"

Charles looked at her. "Of course."

"Nothing in life is certain and as we don't know how long we're here for, you can't even say you'd have grown old together."

"True, all true," agreed Charles wearily.

"Lady Emerson has left you the most precious gift she could – your daughter. Do you really think she'd want Cassandra looked after by strangers? Lady Emerson," Charles interrupted. "Please, she was your friend, call her Lizzie."

"All right," said Kate. All I was going to say was Lizzie and I painted here together sometimes and chatted about this and that. She was so positive about everything. There were no grey areas with her and she was thrilled about being pregnant, talked about the baby incessantly." Kate smiled. "She even wondered if one day he or she would paint here as well."

Charles looked intently at Kate. "Did she? I know what you're trying to say and in some ways I can understand, but I feel totally and utterly out of my depth at the thought of looking after a baby. Surely you can see she would have a better chance with parents who would love her?"

"She has a father who will love her and a mother who has given her a beautiful name which if she were adopted would, in every likelihood, be changed. Cassandra doesn't deserve that, does she? I don't think Lizzie does either."

Kate wondered if she'd said too much but Charles just shook his head. "I suppose not."

They continued talking and every time Charles spoke of '*the baby*', Kate gently reminded him of her name so that by the end of their chat he talked of his daughter, Cassandra, with a warmth and affection that surprised him. He looked at his watch and realised that they had been chatting for nearly two hours. "Kate I think – no I definitely have made my decision." He paused. "Although I'm a little unsure if this decision is for better or for worse! But I **will** bring Cassandra home." The words 'Cassandra' and 'home' sounded so right now.

Kate smiled at him delighted at this news.

Then with a degree of effort, after having sat on the grass for so long, he struggled to his feet and helped Kate up. "Well, I'd better go back and break the news," said Charles.

"One thing," said Kate as she bent to pick up her holdall. "Who do you have to look after her? Have you got a nanny? They're not that easy to get and you have to be absolutely sure you get the right person for Cassie!"

"Cassie!" repeated Charles. "Oh, I rather like that, I really do; a nickname, Cassie, a lovely idea." He smiled then his brow furrowed. "A nanny, you say!"

Charles was a little perplexed at this suggestion and thought for a moment or two. "Will I require a nanny do you think? I hadn't really thought. I mean will Mrs. Pearson not manage with my help? Possibly not. Neither of us is getting any younger. I'll have to think this out a little better," said Charles, more to himself than Kate. "I suppose I was just a little carried away."

Charles stared out over the lake hoping for inspiration when after a little while he suddenly let out a mighty "Yes!" and all at once looked ten years younger. He had what he thought was a brilliant idea. Kate jumped in response but smiled back. All of a sudden he looked so different.

"Kate, you said you hate working at Wilsons. Have you any experience of children?" Not waiting for a reply, he continued. "Sorry, of course you do, you have a younger brother don't you? I seem to remember you hauling him around the village bossing him constantly as only an older sister can!" A vision of his own childhood with Lydia springing to his mind. "Well Kate, how do you fancy becoming Cassie's nanny?" asked Charles anxiously.

Kate looked at him, incredulity spreading across her face. "I'm not sure. I mean I don't have any experience or anything. Looking after a little brother is a different thing and I really want to go to Art School. That's all I've ever wanted: to go to Art School.

Charles looked thoughtful. "I know, but I'm sure you'd be excellent with Cassie and it would only be on a temporary basis. Just until I get sorted."

Kate smiled shyly. "If you're sure, but just until you can get a full-time nanny."

"Splendid," said a relieved Charles, "and whatever you get at Wilsons I will increase so you can save for Art School. I would need you to live in but there is plenty of room and your only duties would be to look after Cassie. Oh, and there is a summer-house, well more of a shed, well whatever, it can be your studio for your painting but we can sort all that out once you see it and if you like it. Do you have to give notice to your employer?" asked Charles.

"Not really," said Kate with a slightly guilty look upon her face.

"Come on, Kate. We have to do this properly. We can go and see the chap at Wilsons tomorrow. Right now I had better go and make peace with my sister. I'll telephone you later this evening and make arrangements for tomorrow and Kate, thank you, thank you so very, very much."

"No problem," smiled Kate. Hitching her canvas bag onto her shoulder and picking up her easel, she asked, "I'm going that way, if that's okay?" pointing to the right.

Charles gave a slight smile and nodded. "Of course. See you tomorrow."

Lydia glanced out of the drawing room window and saw Charles stride purposefully across the lawn. His back was straight and his face had lost the haunted look of the past weeks. He looked, if not happy, then at least more at peace with himself. She went to the door to meet him.

"Lydia, I don't know how to apologise," said Charles, kissing her on the cheek. "My behaviour today was appalling, not only today of course. I am well aware of how I've been of late. However, things will change, in fact things are about to change," he said, ushering a very surprised Lydia into the drawing room. "Fancy a drink before lunch? I know I could do with one. Gin and tonic?"

Lydia was grappling with this change but replied, "Mmm that would be lovely."

As Charles was organising the drinks he continued. "You **are** right. My daughter does need to be with me. I will telephone the hospital and arrange to bring her home. However, firstly, I had better check with Mrs. Pearson and Benson that they will help but I am sure they will, and no doubt you will be putting your oar in at regular intervals," he said looking at her with affection.

"Charles, what on earth has brought about this transformation?" asked a puzzled Lydia.

"It's Kate's idea," said Charles, handing Lydia her drink.

"Kate?" repeated Lydia, "Who's Kate?"

Charles then realised that he was making no sense at all. So, sitting down on the sofa beside Lydia, he told her what happened at the lake; explained his fears and how Kate appeared to have had answers for each one.

Lydia vaguely knew Kate Brewster but had felt a fleeting twinge of irritation that Charles appeared to have unburdened himself to this girl and not her. Quickly she decided she shouldn't care, and should just be grateful in the change that had taken place in her brother, in what seemed only to be a matter of hours. She realised Charles was still speaking.

"Sorry, Charles what were you saying?"

"How different this will be. How very different from what Lizzie and I planned. We had so many plans and now..." his sentence tailed off. Sighing, he stood up and went over to the window. Shoulders hunched, he looked out over the lawn, trying to envisage a little girl running around or learning to ride her first bicycle, playing with her toys. Nothing came into his mind.

Silently, Lydia was beside him. She put her hand on his arm, staring ahead as if trying to form her own pictures. "We'll all help. In our own way we'll help and support you in every way we can. We'll make Lizzie proud."

Charles continued staring ahead but squeezed her arm and said quietly. "Thank you."

Sensing his desolation, Lydia tried to change the mood. "However, there is much to be done," she said, briskly. "Babies require a huge amount of all sorts of paraphernalia."

Looking down at her he gave a soft smile. "We need to make a list." And before long there were about five pages of '*list*'.

Charles looked at the pages before him and wondered if Lizzie had had any inkling that something was wrong with her. She had not wanted to decorate a room for a nursery or buy any baby clothes. He remembered he thought this was a little strange but she had said she thought it was bad luck and felt it was something that all three of them should choose. Charles was a little unsure as to what input Cassie would have on this but decided he would adhere to what had, after all, been Lizzie's wishes, and so he would take Cassie shopping with him. First thing to do, therefore, was to collect Cassie from the hospital. His quiet and ordered life was about to be shattered, and rather unexpectedly, he was decidedly pleased!

He insisted on going into the hospital to collect Cassie on his own and very graciously, Lydia allowed him to do that, having owned up to having popped into the hospital occasionally to see her niece without Charles's knowledge.

Charles could not remember ever having held a baby before. Suddenly he became a little nervous at the prospect. What if he dropped her? What if she took one look at him and screamed the place down? What if, what if, what if. As the enormity of the situation hit him he resolved to deal with each 'what if' as it arose, so taking a deep breath, he strode into the hospital exuding a confidence he certainly was not feeling.

Nurse Smyth, the nurse who had been so kind to him when Lizzie had died, was waiting for him. She led him into the nursery and there, in the corner crib, with a little teddy bear beside her, was his daughter. He felt badly that he hadn't thought to bring a toy and experienced a moment of jealousy that her first toy was not from him but he vowed he'd make it up to her, he really would.

He sat down on the edge of the chair and, trying not to look too scared, tentatively waited to hold his daughter for the first time.

Charles was totally unprepared for the feelings that flooded over him as he held her in his arms. This was total and absolute unconditional love. He was completely besotted and totally oblivious to Nurse Smyth in the room. He kissed his daughter on the forehead and cuddled her close to him. "Oh Lizzie, she's beautiful, so beautiful," he said quietly. Tears welled up in his eyes. "How I so wish…" He stopped as Cassie gripped his finger tightly with a strength he did not know babies possessed, and looked up at him intently as if to say, don't you ever leave me like this again. He smiled and stroking her cheek, promised his complete and utter devotion to her. In the space of a moment she had him literally, round her little finger, and with pleasure he realised that is where he would be happy to remain for the rest of his life.

Nurse Smyth looked at this scene and felt a lump rising in her throat. She had never given up hope that Lord Emerson would come round to the idea of looking after his daughter but today she had been quite taken aback by the transformation in him. It was wonderful to see.

Charles said to Cassie, "I'm going to take you home now. You have a doting aunt, nanny and assortment of other people who are going to help us. So, let's go." Charles, well aware that his imagination was taking grip, fancied that Cassie smiled at him and nodded. Others, with a slightly more cynical opinion, would say this was caused by 'wind', but Charles knew better!

"Thank you so much for your patience and understanding and for taking such good care of my daughter. I am extremely grateful to you," said Charles to Nurse Smyth.

"Please bring Cassandra back occasionally to see us. We've all grown very fond of her," said Nurse Smyth, tickling Cassie under the chin. Cassie gurgled back contentedly. She was going home!

"Of course we'll be back," said Charles. "Now young lady, home we go." He carried her tenderly to the car and, with great care, placed her in the car seat. This manoeuvre being supervised by Nurse Smyth and of course Lydia, his new child-care expert! When Cassie was eventually secured in her seat and after further thanks, Charles got into the car and, with a wave, drove off.

On their way home Charles remembered he had still not registered Cassie's birth so thought now would be as good a time as any. Remembering Lizzie's words he told Lydia to stay put, and picking up his daughter marched proudly into the registrars.

Back in the car Charles handed Lydia the birth certificate and when she read it she was completely taken aback. Normally a person in control of any emotion, she was unprepared for what she saw and tears pricked her eyes as she smiled at the names before her; Cassandra Elizabeth Lydia Emerson.

"Thank you, Charles. You didn't need to do that."

"Well I didn't for a moment imagine that you'd be keeping in the background of your niece's upbringing. And as you are likely to be, and I very much hope you will be, an important influence in her life, it seemed appropriate she bear your name." He smiled at Lydia. "It's also my way of saying thank you."

Charles continued, "I thought I would get Cassie christened in the chapel. If we do it soon, she might even be able to wear our mother's christening robe. We were both christened there and I think it would be a nice tradition to continue."

Lydia looked in slight disbelief at what she was hearing. "Don't look at me like that," smiled Charles, "I know belief is not my strong suit, but I still think I'd like to do it. Before you say anything, would you agree to be Cassie's godmother, that way you can make sure her religious upbringing is being suitably attended to!"

"I'd be thrilled Charles, thank you so much for asking," beamed Lydia.

They continued the journey home in silence, each immersed in their own thoughts. Charles felt tension mount and his stomach started to knot at the irrevocable decision he had made and, once again, doubts surfaced as to his ability to care for his daughter. *Oh Lizzie, have I done the right thing? I so wish I knew*, he wondered.

Chapter 3

Leaving the nursery door ajar, Charles tiptoed across the hall and went into what had been Lizzie's dressing room. It felt stuffy but if he tried hard enough he thought he could still smell her perfume and therefore for that reason was loathed to open the window that might banish her smell. But he did. He then opened the wardrobe and upon seeing her clothes all the memories of the first time they had met tumbled out.

It seemed a lifetime ago that Lizzie had arrived, seemingly from nowhere, but in answer to an advertisement he had placed in the local newsagent requesting help with typing, as his usual typist in the village had got married and left the area.

Charles, an author specialising in history, had been writing a history of the village of Harrington. He was reasonably successful but it was more a hobby rather than a career, as money was never a concern for he was lucky, the estate generated all the income he required.

Despite Lydia's numerous match-making attempts over the years Charles had never married and although the ladies found him attractive, he was always off on one or other of his research projects for his books, so he never found the time for romance. He felt that he was now too set in his ways and had resigned himself to becoming a crusty old bachelor, being looked after by Mrs. Pearson and Benson, his butler and general factotum!

Lizzie had answered his advertisement and arrived for her interview on a ramshackle old bicycle, dressed in sandals and long flowing garb. She only required beads in her hair to complete the picture of the sixties hippy. He had, however, been instantly bewitched by her. She had big soft brown eyes and titian-coloured hair that flowed in ringlets down to her waist. She was softly spoken and had a somewhat ethereal quality about her. She quite mesmerised him.

She told him she was a struggling painter and was nearly twenty-two years old. She had no family apart from a distant cousin in New Zealand as her parents and sister had been killed in a car crash some years previously said, he remembered, without emotion. She was looking for work and at the moment lived with some others in Chornley Lodge, about ten miles away. Charles remembered that at the time he had thought the Lodge had been boarded up and then realised she and the others were probably squatting. She did not tell him so but said the others she lived with were also artists of some kind or another but naturally they required money to live on, hence her reply to his advertisement.

Every instinct told Charles not to employ her but he could not stop himself from saying, 'When can you start?' The look of joy on her face was reward enough for him.

He remembered that on the days she came to work he had got out of bed with a spring in his step and took particular care with his appearance – a ridiculous thing to do. At that time he was prone to perform critical appraisals in front of the mirror. Age forty-six, nearly forty-seven, height 6'1, slim (ish), with just the beginnings of a slight paunch but nothing too drastic and when he pulled his stomach in, nothing at all. His grey-blue eyes required the assistance of reading glasses and his dark wavy hair, which had a mind of its own, possibly through lack of any visit to the barber – had streaks of grey through it, but there was no hint of baldness for which he felt quite cheered. He remembered that although he felt he kept in good shape his clothes left a great deal to be desired. Typical bachelor attire; baggy cords, baggy cardigans, in fact if he were honest, a fairly unkempt picture. When he eventually got round to buying new clothes, and even went as far as going to the barber, Lizzie had grinned knowingly and asked if there was a new lady in his life. Charles smiled at these recollections. How happy he had been then. Like some love-struck teenager.

Lizzie had typed draft after draft and on occasions he found himself changing things in the text just to make sure she had to come back.

Charles thought back to when he realised he had fallen in love with her.

She had arrived one day on her bike, as usual, but with red-rimmed eyes and a pale drawn expression on her face. He had been his usual solicitous self and was genuinely alarmed by her appearance. She had brushed off his concern with slight irritation and said she had a cold. Charles, not usually perceptive in the ways of women, suspected this to be a lie. Lizzie eventually confessed she was miserable because her boyfriend, who was also an artist, had won a scholarship to work with some famous artist in California and was leaving soon and would be away for at least six months. Lizzie was heartbroken. Charles had a different emotion. Joy would be perhaps too strong a word but he certainly wasn't unhappy at this news.

She had been in floods of tears, so what was a man to do? Offer comfort. Charles knew that was what was required, but he was a little unsure what to offer. It soon became obvious, even to Charles, that she had to wipe her eyes so he gave her his handkerchief and then tentatively put his arm around her shoulders whereupon she let out a heart-wrenching sob and flung herself at his chest. He had hoped she would not notice that his heart was pounding completely out of control as he put his other arm around her and tried to soothe her, meanwhile thanking whomever had arranged for David, her boyfriend, to go away and so delightfully far away!

Charles remembered having been thrilled, which he knew was wrong when Lizzie was so distraught, but if he were being honest, thrilled is what he felt. Alarmingly, another emotion came into force as he held her in his arms, for he realised how much she had come to mean to him, how much he needed her for he could not remember life before her and could not envisage life without her.

He had held her, and allowing sense to prevail for once, realised that this was perhaps not the time to declare his feelings to her, so had just basked in the knowledge that at this moment she needed him and was in his arms. However the moment of exquisite pleasure had sadly come to an abrupt halt with the arrival of Mrs. Pearson bearing the tray with coffee for elevenses. Charles remembered it all as if it were yesterday.

Dear Mrs. Pearson – although she was only slightly older than he, that is what he always called her. He could not remember her first name although thought it was something like Euphemia but she was always Mrs. Pearson or, if he was taking a liberty, Mrs. P.

She had been employed as a maid in his father's time and was now Housekeeper/Cook. She lived in the east wing of the house and, as she did not have any close relatives, this was her home and as far as Charles was concerned it would be for as long as she wished.

She had looked the same all the years he had known her. Charles decided her height must be about five foot two or so, fairly plump with permanently pink cheeks and hazel eyes. She had grey hair, only ever seen in a bun, usually with wisps struggling to escape, but she always wore a crisp white apron over her grey dress and sensible black shoes with laces, which were worn summer or winter. He had suggested this uniform was not necessary but she had looked with such horror and had muttered something about falling standards that Charles decided she could wear whatever she liked and she did; unchanged for the last thirty years.

With a sigh, Charles returned to the present and resumed the task of looking through Lizzie's things.

The only thing of monetary value that Lizzie had brought with her to Harrington Hall was a ring. Charles now wore it on his little finger, next to his signet ring. Charles knew the type of ring had a name but he could not for the life of him remember what it was. It was gold, with the appearance of two or three rings twisted together and had five small diamonds stuck to each of the strands. Lizzie had always worn it and one day Cassie would wear it; he was only the temporary custodian.

He looked through Lizzie's clothes, they looked as if they had come from another era and he wondered if even the charity shops would want them. He decided to put them in a trunk in the attic for Cassie to look at when she was older. Charles was unsure if he was being entirely sensible about this but could not bring himself to give them away – not yet.

Being a methodical man, Charles accomplished the task quickly; with everything neatly sorted out. There were only two boxes to go through.

The first was a smallish box and in it a sketch pad and some letters. He flicked through the sketchpad. She had been so talented and his heart ached at what she might have achieved but knew that one day Cassie would love to see it. The letters he left in the box where they were. He would not read them. That he felt would have been an intrusion. Perhaps when Cassie was older she may wish to see them. He placed them in the trunk.

He looked at his watch, nearly time for tea. He opened the second box. There was tissue paper protecting what was beneath. He then realised what it was: Lizzie's wedding dress. He touched the silken material, recalling the first time he had touched it and how radiant Lizzie had looked on that day. How happy he had been.

With a last lingering look Charles tucked the tissue paper around the dress, and putting the lid back on the box, tried to shut out the painful memories of the past.

Chapter 4

The years sped by with Cassie growing more adorable and wonderful by the moment, according to her father at least! To Charles, Cassie could do no wrong and it was left to Lydia to admonish her niece when the occasion demanded. Charles reflected on the various events in Cassie's life. He knew there was nothing he could have done to save Lizzie and was lucky Cassie had survived. A shiver went through his very being at that thought. His life was now one of such inexplicable joy that he could not bear to think of what might have been.

After the first anniversary of Lizzie's death Charles felt emotionally stronger. The intense feelings of loss had now started to slowly recede and he could now talk about Lizzie without feeling he would break in two and Harrington Hall, which previously he had felt no great emotion for had, with Cassie's presence, become a warm and welcoming home.

When Cassie was nearly five, changes were taking place at The Hall. Kate and Robert, his Assistant Estate Manager, had decided to get married. Cassie was beside herself with excitement – she was going to be a flower-girl!

After an evening in London, Charles came home the next morning to find the house in a state of great excitement at the thought of the forthcoming marriage and with Cassie bouncing up and down bursting to tell Charles her news.

"Daddy, Daddy," she said as Charles scooped her up into his arms.

"Hello, my little princess, what's the excitement?"

"I'm going to be a flower-girl. Kate and Robert are going to get married. He asked her last night, and she's got a ring and its lovely." All this tumbled out in a breathless rush.

Kate, running down the stairs, came to a sudden halt as she realised Cassie had broken the news that she herself was going to tell him. She blushed a little as Charles smiled over Cassie's head at her.

"Well, well, Kate, you're a dark horse." He was aware Kate was looking at him, not knowing if he was pleased or what he was thinking.

Charles put Cassie down and, walking over to Kate, put his arms around her, kissed her and said, "Don't look so worried, I'm delighted, absolutely delighted but wait till I see that Assistant Estate Manager of mine; now I know why he always seemed incapable of using the telephone!" Kate blushed.

"Now Kate, we need to celebrate. What are your plans?" asked Charles.

Before Kate could reply Cassie piped up, "They aren't doing anything, Daddy, because they're saving to get married."

Kate glowered at Cassie who completely ignored her. "That's not fair is it, Daddy?"

Charles agreed it wasn't fair.

Kate interjected before Cassie would feel the need to continue. "We, Robert and I, just thought we'd have something really quiet. We don't want loads of people or a party or anything."

"Oh, that's not fair, I love parties," moaned Cassie.

"Well, I don't," retorted Kate.

"All right Kate, it's your engagement but may I make a suggestion?" enquired Charles. "How would you like to have dinner here, in the dining room, the full works and invite anyone you'd like?"

Kate had never eaten a meal there. It was used infrequently and only for formal occasions of which Charles was not particularly fond.

"Are you sure?" asked Kate who was a little taken aback at the suggestion. "I'd love to, but the people I'd like to invite are all here," smiled Kate, a little shyly.

"Does that mean me as well? Would I get to stay up?" demanded Cassie, delighted that Kate seemed to be changing her mind about the party.

"Who would you like at your party Kate?" asked Charles gently. "And you," smiling down at Cassie, "Not a word."

"Well," said Kate, "I'd like it to be just you, Mum of course, Benson, Mrs. Pearson, Lydia and Robert of course. I think that's all, I can't think of anyone else," grinned Kate.

"Yes you can, please yes you can, you've got to have me," said Cassie tearfully.

Kate bent down and picked Cassie up. "I'm sorry, just teasing. Of course you'll be with us. You'll be the most important person there." Cassie beamed and Kate looked across to Charles in the hope he would agree.

Cassie's big violet eyes looked at her father, pleading with him to say yes.

Charles smiled, "Yes Cassie, it wouldn't be the same without you but you'll have to have excellent table manners and behave like a lady. Do you promise?"

"Yes, yes, I will, I'll be excellently behaved, I really, really will, and, I'll put on my best dress as well," replied Cassie, thrilled at the idea of her first grown-up dinner party.

"I have an idea," said Charles. "I will cook the meal for you all, perhaps with a little help from Mrs. P. and Lydia can help. We will cook and serve you all. Yes, that's what we'll do. I'm actually not too bad in the kitchen. You all look after me, it's my turn to show you my appreciation." Charles stopped and grinned. "On second thoughts, perhaps we should wait until you've tasted my meal before you decide if its appreciation I'm showing. When would you like this gourmet extravaganza, Kate?"

"Gosh, I don't know, whenever you like would be lovely, you say, please."

"Friday is always nice for a 'do' don't you think. Today's Wednesday so I've two days to conjure up some fabulous menu, so is Friday fine?" asked Charles.

Kate just nodded, a little astonished by the proceedings said, "Lovely, thank you."

Charles laughed. "Kate, it isn't often we have you speechless, I must do surprise dinners more often. Had you better not check with your fiancé? And when you see him, tell him I want to see him, no hurry, just as soon as he can! I will now leave you ladies to discuss weddings and all that involves. I have some work to do, menus to think up, that sort of thing," and off he went to his study.

Kate looked at him as he walked across the hall. She thought he was one of the nicest and kindest men she had ever known. She looked down at Cassie, who was bursting with excitement. "Come on you, let's go upstairs."

Cassie would not stop asking questions which Kate tried to answer as patiently as she could. She explained the wedding ceremony; the '*I do*' bits and such like but then added, "It may not be the same in the Registry Office." Cassie wanted to know what that was and thought it did not sound nearly as good as being in a church with the music playing and everyone dressed up.

Kate secretly agreed with Cassie. She would have loved a church wedding but she and Robert could not afford anything grand. They didn't want to ask his parents for money and she couldn't ask her mother so she was pretending this is what they wanted. Kate tried to explain to Cassie that she could still dress up but there wouldn't be music and Kate wouldn't be in a fancy wedding dress or anything like that but that it would still be lovely. Cassie looked at her with horror. This was all going terribly wrong. Kate tried to further explain about not having anyone to 'give her away'. This was because her Dad was dead, her brother John was in Australia and she didn't have any uncles and so all in all this was the best plan.

Cassie thought to herself, *this stinks*, but did not say it out loud because she knew she'd get a row.

"What kind of dress are you going to wear?" asked Cassie, who after such initial excitement was feeling a bit down about everything. She suspected Kate wasn't really telling the truth, for whenever Kate had read her stories about brides she had always gone all gooey and said she wanted a fancy wedding; fancy cars, fancy dress, fancy everything and now here she was changing her mind. It was very, very weird.

Kate hadn't been paying attention. "Sorry, what were you saying?"

"Your dress, what is it going to be like?" asked Cassie again.

Cassie got more than she bargained for, when Kate looked at her she promptly burst into tears. Cassie was unsure what she had done. She didn't think she'd done anything wrong but wasn't really sure. "I'm sorry Kate, please don't cry. Will I get Daddy for you?"

Kate who was struggling for control looked down at Cassie who was looking anxiously back at her. "It's nothing you've done, I promise. I have a headache that's all. Do you mind going to play on your own for a little while. I'll lie down and then come and play once my headache has gone. Is that a plan?" asked Kate.

Cassie nodded just wanting to escape. "Feel better soon," said Cassie and blew Kate a kiss.

Kate blew one back and the moment Cassie closed the door, started crying again.

Cassie wandered downstairs. She'd speak to her Daddy. He'd know what to do.

She went to his study door; was just about to go in when she remembered she was meant to knock.

"Come in," answered Charles looking up from his desk. "Hello Princess, what's wrong? You're looking very glum."

Cassie went over and stood beside Charles. "Kate's crying. She's not getting married in a church, she's not having a lovely dress and she's not got anyone to put her away."

"Put her away?" enquired Charles a little baffled by the apparent change in Cassie's mood.

"You know," said Cassie with a hint of exasperation, she doesn't have a Daddy or uncles or anyone to put her away."

"Ah, give her away," said Charles at last gleaning what Cassie was talking about.

"She's not having a bride's dress or anything like that, it's going to be just ordinary in an office or something, it won't be so good will it?" said Cassie.

"Perhaps that is what Kate wants," said Charles.

"She's pretending, I know she is; anyway, I wouldn't," replied Cassie. "I want the biggest wedding and lovely cars and lovely yummy food and dancing and parties, that's what I want."

Charles smiled at this thought.

"Will you promise me something?" asked Charles. "It's got to be our secret that you've told me this, do you think you can keep this a secret?"

"I can, I can do that, I really will, I'll not tell anyone," promised Cassie earnestly.

"All right, off you go and I'll see what I can do," said Charles. "I'll let you know, but don't tell Kate, promise?"

"Cross my heart," replied Cassie.

"Good girl. Now run along and I'll think up a plan," smiled Charles. "And Cassie, well done for telling me."

Cassie beamed back at her father.

It didn't take Charles too long to realise what was going through Kate's mind – money. Robert was a careful chap who would think of this as unnecessary expense. To his mind it would be like frittering away hard-earned money. The fact that it was his wedding would not come into the equation. Charles was trying to work out how he could solve this without Kate and Robert thinking they were indebted to him in any way.

He then had what he thought was an inspirational idea. The other thought he had was about Kate being 'put away' as Cassie called it. These thoughts were careering around his mind when there was another knock on the door.

"Come in," said Charles who looked up as Robert arrived.

Charles stood up and went round the desk to shake hands with Robert. "My congratulations, Robert. You have chosen a lovely girl, you could not have chosen better."

"Thank you," replied Robert smiling broadly. "And I have to say I agree."

Charles then told Robert about his plan for their engagement party. Robert was a little unsure but Charles pointed out that the ladies had thought this was an excellent idea.

Charles then handed Robert an envelope. "This is a little something for you for your forthcoming marriage and as a thank you for all you do on the estate."

Robert had no idea what was in the envelope but thanked him all the same.

"When are you thinking of getting married?" asked Charles.

"We're going to see when the Registry Office can take us, sometime May/June time I would think," said Robert.

Charles feigned surprise, "Is that what you two want? I thought Kate would want a church wedding."

Robert hesitated before replying, "We have other priorities and, well I suppose I think it would be unnecessary expense."

Charles leant forward. "Robert, hopefully this will be the one and only time you do this. My experience of women is zero, I would be the first to agree, but even I know their wedding day is meant to be something special. If you want a small wedding, why not use the chapel on the estate? We can get thirty or so in there with no problem and then, and this would be my present to you both, wedding breakfast here and a dance in the Great Hall. What do you say?"

Robert looked at Charles, "I don't really know, do you think that is what Kate would like?"

"If you'd like the chapel, I would be delighted. That is what it's there for; to be used," smiled Charles. "I suspect I may be right about this, women like a bit of a fuss, especially on their wedding day."

Robert stood up. "I'll speak to Kate but that sounds lovely. Thank you, thank you very much, and thank you for Friday."

"Wait till you've eaten before you say anything about Friday," laughed Charles. "Oh, remember to be all dressed up, the ladies will be and Cassie, most certainly."

"We can't let the ladies down then," said Robert.

He went off to find Kate. She was coming down the stairs as he came out of Charles's study. He beckoned her over to the front door.

"Kate," he whispered, "Let's see what's in here." Looking at her he asked anxiously, "Are you all right?"

"Headache, all the excitement I expect," said Kate.

They went off round to the side of the house for a little bit of privacy whereupon Robert opened the envelope. He went ashen. "Good God, look at this Kate."

In the envelope was a cheque for £5,000. "Why did he give you that?" asked Kate.

Robert was grappling with the amount. He stammered, "He said it was partly a wedding present and partly for doing well on the estate." Robert was still reeling a little from the shock. "Oh, he also asked if we want to use the chapel for our wedding and as a present, excluding this I suppose, we can have the wedding breakfast here and then a dance at night in the Great Hall."

Kate just stared open-mouthed at Robert and burst into tears. "Really, did he say that? Oh Robert what did you say? Did you say yes?"

Robert realised Kate was delighted at this news. "Well, I said I'd speak to you, but yes, I thought we'd love that. Was it all right to say that?"

Kate just nodded and flung her arms around Robert who silently thanked Charles for his undisputed wisdom in this matter.

"I'll have to go back to work. Should I go back in and thank him? What do you think?" asked Robert.

"I'll go, and we'll also thank him together in another way," said Kate.

"What way is that?" asked Robert.

"I haven't a clue as yet," replied Kate. "All I know is I want to do something to thank him for not only this wonderful cheque, but for everything else he's done for us. You know something Robert, he's the second most wonderful man I know."

Robert smiled and asked with slight hesitation, "I am rather assuming I'm the first?"

"Of course," said Kate kissing him again.

"Work, I have to get back to work. See you later," said Robert and looking round to make sure no one would hear said, "I love you!"

"Sorry what did you say?" asked Kate loudly.

Robert smiled and blew a kiss.

Kate went back into the house. She could not remember having felt happier in her entire life. Her headache had miraculously vanished and she felt on top of the world. Now that she was getting married in the chapel she pondered whether she could ask Charles to give her away but was concerned he might think her too presumptuous. She was debating this when Charles emerged from his study, deep in thought. He looked up at Kate and smiled. He then eyed her up and down. Would it be suitable? Kate, who was starting to feel a little disconcerted, wondered what was he doing?

"Ah Kate, I won't be a moment, would you have a minute to chat? I've just got to find Lydia, won't be a tick, wait in the study, won't be long," said Charles rushing off.

Charles found Lydia in the flower room doing a rather spectacular floral arrangement.

"That's very good, where is that for?" enquired Charles.

"Drawing room, I thought we might have some champers to celebrate Kate and Robert's engagement. What do you think?" asked Lydia.

"Splendid, absolutely splendid," said Charles. "When are we doing that?"

"Lunchtime I thought; just us. Mrs. Pearson is doing wonders in the canapé department ably assisted by Cassie of course," smiled Lydia. "Cassie seemed to be in the depths of despair, something to do with Kate but she said it was a secret, so I've no idea what it's all about."

"Ah," said Charles. "It's because of Kate I need your thoughts – can we have a quick chat?" Lydia nodded continuing with her arrangement. "Money, as you can imagine, is a little tight for the youngsters, so I have suggested they marry in the chapel; they were going to go to the Registry Office – can you believe it?"

"Oh, that's a lovely idea, well done Charles," said Lydia.

"Anyway, I was wondering; what do you think of her wearing our mother's wedding dress. Kate's about the same height and Margaret could take in bits or let out bits or whatever one does. What do you think? Should we ask if she'd like to?"

"I think she would really suit it, but you know Kate, she may be overwhelmed by all this. Tread warily. There is another alternative." Lydia pondered for a moment and Charles could not make up his mind whether she was thinking where to put the next stem or just thinking. "Margaret could perhaps make one." Lydia paused, "No that may not be quite so satisfactory. I suppose the material would be expensive and then that would be tricky trying to give them money for material. All right, good plan, ask Kate but the only reservation I have is Cassie. If she gets married she may want to wear it," said Lydia.

"You may be surprised to know that I had actually thought of that," said Charles. "My only stipulation for wearing mother's dress will be that it is not radically altered. Is that fair do you think?"

"Very bright, Charles. You sometimes surprise me, you really do."

"Praise indeed," said Charles. Kate's in my study, I'll go and have a chat. Does she know about the champers at lunchtime?"

"No," said Lydia, "Let's meet in the drawing room at 12.45. I'll find Robert and tell him. It will just be Margaret, Benson, Mrs. P. and us.

"Sounds good to me," said Charles and went off to speak to Kate.

Charles entered the study to find Kate gazing out the window. She jumped when he came in.

"Sorry Kate, I didn't mean to startle you. Wedding plans whizzing through your mind?"

Kate turned round. She looked so serious. "I don't know how to even begin to thank you for firstly the cheque, the chapel, the…" but Kate was stopped by Charles.

Taking her hands he said, "Kate, please don't say anything. There are two people I had always hoped would one day get married in the chapel. You must know who they are, you and of course Cassie. My two favourite young ladies." He smiled at her with affection.

"Kate, this is your home. There is nothing that would give me greater pleasure than for your marriage to take place in the chapel. There is something else," continued Charles. Kate looked at him with a slight feeling of apprehension, she wondered if there was something wrong for he seemed to hesitate.

Kate looked expectantly at Charles who smiled at her. "Kate, if you are happy to be married in the chapel," Kate nodded. "I wondered if, well what I am trying to say is, I would be honoured to give you away. I know that John can't make it and I could be the surrogate dad or uncle, call me what you will, that is if you hadn't thought of anyone else."

Kate's eyes filled with tears and before she knew what she'd done, she flung her arms around his neck.

"Is that a yes, then?" laughed Charles.

"Gosh, sorry, I'm sorry," said Kate blushing trying to untangle herself.

"Don't be, don't be at all," replied Charles and hugged her once more.

Kate wiped her eyes. "Are you sure? I can't think of anyone I'd like more."

"Excellent, I really hoped you would ask, sorry for jumping in first, but I would be thrilled, I really would, and lastly, now don't look so worried. Lydia and I were wondering if you haven't organised a wedding dress or anything whether you would care to try on our mother's. You've seen it, cream lacy thing, I can't describe it properly as I have amply demonstrated, but if you wish, go and have a look with Lydia and your Mum and see what you think."

Kate just stared unblinkingly at him and promptly burst into tears yet again. She couldn't take all this in at once.

Charles put his arm around her. "I think its going to be a fabulous day, I really do. Kate, I have an enormous amount to thank you for, never forget that. Without you..." he paused. "I will always, always be indebted to you for making me see sense about Cassie. You must know that and to have you married in the chapel will make me very, very happy, not to mention a certain young lady!" Kate wiped her eyes and smiled at him.

Looking at the clock Charles realised that it was nearly time for the celebrations. "Kate, trust me on this, but I think you should go upstairs, powder your nose or whatever the expression is nowadays and rush downstairs again." Kate looked a little surprised at this suggestion but Charles, ushering her out of the room, said, "Hurry, two minutes and back down here."

Kate raced upstairs to her room and on looking at the mirror decided Charles had a point; she looked a bit red-eyed. She applied some make-up and raced downstairs again. Charles was at the door looking pointedly at his watch.

"Well done, Kate. Your transformation has been accomplished in under two minutes. You look fab, as you say!" Offering his arm he escorted her to the drawing room.

He opened the door for Kate who was surprised to hear everyone shout "Surprise!" and Robert came forward.

Taking Kate's hand Robert said, "I didn't know about this either, I promise."

"We decided to have a little drink at lunchtime. We couldn't wait until Friday," said Lydia leaning forward to kiss Kate.

Cassie was jumping about excitedly. "I did the nibbley things, the cannabis things."

Mrs. Pearson looked aghast at Cassie's mispronouncing. "Canapés, Cassie. Not cannabis."

Everyone laughed. Cassie who was a little unsure as to what was so funny decided to laugh as well. Everyone looked happy, especially Kate. She looked over to her father. Charles winked at her. She grinned at him as she ran over to where he was standing. He bent down and whispered just one word, "Fixed!" and winked again. She tried to wink back which came out as a blink, but beamed at him and ran over to Kate.

Kate took Cassie's hand, "Sorry I was Miss Grumpy earlier, forgive me?"

Cassie gave her a big kiss. Then there was a loud 'pop'. Cassie went over to Benson and looked up expectantly. Smiling he looked over to Charles who indicated a thimbleful amount.

"Be careful with the glass and don't drink until we all say 'cheers' all right?" said Benson.

Cassie nodded as she watched her glass be topped up with lemonade and then bubble and fizz. She decided there and then, she loved parties and when she was older she'd have a party every day!

Charles went over to Benson, "Have we all got a glass? Mrs. Pearson, where's your glass?" Smiling, he shook his head, for in Mrs. Pearson's mind the impropriety of the situation was just too much. "Just this once, for Kate, for me?" he tried to win her over with what he hoped she'd think of as boyish charm.

"Very well, Master Charles, just this once," responded Mrs. Pearson through pursed lips.

"When are we saying the 'cheers' word?" asked Cassie, who could not contain herself any longer. The bubbles were going up her nose and tickling her. This was lovely, so much nicer than ordinary juice she decided.

Charles smiled at her and mouthed, "One minute, okay!" Cassie nodded back.

"Ladies and Gentlemen, I would like to propose a toast to Kate and Robert. Robert, you are a lucky, lucky man but I think you know that." Robert nodded and put his arm around Kate. Charles continued, "Robert I feel very lucky having you here on the estate, not only because of your work, but also because it means that Kate, if not here at The Hall, will be close by.

Kate, the affection I feel for you cannot, I think, be adequately described. I have so much, so very much to thank you for." A cough from Lydia prompted Charles to bring his speech to a close.

"But, before I am told off for going on too long," he said, looking pointedly at Lydia, "I would like to propose a toast for the future happiness of Kate and Robert."

"Kate and Robert," they all chorused.

"Is it cheers nearly yet?" asked Cassie.

Charles smiled at her and raising his glass said, "Cheers."

Two days later the 'dinner party' took place. Mrs. Pearson, initially aghast at Charles's suggestion of his doing the cooking and waiting upon her, had eventually calmed down and the evening had been voted a resounding success, thanks in part, to the amount of sherry she had consumed whilst over-seeing operations in the kitchen.

Cassie had risen to the occasion beautifully. Her manners had been impeccable, sitting up in her chair, back straight, like a little princess. She saw Charles at one juncture, with his elbow resting on the table and informed him in, one might suspect, a voice impersonating Lydia, that, "All joints on the table would be carved!" Charles, suitably chastened, apologised.

All too soon, it was time for Cassie to go to bed. She had had a lovely time but although she hated to admit it, was quite pleased to be going to bed but before she went upstairs she went round everyone and kissed them goodnight. Charles surveyed the scene. Cassie was surrounded by love from all the people at the table and they had all contributed something to her development. He hoped Lizzie would approve of their daughter's upbringing. He felt sure she would.

Cassie, although exhausted, was trying to put off the inevitable as she chatted to Benson. Charles went over and said, "Say, goodnight, **now**."

He picked Cassie up, who with expansive kisses being blown to everyone around the table, eventually waved goodnight as they disappeared from the room.

Chapter 5

The next few weeks passed in a frenzy of activity associated with the forthcoming wedding. Charles was bemused by most of what was happening and was delighted that everything seemed to be taken out of his hands apart from signing cheques. He had no idea that caterers, florists, in fact anyone, it seemed, who was remotely connected with weddings seemed so expensive. He did not begrudge Kate this for one moment but it did make him think he should make contingency plans for his finances for when it was Cassie's turn.

Cassie was having a wonderful time and would regale Charles at bath-time of the day's events.

"Daddy," asked Cassie earnestly as she set about washing her leg. "Where will Kate live if she's not living here?"

"She and Robert will live together in Robert's house," said Charles.

"But why can't they stay here, its much bigger and that would be better, then I would see her every day," replied Cassie.

"Well, when people get married they like to be on their own for some of the time," said Charles, "and anyway, you don't need a nanny anymore, you'll be off to school soon."

"How long do I have to go to school for?" asked Cassie.

"About twelve or thirteen years," answered Charles preoccupied in the task of retrieving items of clothing Cassie had abandoned en-route to the bath and was unaware of the look of horror on Cassie's face. "But, you'll see Kate lots, you know you will." Charles stooped to pick up a sock. "You know, Cassie, I would very much appreciate it if you could fold your clothes yourself instead of scattering them everywhere. Do you think you could try please?"

"I'll try," replied Cassie a little distracted in her reply. "Kate could teach me."

"You'll love school, you really will. Now, what about the dress Mrs. Brewster's making for you? Is it nice," asked Charles, desperately trying to change the subject.

"I'm not allowed to tell you about it," said Cassie. "I'm like Kate, she's not telling Robert. She says it's bad luck, so I'm not telling you either, so there."

"Right you are, I will look forward to seeing it on the day. Out you get." Lifting Cassie up he dangled her over the bath and shook her. "Drip dry time. Gosh, you're soon going to be too heavy for that my lady."

Once Cassie was dried she ran through to her room and said, "Come through Daddy but shut your eyes. I'm going to show you something."

Charles did as he was told. "Open them now." Cassie looked at him smiling proudly. "I've done this picture for Kate and Robert for their house. It's my present for them. Do you like it? Please say you do. If you do, will you frame it? Please, please, please," said Cassie jumping up and down excitedly.

Charles picked up the picture, aware that Cassie was looking at him intently. It was a picture of Kate and Robert, and even at Cassie's tender age, she had, amazingly, managed to capture their likeness. He was astounded. "It is excellent, really excellent; you're incredibly clever."

Cassie thought she was going to burst she was so pleased. She had been planning it since she had known about the wedding.

Kate now let Cassie into her studio, which Charles had refurbished for her when she arrived at The Hall. To Cassie it was like being allowed into Aladdin's Cave, It was wonderful, all the different colours of paints and Kate's work propped up around the walls. When Kate was working on something, she'd give Cassie either paints or crayons to keep her quiet and it worked. Cassie was completely absorbed in what she was doing.

Charles remembered Kate had said how talented Cassie was but he had thought she was saying this to please Cassie and hadn't really paid much attention. Looking at this, it was definite; Cassie had indeed inherited her mother's talent.

"Do you know what we are going to do?" asked Charles. Cassie shook her head. "**I'm** not going to put it in a frame." Cassie's face fell. He smiled. "I think this is so good, absolutely wonderful in fact, that when you have completely finished it we are going into town to get it framed properly. That's how good I think it is." Cassie let out a yelp of delight.

"Really, are we really going to do that?" asked an ecstatic Cassie.

"We certainly are, then we are going to find the nicest paper and get ribbons and bows and parcel it up as beautifully as we can and then you will give it to Kate and Robert. They will be thrilled, absolutely thrilled," said Charles proudly.

Eventually the great day dawned. It was a beautiful June day. Cassie had wakened at about five and had gone running through to Charles. She informed him she couldn't sleep and wondered if it was nearly time! After much persuasion she went back to bed until she could stay no longer. She went back through to Charles who relented and got up. It was 7.00; he felt it might be a long day!

He went downstairs and gasped at the transformation; there were flowers everywhere and a stage erected in the Great Hall to accommodate the band for the dancing in the evening. The dining room was set for the wedding breakfast and there were presents galore in the library and sitting room. He went to the kitchen. It was full of people. Nodding to some strange person, he helped himself to coffee and then saw Mrs. Pearson.

"Is there anywhere not invaded by people, Mrs. P?" Charles looked at her. She somehow looked different.

She saw him staring. "Something wrong, Master Charles?"

Charles suddenly realised what the difference was, "Your hair, its different. It's lovely, really nice," he smiled at her.

"Master Charles, fancy you noticing, well, I never," she was blushing slightly but was pleased as could be that he had noticed.

"I've been booted out of my own kitchen. Can you credit it?"

"That's because for once you can sit back and enjoy the day. Kate wanted you to be at the chapel, to relax and enjoy her day. I know the catering will not be up to your standard, but it's only for the one day. Back to normal tomorrow. Now, where can I escape to?" asked Charles.

"Well I'm going to my room, that's where I'm going," said Mrs. Pearson.

"May I join you, just to have my coffee in peace?" asked Charles. "We haven't had a chance for a chat in peace for ages." Mrs. Pearson nodded.

"Let's nip up the back stairs so we're not spotted. But before we do…" Charles quickly popped a couple of slices of ham and some bread onto a plate before the caterer noticed and with a conspiratorial wink at Mrs. Pearson, they went upstairs.

Within the space of only a few hours the chaos of the morning was transformed, if not into peace, then at least a modicum of calm had descended upon the house. Everything was in readiness for later.

Charles felt it was time he should get ready. He was dressing when there was a knock at the door. "Come in." The door opened and there stood Lydia with Cassie beside her. Cassie was beaming at him. "Don't I look gorgeous?" She twirled round to show Charles her bridesmaid's dress which was pale blue with a midnight blue bow.

Lydia laughed, "Cassie, it is for others to say that, not you."

Charles bent down as she came hurtling into the room. "Hey, watch you don't crease your dress," he said as they hugged. "But I agree, you look absolutely beautiful, you are indeed my little princess for that is what you look like today, a princess." Charles felt his throat become tight and he swallowed hard.

"Look what I got. I got it from Kate, for being a flower-girl. Isn't it lovely?" gushed Cassie.

Charles looked at the gold bracelet Cassie was proudly wearing. "That was kind of her; it's something to always remember this day by, your lovely bracelet."

Charles then winked at Cassie. "There is also someone else who is looking rather super don't you think?" Cassie nodded and pointed to Lydia.

"I helped her chose the dress, me and, well it was mostly me," decided Cassie.

Charles and Lydia laughed. "You look lovely, Lydia." Looking down at Cassie he said, "I think I am an extremely lucky chap to be in the company of two such beautiful ladies. I hope I will have the pleasure of a dance with each of you this evening." The ladies both agreed.

"We'll let you finish dressing," said Lydia. "Come on Cassie, we'll go downstairs and join the others."

Charles finished dressing and went along to Kate's room. He knocked on the door. "I am obviously going to be surrounded by beautiful women today. You look lovely, Margaret. I'm going downstairs. I'll wait in the hall for the bride. We have plenty of time but I was going to have a little something before we go to the chapel. Do join me if you can."

Margaret smiled at him and said, "We'll try."

Charles went downstairs, surprised that he was feeling a little nervous.

Cassie heard him on the stairs and ran out from the study. She looked at him and with incredulity in her voice said, "You look gorgeous Daddy, really gorgeous." Lydia who was following her had to admit to agreeing with her. Charles was looking very handsome indeed, resplendent in his morning suit.

"Thank you," smiled Charles. "But you don't have to sound quite so surprised. It's also more usual to say the man is handsome, and the ladies are gorgeous, but thank you nevertheless." Looking at Lydia he said, "I confess to feeling quite pleased I could still get into this. Button-hole, do I have one?"

Lydia replied, "Of course, it's in the fridge, I'll just get it!"

Charles was going to ask why the fridge but decided against it and took himself off to find the sherry decanter. He checked his pocket for his speech for the umpteenth time. Lydia had insisted on reading it and it had been pared down to about half a page. It was not for him to be verbose she had said. Charles hadn't thought he had been, but as usual, was doing as his sister told him! He read it again. He so wanted to convey what Kate meant to him and to the family. As there was no time to change it he decided Lydia was right, it was fine. Lydia came back with the flower followed by Mrs. Pearson and Benson.

"Mrs. Pearson, if I may say, you look lovely, don't you think so Benson?" said Charles.

"I've told her that already," he replied. Mrs. Pearson, a little embarrassed at all this attention was nonetheless, loving every moment of it.

"Well did you have to hire one?" chuckled Charles.

Benson smiled back, "No, although it was a bit of a tight fit but thankfully it's easing off a little now."

"Good man, me neither."

"The carriage is waiting to take us over to the chapel," said Benson, "Are you ladies all set?" They nodded.

"Now, Cassie," said Lydia. "Do you remember what to do?" Cassie nodded gravely. She was certainly going to take her duties very seriously for Kate had decided that she only wanted one attendant and that would be Cassie. Cassie knew this was an incredible honour and was not going to let Kate down.

"Cassie, the carriage will come back for you and Margaret," said Benson. "Good luck, you'll be terrific."

Cassie, who decided she was a little nervous, was going over in her mind what she had to do at the ceremony.

The carriage came back for Margaret and Cassie. Cassie suddenly looked incredibly scared and Charles realised that no matter how much she was looking forward to it, now the time was upon her, it was a little daunting for a five-year-old.

He bent down and kissed Cassie. "Are you a little nervous?" She nodded. "So am I," said Charles. Cassie looked surprised. Her Daddy, nervous! Charles continued, "But it's a good thing to be a little nervous, trust me it is, but we will both be excellent, we really will, so don't worry," and with that he kissed her again and escorted them both to the carriage. He lifted Cassie in, who looked back at him with still a look of apprehension on her face. He mouthed to her, "You look beautiful."

She mouthed back to him, "So do you," as the carriage set off.

Charles smiled and went back inside just as Kate was coming down the staircase.

He gasped when he saw her for she was beautiful, quite, quite beautiful. Having normally seen Kate dressed casually and more often than not in jeans, this transformation was spellbinding.

"Kate, you look absolutely glorious, beautiful," said Charles dazzled by this vision before him. "I will be the envy of all when I escort you down the aisle." He tried to keep the conversation light because he was suddenly feeling quite overcome with the emotion of the moment. "I was just having a little sherry. Would you care for something? I have champagne."

"No, thank you, I'm fine. I don't want to breathe alcoholic fumes all over the vicar. He wouldn't approve." Kate smiled at Charles. "Thank you, thank you for today."

"It is entirely my pleasure," said Charles, looking out of the window. "That's the carriage. Are you ready?" Kate smiled. She was looking completely composed. She took his arm and he led her to the waiting carriage.

Cassie and the vicar were waiting at the entrance to the church. When Cassie saw Kate and her father arrive, she started to wave excitedly at them.

The vicar greeted them and went off down the aisle to alert the organist of the bride's arrival. Meanwhile, Cassie busied herself checking that Kate's dress was sitting nicely. So far so good, she was remembering all her duties.

The music then changed and Charles said, "Okay Cassie, walk behind us, and be careful you don't get too close to the train and when I count to three, off we go." Cassie nodded.

Charles looked at Kate and squeezing her hand, said, "One, two, three," and in perfect step, they proceeded slowly down the aisle. At the appointed time, Cassie laid down her basket of flowers and went round to Kate's side to take her bouquet.

Charles was bursting with pride at how wonderfully Cassie was coping. She was remembering everything. He turned to her and mouthed, "You're fab!" She let out a little giggle of pleasure and then resumed her duties with all seriousness.

After the ceremony, the bridal party walked back to The Hall in the glorious June sunshine while the older guests returned by carriages.

Charles started the proceedings. "Ladies and gentlemen, welcome to Harrington Hall and to the marriage of Kate and Robert. I have been given strict instructions to keep this short and sweet so I will try and obey that command! Firstly, Kate I just want to say how beautiful you look," – everyone shouted their agreement at such an obvious fact! Charles continued. "Although I have known you all your life, since you came to The Hall five years ago, I have grown to think of you as, and I hope you don't mind Kate, as an elder daughter. As I escorted you down the aisle I don't think I could have felt more pride than had you really been my daughter." Kate blushed and smiled with affection at Charles.

"Kate has lived at The Hall since Cassie was born and along with the others here, has been instrumental in making it very much a home. I, and I'm sure I speak for the others here, will miss your presence very much indeed." More agreement was murmured. "Happily though, you aren't too far away – just across the field.

"Robert as we all know is a fine chap who is admired and respected by you all." Guffaws from his friends indicated that they were a little unsure of this fact. Charles grinned at Robert and continued. "Finally, you will all be relieved to hear, although I should not be mentioning this in my speech, you will have to indulge a proud father, for there is one young lady whom I certainly wish to mention and that, of course, is Cassie." Everyone clapped loudly and Cassie revelled in the moment. Charles smiled at her and continued, "I am sure you will all agree that she carried out her duties to perfection and I thank Kate for giving Cassie that trust."

The day was deemed a huge success. An exhausted Cassie declared just before she fell fast asleep, that this had been the best day of her entire life!

~~~~~

Two months after Kate and Robert's wedding, Cassie's first day at school loomed. She seemed very subdued, which puzzled Charles as he had thought she would really enjoy school. Sarah, her best friend, would be starting as well but no amount of encouragement from Charles, Lydia or anyone else at The Hall seemed to allay her apprehension. Charles was so concerned he decided he would give Cassie a week to settle in and if she still seemed unsettled he would go and see her teacher.

Before the big day, Kate came over with a pencil case for Cassie which featured various puppies from 101 Dalmations adorning every item comprising; pencils, coloured pens, rubber, etc. but Cassie just looked at everything, unseeing it seemed, and put it to one side. Even Kate couldn't find out what was wrong. When Benson, Margaret and Mrs. Pearson presented her with her new schoolbag Cassie took one look at it, burst into tears and ran upstairs to her room.

Charles went up and sat down on the bed trying to comfort her. He noticed that on the floor she had a little case neatly packed with clothes and her Little Mermaid rucksack seemed to be bulging complete with teddy with his head poking out the top.

"Are you going somewhere?" asked Charles.

Cassie let out another heart wrenching sob. "You know I am, I hate you for doing this, no one cares, no one is going to miss me and I'm going to miss all of you. I don't want to go, please don't make me. I'll be really good, all the time I'll be good but just please don't send me away," said Cassie gulping out the last few words.

Charles was still mystified by Cassie's obvious anguish. "Cassie, please turn round and look at me. I really don't know what is wrong. You tell me and I'll try and fix it. I will, you know I'll try but I don't know where you're going or why you're packed."

Cassie looked at Charles with such distress. He hated seeing her like this; she appeared tortured by something.

"Please Cassie, try, just for me," said Charles gently as he cuddled her close to him.

Her tears abated and she looked up at Charles with her big violet eyes which had a tear balanced precariously on the bottom of each lid. "You'll be so old when I come home, everyone will be so old, maybe even..." she couldn't bring herself to say the word out loud and whispered, "Dead." Cassie looked frightened by this thought.

Once again, Charles tried to calm her but he was becoming slightly exasperated. "Cassie, where for heavens sake, are you going?"

"School, you said I had to go to school for twelve or thirteen years. I'll be an old lady then, you'll be old, everyone will be old..." Cassie ran out of breath and Charles now thought he understood what all this was about.

His first instinct was to laugh out loud but he tried to keep a straight a face as possible. "You'll only be away for three hours!" He smiled at her and wiping away her tears continued. "I will take you there at nine in the morning and will be there at the school gates, along with all the other parents, to bring you home at twelve. For the whole of September that will be the routine then, from October you and all the other children will stay until three in the afternoon, where, again, all the parents will be waiting at the school gates to take their children home. You will only be at school for three hours tomorrow, that is all, I promise. Is that all right?"

Cassie just looked at him trying to take this revelation in.

"What made you think you wouldn't be coming home?" asked Charles who was still struggling not to laugh out loud.

"You said it, you did, when I asked why Kate couldn't be here. You said I'd be at school for twelve years. You did, I remember," said Cassie whose mood was now changing to one of fury for she suspected Charles was now laughing at her.

"Well, that was just a misunderstanding and I'm sorry you were so upset and worried about it, but there is no way I could ever send you away – you know that. I would be heartbroken. I'd miss you, Aunt Lydia, Kate, everyone would miss you. Goodness me, we even miss you when you stay at Sarah's overnight, just like Sarah's parents miss her when she stays here overnight. Yes? So why don't you unpack, then we'll go down and thank everyone for their nice presents," said Charles.

Cassie nodded but wasn't entirely sure. "Suppose," she muttered.

"Right, as a big treat before school tomorrow what about one of Mrs. P's super-duper fancy ice cream pyramid things with all that gooey revolting stuff you and she insist putting on top? Sound good? In fact, we'll all have one," said Charles whose stomach lurched a little at the very thought.

Cassie immediately brightened at this news and she and Charles went downstairs for this feast. Before anyone could ask what had been wrong, Charles quickly conveyed to them that there had been a misunderstanding and everything was now hunky-dory and it was time for ice creams all round.

He'd tell them later, once Cassie was safely in bed and out of ear-shot.

Chapter 6

To Charles, the seasons seemed to change in the blink of an eye. Cassie, he realised, with a slight tinge of regret was no longer his 'little princess'. That was totally and utterly 'un-cool' and he had to promise never to use that expression, especially in front of her friends. She would die; absolutely die if he did. He promised his little drama queen that he would never do that.

His own name had changed as well. No longer 'Daddy', which again was deemed 'un-cool' he was now called 'Pops!' He confessed to rather liking it – he felt 'hip and happening' upon hearing it then he remembered he wasn't allowed to use that expression either – something from another planet apparently.

For Cassie's thirteenth birthday she and her best friend, Sarah, were going to share a party. The village hall was considered far too gross so the party was to take place in one of the disused barns. The girls duly cleaned the barn, although not without coercing a vast array of their friends in to help until it was deemed habitable.

Sarah, who was going to spend the night of the party at The Hall, had arrived in the afternoon! After what had seemed an eternity, the girls eventually emerged in their party attire. Charles thought he was going to have a heart attack, for coming down the stairs were certainly not the two girls who had gone up. Two eighteen year olds came down instead.

"How do we look, Pops?" asked Cassie.

"Very nice, very nice indeed, but won't you get cold?" asked Charles.

Both girls looked at each other. Sarah giving Cassie the look that said 'you poor thing, he's so sad!'

Peter then arrived and although a GP, and well versed in the ways of thirteen year olds, was a little taken aback at the appearance of his own daughter and her friend. His eyes were out on stalks. "What on earth are you wearing and what have you got on your face?"

It was Cassie's turn to give Sarah the pitying – 'parents are such an embarrassment!' look.

The only person who seemed to take the girls appearance in her stride was Lydia, who came out of the library and smiled expansively at them.

"Girls, you look simply stunning, don't you think…" but she tailed off when she saw the look on the faces of their fathers. She winked at the girls and repeated, "Stunning – have a lovely, lovely time."

"Right," said Charles. "Off we go. Everyone get into the car, I've just got to tell Lydia something."

He ran after Lydia. "Lydia, Lydia, come back."

Lydia stopped. "What on earth's the matter Charles?"

"You've seen what she's looking like." Charles was looking frantic and looking slightly deranged, "Have you done the sex talk? You know, talked to Cassie – you were meant to, have you done it? Does she know about boys – and things, God – does she, have you?"

Lydia smiled at her demented brother. "Yes Charles, years ago, we are now onto contraception, STDs, etc. etc."

Charles could only stammer. "What? Contraception – oh God, she doesn't need it, tell me that, please tell me she doesn't need it." There was an impatient toot on the horn.

"Charles, they are waiting for you. Relax. Cassie won't let you down. She herself feels she is too young for a sexual relationship." Charles looked at Lydia wide-eyed. He could not believe what he was hearing.

"She looked stunning, they both did. They'll be boys at the party. Are you sure she'll be all right?" There was another impatient toot.

"Absolutely," said Lydia. "Now go, and don't make a complete idiot of yourself." And with that she shoved him out the door.

The dance passed without any apparent mishap. The next day the girls emerged downstairs at lunchtime looking, much to Charles's relief, like thirteen year olds again. The party was considered '*brill*'. All afternoon the phone was red-hot with teenagers over the county confirming how '*brill*' it had all been.

Charles wondered how on earth he was going to cope with the 'teenage' years. He suspected – badly!

However, both Charles and Cassie progressed through the years relatively unscathed and all too soon it was time for Cassie to go to art school in London.

Cassie asked Kate if she was envious of her getting the chance when Kate had so wanted to do this. Kate allayed her fears, saying she would bask in the reflected glory, realising it was the truth for she could honestly say she wasn't at all envious. Even when her children were young, she managed to continue painting and sold her paintings to the local tourist shops where her work was quickly snapped up. She felt she had the best of both worlds. She loved her life here on the estate. She had a husband whom she adored and four children who were the apple of her eye and, as a bonus, had wonderful friends in Harrington, especially on the estate. What more could she want?

Kate smiled at the thought. There had been quite a few changes on the estate. Even her Mum was now happy for she and George; Kate always found it difficult to call him that after years of saying, 'Benson', had married. The cottage beside the barn, which had been Kate and Robert's first home, had been fairly cramped with four children. The solution to this had been that Lydia move out of her home with its many rooms, and into rooms in The Hall and Kate and the family moved into her house. Surprisingly it all worked out well, even though Charles and Lydia were more often or not sparring partners, they were also best friends and The Hall was large enough for them to keep out of the other's way should the need arise.

When Harry, the Estate Manager of forty years, retired, Robert was promoted to the post. He loved his job and was absolutely delighted, revelling in the increased responsibility. He and Charles had an excellent relationship and Charles was more than happy to give Robert free rein on any ideas he had for the estate.

Kate recalled something Charles said, "They were a happy little band!" She wholeheartedly agreed.

However, all this was now about to change with Cassie's departure. Kate wondered how Charles would cope, how any of them would cope for that matter. Kate would miss her very much, for she thought of her as a little sister. However, it was Charles she would need to concentrate on.

Charles woke with a knot in his stomach. The day he was dreading had arrived. He knew he was being selfish because he really was so proud of her. It was an incredible achievement for not only had she secured a place at Art School in London, but she had also won the coveted Leonardo Scholarship to study in her second year at the Michelangelo School in Florence.

Cassie had assured him she would come home at weekends but Charles had been equally firm in telling her that wasn't to be. She had to make friends and socialise and generally have a fabulous time.

Charles had gone to Cambridge where he had read English and History and thoroughly enjoyed the experience. He was sure Cassie would also enjoy the student life. He had then gone to Sandhurst – all sons in the family had gone there. He hadn't wanted to, but his father had told him that is what he'd do and so to spare his mother any anguish had obeyed. Unfortunately, this had coincided with the Korean War. Much to his dismay he found himself sent there, but happily he had returned unscathed.

Charles got up and prepared to face the day. Once dressed, he went along to Cassie's room and knocked.

"Come in," said Cassie. "Oh, Pops, it's you. Well, today's the day. How are you feeling?"

Charles had been practising his bright and breezy approach for days and hoped it was honed to perfection.

"Not bad, pretty good," he said sitting down beside her. "I remember my first day at university, such an adventure. You officially become a grown-up, all that kind of thing. You eat garbage, live in squalor, stay up all night – it's great. Of course do try not to do that too often! You'll have a wonderful time. You really will. When I come up to London on business I'll treat you to lunch; some decent food, but don't worry, I won't be zipping up every five minutes."

Cassie looked anxiously at Charles. If, at that moment, he had asked her not to go she would have had no hesitation whatsoever, but she knew he would not do that.

Her eyes filled with tears. Charles, struggling for control as well, put his arm around her and hugged her to him. "It will be fine, I promise you and I've never broken a promise to you have I?" Cassie just shook her head. "I know you'll maybe feel a little homesick for a while but that will soon pass, really it will, and if you feel a bit low then pick up the phone." From his pocket Charles produced phone cards. "So there is no excuse, I have bought you these. I'll replenish them every so often when I write."

Charles stood up and looked around the room. Cassie's belongings were stacked up near the door, ready for packing in the van.

"What time is your friend coming with the van?" asked Charles.

"Half ten, but he's always late," replied Cassie.

"Its very kind of whatshisname, what actually is his name?" asked Charles. "I seem to remember its something weird."

"Its Sputnik," said Cassie.

"I can't call him that. What's his proper name?"

"I don't know to be honest," said Cassie, "He's just always known as Sputnik."

"Well whatever, its kind of him to take you. It's nice that you know someone already and can travel up together; and you like him, don't you?" asked Charles anxiously.

"Oh Sputnik's great, a right laugh. Initially we'll even be in one or two classes together. Yes, it's good he's there as well. Don't worry Pops, I'll be fine. I've just got a bit of the collywobbles, that's all."

Her eyes filled with tears again, "I'm going to miss you so much," she said, trying to wipe away an escaping tear.

"Me too, we all are," said Charles with a voice thick with emotion. Then trying to lighten the moment he said, "How about breakfast, do you fancy some?" Cassie just nodded.

Charles looked down at his ring and wondered... "Before we go down, what about having your Mum's ring now? I was going to keep it for your twenty-first, but this may be as good a time as any. She would have been so thrilled at your going to College. It will remind you of us and that you'll be constantly in our thoughts!" Taking the ring off he slipped Lizzie's ring onto Cassie's finger. "Good – a perfect fit," said Charles.

"Oh Pops, thank you, thank you but will you not miss wearing Mum's ring?"

"No, I was only looking after it for you. I don't know why I thought of giving it to you now – possibly you're the same age your Mum was when she was given it – who knows, all I know is that she loved wearing it, in fact I don't remember her ever taking it off. It's yours now, enjoy!"

Cassie kept touching the ring. She was thrilled and especially now for if, or rather she suspected when, she felt homesick, this ring would be like her lucky charm. Ridiculous notion she knew, but it helped for the moment.

"Right," said Charles, trying once more to inject a little lightness into the moment. "One last hug and then onwards to breakfast."

Breakfast, however, wasn't the usual light-hearted event it normally was. No one was particularly hungry and conversation had a forced gaiety about it.

All too soon, Sputnik arrived and as Cassie remarked, for once, too early.

The van was duly loaded and then it was time for the goodbyes. Cassie was thankful that Kate and the family had been over the night before so now it was just the family at The Hall who were now all congregating in the drive.

Firstly Mrs. Pearson, who came out staggering under the weight of a box of goodies she had made for Cassie. She then proceeded to give her a lecture on eating properly and taking care of herself. Choking back the tears, she gave Cassie a hug and quickly disappeared back into the house.

Next Margaret, Kate's Mum, then Benson – he had been like a favourite uncle to her. Benson was swallowing hard as he gave Cassie a tight hug. By now Cassie could control the tears no longer and they cascaded down her cheeks unchecked.

Aunt Lydia, her heart breaking but as composed as ever, thrust an envelope into her hand and smiled. Kissing her on both cheeks she said, "Safe journey, lots of love and have loads and loads of fun."

Cassie could not speak and gave her aunt one last hug and a muffled, "Thank you," and then, looking over at Sputnik, indicated to him to start the van.

She looked at Charles; neither said anything. Charles wrapped his arms around her, not wanting to let her go. He kissed her on the forehead and taking a handkerchief from his pocket, gently wiped away her tears. "Goodbye, take care," he whispered.

Cassie turned away and quickly climbed into the van. With a final wave, they were off.

Charles watched until the van disappeared from sight and then with head bent, walked across the lawn in the direction of his place of refuge, the lakeside.

Lydia watched him go, her heart aching for him. Today was ghastly, tomorrow would be better and once he heard from Cassie and knew she was fine, then he would be as well.

It had been nearly a month since Cassie left and the house was so quiet. They all missed her so much but from her numerous phone calls it sounded as if she was loving her time. She was like a sponge, absorbing everything she learned and was thriving in the atmosphere.

If truth be known, Cassie was terribly homesick, not only for the people but for the familiar countryside around Harrington. She loved the many galleries and museums she found in the city but she felt London itself was horrendous; it was so noisy and dirty. She couldn't wait to go home but had promised her father she'd stick it out for at least two months before returning for a visit. The two months would soon be up! She couldn't wait.

Cassie's first year seemed to race by and it was now time to confront Italy. She thought she would be incredibly lonely although she could speak Italian reasonably well, it would be sad not seeing everyone. She hadn't, however, realised that at some point everyone would be coming out to see her, news that delighted her.

Kate, Robert and family had booked to go to a campsite just outside Florence; Lydia and her friend Beth said they would definitely be paying a visit, as would Margaret and Benson. Cassie asked Mrs. Pearson if she would be visiting as well but was told she had no intention of stepping off these shores and anyway, she did not possess a passport nor had she any intention of having one.

"What about you, Pops? Will you be coming out to Florence? Everyone else is, well everyone apart from Mrs. P that is," said Cassie.

"I suppose I could write a history of the Ponte Vecchio, not that perhaps one has a great deal to write on the subject of a bridge, but I could try. Perhaps the people who have crossed it would be more interesting material. It's a thought."

"What, really, are you really? That would be wonderful. We could get a flat together somewhere overlooking the Arno, gazing at the Duomo in the background. Let's do it, let's," said an enthusiastic Cassie.

"No cheap little back street for us I see," laughed Charles. "I'll certainly be coming to Italy, you can count on that. But you will have to study. You're also given accommodation and anyway you'll be in Florence, a wonderful city – I might cramp your style!"

Cassie's face fell and she blushed, "No you wouldn't. I'll be too busy with my art!"

"You'll have a magnificent time, just you see. I can't think of anywhere lovelier, I really can't. I'll pop over for the odd weekend and then if you have some time off, a week perhaps, we could hire a car and tour the area. That would be good. An even better thought, now that you've passed your test, you can drive and I'll be able to sample the produce of the vineyards. This gets better and better. Time will whizz by Cassie, it really will. I, for one, can hardly wait."

Cassie was immeasurably cheered by this news as well.

Italy for Cassie proved to be a resounding success, both study wise and socially. She settled in quickly and loved the city, the people and the food. Mrs. Pearson was aghast on hearing about the food and was quoted as saying 'foreign muck, this pasta business'. Cassie did not have time for any homesickness in Italy for the promise of visitors was indeed true and she had a steady stream for the whole year. She stayed with one of the tutors on her course, Signor Lorenzo. He, his wife and children made her more than welcome and within a short space of time she felt like one of the family.

A few months after Cassie left, Charles went to visit the Lorenzo family, who had a sizeable house, insisted that he stay with them and would not hear of him using a hotel. Signor Lorenzo and Charles became instant friends, although neither of them was particularly fluent in each other's language. Their common bond was 'the grape', and they had many an interesting discourse on the subject with much sampling required for each subject matter!

Charles felt happy to see Cassie so obviously enjoying her stay and relaxed knowing she was being well looked after.

All too soon, Cassie's year was up and it was time to leave people she had grown so fond of. On her arrival back at Harrington, she unpacked and caught up on the gossip of the village. Then Kate arrived, delighted that her friend was home.

"So," said Kate. "Let's hear all about your romances in Italy. Go on Cassie, you can tell me." Kate started to tease her. "You're not telling me that you spent a year in Florence without falling hook, line and sinker for some gorgeous Italian. I can't believe it, I don't believe it."

Cassie blushed.

"Ha! Knew it," exclaimed Kate.

"You know nothing of the sort," replied Cassie indignantly.

Kate looked intently at her. "You know you want to tell me."

"Well, there was one. His name is Gian Carlo and he is the Lorenzo's eldest son. Okay, satisfied?" asked Cassie.

"No, of course not, I want to know details," laughed Kate. All right, I'll stop – I'm being rotten. As long as you had a wonderful time, that's all that matters," and she hugged Cassie to her. "Oh how I've missed you. It's not the same without you, really it's not. You know one of the things I miss most. It's not having anyone to talk with about art. Are you too tired to go to the studio?"

"Never too tired for that," replied Cassie.

Charles watched from the window. It was so good to have Cassie back. Cassie, he thought, had grown steadily more and more beautiful – even accounting for a father's bias!

She didn't look like Lizzie at all, for she didn't have her mother's titian hair or her brown eyes. No, she looked more like Charles although more in mannerisms that actually looking like him. Charles had looked through the family albums to try and see whom Cassie resembled. He decided that she perhaps looked quite like his mother's sister, with her dark wavy hair and similarly shaped nose and mouth, although no one had eyes like Cassie. Where they came from he did not know. All he knew was his daughter had turned into a stunning young woman.

Her month at home passed all too quickly and it was time for her final year in London. Although she had enjoyed her time, and especially in Florence, she looked forward to leaving the city life. She did not really think it was for her. She decided that the country life was more her style.

Cassie's ambition was to be able to support herself by becoming an artist but she was realistic enough to know that this would not be an overnight achievement and that she would have to find some other work for the immediate future to supplement her income.

With this in mind, when she had last been home she had gone to see Pierre Gabriel who owned the Gabriel Gallery. The gallery, which was in the town of Piltonsby, about fifteen miles from Harrington, was a prestigious gallery where artists clamoured to have their work exhibited first before transferring to London. Cassie didn't really know if Gabriel's required an assistant but she thought she'd go to the top first and then work her way down!

Pierre Gabriel was an astute businessman with 'an eye' for art and especially for up and coming talent. He had agreed to see Cassie more out of curiosity than anything else, as he had no intention of hiring her. He ran the gallery himself and did not require any of what he thought as interference.

Cassie arrived, bringing some work to show him. He was deeply impressed. Somehow, over the next hour, Cassie had convinced him that not only would he hang some of her work, but that he did require her services as his assistant! She had him so mesmerised that he was at a loss to understand how he had coped on his own for so long!

When Cassie eventually owned up to Charles, he felt complete empathy with Pierre. For the scenario reminded him of a certain young lady who had turned up on his doorstep twenty or so years ago, saying she was a typist!

Charles was of course thrilled and after her graduation a new era started at Harrington Hall: that of the working girl.

Cassie was delighted to be at the gallery and loved the work and the people she met. Pierre was clearly enchanted by her and Cassie extremely fond of him. Cassie thought she knew lots about art but Pierre, in a kindly way, demonstrated that she had only scratched the surface. He was fascinating and Cassie was indebted to him for his patience in explaining things to her. He was an excellent teacher, and she a very willing pupil.

Although she frequently came home from work exhausted, not from the physical work, but from the sheer amount of information that she had learnt that day, this wasn't a complaint, it was a delight. She would go to bed at night, looking forward to work the next day. She knew how lucky she was, for so many people dreaded going to work – she could not relate with that at all.

Charles loved when she came home from work and regaled them with stories, inevitably embellished, of her customers at work or what had amused her.

Charles had initially been concerned that living at The Hall she may miss the buzz of city life but no, that wasn't the case. She admitted to being far lonelier in the city than she ever felt at Harrington and Charles could quite believe it for there was a steady stream of young people trooping in and out. Lydia seemed to know them all. Charles was always a little vague as to who everyone was but was always most welcoming.

"Is there anyone in particular that Cassie likes?" enquired Charles to Lydia as he watched from the window as Cassie jumped into the back of a car with three males.

"That chap Paul was on the go for a while but I think that's finished. I'm sure she mentioned it was – I sort of lose track to be honest," said Lydia.

"Hmmm," said Charles not really sure if that was a good or bad thing. "Do you think she's happy?"

"Charles, it's obvious to a blind man that she is. She's young, she's playing the field, relax," replied Lydia.

Lydia was right, Cassie was truly happy. Could anything mar her happiness?

Chapter 7

Peter watched from the surgery window as Charles made his way to the car. There was nothing in his gait to suggest that he had been given the news he had, for his bearing was, as ever, erect and his stride purposeful.

Peter thought back to his first meeting with Charles over twenty years ago. He had been the brash, enthusiastic young doctor ready to change the world, or if not the world, certainly the village, and in the process had very nearly alienated most of the villagers. It was Charles, in his usual diplomatic way, who had guided the young man in the ways of the village and its inhabitants and had introduced him to the country pursuits of which Peter was now so fond. The villagers eventually forgave him his clumsy beginning and warmed to him, for he was an extremely affable, kindly and caring man who entered into the spirit of village life with a zeal that endeared him to the community. He and Charles quickly became close friends and Harrington Hall was a second home to Peter and his family.

Peter had been dreading Charles's visit. The results sitting before him bore the news he did not know how to impart. However Charles, sensing Peter's unease had smiled at his friend and said, "Not good is it, perhaps even worse than we thought?" Peter nodded. "All right then, are you able to put a time limit on how long I have?"

Peter tried to speak but his voice cracked. He smiled weakly at Charles and shook his head. He was trying to be in control and not so unprofessional but it was nigh on impossible when sitting before him was one of his closest friends.

"I can't do that for sure, but I think we are talking months rather than years." He looked at Charles, trying to gauge if he wished to continue. Charles sat impassively. Peter continued, "I'm so very, very sorry but the tumour is inoperable. This particular cancer is, unfortunately, notorious for being insidious." He hesitated, letting that news sink in. "We should perhaps consider some palliative options so we do need to discuss chemo and radiotherapy, that sort of thing."

Charles nodded, for he was now thinking of Cassie and how on earth he would tell her.

As if reading his thoughts, Peter asked, "Do you wish me to talk to Cassie?"

"No, no thank you," replied Charles. "I will tell her but there are one or two things I need to sort out first. By the way, are you still on for golf on Saturday? I think we have a good chance to win the trophy from Carstairs and Kemp."

Peter grappled with the complete change of conversation. He knew Charles well enough to know that when he wanted to talk he would. Right now he obviously didn't.

"Yes, of course I am. I've had Lawrie sort out my slice and now apparently I have an 80% success rate so hopefully I won't let you down."

A look passed between them. "There is no fear of that, you never have." Charles stood up and, with affection, squeezed Peter's shoulder. "I'll pick you up around eight then." Walking to the door he turned, "Bye and thank you. I know this hasn't been easy but you know how much I hate hospitals and I'm afraid that here feels much the same to me. Perhaps we can have a chat about things later. I suggest over a good claret, what do you think?"

"No problem, pop round to mine if you like because I'm on my own for the next few days. Rowena and the children are off to her sister's but phone first, I might be on the course practising my swing before Saturday," smiled Peter.

"Will do," said Charles.

In the hallway Peter heard Charles speak to Carol, the receptionist, asking how her new baby was – so typical of the man. God, he was going to miss him so much. At that thought, tears pricked his eyes. He wiped them away. He had other patients to see and he had to be in control. He pressed the intercom on his desk.

"Carol, can you show the next patient in now please." He opened the door just as his next patient arrived, "Ah, Mrs. Thomson, and what can I do for you today?" He shut the door and, for the moment, the problems of his friend from his mind.

Chapter 8

Charles drove up to Beeches Hill, parked took his Barbour from the back seat, put it on and started to walk. Down in the valley was the village. Seeing it like this he realised how much it had spread out. The new houses on the outskirts had been such a bone of contention with the old timers in the village but remarkably the two factions had eventually gelled. There was now a friendly rivalry between the customers of the oldest pub in the area, The Black Bull, dating back to 1650 or thereabouts, whose customers were usually the locals from the original village and the pub the locals called the 'newish one', The Trout, having been established as recently as 1882! It was generally frequented by those on the estate who, for at least a couple of generations, would still be considered newcomers. Darts and football matches had sprung up between them and in the summer the village green doubled as the cricket pitch.

Up the hill from the village and built, Charles fancied, to give an air of superiority, was Harrington Hall. It had been built in George III's reign. The addition of the west wing was courtesy of the Victorian era but the two blended together beautifully so that the overall result was pleasing to the eye.

From this vantage point Charles could see the area of land over which he presided. He tried to think of his estate. It was vast, with many people in his employ and it was the people whose livelihoods were in his hands, that he had to base his decision on. Cassie, who loved the house had absolutely no interest in the workings of the estate, although was more than happy to spend the money generated from it!

Her love, inherited from her mother, was painting, although unlike Lizzie her specialty was portraits, at which she excelled. For his birthday she had presented him with a portrait of himself. He felt it was a little flattering but everyone else had kindly said it was an excellent likeness. She insisted it be hung in the Great Hall. He would have been happier if it had not been in quite such a prominent place but Cassie had said there would be appropriate – amongst all the other fossils on the walls! Such disrespect for her elders he had said but she had just laughed, running off to drag Benson in to help with the ladder and before, he could say 'picture hook', he was well and truly hung!

Charles sat down and lit a cigar. He inhaled deeply. After all those years of not inhaling he thought, *what the hell*. He then remembered why he didn't inhale, as he initially spluttered and felt distinctly light-headed, but the feeling was not an unpleasant one and in some ways the light-headedness made him disassociate himself from his problems. He rested his back against the wall, gazing out over the valley and blew smoke rings, spending a pleasant few minutes thinking about nothing in particular.

Finishing his cigar he thought about Peter's revelation and struggled to comprehend that nothing could be done. He hoped Peter hadn't realised the extent of the despair that had descended upon him on hearing the prognosis, for Peter's words had shocked him to the core. What a fool he'd been. If only he'd gone to see Peter sooner. And then a deep and overwhelming sadness enveloped him for he realised he would never see Cassie mature, maybe marry, have children. None of the things he had taken for granted and at that realisation Charles bent his head and sobbed uncontrollable sobs at what might have been; sobbing for the legacy he was leaving her, a legacy she wouldn't wish. He shuddered. "Oh what can I do, Cassie?" he asked out loud. "I'm so, so sorry. I've let you down. Totally and utterly let you down." He bent his head and let the tears fall. Some minutes passed before they eventually stopped and, wiping his eyes, he struggled to his feet and looked across to Harrington Hall. "I have to find a solution for you, my dear, dear Cassie," he said, "But I'm unsure where to even begin." He walked aimlessly for some minutes and thought about Robert, who had been his estate manager for the past ten years. He was an obvious person to run things temporarily. He and Kate had been married now for over fifteen years. Charles could not believe how time had flown by. Kate had never gone to art school but seemed happy and totally absorbed in bringing up their four children. The problem with that idea however, was not that Robert would be unsuitable – far from it – the problem was one steeped in three hundred years of tradition, as the Emerson's had lived on this land all that time but this was the first generation where a son was not, so to speak, waiting in the wings.

His next idea was that Cassie might marry, have a son, and the son would inherit. However, this seemed unlikely to happen in the immediate future.

Charles shivered and, looking at his watch, realised he had there for nearly three hours. No wonder he was cold and not thinking clearly. Walking back to the car, he put the heater on full blast and drove back down the hill.

As he approached The Hall, he saw a navy blue Lotus parked in the drive. *No doubt one of Cassie's friends*, he thought. On entering the house he was informed by Benson that a gentleman was waiting in the library.

Charles entered the library and the 'gentleman' rose and extending his hand said, with a hint of an American accent, "Hi, I'm David Coleridge."

They shook hands. There was something vaguely familiar about the name but Charles could not place him.

"Good evening, and what may I do for you?" enquired Charles, indicating to his guest to have a seat.

"I'm really sorry barging in like this but I was in the country sorting out my mother's estate. She died over six months ago but everything is taking such a heck of a long time, that I thought if I came over I might be able to speed things up a bit, with little or no success I may add. I needed a break from it so as I was fairly close I thought I'd pay Lizzie a call; we sort of lost touch when you and she got married. I haven't been back since I left all those years ago so I thought it was time to catch up on some old friends. I hope you don't mind," said David.

Charles just stared at him: the eyes so familiar to him.

David was beginning to feel a little uncomfortable. "Look, I'm really sorry I shouldn't have just arrived without phoning first."

Charles gathered himself together. "I'm so terribly sorry. I really don't know how to say this. Lizzie died; she died over twenty years ago."

David paled and clutched the arms of the chair. He had always assumed the reason Lizzie had stopped writing was because she wanted to sever ties with her past life when she became 'Lady of the Manor'.

"I wonder," asked David. "May I have a drink please? I'm not really taking this in. Lizzie, I can't believe it; I just can't. What happened, was it an accident or something?"

Charles shook his head and asked David what he'd like to drink. "Whisky, brandy, whatever you like." Charles was trying to buy a little time before he had to relate the events of Lizzie's death.

"Scotch would be fine, with a dash of soda if you have some," replied David.

Charles poured a hefty measure for David and felt the need to do likewise for himself.

Simultaneously they took a large gulp and David asked the question again. "What happened?"

Charles then proceeded to go over the events of Lizzie's death.

In response David just shook his head uttering, "I just can't believe this – I really can't. I thought it would give her such a kick to see me again. I've changed just ever so slightly since I was last here," he smiled ruefully at this recollection. "I was going through a sort of punk phase I suppose you'd call it – went with the image of living in the commune. Did she tell you about it? I suppose she did." David was speaking more to himself than to Charles.

Charles looked at the whisky bottle. "Dinner will be in about an hour but I think you should stay the night. You can't drive back. We've had quite a lot to drink."

David looked at Charles. "If it's not too much trouble I really would appreciate that, thanks."

Charles rang for Benson and informed him that they had a guest for dinner and that the guest was staying the night. Benson looked David up and down and invited him to follow him to the guest room.

"Why don't you have a nap? I'll give you a shout when dinner is ready," said Charles.

"I might just do that," as he followed Benson out of the library.

Charles felt exhausted and emotionally drained by the encounter with David. *Today of all days*, he thought and was glad that he would have a 'breather' for an hour. He felt so very, very tired and decided that it might be a good idea to have a nap as well, so settled down in the large leather chair in the library and within a moment, was fast asleep.

After what seemed only a minute, Benson entered the library, to inform Charles that dinner would be served in approximately fifteen minutes and should he inform their guest. Charles rose wearily and told Benson he would see to their guest himself.

He climbed the stairs to the first floor and knocked on David's door. Immediately there was a response.

Charles entered to find David standing at the window gazing out over the lawn down to the lake. "Did you manage to have a nap?"

"Couldn't sleep," replied David. "I had a cold, well coldish, shower instead. Just trying to clear my mind. You know I did love Lizzie, I really did. I was just too selfish. I thought I could have everything and that she would be as thrilled as I was about my going to America. Wrong about that, wasn't I? Women don't really see things the same way as us, do they? It was only meant to be for six months but it seemed that no sooner had I left than she got married to you. I really resented you but I imagine you would have guessed that."

"She was distraught when you left," said Charles.

"Hmmm, not so distraught that she didn't leap into marriage in a blink of an eye. It sure was some whirlwind romance," countered David with a degree of sarcasm in his voice.

He looked at Charles and immediately felt guilty; thinking how the man had suddenly aged since their first meeting only an hour or so ago. David knew he wasn't being fair. It wasn't Charles's fault. He had been nothing but courteous and hospitable and did not deserve David's petulant behaviour.

Gently he said, "Sorry that was uncalled for. In her last letter she told me about your marriage and how lucky she felt knowing someone like you."

"Thank you. Shall we go down to dinner?"

They walked down the sweeping staircase and into the Great Hall. "It's some place you have here. Nice, really nice." David murmured, a little distracted as he looked at the portraits. "Interesting works you have. I wouldn't mind a closer look after dinner. Portraits are my field. I love trying to capture the essence of the person. The eyes, now they are really tricky to do, the windows of the soul as they say, but whoever did your portrait is good, I don't know you but I think the artist has done pretty well. Lizzie, now she was wonderful at skies, amazing. Do you have any of hers? I'd love to see them if you did."

Charles, disconcerted by what he was hearing, was trying desperately to change the subject. He ushered David into the dining room with the promise that they would go after dinner and look at Lizzie's paintings, which were hung in the sitting room; his favourite room. Right now he really wanted to get off the subject of art.

Dinner was, as usual, excellent. Mrs. Pearson had, in the limited time available to her, even tried an American theme for the main course of fried chicken and corn fritters. David was very appreciative and relished every mouthful.

"Was it a local artist, the one who did your portrait?" persisted David oblivious to Charles's reluctance to pursue the subject.

"No, no it wasn't, it was actually my daughter. She painted it as a present," admitted Charles a little reluctantly. "If you are finished, shall we adjourn to the sitting room and I'll show you Lizzie's work."

But David kept reverting back to Cassie. "Will I get to meet her?"

"I'm not really sure," replied Charles, as they crossed the hall to the sitting room. "You know what young people are like, out to all hours and parents are often the last to know when they'll be back," he said with what he knew sounded like a forced laugh.

"I wouldn't know," said David. "I would be useless at being a parent. I have enough trouble looking after myself," he laughed.

Charles also laughed, although perhaps more than would normally be required, for he was conscious that David looked at him rather strangely but Charles hoped he would think this is how the British aristocracy normally behaved!

David looked quietly at the pictures round the walls. They were all Lizzie's. "Such a waste," he said, more to himself than Charles. "She had such talent, such an incredible talent." He paused before one she had done of the lake at sunset, Charles's favourite.

"Gosh, I remember her doing this. She was painting this just a little while before I went away. She loved the lake and had the amazing gift of memorising the colours exactly and then putting them on canvas. Some artists take photographs, I don't suppose Lizzie could afford to do that, we were always broke." He smiled at the recollection. "They really are wonderful, quite, quite wonderful. How lovely, your daughter has inherited her mother's talent."

"Yes," replied Charles, for that was all he could think to say.

"Would you care for a night-cap? I think I would," said Charles.

"That would be great," responded David. "Brandy please."

"I think I'll join you in that," replied Charles.

"Look," said David, warming the brandy glass in his hand. "You have been so kind, putting me up and the lovely meal and everything that I would love to take you and your daughter out for a meal tomorrow. That is if you are free, just as a way of saying thanks."

"Oh, there is absolutely no need for that," replied Charles grappling as to why this was such a horrendous idea. "You have been no trouble at all."

"Please," persisted David. "I won't take no for an answer."

"The problem," said Charles struggling with what the problem could be, "Is that my daughter, Cassandra that is, well we actually call her Cassie, Lizzie wanted her named Cassandra." Charles tailed off, he had completely lost the thread of what he was saying.

"Ah… what was I saying, yes, Cassie…"

With that a voice said, "Is that my name being called in vain? Hi Pops," Cassie burst into the room and planted a kiss on the top of Charles's head. Noticing David she said, "Hello, who are you? Aren't you going to introduce us?"

"I would, if you would give me a moment," retorted Charles, trying to find his voice.

David stood up and extended his hand and smiling warmly said, "Allow me to introduce myself. My name is David Coleridge, I was a friend of your mother's a long time ago. She was an amazing lady, your Mum."

"I'm afraid I didn't know her so I don't really know what I missed, but Pops has told me all about her." Glancing over at her father she thought that all of a sudden he looked so vulnerable and continued, "But I do know I've been incredibly lucky because I only have THE most fab father in the whole world, don't I Pops?" She looked over at Charles and smiled. "Are you all right?" He looked so old.

Charles looked at them both and felt his heart lurch but managed to smile at Cassie. "It's been quite a hectic day and David and I have been going down memory lane, bed time for me I think. Would you both excuse me?"

David said, "I think I'll turn in as well. Your Dad and I also demolished a fair amount of scotch. Luckily for me I am staying the night so I do hope I may see you in the morning?"

"Yes," said Cassie, "But not too early. Night."

Charles wanted to escape to his bedroom to think about all that had happened that day. However, sheer exhaustion took over and he fell asleep as soon as his head hit the pillow. When he awoke it was nearly seven o'clock. He couldn't believe it. He hadn't slept this well for ages, although he did appreciate that the combination of whisky and the night-cap of brandy may well have been contributing factors to this state of blissful slumbers!

He got out of bed and drew back the curtains. He never tired of this view of the lake. He knew he wouldn't be able to sleep again so got up, shaved, showered, dressed and went downstairs. He would go for a walk and have an appetite for breakfast. He rather fancied a fry-up so left a note for Mrs. Pearson saying: *'Gone for a walk, no healthy breakfast today – bacon, eggs, in fact, the works, please'.* He underlined the word please in the hope she would take pity on him.

Cooked breakfasts had, in the past, been the order of the day before doctors had gone health mad. Mrs. Pearson had been given a lecture by Peter to say that matters of cholesterol were to be considered and healthy was to be the by-word at Harrington Hall from now on. Charles was appalled by this and loathed with a passion the homemade muesli foisted upon him in the interests of health! However, he felt Peter wouldn't mind too much about his lapse today. He was so looking forward to breakfast and with that thought strode across the lawn.

The leaves were starting to fall. Autumn was well and truly here. He looked at the golden and amber colours and wondered if he would ever see another autumn. He knew it unlikely but he did hope so, he really did. He could have become maudlin but instead pulled himself together and thought about breakfast!

On his return home the smell of bacon wafted towards him as he entered the back door. Was there ever a lovelier smell? At this moment he certainly couldn't think of one. He went into the kitchen where Mrs. Pearson was piling bacon onto a warmed ashet. Charles went over to her and planted a kiss on her cheek. "You are a treasure, Mrs. P. An absolute treasure. My thanks know no bounds," and with that he kissed her again.

"Master Charles behave. I don't know what Doctor will say, I really don't," said a slightly flustered Mrs. Pearson.

"Ah," said Charles. "We won't tell him, and anyway, a little of what you fancy and all that. Are the others up yet?"

"Yes," said Mrs. Pearson, "Mr. Coleridge is up. He was requiring an aspirin." She gave Charles a look of such disapproval that it transported him back to when he was a boy.

"Sorry, we needed a little drink yesterday. We won't be naughty again," said Charles mischievously as he grabbed a piece of bacon and popped it in his mouth. "Delicious, quite delicious."

Charles entered the dining room to find David already there. "Good morning. Sleep well?"

David smiled a little sheepishly and confessed to having had to ask Mrs. Pearson for an aspirin. "She's quite scary, but I was desperate. My apologies for drinking you dry last night."

"I think we both required a little Dutch courage yesterday," replied Charles. "Can you face breakfast?"

David felt he could and so they sat down to eat. They had both just finished when Cassie came bounding in.

"Hello Pops, David. Have you both recovered from your binge drinking last night?" asked Cassie helping herself to some coffee. She looked at her father who was looking at her strangely. "Are you all right?"

Charles nodded. "Was there a mention of dinner last night?" Cassie asked looking at David. Both men groaned simultaneously. "Oops, sorry," grinned Cassie. "A little fragile are we? How long are you here David?"

"Not sure," he replied. "But back to our dinner date; maybe not this evening all things considered, but certainly soon, I want to take you both out."

"I look forward to it," said Cassie. "Well, I'm off. See you Pops. Bye David."

"Where are you going?" asked Charles.

"Oh, loads of places. Got to dash, but I'll be home for dinner. Can you tell Mrs. P. for me?" And with a wave she was off.

"I had better hit the road as well. May I have your telephone number?"

"Yes, of course," said Charles and scribbled it down on a piece of paper.

They walked out to David's car. "Thanks for everything. I'm really pleased to have met you. I often wondered what you'd be like. I cannot begin to imagine what it must have been like for you when Lizzie died, but in some ways you are lucky. You have Cassie. She's a great girl. She reminds me a little of Lizzie and although fleeting, it was lovely meeting her."

Charles smiled and said, "Yes, I am lucky, she is a lovely girl."

David smiled back and said, "Once again, I'm sorry I just barged in yesterday and thanks, again." With that he got into his car and, with a wave, he accelerated down the drive.

Charles shivered, he suddenly felt chilly. He went inside and poured himself another coffee, relieved that his ordeal was over, at least until the next meeting. He sat in contemplation. He had to allay his suspicions so perhaps it was now time to confront the past and go upstairs to the attic.

Chapter 9

In Charles's youth the attic had been his playroom and, perhaps more especially, a sanctuary from his father. It was huge. In one corner was a sitting area. He noticed this was now very changed. Cassie had painted the walls yellow and blue. A little startling perhaps, but a big improvement on sludge brown; his attempt as a youngster. He walked further down the attic and came across the trunks put there all those years ago. In his meticulous way everything was labelled. He took out a key and opened one of the trunks. Inside was a box that held letters, a little jewellery and a small sketchpad; Lizzie's things.

He closed the trunk again and, carrying the box, went over to the sitting area of the attic. He looked around. Cassie had made it rather nice. There were rugs on the floors, some of her early attempts at art, a little table and a lamp. He switched on the lamp and opened the box again.

After Lizzie had died he had found the box at the back of her wardrobe with her sketchpad and some letters in it and without having ever read the letters, had put the box in the trunk. Now he felt guilty. This was such an intrusion on Lizzie's life but now he had met David; he had to know.

A little tentatively, Charles picked up the first envelope and took out a letter; there were five airmail letters in all, this was the first.

It was a letter from David. It was filled with enthusiasm for America: what he was learning, the paintings he was doing and carried on in that vein. A rather selfish vein Charles felt, but then he was slightly biased! He felt incredibly sad, thinking how Lizzie must have felt upon receiving it, as only in the last sentence was there any reference as to how Lizzie might be.

Charles started to feel angry. How could David have been so cruel? Then sense prevailed. This letter was written by someone young, enthused with life and, with the typical arrogance of youth, totally self-centred. Most young people had moments in their lives when they acted like that so why not David? Here was a young man who was getting the chance of a lifetime and not comprehending for one moment why his girlfriend wasn't as overjoyed as he!

The letter looked as if at some time it had been crumpled up. Charles suspected Lizzie would have thrown it away in a fit of pique or perhaps more likely, an explosion of temper.

He opened the second one. The gist of this was that David could not understand why she had written such a cold letter and was asking when she was coming over. He would try and help financially with part of her fare. David said Lizzie's attitude was completely beyond his comprehension. Here was a man doing everything in his power to be understanding and show how much he cared. He wanted her to join him and could not understand why she wasn't leaping into action at the very idea. Why was Lizzie behaving like this, he enquired?

The third letter was written obviously in response to a couple of letters Lizzie had sent. In this one David sounded hurt and totally bewildered by what was happening. He pleaded with Lizzie to change her mind. Charles was unsure as to what he was referring but assumed that Lizzie had written breaking off their relationship. He continued the letter, telling her there were fabulous opportunities in the States. Charles began to feel a little sorry for David and wondered how Lizzie had reacted to this letter.

The fourth letter from David was different. It was written in anger and, perhaps, in disbelief as to what Lizzie had last written to him, for she had obviously mentioned her forthcoming marriage to Charles.

David had gone into a tirade regarding this subject; calling Charles for everything. The letter finished with David saying he didn't care what she did; as far as he was concerned, their relationship was history.

The final letter, written months after the previous one, was full of apologies, begging her to reconsider. It ended with him saying that although he did not understand why she would wish to marry someone like Charles, he nevertheless wished her happiness. As a postscript to the letter he had added that if he did not hear from her again he would understand that she wanted to sever connections with her past life and perhaps him in particular, and that he would try and respect that. He signed it 'All my love, forever, David'. Charles turned the envelope over and looked at the postmark. She would have received it about two weeks before she died. He was glad.

Charles flicked through the other letters. He did not understand. The rest of the letters were all in Lizzie's handwriting but had not been sent. They were all addressed to David.

With trembling fingers he opened the first envelope, guilt-ridden at what he was doing. The letter had been written after they had married. He smiled at the recollection of all those years ago. He had proposed very much on the spur of the moment and to his amazement she had not only agreed to be his wife, but had thought there was no point in waiting to get married; suggesting they get the appropriate licence and marry as soon as possible. He had been astonished, but thrilled and bowled along by her apparent enthusiasm had, much to everyone's amazement, complied with her wishes. Tongues had wagged in the village but the tongues wagging the most, were in his own home!

Although everyone at The Hall knew and liked Lizzie from her work as Charles's typist; being Lady of the Manor was decidedly different. However, before too long Lizzie had weaved her magic spell on those around her and wagging tongues were laid to rest. Besotted Charles had no idea how this had been accomplished but was absolutely thrilled.

He smiled at the memory and started to read the letter but he quickly stopped. He suddenly felt ill. He couldn't breathe. He loosened his tie and undid the top button of his shirt. He thought he was going to be sick.

He ran his fingers through his hair. It must be a mistake. Please God, he thought it cannot be true. In the letter before him something he had suspected, but had not wished proved, was staring him in the face. Letting out a yell of anguish he read the sentence over and over again. Realisation stared back at him. Lizzie had known she was pregnant when she had agreed to marry him.

Cassie, his wonderful, talented, funny, beautiful daughter... wasn't his daughter.

He couldn't bear this thought. Standing up he yanked the lamp from its socket and flung it across the attic. For a moment he felt a sort of release at throwing something, but only for a moment. He slumped back in the chair and stared at the letter, reading the line over and over again, hoping upon hope the wording would miraculously change. Charles had no idea how long he had sat staring at the letter but he decided he needed air, a drink, or both. He went down the stairs and, remembering to lock the door to the attic, went firstly to his bedroom to splash water on his face. He decided he would lie down for a moment, just a moment he thought. However, sleep soon came upon him and he did not hear Lydia enter his room.

Lydia looked at her brother lying there. Even in sleep he had a troubled look on his face. She had seen him leave the surgery yesterday when she had passed in the car on her way to spend the night with a friend. She was late so hadn't stopped but it had troubled her. She knew Charles would call this her interfering nosiness. She preferred to call it concern. She realised it could have been a social call for she knew he and Peter were playing golf at the weekend but she suspected not, for some time now she hadn't thought her brother looked himself. She had asked him repeatedly if he were feeling well but was always given the same answer. He was fine and to stop nagging. But she knew something was wrong and she was determined to find out what.

She tried to tiptoe out the room but he woke and was less than pleased to find her there. "God damn it woman, can't I even have five minutes to myself?"

"Temper, temper Charles," retorted Lydia. "I'm concerned about you, that's all. What's wrong? Because there is something, I know there is. I saw you leave the surgery yesterday. I was on my way to Beth's and couldn't stop."

"Well, at least that was something," said Charles trying to sit up. As he did a sudden pain caught him by surprise and he winced. He very much hoped this would go unnoticed by his sister. It didn't.

"Are you in pain?" she demanded to know but with concern on her face. She sat at the edge of the bed. "Please, Charles. Is there something wrong?"

Charles looked at his sister and patted her arm. "Give me five minutes. You go downstairs and join me for a gin and tonic before lunch. How does that sound?"

"It sounds," said Lydia, "very much as if I am being palmed off but I won't be."

"I know, I am well aware of that. Please, five minutes and then we'll talk. I do actually need your help." He smiled with affection at Lydia.

"Five minutes then," Lydia retorted as she left the bedroom.

Charles was annoyed that she had seen him in pain. She would just worry. He had managed to hide it so well up till now. It was possibly his liver rebelling after yesterday's rather excessive alcohol intake. He'd better just have a small gin and tonic!

He splashed some ice-cold water on his face and, tidying himself, was ready to face his sister; or so he hoped.

He entered the drawing room just in time to hear the tinkling of ice in the glass.

"Perfect timing," said Charles taking his glass. "Cheers!"

"Now, Charles," started Lydia.

"Stop," said Charles. "I require no interjections or interruptions of any kind. Do I make myself clear?"

"Crystal," replied Lydia.

Charles then proceeded to tell her of events yesterday, starting with his visit to Peter.

"You are correct. I did go to see Peter as a patient." Charles looked at Lydia tenderly. "I need you to be brave; very brave." Lydia just nodded.

Charles continued, "I was seeing Peter to get test results back. I have cancer, Lydia. Its fairly advanced, so operating is not an option."

Lydia looked at Charles and her eyes filled with tears. "Oh Charles, I…" and with that she tailed off, unable to finish.

"Stiff upper lip old girl," smiled Charles. "For me? It's the only way I can cope."

Lydia straightened her back and blinked away the tears. She was devastated at his news but that would be the only time Charles would see her falter. In his presence, she would be strong for him; she wouldn't let him down.

"Thank you," said Charles and putting his arm around her shoulder, hugged her to him. "We're a good team, we'll get through this! It's the estate I'm worried about."

"Charles, for God's sake. Forget the estate. Concentrate on getting better," said Lydia with exasperation in her voice. She looked at Charles. Their eyes met and she then understood. She nodded, unable to speak, not confident that her voice would not give away what she was feeling. She squeezed his hand, "I see."

"And Cassie, what have you told her?" asked Lydia.

"I haven't," replied Charles. "I'm not sure what to say or what to do. I didn't have an opportunity to speak to her last night because we had an old friend of Lizzie's here. It was quite a surprise and, I confess, quite a strain because he didn't know Lizzie had died. He wanted me to tell him what happened and just kept repeating how he couldn't believe it. You know it still hurts speaking about it, even after all these years."

Charles didn't know whether to continue and tell Lydia what he had discovered in the letters but thought she had maybe enough to cope with today.

He continued. "He was a nice enough chap; an artist living in the States, went there twenty or so years ago. Just back to sort out his mother's estate. He wanted to see Lizzie's work and remembered she had been painting the lake picture just before he left for the States. They had obviously been pretty close once but I suppose had drifted apart when he left." Charles hoped his voice would not betray what he really was feeling.

"What sort of artist is he?" asked Lydia.

"Oh, heavens, what was it he said? Ah yes, I believe he said he specialises in portraits," replied Charles as casually as he could muster.

Lydia looked at him. "What name did you say?" enquired Lydia, equally casually.

"I didn't," replied Charles. "But it's David, David Coleridge".

Charles saw the look that flitted across Lydia's face. He looked intently at her but the look vanished as quickly as it appeared. He surely must have imagined it so decided to change the subject.

"Lydia, I don't know what to do about the estate. Of course I've thought about it over the years but not in any serious way. I suppose I didn't think I'd have to do anything drastic for a long time. Stupid really, I should have had a plan because I now realise I can't put off the inevitable. I've been wracking my brains. Who will I put in overall charge, someone to guide Cassie and manage the estate? I just cannot come up with a solution. Have you any idea?" asked Charles.

"Not one that immediately comes to mind," replied Lydia, "But I'll try, I really will."

"I tell you what," said Charles. "Why don't we call a halt to this discussion and sleep on it and chat about more pleasant things. Firstly, how about another G&T?"

"Sounds good to me," replied Lydia, holding out her glass. "Let's have some sandwiches as well, it will soak up the drink. I'll make some, I won't be a moment."

She was glad to do something. She needed a little time to herself. She could not believe what Charles had told her. In truth, she did not want to believe what he had told her. She had pretended to him to be strong but inside, she was falling apart.

Although both she and Charles would be considered old, he was her "little" brother and she hated to see him ill or hurt. All her life her coping mechanism had been to appear to have a 'devil may care' attitude to people and life in general and she could, at times, appear brusque. Only one or two people, who had broken through the barrier, knew this to be a front! She just hoped she would be able to carry it off in front of the most important person in her life; Charles.

She went back to the drawing room with a tray of sandwiches and she and Charles spent the next hour or so chatting about nothing in particular and consuming one or two more gin and tonics! They were at the reminiscing stage, giggling like a couple of school children when the moment was interrupted by Cassie, who came bouncing in to the room to find her father and aunt who had so obviously been drinking, look suitably guilty.

"Hello Cassie," they said in unison.

"You're back early, I wasn't expecting you so soon," said Charles who rather spoilt the sentence by slurring his words just ever so slightly.

"That is more than evident," said Cassie frostily. "Aunt Lydia, I do believe you are encouraging him. This is the second time I have come home to find you 'squiffy'. Are you becoming an alcoholic?" She glared at her father.

Charles could not in all honesty come up with an answer so just grinned sheepishly.

"I was just leaving," said Lydia who was concentrating intently on pronouncing her words correctly. She got to her feet, hiccuped, grinned at Cassie and said, "Pardon me," and proceeded to hiccup again. "I'll see myself out."

Cassie, looking a mixture of concern and annoyance at the behaviour before her, informed her aunt, "You actually live here, if you remember!"

"That is what I meant," replied Lydia indignantly. "I will see myself out of the room. It is self-evident that is what I meant. I will then proceed in a westerly direction towards the stairs whereupon I will endeavour to walk up them. I will turn right at the landing and go to my rooms. Satisfied!"

"All the best then," grinned Charles.

"Thank you so much," replied Lydia.

Cassie just groaned at this performance and, dragging her aunt by the arm, said, "Come on, I'll escort you. An afternoon nap for you both I think."

"See you at dinner," said Lydia, waving regally to Charles as she was guided from the room.

Charles sobered up immediately. The light-hearted mood of the last few hours had vanished and it was now time to face reality again.

He wondered if he had had a sufficient amount to drink in order to tackle the demons in the attic again. He decided he had.

He went up the back stairs in order to avoid Cassie whom he felt sure would start nagging again. Once inside the attic he locked the door.

He looked at the box with Lizzie's letters in them. He hoped the alcohol would dull, even slightly, the pain of the revelation before him. He picked up the letter and started to read.

> *My dear David,*
>
> *I hope you are well. I do not know why I ask that, for I do not think you will ever see this letter but I want to write to you as I would a letter.*
>
> *I am now married and I am so lucky, for Charles is a devoted and attentive husband. I could not wish for more.*
>
> *You will possibly never understand why I have married Charles but that is because you do not know the man. He is a kind, generous, caring person, much respected and admired by those who know and work for him. I feel very lucky, I really do.*

*I also know he will be a wonderful father to our child. Yes,
David, I am going to have your baby. I know you will never believe
me but honestly, I only knew after you left. I promise.*

*Can you even begin to imagine how you would have coped with
this news if you had known? I do. You would initially have been
filled with your usual enthusiasm but once reality set in you would
have quickly lost interest.*

*Marrying someone like Charles will enable our child to have the
best in life.*

Please give us – give us all, your blessing.

All my love, Lizzie.

Charles read it this time with little or no emotion. She had used
him, his Lizzie, whom he adored, had used him. He picked up the
next letter.

My dear David,

*Today, I felt movements for the first time. Charles and I went to
the hospital for an antenatal check. Everything seems fine.*

*Charles will be a wonderful father. He is, I think, rather
pleased about the baby. He wants to rush out and buy things. I don't
want him to. Not yet. It's meant to be bad luck and I don't want to
tempt fate.*

*His sister, Lydia, questioned me about my dates. She seemed a
little suspicious and remembered you. I was as vague as I could be but
she is persistent. I do want to confide in her but I don't know if I
have the courage.*

*Weather here grey and dull. No doubt the sun is shining where
you are, lucky thing.*

Well, I had better go – things to do. Take care.

Much love as ever, Lizzie.

The letters continued in a similar vein although there were some
subtle changes, of which Charles initially wasn't aware but at least
there was no more mention of Lydia. Charles wondered if they had
talked. Reading the letters, it was as if Lizzie was trying to distance
herself from the past. He wondered if her life with David seemed to
be slowly but surely receding in her mind. He rather hoped it had
been. She talked about her art and what she was hoping to achieve

with her paintings more than she did about the baby. Charles was ridiculously pleased, which was foolish, considering David had never seen the letters!

By now Charles had looked through about ten or so letters: only one more to read.

He picked it up and upon opening it realised what one of the changes were:

> *Dear* (instead of My Dear) *David,*
>
> *Not long now. We are so looking forward to the 'big' day. I do hope I cope and don't make too much of a fool of myself during labour. Needless to say I have been regaled with horror stories regards the pain and one or two of the other indignities that giving birth will involve, but I am so excited about it, I don't care.*
>
> *Charles has been marvellous and has even attended the father's classes. He is the oldest there **but,** I am proud to say, certainly the most handsome! I've seen one or two of the others sneak a sideways glance at him and have looked at me with envy. I am so, so lucky and he has said he will be there with me; some of the other dads have declined — too gory, they said. I do hope when it comes to it, he will still want to. I think he will. I do want him there. I need him to be there so much. I don't want to be alone.*
>
> *I think he secretly wants a girl so needless to say that is what I am hoping for as well. I want her to be called Cassandra, and Charles has agreed. I read it in a book and thought it sounded just right, Cassandra Emerson; it has a lovely ring to it, don't you think.*
>
> *You know David, and this is a terrible thing to say to you, but I don't think of this baby as yours any more. If truth be known, I haven't for ages. It's mine and Charles's. Oh, I know that one day I may have to tell him or her (we don't want to know the sex until 'its'; I hate saying 'its', born), but I hope not. I would have to tell Charles first and I could not bear the thought of hurting him like that.*
>
> *Life with Charles has been more wonderful than I imagined possible; and not for the reasons you are thinking, if knowing you, you are thinking mercenary thoughts.*
>
> *I don't really know if I can describe properly what I feel. A feeling of belonging perhaps. No, I think its more than that. I just know I am happier now than I have ever been, even, if your ego will take it, than with you. I think that at last I realise I cannot*

*contemplate life without Charles. The bottom line, as they say, is that
I love him. I really, really do.*

*It is not perhaps the love I had for you; which I suspect was a
combination of first love and a great deal of lust; but a love which has
grown and grown with, if you want to know, many occasions of lust!
It's possibly true what they say; the older ones are the best!!*

*I shouldn't be speaking like this, a nearly-to-be mum! I had
better close now. I have chattered on enough and I think I will have a
lie down as I have a bit of a headache. That is the only thing that is
a bit of a downside of pregnancy; the headaches, but I have been
lucky, they have only recently started.*

*I'm going off to find Charles to remedy something that is long
over due. I've never told him what I feel about him, never ever, not so
much as a hint. Can you believe it?*

*David, I don't know whether I will write to you again, (who'll
have the time), so in case I don't, I wish you all the happiness and
success in the world and thank you, thank you for my youth. It was
wonderful, but its now nearly time for me to be a grown-up and do
you know something? I can hardly wait.*

Bye,

Lizzie x

Charles stared at the letter. Simply sat and stared. Then the
realisation of what he had read hit him. He said out loud. "Lizzie,
Lizzie, Lizzie; thank you, thank you from the bottom of my heart."

For now he knew. He had never really understood why she had
married him. But she had cared for him, even, had loved him. She
had been on her way to him.

Sadly she had never been able to tell him. Why had she been so
cruelly denied that? For on the day the letter had been written was
the day she had died. The memory of that day still etched on his
mind, as if it was only yesterday.

He remembered she had been coming out of their bedroom as
he came up the stairs. She had looked at him strangely and holding
out her hands to him had only managed to gasp *Charles,* when she
had collapsed into his arms. He had shouted for help and then in
what seemed to be a moment Lizzie was taken out of his arms and
became the responsibility of others as they tried to save her. So long
ago: so very long ago.

His mind was in turmoil. He read and re-read the letter. This was the only letter that mattered to him. Charles wondered if Lizzie had felt unwell, if she had an inclination things were not right, for the letter in some ways seemed prophetic. Rather selfishly he could not bear this thought and banished it from his mind.

He put the letter into his shirt pocket and tidied the others into the box and put it away in the trunk. He wanted to speak to someone. He did not know what to do for the best. He could not bear the thought of hurting Cassie. He smiled, his daughter, but was it unfair, especially now with him so ill, to deny her a father? Was he being selfish? Yes, possibly he was, he thought.

He went down the attic steps, unlocked the door, and walked slap bang into Cassie.

"What on earth have you been doing? I've been searching high and low. Why were you in the attic?" demanded Cassie.

"Ah, Cassie," said Charles stroking her cheek. "You are the light of my life, you really are. Don't ever change, never," and off he went towards his bedroom.

Cassie followed him. "Pops, are you feeling all right. You look a bit weird, if you don't mind me saying."

"I'm fine, just fine. Please don't worry. What are you up to this evening or shouldn't I ask?" smiled Charles.

"I'm going to Steven's house after dinner," replied Cassie.

Charles did not have the strength to ask who Steven was so just nodded. "When your aunt wakes can you tell her that I'm going over to Peter's. He asked me for a drink; and yes, before you say anything, another drink, but tell her I won't be in for dinner." With that Charles retreated into his bedroom.

He picked up the phone and rang Peter, who sounded delighted at this interruption and looked forward to seeing him.

He then showered and tried to look a little more respectable before he went downstairs.

He went firstly to Benson to ask him to drive him to Peter's and collect him later. Unfortunately Benson, Margaret, and Mrs. Pearson were all in the kitchen when this request was made, and Charles knew that there would be looks passing between them, especially when he disappeared down to the wine cellar and returned with two bottles of claret.

Charles just smiled at the ladies and said to Benson, "Shall we go? Goodnight, ladies."

Chapter 10

Peter watched with 'his doctor's eye' as Charles got out of the car. His friend looked strained and Peter wondered if he had spoken to Cassie or Lydia. He suspected not, but wouldn't pry and decided he would let Charles set the agenda for this evening.

He opened the door and Charles handed him a bag. "For us."

"Priorities straight as ever," responded Peter with a smile, for he suspected there was a delight in store by way of an excellent wine or two to enjoy. He looked in the bag and let out a gasp of sheer delight as nestling in it were two bottles of the '90 Pichon Comtesse de Lalande.

"Good grief, a treat, an absolute treat. You are undoubtedly spoiling me," said a thrilled Peter. "I am rather glad I have taken steaks out of the fridge. Do you fancy one later, with of course... a side salad?" grinned Peter.

"I suppose chips are out of the question then?" enquired Charles.

"Hold on, I'll see what's in the freezer," said Peter. He rummaged around until he found what he was looking for. "Oven chips, will they do?"

"Excellent, that's more like it," said Charles.

Charles opened the wine while Peter got the glasses and then settled down on either side of the fire with their wine.

"Gorgeous, simply gorgeous," extolled Peter as he savoured the wine. Charles nodded in agreement.

After a few minutes of catching up on things, Charles leant across and said to Peter, "I need your advice; it's not about the cancer, we can talk about that some other time, something else has come up. Never rains but it pours, as they say," he said, trying to smile.

Peter knew, whatever it was made Charles feel decidedly uncomfortable.

"Well, here goes," said Charles. "Now, just say if you'd rather not discuss it or if you are embarrassed, you know, anything at all and I can stop."

"For God's sake man, I haven't a clue what you are talking about. You're wittering; go for it!" More gently Peter said, "Whatever, I'm sure it's not as bad as you think."

Charles looked over at Peter and nodded. Taking a deep breath he then took a sip of wine and said, "Worse, actually." He continued, "Lizzie, did you ever hear any rumours about Lizzie?"

"What kind of rumours?"

"Oh, you know," said Charles, "Our age difference, that sort of thing."

Peter looked at his friend, who was obviously finding this so difficult. He didn't know what to say to him.

"A village like ours always has rumours, you know that," said Peter as diplomatically as possible. "There were the usual gossips who talked about the age difference but Charles, it was more than obvious to anyone who was in the company of you and Lizzie for more than five minutes that you had a special relationship, it really was."

"How special?" countered Charles. "No one ever mentions the "love" word. Do they?"

It was Peter's turn to look a little uncomfortable for, in truth, he had been a little surprised at the marriage, but Charles had been so obviously 'head over heels' that he never ventured a comment.

"It doesn't matter, though because I know she did, I have proof which I want you to see. I found it today, a letter," said Charles as he took the letter out of his pocket.

"Something so personal, are you sure?" asked Peter. "Please think about this. Let's start the meal and once we have eaten, if you still want to show me then fine, but as you said yourself, you have only seen the letter today. Think carefully." He stood up. "Let's go to the kitchen and prepare the meal. Oh, and while you are thinking," he smiled. "You are in charge of the chips. How many do you want?" he asked, opening the bag and pouring some onto the tray. Not waiting for a reply he continued. "They look so good, I'll have to have some as well! I love chips," and he poured the rest onto the tray and put it in the oven.

They both busied about preparing the meal. Charles opened the second bottle of wine and they sat down to enjoy their meal.

"That was delicious, compliments to the chef," said Charles as he raised his glass to Peter.

"My pleasure, although even I can manage to rustle up a steak; mind you its about the only thing I can do," replied Peter.

They quickly tidied the kitchen then settled down in front of the fire to finish off the wine.

Charles looked across at Peter. "I've done as you suggested; I've thought, just in case you imagined that befuddled by drink, I'd forgotten," he said smiling at him, "And I still want you to read the letter." He handed it to Peter. "Please, I really do need your advice."

"Okay I will, but I still feel uncomfortable reading it," said Peter.

"I want you to," persisted Charles.

Peter put on his reading glasses and settled down to read Lizzie's letter aware that Charles was scrutinising him for any reaction. He hoped his face was an unreadable mask.

Peter took his glasses off and handed the letter back to Charles. "That is a lovely letter, thank you for sharing it with me. I feel privileged."

"Are you surprised at the content?" queried Charles.

Peter gave Charles half a smile saying, "I won't insult you by pretending I don't know to which bit you are referring. Lizzie wasn't my patient, but yes, I would be lying if I said I hadn't wondered. But Charles, that is all in the past. You are the one who brought Cassie up: you are the one who is her father. That is what matters. Does she have to know?"

"He's here. He's about ten miles away. David, her real father. I met him for the first time yesterday as, I may add, did Cassie," said Charles, displaying no outward show of emotion.

"Oh God, how the hell did you cope with that?" asked Peter.

"By getting a little drunk," replied Charles. "I would not think for a moment he suspects. He didn't even know Lizzie was pregnant. But it is only a matter of time, I really think if he stays for too long, a seed of suspicion will form. It will. Also, he is an artist."

"Yes," interjected Peter, "But so was Lizzie, that doesn't mean a thing."

"Specialising in portraits," continued Charles.

"Ah, I see."

Charles looked across at Peter and smiling slightly at the thought said, "I can see myself spending my remaining months on this earth in a completely inebriated state. It's going to be the only way to get through this nightmare." He looked at Peter. "Joke, just a joke, although goodness me, its tempting, really tempting. Have you another bottle we can crack open?"

"Good plan," said Peter and went off in the direction of the kitchen to find another bottle of wine.

He poured out another two glasses and Charles, taking a sip, said, "They have the same violet eyes and even a similarly shaped nose. Anyone seeing them together will suspect. I am sure of that."

"It was twenty years ago, no one is going to remember. Lots of people look alike who aren't related," said Peter.

"This will be interesting," said Charles. "Who exactly?"

"Loads, simply loads. I've just forgotten their names, that's all. Too much wine, it will come back to me, really it will."

"Not a patch on yours of course, possibly even an insult to serve after your sublime offering, but not too bad. Not bad at all" said Peter taking yet another sip. "Mind you, my palate doesn't really know what the hell its having now. What do you think of the wine?"

Charles, who hadn't really been listening, said, "Peter, is it fair, considering my state of health, to deprive Cassie of knowing David as her father? Would you not want to know? When I die, who will she have? Lydia – but who knows for how long, she is older than me. Perhaps some very distant relatives, whom we are not really close to? Cassie will be a very wealthy lady but dealing with finances is not exactly her forte. I need to be sure that she has someone who will be there for her."

"Charles, you know that Rowena and I will look after her. You have to know that," replied Peter.

"Good grief, I rather arrogantly assumed," said Charles. "I know you will, as will Kate and Robert and, of course, Benson and Mrs. Pearson, bless her. But none of us are getting any younger. Cassie has friends of course and young men waltz in and out of the house with monotonous regularity but painting, painting is her first love. When she is painting everything and everyone is forgotten. I'm just concerned that someone will latch on to her for her money. You can understand my concerns. Surely you can?"

"Of course I do," said Peter. "But what about Cassie? Have you any idea how she is going to react to firstly, being told how ill you are and secondly, being told she has another father? You can't do that to her, Charles. You just can't."

"Maybe you're right. I don't know. All I know is that I don't have too much time to decide," responded Charles wearily. "I just wish I did."

Charles stretched his legs out in front of the fire and closed his eyes for a moment.

"Help me, Peter. Please help me. I want to do what is best, you know that, but my mind is in turmoil. He, David, I mean, seemed a decent enough chap and he and Cassie seemed to get on quite well."

Peter looked in disbelief at his friend. "Charles, you are basing your opinion of him on one, if I may say, drunken evening and, by your own admission, a fleeting moment or two with Cassie. Forgive my saying this but it does sound as if you are clutching at the proverbial."

"I know. I'm just a bit desperate. It was a nice letter though, really nice." Charles was suddenly hit by a feeling of overwhelming tiredness from the day and by the alcohol.

"Come on, up you get, you can stay here tonight," said Peter, trying to haul Charles out of the chair.

"Can't, can't stay," slurred Charles. "Benson, he's coming for me, I just have to phone. One call and in two shakes, Benson, good old Benson, will be here and off I go. Terrific chap, don't know what I'd do without him." With that Charles slumped back into the chair. Opening one eye he said, "Sorry, squiffy again, making a habit of it I'm afraid, what the hell, that's what I say… what the hell. Excellent meal though… truly excellent," and with that he grinned and closed his eye again.

Somehow, although Peter was a little unsure how, he managed to get Charles upstairs and into bed. Considering how Peter himself was feeling, he felt it was a huge accomplishment! He even managed to phone Benson and say, in as sober a voice as he could muster, that Charles was staying. Benson had thanked him for his call but there had been a slight note of disapproval in his voice! Peter stifled a giggle and feeling suitably chastised, managed to find his own bedroom and crashed out on top of his bed.

The next morning Peter woke to the smell of bacon cooking. He sat bolt upright in bed. For one awful moment he thought Rowena was home. Then calmed himself with the realisation that she was safely away at her sister's. He gave up a silent prayer. Charles, his 'so called' friend: what did he think he was doing?

However he had no more time for that thought, as the feeling of nausea he had on waking was now turning into the distinct possibility of throwing up. With some effort he got out of bed and ran to the bathroom.

He felt a little better, notwithstanding the pounding head and a mouth that tasted of goodness knows what but decided re-hydration was the answer to this problem. He made to go downstairs, and with a concentrated air, held onto the banister and with a slow shuffling gait arrived in the kitchen to encounter the sight of his so-called friend, tucking into an enormous plate of bacon, eggs, and black pudding.

Charles looked up, "Good morning, sleep well? You don't look great. What you need is breakfast, that would help," he said through a mouthful of bacon and eggs. "Fancy some bacon? I hope you don't mind but I was a bit peckish so just rooted around till I found things. This is excellent by the way, first rate."

Peter slumped into the chair and looked in disbelief at Charles who had his forked poised with another pile of bacon. Glaring at him he said, "I want you to know, you are a bastard; truly you are. I just wanted you to know that. You are no friend of mine. A true friend would not sit there devouring a fry-up. He absolutely and definitely would not. That is why you are no friend of mine. I am now going back to the bathroom." And with that Peter hurtled out of the kitchen again.

Charles grinned after him and carried on with his breakfast!

Eventually Peter came back. "Hello, still here? Oh, goody," he said sarcastically and plonked himself into the nearest chair.

Charles placed a pint mug with water in front of him. "Drink up, all of it, you will feel better." After his third pint of water Peter did feel better.

"What a night. I can't take the pace. I haven't felt as bad since I was a medical student," said Peter, holding his head. "Did you know, I have an orchestra in my head, playing the entire symphony no less. Of course it is not something soothing, no they are playing some discordant garbage." He looked at Charles. "It isn't fair, is it?" Charles agreed it wasn't fair.

"The other thing I want to know," demanded Peter. "How the hell are you feeling so bloody all right? That is something else that isn't fair."

"Have some coffee," said Charles, "and I've made you a little omelette and toast. You'll feel better, I promise."

Peter glowered at him and tentatively at first, picked at the first piece of egg but after one or two mouthfuls grinned up at Charles. "I'm feeling better, much better, this is good. You can be my friend again!"

"I'm relieved to hear it," replied Charles smiling back.

After breakfast Peter felt like a new man. They made another pot of coffee and went out into the garden where, if in a sheltered spot, it was reasonably warm.

"Thank you for looking after me last night," said Charles. "I'll have to make my peace with Benson. I don't suppose you remembered to phone?"

"Well you suppose wrongly," replied Peter. "However, you are in big trouble. I felt like a little boy again after I had spoken to Benson. He did not approve."

Charles smiled, "I felt like that last night when I was getting the wine; all eyes on me, all disapproving. I tell myself though that its because they care!"

"And they do," agreed Peter smiling at the memory of his call to Benson. "Changing the subject, do you want to continue last night's discussion? I do remember it in case you are wondering!"

Charles smiled back at his friend. "I really think I should speak to Cassie about my illness. I'm dreading that, I really am." Charles gazed out across the garden deep in thought. Dragging his mind back he continued, "I've been so lucky though, I really think we have a good relationship, considering our start!" Peter looked at him blankly. "Oh, you won't remember," continued Charles, "although perhaps you heard the village rumours." He looked at Peter, "Such a long time ago it all seems."

Peter said, "I'm trying to think why I wasn't around then. Can you?"

Charles shook his head, "No, but then that period of my life is a little bit of a blur in some ways."

"I remember now," said Peter. "I met Lizzie when I was here as a locum: you two had just got married, it was a party or something. Then after my stint here I had to go back to Edinburgh to finish my last six months as a trainee, so that by the time I came back to take over from Dr. Murdoch, everything was sadly different, very different."

They both sat in silence, each contemplating that time, all those years ago.

Charles broke the silence. "Initially I wouldn't accept her, Cassie I mean. Can you believe it? Took ages, well it seemed ages but it was about a month or perhaps a little more. What a waste, what a stupid waste." He felt so sad at that thought. Pulling himself together he continued. "However, no point in going over that again. Well my friend, do you think I should speak to Cassie tonight?"

Peter hesitated before replying, "You and I need to have a chat as well about treatments, I wonder if we should do that first. That way you can have all the facts before you."

Charles shook his head. "The treatments aren't cures though, are they? In fact they may be even worse than the cancer."

Peter continued. "I can understand your concerns, but, and I grant you this is a big but, they may give you extra time. Would you think about speaking to the oncologist? You have nothing to lose and perhaps something to gain. There are new treatments all the time, even trials you could go on. I know I'm not 100% au fait with all the new developments. I don't want to pressurise you but I do want you to know of all the options available. As your doctor I would not be doing my job if I didn't. As your friend, I will respect whatever you wish to do. All I ask is that you think about it please."

"I will," said Charles thoughtfully. "I really will. I suppose its because I'm such a coward; I'm so scared of hospitals, pathetic I know."

Peter chuckled. "People would laugh at the name of Charles Emerson and the word coward mentioned in the same breath. May I just say Korea at this point? Medals for valour, etc. etc. Need I go on?"

Charles looked at Peter. "You'll think I'm mad but right now, the thought of Korea seems easier than facing Cassie, oncologists, hospitals or whatever. Told you I was crazy."

Charles glanced at his watch. "Do you know what time it is? It's nearly lunchtime. We have been talking for ages. I'd better be going now. Can I phone Benson? Oh, can I also add to my list after hospitals, Lydia, Mrs. Pearson and Benson!"

Peter laughed. "Now them – I can understand. I don't envy your reception when you go home."

Charles tried to look appealingly at Peter, "I don't suppose you'd care to come for lunch? Safety in numbers and all that!"

"You're on your own chum. I don't have the strength plus, I will have to do some things in the house before Rowena comes back or else they'll be hell to pay, but I'll be thinking about you. Come on, I'll run you home."

"Drive slowly, then," said Charles.

All too soon they arrived at The Hall. "Well, here goes. Wish me luck," said Charles. Getting out of the car he continued, "I think I'll speak to Cassie tomorrow, when I'm more in control of my faculties! I may make more sense then." Smiling at Peter he said, "Excellent evening as ever. My thanks. I don't know what I'd do without you," he added quietly and with that he closed the car door.

Peter looking at him with affection, mouthed, 'all the best!' as he drove off.

Chapter 11

Charles had hoped to sneak in and thought all was well that was until he began his ascent up the stairs, for at the top was Benson.

Whoops, thought Charles. "Benson, ah, there you are. Lovely day is it not," Charles smiled up at him.

Benson nodded and said, "Good afternoon. I trust you had an enjoyable evening."

"Yes, yes thank you we did. I thought I'd stay over so as not to drag you out at some God awful hour," said Charles, totally understanding how Peter had felt last night after his call to Benson. Benson was making him feel like a little boy.

"Most considerate of you but it would have been no trouble, no trouble at all."

"I'll remember that for the future then, thank you Benson," said Charles.

"Is there anything you require, Sir?" enquired Benson.

"Thank you, nothing, and no lunch as I had a late breakfast. I'll call should I wish anything," replied Charles and went into his room.

He closed the door with relief and hoped he could now have some peace. He remembered this was Lydia's day for good works at the charity shop so she wouldn't be back for some time. Cassie would be safely at the art gallery. *Excellent*, he thought, *Peace and time for a snooze without interruptions!*

He lay on top of his bed but after a minute or two felt cold so decided to go the whole hog and undress and get into bed. As his head touched the pillow he let out a contented sigh and within a very short time fell asleep.

It was dark when Charles woke and he was a little disorientated. He then remembered where he was. Looking at his bedside clock he realised he had been asleep for nearly five hours. He felt much better. Cassie and Lydia would be home soon so he thought he'd better get up and shower to be presentable for their return otherwise there would be yet another inquisition. After his ablutions he dressed and went downstairs. He heard a car screech to a halt – Cassie was home!

He went to the door just as she came bounding in. "Hello Pops. Have a good time at Peter's last night?" she asked kissing him on the cheek. "What time did you get home?"

"Yes and can't remember," in answer to your questions replied Charles and then, trying to divert her further interrogation, "How was the gallery today?" putting his arm around her shoulder.

"We sold a Fletcher, what do you think of that?" replied Cassie.

"I think," responded Charles, "That some people have more money than sense. How much?"

"How very rude. You'd better sit down then," replied Cassie, laughing. "Ready for this?" Charles nodded. "10,000 smackers, can you believe it? Don't look so stunned Pops but I'm with you, it is incredible."

"It's not incredible it's obscene, quite obscene," said Charles. "You know I met him once, that Fletcher chap, at one of your *do's*. I was looking with, I may add, some incredulity at his work and he came across. I hadn't a clue what to say to him so said the token *'interesting'* and asked him how he did it. I had always thought that he must pick up a tin of paint, fling it across the canvas and then perhaps invite a few people in to do a war dance on top of it and do you know that's exactly what he does. He told me, he really did."

Cassie laughed, "You're kidding."

Charles laughed as well. "Perhaps not the war dance bit but he flings the paint. He said that after he has thrown the paint he then decides which way the paint seems to flow and his body then reacts with that. He apparently lies on top of it as if swimming, I suppose and then, hey presto, you get some complete moron thinking it's 'the in thing' and has to have it. More fool them I say. I think after dinner I must go to the shed to see if there is any paint kicking around and chuck it about – may make a fortune! Speaking of dinner will you be gracing us with your presence or not?"

"Yes, in tonight," said Cassie.

"Oh good, that's nice. We haven't had the chance of a chat for ages."

"Well, actually Pops, I had sort of thought I'd go to the studio afterwards. There's something I'm working on. I'm itching to get back to it. You don't mind do you? Aunt Lydia will be in." Charles raised his eyes heavenwards. "Don't look like that," said Cassie. "Yesterday you two were getting on like a house on fire, no bickering at all. I was very pleased with you both."

"Thank you, how kind, but that was yesterday," replied Charles. "Anyway, what are you working on just now that's so important?"

"Promise me you won't come to the studio."

Charles raised an eyebrow at Cassie. "Why, what's the secret?"

"You've got to promise first. I won't even give you a hint unless you do," said Cassie.

"Cross my heart, Scouts honour and anything else you'd like," responded Charles.

"Well," said Cassie, just a little coyly. "It was meant to be a surprise for you. Now before you say anything," she added quickly. "I know you hate surprises, but you'll like this, I really think you will. So you won't bug me about it – please, pretty please."

Cassie batted her big violet eyes at him and once again, as with all the other times previously, Charles laughed, succumbed and promised he would not go near the studio.

She flung her arms around his neck and said, "I knew you'd say that. You won't regret it," and gave him another kiss.

They were both unaware that Lydia had been standing at the door witnessing this scene between father and daughter – how happy they appeared – how sad she felt, knowing that time between them was so limited. She felt tears prick her eyes. Life at times could be so unfair; in fact, she hated to use the word, so unlady-like, 'a total bugger'. There, she'd said it. She felt better for it, feeling angry was so much better than feeling sorry for oneself.

"Hello you two, what are you up to?" asked Lydia. Before either could answer she continued, "Charles when did you get home from Peter's last night? I didn't hear you."

"Tiptoed in that's why. Fancy a G&T? What about you, Cassie?"

Aunt and niece both replied in the affirmative. Charles poured the drinks and then they all sat down to talk about their day, well really only Lydia and Cassie with Charles contributing the occasional 'mmmm', until Benson came in to tell them that dinner was ready.

After dinner Cassie went off to the studio and Charles and Lydia adjourned to the sitting room.

"Have you told her?" asked Lydia.

"No," sighed Charles. "I know I have to, I just didn't want to spoil tonight. Peter and I talked last night. He wants me to see an oncologist – you know, keep all avenues open. I've said I'll think about it but you know me and hospitals; can't bear the thought. Night-cap?"

Lydia nodded, "Brandy and with a splash of ginger please."

Charles poured them both one.

"You look tired Charles, you should have an early night. You were obviously late last night!"

Charles smiled back at her. "I may do just that."

"I know it's none of my business," said Lydia tentatively.

"This will be good," responded Charles, "Because that will be a first! Just teasing. What is it?"

"I agree with Peter," Lydia continued, "I would like you to explore all avenues. Please, at least think about it."

"I will, I promise I will," Charles gave a slight smile. "It's just you read that the cure, although in this case there won't even be a cure, but the treatment shall we say, is worse than the actual disease itself. It's scary, that's all, but if its any consolation, I had thought I'd see the oncologist just hear what he has to say. I'll phone Peter in the morning and fix up an appointment."

Lydia gave a relieved smile. "That's all I ask. No stone unturned as it were. Think of Cassie."

"If I do that," replied Charles, "I'll totally crack up. I'll phone Peter tomorrow, I really will. Now, completely changing the subject, what are you up to tomorrow?"

"No plans," replied Lydia.

"Excellent, I'll treat you to lunch at Les Maison. What do you say?" asked Charles.

"That will be lovely, I look forward to that," said a delighted Lydia. She was just about to ask why, when the phone rang. "I'll get it."

"Say I've emigrated," said Charles.

"Hello, no it's her aunt speaking. Charles, um, I'm not sure where he is at the moment. May I ask who's calling? David Coleridge!" Lydia looked over at Charles who was giving frantic signals that he did not wish to speak to him. "When he returns I'll ask him to call you. Does he have your number? If you let me have it then, yes, I've got it. I'll let him know. Thank you for calling. Goodbye."

Lydia replaced the receiver. "That was the chap who was here the other evening, wasn't it, Lizzie's old friend?" Lydia saw the troubled look that clouded Charles's face. He ran his hand through his hair. Since he was a little boy he did that when worried.

She went over and sat beside him. "Charles, please, if I can help I will. There is something wrong. I know there is." Charles looked at her and nodded. "For once though, I'm not going to nag. Surprising as that may be! When you are ready, I'll listen, but only if you want me to."

Charles smiled and, patting her hand, said, "You know something Lydia, you can at times be a pet and a poppet." He lay back on the sofa and ran his hands through his hair again. "God, the last few days have been absolutely bloody, totally and absolutely bloody. I don't know how much more I can take, I really don't. I feel I'm on an emotional roller-coaster which I would really like to get off." He smiled grimly, more to himself than Lydia. "This evening was so pleasant, just like the old days chatting with my two favourite ladies over dinner. I quite forgot everything until he phoned. Damn him, absolutely damn him. You know something? I wouldn't care, but he's actually quite pleasant and under different circumstances I may have even quite liked him."

Initially Charles wasn't making a great deal of sense to Lydia but then, slowly but surely, it dawned on her and in the mists of her mind she began to remember what she had suspected a long, long time ago and wondered. She looked at Charles, their eyes meeting.

It was Charles who broke the silence. "What do you know?"

"What do you mean, what do I know?" asked Lydia stalling for time, trying to remember what she did know.

"David, David Coleridge, that name means something to you. Did Lizzie ever speak to you about him?" persisted Charles. He looked at her intently as if imploring her to remember.

"I'm trying to remember Charles, really I am," said Lydia. "We're both tired. Why don't we talk tomorrow? Everything will seem clearer in the morning."

Charles rose wearily. "You are right, as ever." He walked over to the door and looked back. "Still on for lunch tomorrow?"

"Let's see how we feel tomorrow, Charles," replied Lydia, grateful for this reprieve.

Charles started to walk out of the room and saying to no one in particular, "It's amazing, truly amazing how one teensy-weensy phone call can absolutely ruin the moment, the evening, truly amazing. Goodnight."

Lydia watched Charles seemingly haul himself up the stairs with each step appearing such an effort. Lydia thought that if she had David Coleridge in front of her she'd have throttled him, and with that less than charitable thought, went upstairs to bed.

Charles had spent a restless night, sleep denied him, tossing and turning. Music, as ever, was his solace and he had spent the night listening to Bach's B. Minor Mass and St. Matthew's Passion. A night for Bach he felt, whilst reading and re-reading Lizzie's letter. To some a perhaps strange combination, but he found them both comforting. If there was such a thing as a soul, or spirit, he thought it had been at least partially healed. By first light he was a little more at peace with himself and seemed to have gained strength to face the ordeals before him, namely, Cassie, the oncologist, Lydia and David.

He went downstairs in a strangely buoyant mood to find that Cassie was already tucking into breakfast. "Good morning. What time did you get to bed?" he asked, bending down and kissing the top of her head.

"Didn't, haven't as yet, couldn't stop what I was doing," said Cassie through a mouthful of toast.

"Oh, yummy," said Charles. "Why can't we revert back to the good old days of cooked breakfasts?" he asked spooning some muesli into a bowl. "This is like eating hamster bedding. "It's revolting, quite revolting. Have you not work today?"

"Yes, I'll have a quick shower and 'bob's your uncle' as they say, I'll astound the customers with my exquisite beauty," Cassie giggled. "I know, some hope!"

She looked over at Charles. "Why are you looking at me so strangely, Pops? Are you feeling all right? You know something?" Cassie asked biting into her toast, and not expecting a reply. "For the last little while I've thought you have looked a little poorly but in the last couple of days you've looked down right weird. Are you sure you're okay?"

"Fine, absolutely fine, don't you fret," said Charles. "What are your plans for tonight?"

"I've only to work the morning," replied Cassie. "Because I'm doing Saturday morning, so I will be off to the studio. The place you can't enter. Remember?" She grinned at him. She had realised lately that he was looking so much older. She couldn't bear the thought of him being older, of not being there. She shivered, awful thought, quite awful, but there was something, definitely something, that wasn't right but she could not put her finger on it. She'd ask her aunt, she was bound to know.

She leapt from the table, gave Charles a peck on the cheek and went whizzing out the door, nearly knocking her aunt down in the process.

"Gosh, sorry, got to dash. I'm late, got to shower and be out of here in ten minutes!" With that she bounded up the stairs two at a time.

"Morning, Charles. By the look of you I wouldn't say you had a particularly restful night," said Lydia, helping herself to coffee and toast.

"How right you are," said Charles. "This is disgusting, I can't eat anymore of this," and he put his spoon down.

"I think I'll go and phone Peter before surgery and get him to fix things, won't be a moment," said Charles.

Charles came back with a fixed expression on his face. "My good friend has rather pre-empted that call. Sorry, lunch is off. I've got to see the chap at two. Peter decided to phone the doc, just in case I agreed. Kind, isn't he!" Helping himself to more coffee, he continued. "I don't think I'll feel like lunch before seeing him. Will you, as they say, take a rain check? I'm really sorry about this."

"Charles, for heavens sake, we can have lunch anytime," said Lydia. "As you know, I," Lydia was suddenly very hesitant, "Well what I'm trying to say is, if you want company, I'd be pleased to come along but I... well... of course, and its entirely up to you, whatever, but what I'm meaning is – well, you know... I'm available."

Charles grinned. "I don't think you should tell all and sundry that you're available; they'll get totally the wrong impression." Lydia did not smile back and he knew he shouldn't tease. "Sorry, and thank you for your offer, but if you don't mind I'll toddle along on my own. It would look a bit pathetic I feel, having my big sister with me! I'll be all right and will report back, I promise."

They both looked up as they heard a "Bye!" shouted from the hall followed by the door being shut. Cassie was off to work. They heard the car roar into action and Charles looked at his watch. "Amazing, and with two minutes to spare."

Charles and Lydia finished their breakfast. "By no stretch of the imagination could that be called a delicious breakfast," said Charles.

"It's meant to be good for you," said Lydia.

"Quite," replied Charles. "It's been a boon hasn't it?" he said with a wry smile. "Well, what are you up this morning?"

"I've no plans," answered Lydia.

"How do you fancy a walk then," asked Charles. "I rather fancy going to the lake and along to the meadow, care to join me?"

"Mmm, that would be good, it's a lovely morning," replied Lydia. "Give me a minute to change."

"Why on earth do you need to change? Such a mystery to me all this changing that goes on with you women, amazing. I'm going as I am, perhaps a jacket, that's all," sighed Charles.

"Two minutes," repeated Lydia, ignoring him.

Lydia went upstairs. She was happy to do anything that Charles wanted, for she knew he would be nervous about going to see the doctor and wanted his morning filled. Lydia still felt all this was a little unreal. She couldn't believe it was only two days ago that he had given her the horrendous news. She was trying very hard to be brave for him but found it so difficult. She put on the clothes she thought more suitable for their walk and went back down to find Charles pointedly looking at his watch.

"Very good, only twelve minutes – you said two! Are you ready now?" asked Charles impatiently. Lydia nodded and off they went.

The walked across the lawn towards the lake. Charles looked down at Lydia and said, "Thanks for the company, I didn't fancy being on my own this morning."

"My pleasure," responded Lydia, smiling back at him.

They continued to the lake in companionable silence. It was a beautiful autumn day and surprisingly warm. After they had been walking for nearly half-an-hour they rested on one of the bench seats that Charles had dotted around the estate.

"Sorry about this, but I need a little break, can't take the pace any more," said Charles. "Nice place for a breather though," he said as he gazed at the vista before him, deep in thought. After a little he hunched forward and ran his hand through his hair.

Lydia leant forward. "Charles, is it this afternoon?"

Charles shook his head and then sitting back looked at Lydia and smiling said, "Sorry about this but I need your advice again. You should feel tremendously honoured, twice in two days... but that is of course what big sisters are for. I'm about to land yet another bombshell at your feet. Think you can cope?"

Lydia smiled. "I'll try."

Charles gave a slight smile. "Remember our phone call from David Coleridge last night?" Lydia just nodded.

"I think the name is familiar to you," said Charles as he lit a cigar. "You don't mind?" he motioned to the cigar. Lydia shook her head.

"The name is not unfamiliar to me. I wracked my mind last night after his call and yes, he and Lizzie were friends," replied Lydia.

"Friends!" repeated Charles. "No more than friends?"

Lydia chose to ignore the question. "Charles, why are you torturing yourself with this now, especially now. Don't you think you have enough to contend with?"

"It is precisely because of the timing that I need to sort some things out. Do you want me to tell you about David or not?"

"Very well. Go ahead, you're obviously concerned but I'm sure it can be easily sorted." replied Lydia.

"I wish I shared your optimism," said Charles as he shifted uneasily on the seat. "There is no easy way to tell you so I'm going to blurt it out. I have just found out – David Coleridge is Cassie's father."

Lydia turned ashen and Charles thought she might collapse. "Lydia, I'm so, so sorry, are you all right?" he asked with concern.

Lydia was ferreting about in her pocket for her nitro-glycerine spray for her angina. She hadn't had an angina attack for ages; even when Charles told her about his illness. She took two puffs. As ever, a headache of such intensity made her feel worse for a moment or two but then it subsided and her angina was, once again, under control. "Sorry about that," she replied breathlessly, "Haven't had one for ages."

Charles looked with concern. "What on earth am I doing to you, forgive me."

"Nothing to forgive," said Lydia briskly. "I'm fine now it was just the combination of the walk and your revelation, for revelation is surely what it was. Charles, are you sure, absolutely positive?"

"Lydia, tell me honestly. Did you not think there was undue haste for our wedding?" asked Charles.

Lydia felt a little uncomfortable but realised that Charles did not really expect an answer at that precise moment.

He continued. "I did, but you know what Lizzie was like, fired with enthusiasm." He smiled, recalling that time. "I just got bowled along and I was happy to be, I really was. Before I go any further, I want you to know that I would not have changed a thing. I loved Lizzie with all my heart and as for Cassie, I can't turn back the clock, nor would I wish to. She has given me **the** most incredible joy. No father is entitled to so much. I adore her, simply adore her. But initially and only for a moment, a nano-second even, I felt bitter, but no longer than that. I promise."

Charles took a letter from his pocket. "Lizzie wrote letters to David, which for whatever reason, she did not send. Here is her last one. Please, I want you to read it," he offered it to Lydia.

"I don't have my reading glasses," said Lydia.

"I'll read it then," said Charles, putting on his glasses. He read the letter to Lydia, occasionally his voice broke with the emotion of what he was reading. When he finished, he looked at Lydia and was surprised to see tears streaming down her face. He hugged her to him.

"What a beautiful letter, Charles. Forgive this breakdown," said Lydia dabbing her eyes. "It was truly a wonderful letter; thank you so much for sharing it but Charles, think carefully. Does Cassie have to know? She could not have wished for a better father and she adores you. What might this do to her? What about David? Does he know?"

"I don't think so," replied Charles. "I, of course, would have to tell him, in fact I would have to tell him before I spoke to Cassie. God, what a mess. What a mess."

Looking at Lydia, he asked, "You suspected, didn't you? Lizzie mentioned in one of the letters about you quizzing her about her dates."

"Yes I did, I actually tried to speak to Lizzie," said Lydia. "When you two got married I wondered if she was pregnant. Oh, you both looked so happy that day, so very happy. I'm no expert as you know, but Lizzie's bump, shall we say, seemed a little bigger than one might normally expect at the dates she was saying. This is why I was perhaps a little suspicious and then when Cassie was born she did not seem to be premature. But with all that happened, I never considered telling you my suspicions. I suppose I thought I must be wrong and so I put the thoughts away to the back of my mind. I'm sorry, but I don't think I would have done any differently, I really don't."

Lydia patted Charles's hand. "For what its worth, I always thought Lizzie loved you and I am delighted to have been proved right, for this letter proves it without a shadow of a doubt." Lydia looking rather pleased with this knowledge. "Charles, getting back to Cassie: you have brought her up to be the lovely girl she is. It is your guidance, your ideals that she goes by in her life." Laughing, Lydia continued. "She may not have always agreed with them, but she has always respected them."

"That's maybe true, but surely I have to say something to her," repeated Charles. "Don't you think?"

"David Coleridge, how long is he to be here?" asked Lydia.

"Not sure, to be honest. I can't remember if he said. I would suppose it will depend upon how long it takes for him to get his mother's affairs straightened out," replied Charles. "I know I haven't had much time to think about this but I do really think that it's only fair to Cassie that she knows."

Another thought hit Charles. He looked at Lydia with a horrified expression. "God, we have to have dinner with him some time. You can imagine how keen I am on that. You, by the way, will be joining us for dinner – and that is a statement! I'll need all the help I can get." Charles looked so anxious that Lydia could do nothing but agree to join them.

"You know, Charles, I really think this is all far, far too much for Cassie to cope with in one fell swoop," said Lydia. "Please, talk to her about your illness first and let her get to grips with that.

Promise me you will. I know how I'm feeling, so I cannot begin to imagine how Cassie will feel."

"You really think so?" asked Charles. Lydia nodded. "All right, I will bow to your superior knowledge. I won't say anything at the moment. Depending upon what the chap says this afternoon, I may even try and tell Cassie today."

"I think that's wise, Charles, I really do," said a somewhat relieved Lydia.

Charles looked at his watch. "We'd better be getting back. Are you feeling all right for the walk back?" asked Charles anxiously.

"Fine, absolutely fine," replied Lydia.

Deep in their own thoughts they walked back in silence to Harrington Hall.

Chapter 12

Charles was trying to exude a confidence he did not feel but he had to try for Lydia's sake, although he knew that trying to pull the wool over her eyes had always been well nigh impossible.

"I'm off then," he said as brightly as he could muster popping his head round the sitting room door.

"Good luck," said Lydia looking up from the page in her book she had read and re-read at least ten times! Smiling at him, but with a concern on her face that she couldn't quite erase, she said, "I'm sure anyone Peter recommends will be excellent. Take notes, just in case you don't remember everything."

"Perhaps, we'll see!" responded Charles as he made his way to the front door.

"Bye," he called and with that shut the front door, went across the drive to his car and with more than a little apprehension, drove off. He knew it was a ridiculous thing to feel but there was no denying it – he had butterflies in his stomach. He felt as he had in his youth, when he had been off to see the headmaster, that feeling in the pit of his stomach. He hoped he would remember what the doctor was saying. He then panicked. He could not for the life of him remember the doctor's name. How rude. He was sure it was the name of a bird, he considered, sparrow, Dr. Sparrow perhaps. No, that was the name in the Richard Gordon books. What on earth was it? Suddenly it came to him, parrott. Dr. Parrott. He felt a tremendous relief that his memory had not deserted him.

In what had seemed the quickest possible journey, Charles arrived at the hospital and strode along in a purposeful manner to the Oncology Unit. He arrived at the outer office of Dr. Parrott's, knocked and entered. Dr. Parrott's secretary was expecting him and made polite conversation until Dr. Parrott arrived.

"Forgive me, Lord Emerson. I'm a little late," said Dr. Parrott, extending his hand.

"Not all," replied Charles. "It's very good of you to see me. I was early, but your secretary has been looking after me," he smiled at the secretary.

Dr. Parrott opened the door and beckoned Charles to proceed. Once seated Dr. Parrott looked at Charles and asked, "So, how are you feeling?"

Charles went over his symptoms and what pain relief he was taking, finding it far easier than he had thought relating this. Dr. Parrott listened intently, occasionally interjecting with the odd question but was in no way patronising or condescending. Charles warmed to the man who spoke in no nonsense terms and liked his quiet yet authoritative manner.

"I will not insult you by promising you what I can't," said Dr. Parrott, "But, I can perhaps buy you some more time."

"I am concerned that the treatment may be worse than the actual illness," said Charles.

"Many people share your concerns. All I can promise you is that should you find the treatments I suggest become too difficult to tolerate then, if you wish, we stop. Everyone reacts differently to the treatments and it can involve a little bit of juggling around until we get the right combination but you are the one who calls the shots, so to speak, not me. I will continue for as long as you wish. However, by the same token, if things are not progressing as I would hope, then I may say there is no point in continuing and putting you through unnecessary treatments, but we would have continuous discussions regards what is happening." Dr. Parrott smiled over at Charles. "I know this is a great deal to take in. I'll write all this down for Peter, who can go over this again with you and perhaps your family although I would of course be pleased to speak to them. If it is of any help at all to you. If this were me, I would start treatment, but have a think about it and let me know."

Charles looked over at the doctor. "I don't need to consider, I will start the treatment you recommend. When do you propose I come in?"

Dr. Parrott looked at the schedule in front of him. "Would Monday be convenient for you?"

Charles nodded and, hoping his voice would sound normal, said, "Thank you for seeing me and for explaining everything so that even I can understand," he smiled. "I'm very grateful. Do I just arrive here on Monday?"

"No, I'll tell the ward to expect you. We like to see the patients on the ward at eight-thirty. On the first day there are quite a lot of tests; measurements to be done, bloods taken, that kind of thing. Bring a book – it can get a bit boring," said Dr. Parrott.

"Yes I will, thank you. I'll see you on Monday then, eight-thirty prompt," said Charles standing up and shaking hands again. "Goodbye." He nodded acknowledgement to the secretary and left the office.

He made his way quickly to the car and drove off at some speed from the hospital. He just wanted away from the place. He continued for a little while then, stopping at a lay-by, lit a cigar and phoned Lydia. She had sounded relieved he had called and he was glad he had.

He drew deeply on his cigar. He realised that in three days he would have to go into hospital. He would have to tell Cassie tonight for he would also have to tell Benson and Mrs. Pearson, then he remembered also Robert, Kate; the list seemed endless. He hadn't really thought about how many people would need to know. It was only fair that Cassie knew first. Ghastly, awful thought, he really did not know how he would begin.

He finished his cigar and then started the car and drove back to Harrington Hall.

As he entered he heard Lydia say: "He's just arrived, I'll get him."

God, who now? he wondered. Relieved to find it was only Peter wondering how he had got on, he went to the phone. Peter had sounded pleased that he was taking the treatment as well.

"You've made the right decision, Charles, you really have. You're in good hands. Give me a phone if you need anything. Take care," and with that Peter hung up.

Well, thought Charles, *everyone seems to think I'm doing the right thing. I hope to God I am*, and with that he sat down and proceeded to tell Lydia what Dr. Parrott had said.

Firmly in control as ever she just nodded, with no interjections whatsoever. Once he had finished she patted his hand and said "Well done, Charles, one step at a time, but well done."

Charles smiled a little grimly. Agreeing with Dr. Parrott was the easy bit. The hard part was ahead.

"I think I'll have a little nap before Cassie comes home, I feel I'll need all my strength. Just an hour, don't let me sleep longer than that."

Lydia watched him go upstairs. She was so pleased he was going to take the treatment. Although she was sensible enough to know this wasn't a cure, where there was life and all that, was her maxim now. Miracles did happen so who knows, something wonderful might happen to Charles. Sense, she decided, could prevail another time!

Charles woke two minutes after his allotted hour. He felt surprisingly refreshed and ready to face even Cassie.

He showered and dressed and was just about to go downstairs when Cassie came racing up the stairs.

"Hi, Pops, gosh, what a day. Sarah's home so I'm going over there to catch up on all the gossip."

"Do you have to go this evening?" asked Charles. He had completely forgotten that Sarah, Peter's daughter, would be home fleetingly from working in France before going back to university. She and Cassie had been friends all their lives and he could understand Cassie wanting to see her but oh, not tonight.

Cassie looked at him strangely. "You know something, Pops, you don't look very great. I think slightly weird even, well not exactly weird, but not right. Are you okay? You know I haven't seen Sarah for absolute ages. I would just go over for a little while."

"Cassandra, please come in and sit down. I have something to tell you," said Charles.

By calling her that, Cassie knew there was definitely something wrong. He never called her Cassandra unless she had been about to get a row or something serious was up.

"Okay, what's up?" asked Cassie sitting down. It was then she noticed the unmade bed. "Are you feeling all right?" she asked with concern. "You've been to bed haven't you?"

"Yes," said Charles. "I'm not very well. I'm sorry having to tell you like this."

Cassie felt as if someone had just kicked her in the stomach. She was trying to act poised and cope because she suspected what he was going to tell her was something awful, something truly awful.

"Sorry, but I can't think of an easy way to say this." Cassie just nodded.

Charles put his arm around her and quietly told her about his cancer. Tears sprang to her eyes and for a moment she thought she was going to faint but a strength she did not know she possessed came to the fore. She looked at him. This had to be so wrong, so very, very wrong.

"What treatment will you get?" Without letting Charles reply Cassie breathlessly continued. "You know I'll look after you, I really will and once you've had all your treatments you'll be fine. I know people sometimes don't feel very well, and I know you may feel sick and things – but once its finished you'll be better, won't you? Won't you?" she asked again, almost in a whisper. From the look on his face she knew the answer. It was then that they clung to each other and she cried. Charles took his handkerchief from his pocket and wiped away her tears.

"I won't give up hope," said Cassie defiantly. "I won't, I really, really won't. Pops, promise me something."

"I'll try Cassie, I really will try," replied Charles.

"That's what I wanted you to promise. You've promised you said you'd try and you've never ever broken a promise to me, so remember that."

Charles hugged her to him. "This is one promise I would give anything to keep."

He looked down at Cassie who was trying so hard to remain composed. "I'm sorry telling you this way but I've been putting it off. I've hated having to put you through this. Can you be strong?" Speech was denied Cassie at this moment and she just nodded. "I'm going to have to tell Benson and Mrs. Pearson, Kate, Robert and anyone else I can think of before I go in on Monday. Mind you, they'll be a dawdle compared with telling you," Charles smiled gently at Cassie. "Thank you for being so brave. I have to be the luckiest man I know having you." Charles was going to say 'as my daughter' but couldn't quite bring himself to say that.

"Off you go now and see Sarah, I'll see you later."

"I don't really fancy going over now," replied Cassie.

"She's your best friend. We all need friends, especially when we are in trouble," responded Charles. "We can talk later if you wish but it would be good to see her and catch up.

I will confess to you now that Peter and I reverted back to our youth the other night." Charles grinned like a naughty schoolboy. "I didn't get in late. I didn't get in at all, stayed at Peter's. Now you know! But I don't regret it, well apart from the thumping headache in the morning. We all need to do something to have a release when life throws us, shall we say, a bit of a spanner in the works."

Cassie thought she was going to get upset again. This wasn't happening; it just couldn't be. Her Pops, her beloved Pops. Life wasn't fair. It was absolutely not fair. He had to get better; he just had to. He was looking at her anxiously.

"I'm okay, really I am," said Cassie, "I promise you I will surprise you and be strong, really strong." She tried to smile through her tears. I'll do as you say and go out for a little while but I won't be late. Aunt Lydia, Pops, you're her best friend, who will she speak to?"

"We'll all keep an eye on each other," said Charles. "Now off you go, see you later," and he kissed her on the cheek and with a final, 'Go', shut the door.

Charles felt totally and utterly exhausted but that feeling was somewhat tempered by slight relief that Cassie now knew. He might as well tell the others tonight, do everything in a 'oner' as it were.

He went downstairs to find Lydia who was organising two gin and tonics.

"You are a saint," said Charles, taking a glass. "Have you seen Cassie?"

"Yes," said Lydia. "We just looked at each other for a moment – I don't think words were needed. She flung her arms around me and said we'd all look after each other. Then she left, for Sarah's I think. If she wants to talk to me she knows she only has to ask."

"Yes," said Charles. "And I think maybe she will in a day or two. I'm pleased that Sarah is home for a few days; it's good for Cassie to have her friend around just now."

They sat in silence, each with their own thoughts.

"Well, that went down a treat, fancy another?" asked Charles.

Lydia held out her glass. "Please."

"I'm going to have a word with Robert and Kate, Benson and Mrs. Pearson after dinner. I'll have to if I'm going in on Monday. Can you think of anyone else?" asked Charles.

"I don't think so, not at the moment," replied Lydia.

When Cassie arrived at Peter's door, he knew by her face that Charles must have told her.

Peter held out his arms and Cassie allowed herself to be enveloped in the temporary security they afforded. Tears cascaded down her cheeks as she silently wept. Eventually the tears subsided. She dabbed her eyes.

"Cassie, any time you need to talk, are worried about something or just need to recharge your batteries, turn up any time, day or night, whether Sarah's here or not, all right?" said Peter. Cassie just nodded and, wiping her eyes again, smiled weakly at Peter and with Sarah went upstairs to Sarah's room.

"Has your Dad said anything about mine?" asked Cassie.

"No, nothing, only when I said you were coming over this evening did he mention that Uncle Charles wasn't very well and I wasn't to go on and on ad nauseam about France and uni and everything. Is it something dreadful?" asked Sarah gently.

With that Cassie burst into tears again, "It's worse than that, much, much worse," sobbed Cassie. "He's got cancer and I don't think he's going to get better."

Sarah felt tears prick her eyes for she was incredibly fond of 'Uncle' Charles as she called him, and couldn't imagine him not at The Hall. "Cassie, I'm so, so sorry. When did you find out?"

"Just before I came over, he told me then," replied Cassie who was still reeling from the news. "I keep thinking this is some horrendous nightmare and I'm going to wake up; but it isn't and I'm not." She wiped her eyes. "I must be looking excellent, all puffy and red." She was trying to gather herself together.

"You don't look too bad at all," replied Sarah. "A little blotchy perhaps, but that's all."

"Thanks," said Cassie trying to smile. "I mustn't let Pops see me like this. I don't want him worrying about me. He's got enough to think about. Can I borrow some of your make-up before I go home?"

"Of course you can," smiled Sarah, looking at her friend with concern.

Cassie continued. "You know, I've thought he wasn't that great for a little while. If only I had nagged him and made him go to see Uncle Peter earlier, he might have been all right. If only I had done that. It's my fault – I should have made him, I should have." Tears started again. She put her head in her hands and let them flow.

Sarah put her arm round her friend's shoulders. "You know that isn't right. You couldn't have done anything – it wasn't your fault. Don't be such an idiot. You're only saying that because you're so upset. Please don't blame yourself. That won't help anyone, least of all your Dad. Please, Cassie, listen to me."

Cassie raised her head. "I know you're right, I do. I just don't know what to do. He's going in for some treatment on Monday. Your Dad organised it."

"That's good then. They wouldn't do that unless they thought there was some chance, would they?" said Sarah as brightly as she could.

"Maybe not, I don't know," replied Cassie. She looked at her friend. "Sorry, I think I should go home. Do you mind?"

Sarah shook her head. "I'm here until Sunday. Mum's taking me back about eleven."

Cassie tried to smile. "I haven't heard anything about France and all the gorgeous guys. Perhaps I can come back tomorrow?" She went over to the mirror. "God, I look hellish. Do something, Sarah. Try and fix me up to look a little better. I can't go home looking like this."

Sarah attempted to sort her friend out. "Anyway," continued Cassie, "It will give me time to hear every intimate and disgusting little detail about France!"

"As if there was anything like that," replied Sarah trying to sound indignant. She was about to wax lyrical about Claude but decided this was not the evening to regale her friend with stories of her sex life.

"Well," said Cassie, "Go on."

"Not tonight," said Sarah, "It would take far, far too long," she said with a hint of intrigue in her voice. "Anyway, I'm trying to concentrate. There. As gorgeous as ever."

Cassie peered into the mirror examining her face minutely. "It will do, a huge improvement, thanks. Right, here goes."

They walked slowly down the stairs, Cassie as if she were putting off the inevitable.

"Do you want me to come back with you?" asked Sarah.

"No, its okay, it will give me time to gather my thoughts, but thanks," replied Cassie. "Do you mind if I don't go in and say 'cheerio' to your parents? I'll just nip out, say bye for me would you."

Sarah nodded and squeezing Cassie's arm with affection said, "Take care – whoever gets to the phone first phones, yes?"

"Okay," said Cassie and went out into the autumn night to drive back up the hill. She was going to tiptoe into the house for she felt it was quite late, half past ten, but there seemed to be lights on everywhere.

She entered a little cautiously and then heard voices from the sitting room and the library. It sounded as if Kate and Robert were there.

She thought her father would be in the library so went into the sitting room first. There she found her aunt and Kate sitting together with the inevitable drink.

Kate looked up when she saw Cassie. Cassie's face looked haunted. She went over to her and putting her arms round spoke, more in a whisper. "I'm so, so sorry, this is dreadful." Cassie just nodded and held on tightly to her friend. It was obvious Kate had been crying as well. They sat down together on the sofa.

"Is Robert next door with Pops?" asked Cassie.

"Yes," said Kate, "Your father has also spoken to Mrs. Pearson, Mum and George."

Cassie, for a moment, had to think who on earth George was, before realising it was Benson. She hadn't remembered his name; he was always Benson to her.

"Mrs. Pearson's in a terrible state," continued Kate. "I think she thinks of your father as her little boy. She's finding this difficult to take in at the moment."

"Aren't we all," replied Cassie sarcastically. The note in her voice did not escape Kate notice.

"Sorry," said Kate. "I didn't mean – oh, I don't know what I mean. I can't take this in either. You know Cassie, the people your father has told today, us I mean; we are all in shock. I've never seen Robert react as he did. He was as white as a sheet. He's trying to be the big strong man but he's devastated, totally devastated by this.

What I'm trying to say, is that all of us here, we all love your Dad. But…" Kate said smiling at Cassie, "…by the same token, we all love his daughter. We know what we feel for him and how we are taking this news; we are then multiplying that feeling by a zillion at least, to try and even begin to imagine how you must be feeling."

Cassie looked at Kate with her big violet eyes. "Oh, Kate, I don't know. I don't know what to do. I can't bear the thought of him not being here, I can't I really can't," and she put her head on Kate's shoulder as she had done so often in the past when she had problems, and let Kate try and comfort her.

Kate stroked her hair as she used to do when Cassie was little. "You know, Cassie, I remember your father made a speech one New Year. You were still quite young, about four or so, and it was just those of us here today, before the others from the village descended upon us for the party. Your father looked round and said he felt so lucky because firstly, he had his beautiful daughter beside him and with that he swung you up onto his shoulders with you beaming from a great height to us all. Secondly, he said he had his family around him. Us, for that is what he thought of us all. He then told us what it meant to him the way we had all helped him look after you."

Cassie looked a little surprised. "You were my nanny. I thought you looked after me."

"Oh yes, but you had a network of people." Looking over at Lydia, Kate smiled. "That lady was boss, that's for sure. She was the one who made sure we looked after you properly, your Dad included, I might add. What I'm trying to say is that we were all like a family here. A family doesn't have to be tied by blood. Do you understand what I'm trying to say?"

Cassie nodded and Kate continued. "Your Dad certainly felt that, because he said we were his true family. You and Lydia, Mrs. P., George, Mum, Robert and me. We are just like a family and right now the family is in trouble, or at least one of the family is, so we all help; we all look after not only the person who is ill, but we all support each other. Yes?"

Cassie nodded again, tears streaming down her face. "Thanks Kate."

A voice from the chair also said, "Thank you Kate. That is a lovely sentiment."

Cassie and Kate looked over just in time to see Lydia wiping her eyes.

She was aware of them looking. "I've dabbed my eyes more in the last two days than I have in a lifetime, so there."

Taking charge Lydia straightened her back and said, "Girls, stiff upper lip and do let's try to be brave for Charles. He'll be even more exhausted today by having had to tell us all and he'll need all his strength for Monday."

"Aunt Lydia, I think you should go to bed. I really do. We need you at the helm for this one, don't we, Kate?" said Cassie, realising the strain this was also having on her aunt.

"Perhaps you are right, dear," said Lydia. "I'll go up." She kissed Kate and Cassie and, to Cassie, said, "I hope you sleep. Pop in for a chat if you can't. I might not be desperately sensible but I am sure that will be no surprise to you," she smiled at Cassie. "You've been nothing but a blessing to Charles, nothing but a blessing. Always remember that," and patting her on the cheek went up to bed.

Cassie felt tears welling up yet again and struggled for control. "I had better go and see Mrs. P, hadn't I?" she asked Kate.

"It's up to you, but I think she'd appreciate that," replied Kate. "I'll wait here for Robert. May I help myself to a brandy, do you think?"

"Family don't have to ask," replied Cassie smiling at her. "Pour one for me as well please. I'll go and find Mrs. P."

Cassie went to Mrs. Pearson's rooms. Just before she knocked she heard Mrs. Pearson say, "But I've known him since he was a young boy," and then a sob. Taking a deep breath, Cassie knocked on the door and found Benson, Margaret and Mrs. Pearson, who was blowing her nose vigorously, all sitting looking miserable.

Cassie went across to Mrs. Pearson and put her arms around her. She seemed to have shrunk since morning. "I came up to see how you were, how you all were," she said, looking at Benson and Margaret.

Margaret squeezed Cassie's arm. "We're doing fine. What about you?"

Cassie felt the power of speech leave her again and for a moment could just nod until a strangulated 'okay!' came out. She looked over at Benson who had tears in his eyes that he was trying desperately to dispel to be strong for Cassie. Cassie went over to him and put her arms around him. That gesture totally demolished his defences and tears poured down his cheeks. He tried to pull himself together, embarrassed at this behaviour.

"Sorry, so sorry about that," he said wiping his eyes.

"Don't be," said Cassie kindly. "I know what Pops means to you, means to all of you." Looking at the others, Cassie tried to lighten the moment.

"Look at us, I come up here to see how you are, and within two seconds, manage to get us all even more upset, good aren't I? Please forgive me." She smiled through her tears at them.

Cassie then proceeded to tell them what Kate had said downstairs to her about the family, particularly the family here tonight in Harrington Hall. This then prompted everyone to get upset yet again!

Cassie blew her nose and wiped her eyes. "I've been a boon. I've really cheered us all up. Kate's right though, we all have to help each other. We're family. Yes?"

"Yes," they all chorused.

"Kate's poured me a brandy downstairs. How do you fancy joining us?" asked Cassie.

"Not for me, my dear," said Mrs. Pearson. "Your father has already given me one; it didn't help one jot. I'm not going to try that again. But I'm feeling a little tired; I think I'll get ready for bed. It's so late."

"Margaret, Ben…" Cassie stopped herself, "George?" Benson looked at her, momentarily surprised, and then smiled. The rules of etiquette on certain estates, used for centuries between master and servant, were not being broken here, for at this moment Cassie was talking to him as her friend, as family, and he was deeply touched by this tender display of affection.

"Thank you, perhaps another night." Looking at Margaret he said, "We're not as young as you two. We'll go to our rooms as well, if you don't mind, but thank you, thank you for asking," said Benson.

Cassie went over to Mrs. Pearson and, kissing her on the cheek, said, "This is an order which has to be obeyed," Cassie smiled at her. "Long lie tomorrow. We are all perfectly capable of seeing to ourselves. All right?"

"We'll see lass, we'll see." Cassie suspected Mrs. Pearson would totally ignore her but at least she had tried.

Kissing Margaret and Benson she wished them goodnight and went downstairs. Kate was right, Cassie thought. They were lucky, in some ways so lucky. They were all in this together and would be strong for each other.

Cassie went into the sitting room to find Kate with her father and Robert. She had to steel herself to be composed.

"Hello Pops," she said as brightly as she could, kissing him on the cheek.

Robert stood up and went over and kissed her. Neither said anything, for their eyes said it all.

"Have you got my drink, Kate?" asked Cassie, trying to think of something to break the tension she felt in the room.

Kate handed her the drink which Cassie knocked back in one.

"Hey," said Charles, "You'll be squiffy doing that."

"Don't care," said Cassie.

"Well, I do," said Charles. "That's my best brandy. If you want to get blotto, have some plonk instead."

"I have your permission, then?" enquired Cassie, wondering what she'd have for a refill.

"I'd rather you didn't," said Charles quietly.

Cassie looked across at him. What was she playing at? "Just a joke, really. Would anyone mind if I went to bed?"

"No," said Charles. "Off you go and I hope you sleep." He got up and went over to her. "Try to sleep, my little princess."

That was too much for Cassie, he hadn't called her that for years.

When she was younger if she had fallen or been hurt in any way, he'd pick her up and make sure she was all right. She would then ask him if he'd always be there to protect her and he always answered yes, for she was his little princess and he was her loyal subject. Such a long time ago that seemed. She wished that he hadn't chosen tonight of all nights to remind her of that.

She kissed him quickly on the cheek, mumbled a goodnight to Kate and Robert and then ran out of the room.

She got to her room, flung herself on her bed and cried herself to sleep.

The next morning dawned bright and quite warm. Cassie woke to the sun streaming in her room. Right now she hated the sun. When she was feeling bleak and grey how dare the weather be anything other than how she was feeling. She looked down and realised she hadn't undressed before bed. *Gross*, she thought. She then noticed there were great blotches of mascara on her pillow. She got out of bed and looked in the mirror. The sight before her revealed the anguish she was feeling. Her eyes were all red and puffy, her skin white and hair resembling rats-tails. All in all: a vision. She had to rectify this before she faced Pops at breakfast. She stood under the shower for some time in the hope that the warm water would soothe her in some way, in any way possible.

After drying her hair, she dressed and went across the landing to her father's room. She knocked on the door but there was no reply. She went in but he wasn't there. She went across to the window and looking out saw him on the terrace below looking out towards the lake – his favourite view. She wondered what his thoughts were.

She left his room and thought she should check on her aunt. Knocking she heard her aunt say, "Come in!" in a bright voice. Cassie smiled at what she saw. Her aunt was looking a million dollars and she told her so. Lydia beamed.

"I'm trying for your father. Yesterday was the day for tears, we now have to face what is happening and be positive. Best foot forward and all that. What do you say? Can you do that?"

"I'll try, I really will," replied Cassie, a little fearfully, for in truth she wasn't very sure how strong she would be but she would try, she really would.

"Excellent," said Lydia approvingly. "Let's make Charles proud of his ladies. Are we all set?"

Cassie nodded and smiled at her aunt. Thank goodness for Aunt Lydia. As always, in a crisis of any kind, her resilience came to the fore.

"You're amazing, truly amazing. I hope I've inherited some of your spunk or whatever it is." said Cassie laughing, oblivious to the momentary intake of breath from Lydia.

Lydia hadn't thought. It had not crossed her mind for a moment. She could not believe how dense she was. She put it down to the upset of the last couple of days and for good measure, threw in old age. For when Charles had told her about Cassie she had in some way disconnected the fact from her brain that Cassie of course was no more related to her than she was to Charles. She looked at

Cassie who was looking at Lydia for guidance and reassurance. Lydia squeezed her arm. Cassie was her niece and that was the end of the matter. "Come on my girl, Oscar award-winning performance all round." Linking arms, they went down the stairs just as Charles was returning from his walk.

"Well, this is a sight for sore eyes, my two favourite ladies. Good morning to you both. Ah, something smells good, shall we go in?" and with that Charles escorted them into the dining room for breakfast.

Cassie remembered her instructions to Mrs. P the night before. Totally ignored. It was obviously going to be business as usual – good for Mrs. P.

Chapter 13

Somehow, they all managed to get through the weekend and all too soon it was Monday.

First thing on Monday morning the face of Charlie, Kate's twelve-year-old son, appeared at the back door. Charles, after whom he was named, was his godfather and they were the mutual admiration society. His mother had told only his older sister Emily and he that 'Uncle Charles' had to go into hospital for treatment as he had cancer. Charlie was devastated at this news but knew he must not let his godfather see he was worried. He had looked out his lucky penknife – he hoped that would help.

"Can I see Uncle Charles please?" asked Charlie anxiously.

Benson's initial reaction was to say no but decided against that. "All right, but don't upset him. He's having breakfast so just hello and bye, okay?" Charlie nodded in agreement.

He walked across the hall to the dining room. Cassie and Lydia were there with Charles.

"Well this is a lovely surprise," said Charles. "What brings you here?"

Charlie went over to Charles and said. "I know you're going to hospital today for treatment and things and so I wondered if this would help, it's my lucky knife and I'd like you to have it; it brings me luck, so it will bring you luck." Charles was completely taken aback but before he could respond Charlie added, "You could give it back once you're better if you like, 'cause you won't need it then, will you?"

Charles took the knife. "Thank you. I will treasure it, I really will. I'll keep it on me at all times and I promise you that when I don't need it any more, I'll return it to you. Is that a deal?"

Charlie nodded. He then looked over at Cassie who had tears in her eyes. "Oh Cassie, please don't cry, Grandad will kill me. He said I wasn't to upset any of you. Please don't."

Cassie wiped her eyes. "You won't get a row, I promise. That really was lovely of you to do that for Pops. Considering you are normally such a horrendous little monster I was just trying not to faint with surprise, that's all!" Cassie smiled at him and winked.

Charlie grinned back at her and then with a little embarrassment gave Charles a quick kiss and said, "Good luck, then, see you later," and ran out of the room before he might get kissed back!

Charles felt emotion well up. It was the unexpected gestures like that which caught him by surprise and he hoped there would be no more.

Charles stood up and, without looking at Lydia or Cassie, said, "I'll just go and get ready. I won't be a moment."

He was trying to put on a brave face to allay any worries Cassie and Lydia may have been having, although they were both into the 'Award-Winning performance' mode and doing sterling work on that front. Charles was tremendously touched by their respective performances.

After a few minutes he returned downstairs, completely composed. He had previously asked Dr. Parrott if he would be able to drive and had been assured he could. With all at The Hall congregating in the drive to wish him well, he set off, with a little trepidation, for the hospital.

The initial two treatments had not been the ordeal Charles had anticipated. Everyone was extremely kind and supportive and, as yet, he wasn't experiencing the dreaded sickness although he knew this might come. So far he was coping.

Cassie, although feeling she was in the midst of some horrendous nightmare, found painting her antidote, and could blot out the events of the day by going to her studio and becoming totally absorbed in her work. She had two paintings on the go at once. One, she was particularly pleased with, the other she could not get right; no matter how hard she tried.

On the day of Charles's third treatment, Cassie had a day off work and was heading off to her studio when a blue Lotus swung into the drive. For a moment Cassie could not quite place who on earth this could be and then remembered: it was David Coleridge.

"Hello David, nice to see you again," said Cassie.

"Hi," said David. "I meant to phone but things have been a little hectic so I thought I'd pop by – starting to be a habit of mine."

He grinned. "I hope that is all right. I'm here, albeit belatedly, about our dinner date. Is your Dad in?"

"Pops is in hospital actually," said Cassie as casually as she could.

"Gosh I'm sorry to hear that. What's wrong?" asked David with concern.

"He's got cancer," she just blurted it out and before she could stop herself felt tears well up.

David went over to her and put his arm round her. "I'm sorry, so very sorry. He didn't mention it when I was here."

Cassie was trying to compose herself. Smiling weakly she said, "Don't be nice, for God's sake don't be nice. 'Matter of fact', that's our motto at the moment and no, you wouldn't have known, he only found out the day you came here."

David apologised yet again. "Is there anything I can do? Drive him to the hospital or anything. I'd be happy to help if I can."

"That's kind of you David, really it is but no, he is able to drive and he likes being independent so while he can, that is what he'll do," said Cassie.

Unknowingly they were being observed from an upstairs bedroom window. Although Lydia had never met David, she just knew it was David who was talking to Cassie and Charles was right; there was a striking resemblance. She felt a sickness in the pit of her stomach. What would she do? What **could** she do? She decided to confront the situation so went downstairs and going out by the back door went round the side of the house where she just happened to bump into Cassie and David.

"Hello," said Lydia with as much surprise in her voice as she could manage without appearing completely over the top.

"Oh, Aunt Lydia. This is David, Mum's friend from the old days. He popped over to see about our dinner date with Pops," said Cassie.

"How do you do Mr. er..." said Lydia who did not wish to appear too knowledgeable about the man.

David interjected. "David, David Coleridge." They shook hands.

"Lydia Maitland," replied Lydia.

"Cassie was telling me about Lord Emerson, I'm so very sorry," said David.

"David offered any help, to drive Pops or whatever," said Cassie.

"How very kind, but that will not be necessary," replied Lydia haughtily.

Cassie looked at her Aunt. She felt that appeared a rather churlish reply, so unlike her Aunt.

David, however, seemed oblivious to any atmosphere and continued. "Well you just have to give me a phone, but I suppose I'd better be going."

"Thank you for calling," said Lydia.

"No, don't go," said Cassie, who was trying to make up for what she felt were her Aunt's bad manners. "Please come and have a coffee or, better still, come to my studio. You paint, don't you? Well, I need advice and…" Cassie had an inspirational idea. David, of course, he would be the one. She continued, "Would you mind?"

"I'd be delighted and honoured. As an artist I know that one can be a little possessive about one's work. Lead the way." Turning to Lydia he said, "It was lovely meeting you. I hope I'll see you before I go. No, I have a better idea. Perhaps I could take you ladies out for lunch. What do you say?"

"I have a prior engagement, perhaps another time," replied Lydia.

"I'd love to," said Cassie, aware this was certainly not what her Aunt wanted to hear and so it gave Cassie some degree of satisfaction to see her Aunt change her so called 'prior engagement'.

"Actually, may I change my mind? I can easily cancel what I was going to do. I'd love to come along and hopefully hear about your work. Would you mind?" asked Lydia, sweetly.

"It's a lady's prerogative to change her mind," said David, slightly amused at this change of heart by Lydia. "I would be delighted to have the chance to take two such lovely ladies out for lunch."

Said, thought Lydia, *with too much charm for his own good.*

"Shall I book somewhere or will we take pot luck?" asked David. "You know the area, I'll be guided by you."

"Let's go to The Swan. It's by the river and won't be busy mid-week so we don't need to book," said Cassie.

"Excellent," said David and looking at Lydia said, "Shall we aim to leave at about quarter to one?"

"I look forward to it," replied Lydia. "Thank you," and then she headed back into the house, realising what a complete and utter idiot she had made of herself. Cassie was bound to ask her why she had behaved in such an extraordinary way. She'd worry about that later.

"Well, here we are," said Cassie as she led David into her sanctuary.

"This is wonderful," enthused David.

"I share it with Kate. Pops renovated it for Kate when she came to be my nanny. She's an excellent artist – always wanted to go to London, but fell for Robert, had four children and that was the end of that plan, but she wouldn't swap her life for anything. Anyway, this was her domain until I was about four or five. On punishment of death if I misbehaved, I was allowed in. I remember being completely overwhelmed by the smell, the paints, and all the colours; and just knew this is what I wanted to do, even way back then. Kate sat me down, out of harms way I imagine, gave me some crayons and I was in seventh heaven: as quiet as a mouse. From then on they always knew how to shut me up – bring me here," she grinned at David.

"This is my Christmas present to Kate and the family," and she showed David the canvas. It was of Kate and Robert surrounded by their children. She pointed them out to David. "The girl next to Robert, is Emily, she's the eldest, then Charlie. He and Pops are as thick as thieves; always have been, and sitting on the floor are Harriet, or Hattie as she is normally called and Ben, the baby of the family."

David examined the canvas critically, not saying anything. Eventually he looked up at Cassie. "This is excellent. You certainly have inherited your mother's talent. What a wonderful present to give them."

"Well, I hope they like it," said Cassie. "However, this is the problem one and when you see it you may be able to help me."

Cassie flung back the cloth protecting her work. "You recognise the subject?" she grinned at him.

David just nodded. Looking at her work Cassie continued, "I can't get the eyes right. But that is possibly more than obvious to you. I think you have to actually know the person to be able to paint the eyes. Don't you think?"

Cassie was oblivious to David's reaction. He was speechless, for staring out from the painting was Lizzie, his Lizzie or rather not his, but Charles's, Cassie's, but not his. Tears pricked his eyes at the unfairness of it all and he tried to wipe them away.

Cassie looked at him, suddenly contrite. "I'm so, so sorry David. I didn't think. I just didn't think. Please forgive me."

"Sorry, it was just seeing her – you have made her seem real, she'll always seem like that, never old, never anything other than beautiful. I was just filled with a regret of all those years ago. Sorry, I'm being stupid and sentimental," said David, trying to pull himself together. "And that is of no help at all. It was just the surprise of seeing her like that."

"You loved her very much, didn't you!" stated Cassie.

"Yes, I did. Sadly I didn't realise how much until it was too late. Just now I suddenly thought of what might have been. Ridiculous really. No point in doing that, no point at all. Sorry Cassie, you've more than enough on your plate just now, without my being a total pain. How can I help with the painting?"

Cassie looked at him. He looked so melancholy and she felt wholly responsible for this. "May I ask you something, David?"

"Fire away."

"Were you and my mother lovers?" asked Cassie.

David looked shocked at the question, the colour draining from his face. "What kind of question is that?" Trying to lighten the moment he continued. "Good grief, girl, I'm shocked, really I am, completely shocked. I'm old enough to be your father, you don't ask questions like that to someone my age," he said indignantly!

"You're not that old. Anyway, I thought it would help me paint the eyes," said Cassie. "To find out what she was really feeling; lost love, all that sort of thing."

"You have some very romantic notions," said David conscious of the fact that Cassie was staring intently at him. "You know it is extremely disconcerting to have someone stare like that – it's also incredibly rude!"

"Were you? I think you were," insisted Cassie.

"All right, we might have been," replied David, unsure what reply to give.

"You either were or your weren't. There's no 'might have been' about it," said Cassie.

"We were very young – too young – but yes, we were. All right, satisfied now? Can we perhaps look at the painting now?"

"Does Pops know do you think?" asked Cassie.

"Oh God, I don't know. I suppose he might, who knows. Cassie it was a long, long time ago. Let's not delve into the past. It's not a good idea, really it's not. Now, back to the business of the painting." Looking at Cassie, he continued. "Do you want my help or not?"

"You're trying to look stern but you're not succeeding so there. I'll leave it, I promise. Sorry for upsetting you and yes, I would like your help," said Cassie, apologetically looking up at him with her big violet eyes.

David smiled at her. He could well understand Charles's difficulty at reprimanding Cassie. He decided that must have been Lydia's department, for she certainly scared him!

"When are you giving your father this?" asked David as he looked at the colours on the palette trying to decide which colours would be best to try and convey Lizzie's eyes.

"I had thought of Christmas but I'm not sure now," replied Cassie. She suddenly looked pensive. She was trying to rid herself of the thoughts whirring through her mind.

David realised what she was thinking and, putting an arm around her shoulder, said, "Let's see how we get on but I think it's too good to keep hidden in here. Once you are satisfied its finished why don't you give it to him then. It would help his recovery, that's for sure."

Cassie nodded and smiled at David. "Thanks."

David took off his jacket and, rolling up his sleeves, started on the process of mixing the colours. He put some paint on the brush and, tentatively at first, dabbed a little of the colour onto the canvas. Cassie watched in silence. His forehead was creased with concentration as he applied the colours. After about an hour, he stood back and looked at his work. He smiled, more to himself than Cassie.

Cassie looked in disbelief at what was before her. "You've achieved what I couldn't do. You've brought her to life, you really have." Cassie was overjoyed at the difference in the picture but a sudden sadness fell upon her like some dark cloak engulfing her.

She spoke quietly. "I wish I'd known her, how I wish she hadn't died. Will you tell me about her?"

"Of course, I'll be pleased to," agreed David who was now feeling emotionally exhausted. He looked at the picture of Lizzie. She looked as if she could walk out of the picture. If only!

"Come on, we have a lunch date. I'll need to wash my hands. I think I'd get zero out of ten from your aunt if I turned up splattered with paint. Your father will be overwhelmed when he sees this, he really will. Where will you hang her?" asked David.

"In the Great Hall, next to the one of Pops. There have always been paintings of the Masters and Mistresses of Harrington Hall going back three centuries, so, at last, she'll have her rightful place," said Cassie. "I couldn't have done it without you. It was fate that made you turn up, it really was. Thank you," and with that she planted a kiss on his cheek.

"My pleasure, my absolute pleasure," replied David. Looking at his watch, he exclaimed. "We're in big trouble, it is now five to one! Come on, let's run."

Lydia was waiting for them in the hall. "My profuse apologies, it is entirely my fault," said David apologetically.

"No, it was mine, so don't be angry with him, Aunt Lydia. He was helping me with a surprise for Pops. I couldn't have managed without him, really I couldn't. Wait till you see it. You'll be amazed," said Cassie.

"I'm sure I will," replied Lydia, in a voice Cassie very rarely heard. She wondered why on earth her Aunt was being so peculiar.

"The cloakroom is there," said Cassie, pointing David in the right direction. "What on earth is wrong with you?" whispered Cassie to Lydia. "You're making David feel uncomfortable, you must be."

"I very much doubt it," replied Lydia disdainfully. "These Americans just turn up unannounced without so much as a by your leave and expect hospitality: well it won't do, it really won't."

"What on earth are you talking about?" asked Cassie completely bemused by her Aunt's behaviour. "In case you've forgotten, I asked him to stay. He's not American, he's English, and it is **he** who is taking **us** out to lunch. So please stop being so weird. He really seems a nice man. Pops seemed to like him, so there."

131

"Very grown up Cassie, excellent! Ah, David here you are," said Lydia whose tone of voice miraculously changed to one of warm honey!

Cassie just looked at her Aunt and shook her head. Definitely weird. She's worried about Pops, that's what it must be Cassie decided.

"Cassie can you clamber into the back and Mrs. Maitland, would you care to sit in the front," David helped Lydia with her seatbelt and off they set at certainly a more sedate pace than when he arrived.

After a couple of sherries Lydia thawed and, if truth be known, enjoyed her lunch very much. She now insisted David call her Lydia, too stuffy to be called Mrs Maitland when they were now such friends! David was an amusing and entertaining host, whom Lydia had found herself liking despite herself. Cassie relaxed as well. It was good to see her Aunt back to normal, although she did feel a little guilty that Pops could not be here as well. He would have enjoyed himself she felt sure.

Cassie was now itching to get back to the studio. She still had some work to do on the portrait. Eventually they left The Swan and David deposited them back at The Hall. He wouldn't come in as he had loads to do, but Cassie made him promise that if he could, he would return at the weekend if not before. He promised he'd try.

David had, much to his surprise, enjoyed his lunch with the ladies. *Cassie*, he thought, *was adorable*. It was amazing to him that in such a short space of time, he felt so completely and utterly at ease with her, Lizzie's daughter. But he also realised that he felt completely at ease with Lydia and Charles; such a nice family. He really hoped that Charles would recover. He would so like to get to know the man better.

David kept his promise and returned the next afternoon with flowers for both Lydia and Cassie as a thank you for their charming company at lunch the previous day. What lady could resist flowers – certainly not Lydia!

After initially thinking that on first meeting Lydia had not taken to him, in fact positively disliked him, David now wondered if he had been mistaken, for she was charm itself. As Charles was still in hospital and Cassie was working, Lydia insisted on taking the opportunity of showing David around The Hall. She made the history of the place come alive with not only the facts of Harrington and The Hall but amusing stories of their ancestors passed down the generations.

Neither of them had realised the time until they heard a car. Lydia looked at her watch, it was nearly five o'clock – Charles was home.

David watched from the window as Lydia went out to meet her brother. He was shocked at Charles's appearance, for he seemed to have shrunk; his clothes hanging off him and his face drawn with a grey pallor.

David went into the hall and upon seeing him Charles smiled and extended his hand. "Good to see you again. Sorry about this. Feel pretty rotten. To be expected, they said. Only one more treatment in this cycle so it's all catching up with me, I feel a little sick for a while but I'll be fine soon. Stay for dinner – I'd like to hear your news."

David smiled at Charles. "The last time I stayed for dinner I wasn't feeling very perky myself the next day."

"That's the one thing," said Charles wistfully. "I can't enjoy a good claret. Life's not worth living believe me, however, the doc tells me this feeling will soon pass. I'm relieved, I can tell you. I'll go and have a lie down, back in an hour," said Charles as he dragged himself up the stairs.

Lydia looked at the retreating figure. Her heart went out to him. It was so sad to see him like this. Peter had, however, told them that Charles was doing well and tolerating the treatment better than would be expected. Although he felt incredibly nauseated, he wasn't actually sick and that was good. Dr. Parrott was even cautiously optimistic. Lydia held on tight to that knowledge. She had completely forgotten David and was suddenly aware of his presence.

Putting his arm around Lydia's shoulder, David said, "He's looking better than I thought he would, much better. Just a bit tired. I expect you don't get rest in hospital – that'll be why."

"Yes," said Lydia, knowing that David was attempting to cheer her up and failing miserably, but it was kind of him to try. "Care for a sherry?"

"I have the car. I'll have a soft drink, if that's okay, but you have one, it will do you good. It's tough to watch – someone going though treatment. My Dad had lung cancer when I was fifteen, and although he had to go through hell with the treatment, so did the family in a different sort of way, so I have a vague idea what its like," said David tenderly.

Lydia smiled back at him and went to pour herself a sherry and find a soft drink for David. They both looked up as they heard a car screech to a halt – Cassie!

"Hello you two, Pops okay? I saw his car in the drive," said Cassie. "Are you staying for dinner, David?" continued Cassie, without either Lydia or David managing to get a word in. "I hope so, I'd like you to see 'you know what' in the studio," she said, grinning at her aunt. "You'll find out soon Aunt Lydia, I promise."

"Hello, yes, that would be good, in reply to your questions," grinned David. "I thought your Dad looked a bit bushed actually. I don't know if I should stay."

In unison both Lydia and Cassie replied, "Yes." Cassie looked at her aunt. It was nice to see her back to normal with David. "It will be nice for Pops as well, he normally has just us to chat to, he'd enjoy talking to you, really he would."

"How can I refuse then," replied David.

"Excellent," said Cassie. "I'll go and tell Mrs. P."

After about an hour Charles returned downstairs and much to David's relief, was looking better. After dinner, Cassie badgered David to go out to the studio.

"Knowing how long Cassie spends there, I may have gone to bed by the time you come back," said Charles.

"You may not have to wait too much longer for your surprise, Pops," said Cassie mysteriously.

"Intrigue, intrigue," smiled Charles. "I can't make up my mind whether I'm looking forward to this or not."

"I think you'll like it, in fact I'm sure you'll like it," said David.

A look crossed David's face as he said it. Charles could not quite place what kind of look, but a look nevertheless. Charles wondered what on earth this could be.

"If I'm not too late I'll pop in and see you," said Cassie, giving Charles a kiss and dragged David out whilst he tried to thank Charles and Lydia for their hospitality.

Lydia looked at Charles. "Why are you looking at me like that, may I ask?"

Charles smiled at her. "You like him, don't you? Despite yourself, you actually like him."

"Yes, I do, I have to pinch myself to try and remember why I should be wary of him. I confess to having behaved in an appalling manner when I met him yesterday. Did Cassie tell you?" Charles shook his head. "She quite rightly, gave me a row. I was so frosty to him. I suppose I hoped I wouldn't like him. It would be easier then, wouldn't it?" said Lydia.

"Much," replied Charles. "But he's only here for a short time. We can cope with that, can't we?"

"I hope so, I really hope so," said Lydia. "Anyway, enough of David. How are you? How did you get on?"

"Not bad, one more to go, then a break and then reviewed by Dr. Parrott," said Charles.

"Wouldn't it be marvellous if…" Lydia stopped herself, aware that Charles was looking at her indulgently.

"No building up false hopes, all right?" said Charles.

"Of course not," replied Lydia, looking across at Charles.

Across at the studio Cassie was waiting, a little nervously, for David to give his critical appraisal.

At last David stood back, looked at Cassie and, with a slight catch in his voice, said, "I can't give you higher praise than saying that I feel I could walk into this picture and take Lizzie in my arms. You have made her seem alive. I can hear her voice, her laugh, even smell her perfume, just by looking at this. Your work is breathtaking and your father," David hesitated. He would have given anything for this picture, but sadly he would never be the proud possessor of such a masterpiece. "Please… please show it to him soon. You could not give him a more wonderful present."

Cassie, for once, was not her usual exuberant self. She wanted this to be so right, so perfect for Pops. She felt it was the very best she could do. She had never before tried to capture the person just from photographs; she had always tried to get to know her subject and through knowing them, was usually able to capture a quality that was elusive to so many other artists. Her work, for that very reason, was now becoming highly sought after. Looking at her mother, she knew this would be the most important work she had ever done or would ever do and all of a sudden she felt incredibly tired.

"Thank you and thank you for your help. I don't think I could have begun to do her justice without your help. I'll frame her at the weekend and present Pops with it the next weekend. He'll have finished the first lot of treatment and should be feeling perkier. You have to be guest of honour, I insist," said Cassie.

David looked at Cassie and smiled. He knew exactly how she was feeling. All of a sudden, after weeks of sleepless nights and every waking moment thinking of the portrait, it was now finished. It was a sort of anti-climax and he suspected she was feeling absolutely drained. "Would you like to go for a drink? You've been cooped up here and it's incredibly tiring. You need a break."

"I'd like that, that would be good," replied Cassie.

They drove out of the village and about five miles down the road came to a roadside inn called, "The Hare and Hound".

"What a catchy and tremendously original name," said David as he ushered Cassie into the pub. "You get a table. What would you like?"

"White wine please," replied Cassie.

David came over with the drinks. "Cheers and continued success."

"Thank you," responded Cassie, taking a sip of wine. "A little warm, but not too bad," said Cassie.

"How long are you staying?" asked Cassie.

"My mother's estate is, I think and fingers crossed and all that, nearly finalised, so there would be no excuse. I have to go back," smiled David.

Cassie pondered this statement for a moment. "No excuse, what does that mean?" she smiled at him.

She really was quite, quite lovely, thought David. "I knew you'd pick me up on that. What I mean is that I will miss you, I'll miss your father and aunt as well. In such a short time I feel sad at the thought of going away, just when I was getting to know you all. I have to though – I have things to do back in the States."

Cassie looked at David and then, a little hesitantly at first, said, "May I ask you something?"

It was David's turn to look uncomfortable. "The last time you asked me that, I got into hot water if I remember."

"I'd still like to know," grinned Cassie who was now gaining confidence.

"All right, but I can plead the Fifth Amendment. Is that a deal?" smiled David.

Taking a deep breath Cassie started. "David, I know you'll think this rude of me and I know I shouldn't pry or anything."

"But of course you're going to," said David twisting about in his seat. "Just ask, go on, get it over with."

"Well, I've been doing some detective work. I've looked you up in my books. I can't see you. Yet, by what you've done with Mum's portrait, I know how good you are, I certainly know that. I'm just surprised, that's all. No one knows you. I've asked Kate, Pierre Gabriel, I've searched high and low and if truth be known, I even rang the library at the Art College. Are you some impostor with some terrible past? "

David let out a great guffaw. Cassie smiled back but was a little surprised at this response. "What's funny?"

"If you'd just asked, I would have told you. You only had to ask," replied David. "What name did you look up?"

Cassie looked at him, raising her eyes heavenwards. "Which name do you think, David..." and then stopped. "I looked up Coleridge of course. You paint under a different name. Oh, gosh, I see, what an idiot, of course. Well what name do you paint under?"

David looked at her. "I paint under the name of D.F. Risi."

Cassie gasped. "You can't be, you're not – are you, really are you? I don't believe it. I am actually sitting beside D.F. Risi."

"The name means something, then?" grinned David mischievously.

"You rat, of course it does. God, we even had to try and copy your techniques at class. I could die, I really could. I drag you into the studio and hope you might, just might be able to help. You must have been falling about laughing at what an idiot I was making of myself; a not uncommon occurrence I may add. I'm sorry, I really can't believe this."

"Don't be, I was happy to help. Now, would you care for another warm white wine?" asked David laughing. Cassie just nodded.

As he came back to the table he smiled at her. "Recovered?"

"Why didn't you say? Why do you call yourself that? Wait till I tell Kate, Pierre, gosh," kept repeating Cassie. "Why," she also kept repeating.

David smiled. "When I went to the States, all those years ago, my teacher said that I had to have a shorter, snappier name. This was because when I would write David Coleridge, it would apparently take up the whole canvas. Slight exaggeration I know, but anyway I was young, naive, inexperienced and having the chance of a lifetime so of course, I was going to take his advice. He then asked for a quick name off the top of my head. I thought of my initials, DF, David Francis, and then was looking out the window for inspiration I suppose, when I saw an advert for a hair product for baldness – Risi – increases follicle growth apparently, so I thought this will do nicely: DF Risi. And the rest as they say, is history," said David.

"Will you sign the portrait for me, please do, it was a joint effort after all," said Cassie.

David suddenly looked serious. "No, I won't Cassie. It's not because I wouldn't be proud to put my signature to such a work, I would. It is for your father. I don't even want him to know that I put one little dab of paint on. It was all your work. I may have advised but I did not pick up a brush. Do you understand why?"

Cassie didn't really. "I'm not sure to be honest. It doesn't seem fair when you helped me make the portrait 'come alive' as you say. I could not have achieved that without you, you know I couldn't."

David looked at Cassie, whose big violet eyes looked so trustingly at him. "Cassie, you'll maybe think this is bizarre and I know I'm seeing it from a male point of view but I really don't want to remind your Dad too much of my time with your Mum. He may have tried to blot that out. Especially just now, when he's not well. Let's not bring back, what after all, may be painful memories for him. We don't know, he may well have chosen to think of your Mum as having no past. Perhaps, just perhaps, only you and I know differently. Do you understand?"

Cassie nodded, trying to digest this. "I think that's really kind of you David, I hadn't thought." Cassie suspected David was right. "If you really don't mind, I'll do as you say. But you will come to shall we call it the 'unveiling'. You definitely have to. And another thing," said Cassie, "I can tell people who you are, can't I?"

"My work isn't that well-known over here, so the name won't mean a thing, it really won't," replied David.

"Rubbish," replied Cassie confidently. "Of course it will."

"Come on, I'd better take you home," said David.

They drove back to The Hall in companionable silence. "Thanks for the drink, and for the advice," said Cassie, getting out of the car. "Please phone or come by, whatever, make it soon. Yes?"

David smiled and nodded and with a wave went back down the drive.

Cassie was too excited to even contemplate sleep. She hoped Pops would still be awake and so raced upstairs and, knocking gently on his door, she opened it and looked in. He was fast asleep. Tears pricked her eyes as she looked at him for he looked so vulnerable lying there with the bed seeming so huge now. "Please get well, you've just got to," she whispered as she silently closed the door.

She wondered if her aunt would be still awake. Knocking gently on her door she heard a faint, "Come in."

"Hello, dear, did you have a good time?" asked Lydia. Cassie nodded and, sitting on the side of the bed, said, "You'll never believe this, never in a million years believe this. Do you know who David is, do you know who he actually is?"

Lydia was, in a split second, trying to gauge if Cassie knew. She couldn't possibly. This would not be her response, she felt sure of that. As calmly as she could she responded. "No, who is he?"

"He's only D.F. Risi, that's all. Can you believe it? I couldn't," said Cassie. The relief Lydia felt on hearing this news nearly overwhelmed her. Cassie wasn't speaking about him as her father, she didn't know.

"That's lovely dear, really lovely," replied Lydia.

Cassie looked at her aunt in disbelief. "You haven't a clue who I'm talking about, have you? You know, Risi, D.F. Risi – don't be so dense, Aunt Lydia."

It suddenly dawned on Lydia whom Cassie was talking about. "Sorry, my dear, I'd taken my pill, must have made me a bit dopey. Of course I know, the portrait painter from the States. Well I never. You admired his work ages ago. Am I firing on, as you say, 'all four cylinders' now? At Art College you were introduced to his work. See, it is all coming back to me," said a much relieved Lydia.

"I couldn't believe it when he told me, I really couldn't. I was speechless," said Cassie.

"That," responded Lydia, "I would have liked to have witnessed." Lydia smiled fondly at her niece. "It must have been a thrill and to think he helped with whatever you are up to in the studio."

Alarm crossed Cassie's face. "No, you mustn't say that, you must not, under any circumstances, tell Pops that David helped. He advised, didn't help, he didn't lift a brush. Do you understand?"

"Yes, I'll try, I promise," replied Lydia.

"It must be more than 'I'll try'," retorted Cassie. "It must be absolutely and definitely not."

"Very well, definitely not," said Lydia. She stroked Cassie's cheek. "Are you all right, something troubling you?"

Cassie looked at her aunt, she could trust her, may even get a different perspective from her. "Okay, here goes. David doesn't want me to tell Pops that he in any way helped. The reason for this, actually this is a bit tricky to say, but well David and Mum were boyfriend and girlfriend, if you know what I mean."

"In the old days," said Lydia with a twinkle in her eye and stressing the word old, "We called them lovers, you know, people in a intimate relationship of a sexual nature. My dear, sex was not invented by your generation."

Cassie grinned with relief at her aunt. "Well anyway, David thought that maybe Pops had blotted out that part of Mum's life and didn't want to think of her as having, shall we say, a past, with David. He felt he shouldn't be mentioned as having helped me – I'm doing a portrait of Mum and it was the eyes he helped with, in case you were wondering."

Lydia nodded, trying to remain in control at what she was hearing. Cassie continued. "I hadn't really thought of that but I think it was nice of David to be considerate about that and so that's why I am taking all the credit. Do you think that's right to do that?"

"I think David is very right in suggesting that," replied Lydia. "Let's do as he says."

"I'm glad I've told you about Mum and David, but don't tell anyone – especially not Pops," said Cassie anxiously.

Lydia said, "Of course not, now you'd better go, I'm about to nod off. It's exciting though, isn't it? Risi, D.F. Risi, who would have thought, and in our house," she knew this was what Cassie wanted to hear.

Cassie agreed, delighted that her aunt seemed as excited about this as she was. She kissed her on the cheek. "Night and as ever, thanks…" and with that she closed the door.

Lydia sunk deeper into the pillows, another award-winning performance. She decided that she was getting too old for them! She thought about what Cassie had said and wished she could feel anger at David. She had so wanted not to like him, but he was making this impossible. What a kind thought, what a decent and nice man. *Damn him, absolutely, damn him*, she thought.

She thought sleep would desert her but exhaustion took over and within moments she was in a deep sleep.

Chapter 14

David had a last look around his mother's house; his old home. He hadn't been back since he had left all those years ago and didn't have any great feelings for the place. His mother, although initially distraught at him leaving Britain, had quickly realised that she would now have an excuse to travel and needed no second bidding to visit him in America, making a point of seeing him at least once a year. He had enjoyed her visits and because of her had seen more of America than he would normally have. He was glad that she had seen his success and he felt sure that she had bored her friends of the coffee morning set with talk of his various exhibitions. *Typical mother*, he thought fondly! He locked up and, pocketing the keys, went into town for his appointment with the lawyer.

He was a little early for his appointment so sat in the dull, drab waiting area with its out of date copies of Punch, Horse and Hound, and, totally out of character, Cosmopoliton. He picked it up, aware that the receptionist was looking at his choice. He looked up at her, winked, whereupon she blushed and bent her head to her work. At 11 o'clock precisely, Mr. Perkins buzzed for David to be taken through.

"Well Mr. Coleridge, it is a lovely day for the time of year, don't you think," said Mr. Perkins, shaking hands with David. He was a little man with flabby and rather damp hands. David surreptitiously wiped his hand on his trouser leg and in a non-committal way agreed about the day.

"I have the keys to my mother's property," said David, laying them on the desk. "I also believe I have one or two things to sign?"

"Yes indeed," said Mr. Perkins. "How much longer are you staying?"

"Well, I am keen to get back, as you can imagine, but I am willing to stay on if that would expedite things here," replied David who realised he would be rather happy for an excuse to stay on. "Suffice to say another week or so is really my limit."

"We will endeavour to make haste then," said Mr. Perkins. David thought that highly unlikely. Haste did not seem to be in the vocabulary of solicitors.

Mr. Perkins opened his desk drawer and took out a small box. "These items of jewellery are the pieces of value. Your mother had kept them here for safekeeping. He emptied the contents and the accompanying piece of paper onto the desk. Looking through the paper he said, "I note there is one ring missing. Your mother took it, let me see, ah yes, in 1972."

"I have no idea," said David. "I didn't see it amongst her personal effects at home."

"It is described here as having three strands of gold with five diamonds inserted into the gold strands. Here, this is the matching bracelet. Charming, don't you agree," said Mr. Perkins as he handed David the bracelet.

David just nodded. He looked at the bracelet and felt a tightness in his throat. He now remembered the ring. He also remembered when his mother had given it to him. It had been his grandmother's and his mother wanted him to give it to his girlfriend; she was so fond of her, and hoped they might marry. David smiled wryly at the recollection.

"It's quite all right, Mr. Perkins. I remember it. May I take the other items of jewellery?" asked David.

"Of course. We'll be in touch soon, very soon. Do you have a number where we can contact you?" asked Mr. Perkins.

David duly gave him his mobile number and said he'd book into a hotel near Harrington.

"Lovely area, Harrington," said Mr. Perkins, standing to indicate that David's allotted time was now up. Unfortunately this necessitated another handshake, one worse than the first. David felt that a visit to the washroom was in order after that.

David left the building clutching the jewellery and a sudden sadness overwhelmed him. He had, what he supposed, was quite valuable jewellery and no one to give it to. There had been women friends in America but he was, by his own admission, self obsessed and appalling to live with, so his track record on commitment was not exactly a resounding success. The real problem was he had never found anyone quite like Lizzie; no one had come even close to his expectations.

He walked on down the street, a little unsure as to where he was heading. He wondered what had happened to the ring. Charles might know but he didn't like to bother him with that just now.

David suddenly felt terribly alone and wanted to be able to talk to someone. The only people he knew were at Harrington Hall and he didn't want them to think he was becoming a permanent feature there. He needed an excuse and then realised he'd found one. Cassie couldn't possibly frame a picture on her own! He knew this pretext was a little flimsy, but it would have to suffice and he jumped into the car with renewed vigour.

He arrived at Harrington Hall to find it apparently deserted. He went round the back but no one seemed at home. He then decided he'd take a chance and try the studio. As he approached he heard a string of oaths emanating from within. He laughed and shouted out, "Cassie, I take it that's you."

Opening the door he was greeted by the sight of Cassie running her thumb under cold water. "Am I glad to see you. This is a nightmare, can you help? I know, I'm always asking you that, sorry. I've just bashed my thumb and it's hurting like blazes," said Cassie, trying to stem the flow of blood. "You really are marvellous David, you turn up exactly when you're needed, what made you decide to come today?"

"Well I've had things to do today, see my lawyer and such like, but then realised how un-gentlemanly I had been saying last night, 'well off you go and frame the portrait at the weekend'. If I had thought for a moment, I would have realised no one could do that on their own, so I jumped into the car, hoping you hadn't started it and here I am; your willing and able assistant," David smiled over at her.

"You're a God-send, really you are. Even I was beginning to run out of expletives! Now, I have plasters somewhere. Oh, I know," and with that Cassie bent down under the sink. As she did, something on the chain around her neck swung into view.

David stared at her.

"Ah here we are." She realised she was being watched. "David, why are you staring, what's wrong?" He looked at her and then grinned a grin that went nearly from ear to ear. Cassie smiled back although was a little unsure why she was.

"May I ask what you have on your chain? I saw it just now, when you bent down, weird place to keep plasters by the way," said David as a bit of an afterthought.

"I don't know why I keep them there."

David shook his head. "No, I don't care, sorry, I was wondering what's on your chain? It looked like a ring."

"Can you help please?" asked Cassie, handing David the plaster. "It's a ring – Mum's. Apparently she always wore it and when she died Pops wore it and then just before I went to College he gave it to me as a good luck thing, from Mum I suppose. Anyway, when I'm working I always take it off and put it on my chain so I don't damage it."

Cassie looked at David and then she grinned, "No! We always wondered, so it was you," she said as comprehension dawned. "It was you. You gave it to Mum."

Cassie fingered it and, looking a little unsure, asked, "Have you missed it? We didn't know where it came from, really we didn't. Are you wanting it back, is that why you asked?"

"No, oh heavens no. I am so pleased, so incredibly… you can't know how pleased I am that she wore it and now you do, I am delighted," said David. He gave Cassie a quick peck on the cheek and said, "You've made my day, you really have. Now onwards, to work."

They eventually accomplished the task and were both rather pleased with their handiwork.

"Are the arrangements all set for the *unveiling*?" asked David.

"Yes, it's just a few of us," said Cassie. "Kate and Robert, Peter and Rowena, that's the local GP and his wife, big friends of Dad's, my best friend Sarah, that's their daughter, she's also coming – she's back down from uni for a week. Then, there's Margaret, George, you know Benson, Mrs. P., Aunt Lydia and Pops, oh, also, Pierre Gabriel. I think he's sometimes a little lonely and he's awfully good about giving me time off. I mean even today, we weren't busy and he knew I wanted to do the framing and so he let me off early. He's nice like that and I also thought that he'd love to meet you. I hope you don't mind. But that's all. I didn't think we should have too many.

"Does your father have any idea?" asked David.

"Not sure, to be honest; he knows we are having a little dinner party but Aunt Lydia said it was to celebrate him finishing his first lot of treatment," said Cassie. "No great dressing up, what you have will do fine."

"Thank you kindly," responded David. "I'll try not to let you down!"

He was about to tell Cassie about the jewellery when they heard a voice. "Hello, hello."

"Hi, Kate, we're in here," shouted Cassie.

"Kate, David, David, Kate, there we are, you're now introduced," said Cassie.

They smiled at each other, shook hands and said hello, both sizing each other up. David liked what he saw; an attractive slim lady with dark hair which framed her face and laughing eyes. By the same token Kate thought David seemed rather handsome, also rather familiar but she couldn't think why.

"Kate, I was going to surprise you with this but firstly, before I show you Pop's surprise, do you know who this is? Do you? Can you even hazard a guess?" enquired Cassie excitedly.

"Inhaling the meths again I see," laughed Kate. "We've just been introduced two seconds ago."

"No, no," said Cassie exasperated. "David is – ready for this, he's only D.F. Risi – can you believe it? I couldn't. Isn't it amazing he's here, right here in OUR studio. What do you think of that?"

Kate smiled indulgently at Cassie and smiling at David said, "Now that I can get a word in edgeways, it is an honour to meet you. I am a great admirer of your work although, and I apologise for this, I confess it was Cassie who introduced me to it. You have been her inspiration in many ways. I don't suppose you'd do a master class?"

"I might just do that, but I'd like to see your work. Cassie tells me you have an exceptional talent. The three of us need to have a pow-wow some time. What do you think?" asked David.

"I'd love that. Now, young lady, may I have a sneak preview?" asked Kate.

Cassie turned the easel round. Kate caught her breath; the work before her was stunning. She felt tears prick her eyes, overcome with emotion at seeing such exquisite work. She just shook her head, incapable, for the moment, of the ability to speak. She went over to Cassie and put her arms around her friend. "That is the best work you have ever done. He'll be overwhelmed, he really will."

"Although I didn't know your Mum very well she was someone you met once and never forgot, oh yes, you've really got her. It's truly wonderful." Kate kept staring at the portrait. She could not take her eyes off it.

A slightly worried look then crossed Kate's face as she stood contemplating it. "Cassie, I may be wrong in this but I'm not sure if Charles will cope with seeing this in front of us all. It's so incredible; it looks as if Lizzie might walk out of the frame. Why don't you have a private viewing with him on his own before we arrive and then he can be more composed when he sees us, because believe me, never in his wildest imaginings could he envisage something like this."

"Well if you think so Kate, whatever you say. You know I wouldn't want Pops to find this difficult. I just thought this would be one pressie he'd really, really like," replied Cassie. "I didn't really think about the consequences, as usual!"

"I agree with Kate," interjected David. "Because of his illness his emotions will be a bit out of kilter shall we say; it would be good to do it with just the two of you there."

Cassie looked a little subdued for a moment, deflated even. "I wouldn't want to embarrass him, I really wouldn't… but," then, as if bursting back into life again she continued, "But you liked it Kate, you really did?" She stared expectantly at Kate.

Kate laughed, "Of course you chump, it's the most wonderful thing I have ever seen."

Chapter 15

Charles woke and realised that he hadn't felt so good for ages. Who knows, perhaps the treatment was working. It was now five days since his last dose and he didn't have any feeling of nausea or any discomfort at all. He decided it was going to be a good day. He then remembered the dinner party. He was unsure why there was to be an occasion made of the end of his first lot of treatment, but if that is what Cassie and Lydia wished to do then who was he to stand in their way. The people who were coming were mostly family or extended family, apart from David and Cassie's boss, Pierre Gabriel.

Charles got up and, after his ablutions, went downstairs into the kitchen.

"Morning, Mrs. P. How are you today?" asked Charles.

"Very well Master Charles and if I may say you're looking more like your old self. It's so good to see," replied Mrs. Pearson.

"I confess to feeling slightly peckish this morning and do you know what I really fancy?" Mrs. Pearson looked at Charles expectantly. "French toast, that's what I'd like," said Charles. "Do you think that would be possible? I suspect the full works in the fry-up department might be too much for the system to bear but French toast would fill the gap nicely, just one – oh maybe, two slices," smiled Charles. "And, if I'm not in the way I'll have it here if I may."

"With pleasure. It's so good to see you like this," replied Mrs. Pearson as she bustled about preparing the breakfast.

In no time at all his breakfast was placed before him. "This looks so good, thank you," said Charles. He took a bite and nodded. "Excellent," and then further appreciative 'mmms'. until replete.

"That could have been a banquet, I enjoyed it so much. Food hasn't tasted of anything of late so it's nice to see the taste buds are leaping into action again. Who knows," Charles grinned mischievously at Mrs. Pearson. "I may even be able to enjoy my claret again!"

Mrs. Pearson gave a little 'tut' but very much hoped this may mean he was on the road to recovery. "Well, a glass or two may be good; medicinal and all that," she decided.

Charles looked appalled. "Good God woman, you can't call some of my truly exquisite claret, medicinal – you just can't. Sacrilege, that's what it is, sacrilege."

Helping himself to another cup of coffee he smiled as he shook his head muttering, "Incredible, absolutely incredible."

With that Benson came in. "Morning Benson," said Charles. "As tonight seems to be a little bit of a celebration I think we should have one or two nice wines. I leave the choice in your capable hands as you know what Mrs. P. is up to in the cooking department, but make sure that when you are setting the table for us all, you don't forget a glass for this lady," as he gave Mrs. P. a hug. "She knows nothing about the joys of wine. It is therefore my mission tonight to try and educate her."

"We'll see about that, Master Charles, we'll just see about that," muttered Mrs. Pearson.

To enable Cassie to get the portrait into the house, Lydia suggested to Charles that they go for a stroll down to the lake. With Charles safely out of the way, Kate and Cassie brought the portrait from the studio into the library. They set it on the easel and, covering it with a cloth, left the room, remembering to lock the door.

Charles suspected something was afoot when he found the door to the library locked. He had no idea what Cassie had planned and everyone else had seemingly been sworn to secrecy. He was informed by Lydia that dinner would be at seven but that Cassie wanted him to be ready at six for canapés and she would escort him downstairs. He looked at his watch; an hour before he was required – a little nap was in order he decided.

At six on the dot, Cassie arrived at his bedroom door. She looked stunning in a halter-neck midnight blue dress that seemed to further accentuate her violet-coloured eyes.

Charles's gazed at her with nothing short of adoration. "You look beautiful, simply beautiful."

"Thanks Pops, you look pretty handsome yourself," replied Cassie.

Charles gave a wry smile. He'd lost weight that he could ill afford and felt if he were honest, that he resembled a skeleton.

As if reading his mind Cassie smiled and, giving him a quick kiss, said, "I mean it, very handsome and anyway, the lean look is very '*in*'."

"Well being such a follower of fashion that's just me then," smiled Charles. "Now, I have been in suspense too long. Am I to be put out of my misery?"

Taking his arm Cassie said, "This way, it's in the library, as if you didn't know."

Cassie unlocked the library door and looking with anticipation at her father led him to the leather chair situated in front of the easel.

With due ceremony she removed the protective cloth with a flourish, "Ta da," she said smiling at him.

She hadn't considered how she had expected him to respond but by the look on his face she was worried. The colour drained from his face and he just stared at the portrait, speechless.

Cassie went over and, kneeling beside him with alarm on her face, said, "I thought you'd like it, I really did."

Charles didn't say anything. He just continued staring unblinking at the picture before him. Unknown to him he was experiencing the very same emotions David had felt, he really thought that if he went forward and touched the portrait, Lizzie would somehow come alive.

Cassie was by now becoming a little agitated; her big surprise was backfiring in a spectacular fashion. "Pops, please, please say something, anything. Tell me you hate it, anything, but just speak to me, please."

Charles was suddenly aware of Cassie beside him, her young face anxious and troubled. Tears filled his eyes and he cupped Cassie face in his hands and kissed her. "I need a moment or two on my own, please, just a little time." He spoke so quietly Cassie could barely hear him but she just nodded and left the room, gently shutting the door behind her.

Kate, ever perceptive, was waiting in the hall for Cassie. She had suspected that when Charles saw the portrait of Lizzie he would be so overcome he would need time on his own.

Cassie saw Kate and blurted out, "He hates it, absolutely hates it. You should have seen his face. He went white, didn't smile. What have I done? Oh Kate why didn't you stop me?"

Kate shook her head. "Cassie, he doesn't hate it. He loves it, which is why he needs time on his own to take this all in. He needs to go over the portrait and examine it minutely – but he wants or rather he needs to do this in private."

Cassie was looking a little dubious about this. "Are you sure, really sure? You didn't see the expression on his face."

"I know this is an expression you loathe," smiled Kate. "But when you are older or when you have loved as your father loved Lizzie, you'll know what I mean. Really you will. Now, give him twenty minutes or so, then go back in. In the meantime, the others have arrived. They're in the drawing room with Lydia and Robert so let's go in and say hello. You all right?" Cassie nodded.

"I haven't a clue half the time, do I?" moaned Cassie, more to herself than Kate.

Kate laughed. "You underestimate your talent, that's all. By the way," she continued as they walked across to the drawing room. "You look lovely, really gorgeous. It's a rare treat to see you out of your painting garb! Makes a very pleasant change!"

Cassie put on her most animated smile as she and Kate walked into the drawing room. She noticed her friend, who was positively flirting with David, seemingly hanging onto his every word. David looked up when the ladies came in and smiled over to them.

Much to Sarah's obvious annoyance Pierre then came over to say something to David. Sarah excused herself and went over to Cassie. "He's totally gorgeous, an absolute hunk."

Cassie wasn't listening. "Sorry, what were you saying?"

"Never mind," said Sarah, "I was only drooling over David. Are you okay?"

Cassie nodded. "Sorry, just wondering what Pops is thinking about the portrait."

"I'm dying to see it myself. When can we go along?" asked Sarah.

"Soon," replied Cassie, "I hope very soon."

David looked at Cassie, who wasn't looking her usual effervescent self. He went over to Kate. "Is she all right, she looks a bit subdued?"

"She's fine, as I said to her, she underestimates her talent. Charles was, as you can imagine, completely stunned when he saw the portrait. I've told her she'll understand his reaction one day," smiled Kate.

After the allotted twenty minutes Cassie could stand the suspense no longer. "I think I'll go and see if he's all right now."

"He'll be fine, I'm sure. Tell him we're itching to get cracking with the champagne," replied Kate.

Cassie went back to the library and knocked a little tentatively. Charles opened the door and Cassie anxiously scanned his face for reassurance that he wasn't angry or whatever emotion he may have initially felt on seeing the picture. He pulled her to him and covered her face with kisses.

Eventually he stopped and, smiling, he put his arm around her as they faced the portrait. "I don't think I will ever be able to convey to you the joy, the delight, or the wonder I felt when you pulled back the cloth. You have captured the very essence of your mother. The look in her eyes, the way you have her hair, her stance. I remember as if it were yesterday. I can only thank God for your talent."

Cassie looked at Charles with some scepticism. "God! Pops, when did you suddenly become a believer?"

"Well, God or whomever, someone on a higher plane must have given you this gift. I feel sure of that and because of that talent you have been able to give me the most wonderful present I could have ever wished for. I thank you," said Charles quietly. "I thank you from the bottom of my heart."

The relief Cassie felt was palpable. "Thank goodness, you had me worried you know." She hugged Charles enthusiastically. "I wanted it to be the best present. I'm so glad it is. Now, I have a message from Kate: she's wanting to get cracking with the champagne."

"Let's not keep her waiting then," replied Charles as they headed off to the drawing room. Everyone was assembled.

"Sorry for keeping you all. Right Benson, let's start opening the champagne," said Charles. He caught Kate's eye; she was looking at him anxiously. He mouthed at her, 'wonderful'. Kate smiled warmly back at him.

"Now Mrs. P.," said Charles. "I will have none of your nonsense tonight. You must have a glass filled at all times, starting with this," said Charles, pouring out the champagne.

"Well just this once, seeing it's a special occasion and everything," replied Mrs. Pearson.

Charles surveyed the room. He was now poised and in complete control. "Ladies and Gentlemen, may I have your attention please. Cassie, come over here please." Cassie went over and joined her father. Charles continued. "I am assuming most of you knew this young lady was up to something as she seemed to take up permanent residence in the studio. Well, the wait is over. In the library is **the** most wonderful present I could ever have. It's a painting of Lizzie, whom most of you knew. I think when you see the painting you will be as stunned as I was. Pierre, I don't think you knew Lizzie but I feel certain you will be deeply impressed by the talent of the work."

Cassie groaned and under her breath said, "Don't be so embarrassing, Pops."

Charles laughed and resumed his speech. "I will finish my speech in a moment so that you may go off to the library and see what I am talking about for yourselves. David, whom some of you have only met tonight, is a world renowned artist. David, I know you have been honoured to have been allowed into the studio and if you had anything to do with the portrait, I thank you." David shook his head.

Looking at Cassie, Charles said, "I'll finish, you'll be pleased to hear, by saying that my initial reaction at seeing this truly wonderful present was one of utter disbelief. Apparently I had Cassie worried for a moment; she took my silence to be that of one of disapproval. How wrong she was; I have never seen anything that moved me as much." Charles looked at Cassie with pride. "I would like you all to join with me in toasting the amazing talent of Cassie."

"Cassie!" they all responded.

David stepped forward. "Before you all go through to view the portrait I wonder if I might say a few words."

"Must you?" implored Cassie, "Please don't."

David said, "I'll ignore that, Cassie. Firstly I would like to say to you Charles that yes, although I was privy to visit Cassie's sanctuary, it was not to wield a paintbrush. Your daughter can do most things single-handed, but framing is not one of them and my claim to fame for this portrait is holding things as she hammered nails here and there." Holding up his forefinger he continued, "I still have the scars to show on this finger and," showing another finger, "the blood blister on this finger is only now disappearing. Picture framing is not exactly her forte. But, she has the most incredible talent and I predict that in the very near future the name of Cassandra Emerson will be known in art circles, not only in this country, but also all over the world. Cassie, it has been a great pleasure to witness, first hand, your talent at work, and Charles you have every justification to be proud of your daughter. So once again I propose a toast, Cassie."

"Cassie!" everyone repeated.

Cassie went over to David. "Thank you for your kind words."

David looked serious. "I meant them, every one of them."

Kate looked at them. Cassie and David looked so at ease with each other. It was lovely, Cassie had a mentor, she thought. But there was something about them, something she found just a little disconcerting. It was a strange feeling. What was it? She couldn't decide. Before she had time for any more thoughts Robert was at her side, ready to escort her to the library.

"Let's go through together in case I get into hot water," said Robert. "You know I need your help when it's anything to do with art. As you have pointed out on several occasions, I am a complete philistine where that is concerned; so let's go."

"Trust me, you'll love this, you really will," said Kate.

Everyone eventually drifted off to look at the portrait, leaving only David and Cassie.

"You look gorgeous," said David. Taking a box from his pocket he handed it to her saying. "I would like you to have it. It will look good with your dress and also, it matches your ring which I see is on display this evening."

Cassie gasped as she opened the box. "David, are you sure? I can't accept this. Wasn't this your mother's bracelet?"

"Yes, but if things had been different, Lizzie would have got it; I'd like you to have it, please say yes," said David.

"Will you put it on for me," asked Cassie. David bent down and fastened the catch.

"Thank you," said Cassie excitedly, "I'll treasure it, I really will and I'll not only think of you when I wear it but also I'll think of Mum." Placing a kiss on his cheek she said, "Thank you again. I must go and show Aunt Lydia and Kate." And before David could stop her she had run out of the drawing room.

David went over to the drinks table and with somewhat trembling hands, poured himself another glass of champagne. He wandered over to the fireplace and gazed down at the burning embers. His emotions were in complete turmoil for he was trying very hard not to, but it was no use, he was falling for Cassie. He wondered if she was aware, even vaguely so. She had looked at him with surprise when he'd cursed as he fumbled with the catch on the bracelet like some inept adolescent – not his usual suave self at all, and she had been rather quick to escape on the pretext of showing off her bracelet. It would be too much to hope she would feel the same. *Dream on David,* he thought to himself. He downed his glass, another glass beckoned he thought, but on turning from the fire he was shocked to see Lydia staring at him.

"Penny for them," Lydia said.

"Not worth even a penny," replied David. "I was just thinking about my mother, all of you and I suppose how much I have enjoyed my visits here." David was surprised at his presence of mind and astonished at how easily that lie had tripped off his tongue.

Lydia thought he looked so vulnerable. He was bringing out her deeply hidden maternal instincts. "Come on," she said, putting her arm through his, I need an escort for dinner. Will you do me the honour?"

"With pleasure," replied David with a smile and bending down he kissed her on the cheek. "You are a lovely lady and thank you for arriving in the nick of time before I became too maudlin!"

Dinner was a happy affair. Charles loved these evenings when it was just 'the family' as he thought of them all. He even had to admit that the presence of David and Pierre in no way detracted from the evening, far from it, for they had both been amusing guests and had enhanced the evening with their company. He noticed Peter steal the occasional glance at David – he wondered what his thoughts were.

Although Mrs. Pearson had done the bulk of the cooking it was very much a 'all-hands-on-deck' affair so that she could relax and enjoy her evening. Charles, true to his word, had cajoled and eventually persuaded her to sample some of his wines. With anticipation on his face, he awaited her verdict.

She looked at him after she had taken a minuscule sip of the third wine. "Would you be very bothered if I told you that none of them are really to my liking," said Mrs. P. apologetically, "I know they'll be expensive and such like, but I'd far rather have a good strong cup of tea."

Everyone laughed and Charles said, "After forcing you to do that it would be my pleasure to go and get a cup for you," and before Mrs. Pearson could protest, Charles went off to the kitchen to make her tea.

Charles came back from the kitchen bearing Mrs. P.'s tea and with a flourish presented it to her. Lydia thought Charles was looking tired; he was beginning to flag a little after the excitement of the evening. Catching Kate's eye she gave her an indication that they should wind up the evening. At an appropriate juncture Kate, who had taken her cue from Lydia, announced she had a busy morning the following day and would have to think about going home. Charles had noticed the look between she and Lydia and smiled gratefully at them both. He was tired but he didn't want the evening to end although he knew it must.

Mrs. Pearson rose from the table and started to collect the dishes together. "Oh no you don't," said Cassie. "You provided the wonderful meal, we will tidy and do the dishes. Off to bed you go."

"This isn't right," muttered Mrs. Pearson vainly protesting. "Not right at all."

But she was completely outnumbered. Charles went over to her. "As ever, a fabulous meal, a sumptuous feast. Three cheers for Mrs. P. everyone. Hip Hip Hoorah." Everyone joined in. Mrs. Pearson looked for a moment embarrassed, but only for a moment!

"Thank you everyone, goodnight," she replied, as Peter gave her his arm and escorted her from the room.

"What do you think you're doing?" asked Kate.

"I'm helping," replied Charles who was about to attack the debris.

"Oh no you don't," said Kate. "Go and sit down, off you go." Looking at Lydia she continued, "I'll get your big sister if you don't. Lydia, I need your help please. Take him away."

"I'm surrounded by bossy women in my own home," twinkled Charles, "And do you know something? I love it! Come on Lydia, let us old fogies go and have a nightcap."

Together Lydia and Charles went into the library. Lydia shook her head. "I have to pinch myself sometimes. She has an amazing talent. Quite, quite amazing."

Charles nodded. "You know, I don't want Lizzie to go up in the Great Hall quite yet. I'd like her here for a few days. Do you think I'm mad, do you think Cassie would mind? It's just that I adore looking at her. It would save me craning my neck, don't you think?"

Lydia smiled. "I think that's an excellent idea. It would give us all a chance to look at it in detail."

"Brandy?" asked Charles. Lydia nodded. They both gazed at the portrait. Charles continued. "It's breathtaking and in some ways it is perhaps selfish of me not to have it hung in, say, Pierre's gallery or even London for a little while, but I just can't bear not having her here. Crazy I know. Daft as a brush, aren't I?"

"No, I agree and I'm sure Cassie will as well," said Lydia.

"Cassie will what?" asked Cassie who had just come into the room.

"Your father would like to keep your mother's portrait here, in the library for a little while, not have her in the Great Hall quite yet. Is that acceptable to the artist?" asked Lydia smiling fondly at her niece.

"Anything you wish to do Pops, is fine by me. It's your present," she said, giving Charles a hug, "You do with it what you like. I'm just glad you like it. I just popped in to say that Kate and Robert are about to leave."

Charles continued gazing at the picture. "I cannot take my eyes off it. I could never have anything that means more to me than your picture. Always know that."

"Come on, Pops," said Cassie aware that her father's emotions may be about to go 'out of kilter' again. "Let's go and see Kate and Robert."

"Our thanks for a wonderful evening. We'll now stagger back home over the field," said Robert. "As you can see we have come equipped," indicating Kate leaning against the wall at the door putting on her wellies!

"Lovely evening, as always," said Kate. "See you tomorrow."

"Where are the others?" asked Lydia.

"Pierre has gone to bed, Margaret and Benson are having hot chocolate in the kitchen, I don't know where David is; he's maybe gone to bed, that is where you should be Pops, and you too, Aunt Lydia," said Cassie.

"Here we are," said Peter. "We're off as well. Sarah is driving, but," said Peter grinning at his daughter. "I think I've had enough drink to let that experience wash over me!" After being told by Sarah that he could walk, Peter and Rowena went out to the car after thanks and goodbyes had been finally said.

"What about you my dear? You've had a hectic time with all this. Are you not tired?" asked her aunt.

"Still a bit fired up, I don't think I'd sleep," replied Cassie. "I think I'll go to the studio for a little while."

"Goodnight then," said Lydia, kissing her fondly. "A masterpiece," she said quietly, "An absolute masterpiece. See you in the morning. Coming up, Charles?"

"Following you up," replied Charles. He looked at Cassie with moist eyes and put his arm round her, hugging her tightly to him. "Thank you, Princess," his voice husky with emotion. He tried to say more but that was all he could manage. Kissing Cassie on the forehead and with a lingering look at Lizzie, he followed Lydia upstairs.

Cassie heard her father say goodnight to Benson in the hall.

"Sorry, I didn't realise anyone was here. I was just going to tidy and lock up." He smiled at Cassie as he looked at the portrait. "I remember your mother. She was a lovely girl. There's no doubt she'd be proud of you, no doubt at all. It's wonderful Cassie, really wonderful."

"Thanks," said Cassie. "You know, its funny but now its finished, it's a bit of an anti-climax. I feel at a bit of a loss. I can't settle so I thought I'd go to the studio."

"Your sanctuary," smiled Benson, "I'll say goodnight then. Remember to lock up when you come in!"

"Don't I always," grinned Cassie. "Night-night."

She ran upstairs and changed out of her finery into her 'painting togs' as she called them. Hauling on a couple of paint-splattered jumpers, she ran downstairs and out into the chill night air.

It was initially cold in the studio but after the two heaters leapt into action it became cosy quite quickly and within a very short space of time she was absorbed in her work. She had started on a new piece, which was a Christmas present for her aunt. It was of Charles and Lydia sitting on the sofa, gin and tonic in hand! She smiled at it. She hoped they'd like it. She could always paint out the G&T if they felt she'd gone too far!

She heard a tap on the door and, looking up, saw David standing huddled in the doorway, obviously freezing. She beckoned him in.

"David what on earth are you doing? I thought you'd gone to bed ages ago. How long have you been out there? You look frozen," said Cassie. "Come and sit by the heater."

"I couldn't sleep," said David who had stopped shivering and was beginning to thaw. "I thought I might just find you here – and here you are." He grinned inanely at her.

"Are you all right?" asked Cassie anxiously. "You look, well not to put too fine a point on it, you look a bit odd."

"Ah, odd," he repeated. "There we have it then. Odd I am."

"David, come on, I'm going to take you back to the house. It's late and I'm not concentrating," said Cassie as she shut off the heaters and covered the canvas. He got to his feet a little unsteadily and grinned again at her.

"You know something Cassie? Do you? I wonder if you do. It is perhaps one of the great mysteries of life this, and I wonder if you know?" slurred David.

"Why don't we discuss the mysteries of life over breakfast," said Cassie.

"I suspect that was just a teensy-weensy bit patronising. Would I be correct?" asked David as he stumbled out of the studio with Cassie trying to hold on to him.

"David, put your arm around my shoulder. I'll help you," said Cassie.

"I feel a song coming on," said David. "This is my lucky day, my lucky, lucky day… can't remember any more."

"Shut up David, it's nearly midnight. You'll wake everyone. Shush. Come on. Tiptoe," said Cassie.

"Another song Cassie. You've made me think of another song," said David drunkenly. "You'll know this one, really you will. Here goes. Tiptoe through the tulips… tiptoe… ah, can't remember any more. Yet another disappointment for you I fear."

"Please David. Really quiet… please, we're at the front door. Now, God help me, you have to try and negotiate the stairs." Cassie said this more to herself rather than David. "I know, coffee and lots of it. Kitchen first David," said Cassie as she manoeuvred him in that direction.

Eventually Cassie got him to the kitchen without, she hoped, anyone hearing them. Sense suddenly hit David as he plonked himself in a chair. *What was he doing?* he wondered?"

After a few cups of coffee he said, "Cassie I'm sorry. Got a bit tight, Mum, the house, got to me more than I thought. Forgive me?"

"Nothing to forgive. Are you all right? Will you manage upstairs… quietly?" Cassie smiled at him, emphasising *quietly*. All of a sudden he looked like a little boy.

He nodded and at the door of the kitchen turned, "Goodnight."

"Sleep-tight," said Cassie in response and blew him a kiss. She did not notice the look that crossed his face at that innocent gesture.

Cassie had been right, she did find sleep nigh on impossible. She looked at her bedside clock and decided enough was enough; she'd get up and go back to the studio. It was nearly six, so she'd get a couple of hours of painting before joining everyone for breakfast.

She had just started to dress when she saw an envelope being pushed under her door. She rushed to the door and opened it in time to see David go along the corridor. "David!" she whispered but as loudly as she could.

He looked back startled at seeing Cassie. "I have to go Cassie, sorry about last night," he whispered back.

"Hold on, wait," Cassie ran back into her room grabbed a jacket and picked up the note. Racing after David she caught up with him at the front door. Standing in front of the door, barricading his way, she said, "What's wrong? Why are you rushing away? Please stay, at least have a coffee." Grabbing his hand she pulled him to the kitchen.

"Cassie stop this. I have to go, I really do," pleaded David.

"You were going to go without saying goodbye. Were you coming back?" She looked so hurt. She opened the note all it said was, '*Sorry, had to go, will explain later – David.*' "I thought we were friends. Have I done something wrong?"

David just shook his head. It was taking every ounce of willpower that he possessed, not to hold her to him. He ached for her he wanted her so much.

Cassie could not bear the thought of his going. In such a short space of time, he had become so important to her and the realisation that he might wish to leave had never once crossed her mind.

"Why do you want to leave?" demanded Cassie looking at David with tears in her eyes. "Don't you like it here? Don't you like us? Last night was such a happy evening. I really thought you had enjoyed it as well. My bracelet, you gave me the bracelet. I thought by doing that I meant something to you. David I don't want you to go, please stay." She was holding on to his arms looking deep into his eyes, begging him.

Any resistance David had been clinging on to at that moment vanished. He grabbed her shoulders with a ferocity that surprised him, and holding her close to him, felt the softness of her breasts and the pounding of her heart. He kissed her as she had never been kissed before: his kiss searing the very fibre of her being. She clung to him, their bodies mingled as one.

Abruptly David pushed her away. "No Cassie, I mustn't." Cassie looked at him in bewilderment and with eyes that implored an answer. "For God's sake stop looking at me like that," he shouted.

Cassie was dazed, everything was happening so fast. "I love you, I realise I love you. I've never loved anyone like you, David please, please, don't push me away."

David looked at her, it was too late; it was all too late. He held out his hands to her and held her close. "Oh, my love. I never meant for this to happen, you must believe me. That is why I tried to get away, I couldn't stop thinking about you. I want you, I ache for you and that isn't fair to you. I am far, far too old for you and in my moments of sense, which I grant you have been few and far between of late, I have realised that. I really have. Please my love, let me leave now. You have to."

Cassie looked at him with anger in her eyes. "How can you be so cruel? You haven't once asked how **I** feel. It's all you, you, you. I love you, I want you to make love to me, please David, please." She pressed her lips against his and to his shame he responded; responded with a passion that negated any sense that for a brief moment had prevailed.

"Cassandra! David!" shrieked Lydia. They both looked aghast at Lydia standing in the doorway.

"It's my fault," said David as he hurriedly tried to rearrange his clothing.

Lydia looked at him as if unseeing, clutching her chest, she slumped into a chair and with effort said, "My spray, please, I need my spray."

David looked frantic as Cassie raced past him and moments later returned with her aunt's spray. After administering a couple of puffs to her Lydia appeared to recover.

"Thank you." Lydia looked intently at them both. "Cassie, please go upstairs and dress in more suitable attire."

Cassie looked at her aunt and was suddenly aware of her scanty clothing; being only dressed in undies and a jacket. She decided that this was not the time to argue and went upstairs.

"Please Lydia, let me explain," said David. "But firstly, may I get you something, tea, water, anything."

"Nothing thank you," replied Lydia frostily. She was trying to decide what to do.

Lydia looked at David. Here was a man in pain and she realised that when she had seen him last night, alone with his thoughts, it was Cassie that had been troubling him. She felt such sadness for him. She did not doubt his feelings for Cassie; she had no doubt at all. What was awful was that neither of them had any notion why the feelings they felt for each other were so wrong. What on earth would she do? Her eyes filled with tears at the unfairness of it all.

David was immediately solicitous. "Lydia, I can't tell you how sorry I am. I was trying to leave; Cassie caught me," he looked ruefully at Lydia. "I know the age difference, of course I'm aware of that. It's just... I love her, I know its not suitable but I really do love her." He stood up and started pacing the kitchen floor. "I would have thought you of all people might have understood, what with Charles and Lizzie. I mean there was about the same age difference there, wasn't there?"

Lydia nodded. "I think I will have that cup of tea. Care to join me?"

"I'll make it," said David. "Oh Lydia, what a mess, what a God forsaken mess I've made."

"Two people can't always help what they feel for each other," said Lydia with an understanding which quite surprised David.

Lydia came to a quick conclusion. "David, I need to talk to you but not here. It is vitally important I talk to you and equally important that you don't speak to Charles about your feelings for Cassie. Do I make myself clear?"

David looked at Lydia with a quizzical expression, but agreed.

"I can't say anything here David so please, don't try and make me. But we do need to talk. Will you meet me?" David nodded. "One other thing; please don't mention our talk to Cassie or our proposed meeting and for God's sake no more kissing my niece." David blushed and agreed.

"Is that tea not nearly ready?" asked Lydia.

David looked at Lydia. "I really am sorry."

"I know you are, we'll say no more about it at the moment. Leave me your telephone number and I'll be in touch. Now, before I expire, is there ANY chance of tea?" The tension between them had eased for which David was truly grateful and he poured he and Lydia a cup which they drank together in silence until they were interrupted by the arrival of a surprised Mrs. Pearson.

"Good morning, Mrs. Pearson," said Lydia, "David and I were gasping for tea this morning so had an early morning rendezvous. I do hope you don't mind."

"Don't mind me, just here to start the breakfast," said Mrs. Pearson.

"We'll get out of your way then," said David, as he gathered up the tea things. "Mrs. Pearson, once again, an outstanding meal last night. I'm going to miss these wondrous feasts you produce when I go back to the States."

"Well, you'll just not have to stay away for too long," said Mrs. Pearson, who now rather liked the young man. Will you be staying for breakfast?

"I can't, Mrs. Pearson. Sadly I have an appointment, but hopefully another time. I'd better go then," said David, who was now unsure whether he should go, stay or what.

Lydia and David went through to the hall. David looked upstairs and Lydia catching his look said, "I don't think so, do you?"

"Perhaps you're right, but I can't leave it like this. I have to see Cassie before I go," said David forcibly.

"You will, but let us have our meeting first," replied Lydia. David reluctantly agreed.

Lydia closed the door behind him. She felt physically and emotionally drained so decided to go back to bed for a little while, and slowly made her way upstairs again.

David went out to the car. In her room, Cassie heard the car start and rushed to the window just in time to see it disappear down the drive. Her aunt was spiteful and she hated her. Absolutely and definitely hated her. In yet another flood of tears, she flung herself in a dramatic fashion onto her bed. After crying for a little while she decided that of course she didn't hate her aunt and felt ashamed for even thinking such a thing. One thing she did know was that she loved David and he loved her. Life could be so hateful in some ways and yet so infinitely beautiful in others, she decided. She'd better go and make her peace with her aunt.

She went to Lydia's room and knocked. There was no reply so she went in. Her aunt was lying in bed. She looked so pale. Cassie crept over to the bedside to make sure she was all right. She seemed sound asleep. She wouldn't disturb her and crept quietly out again.

When she heard the door close, Lydia opened her eyes. She felt badly pretending to be asleep but she had to formulate a plan; she had to get her mind straight before she spoke to Cassie, or David, for that matter. As David so rightly said, 'what a mess!'

Cassie decided that everything would sort itself out. David would be back in no time at all. She wouldn't tell Pops but she was bursting to tell someone: she'd phone Sarah. For once she had some intrigue for her friend instead of it always being the other way round! She whizzed down the stairs, slap bang into Kate.

"Hello Kate, you're here early, fancy some breakfast?" asked Cassie.

"Came to see if there was anything I could do," replied Kate. "Did David not stay the night? I don't see his car."

A look crossed Cassie's face that didn't go unnoticed by Kate. "What went on here after we left?"

Cassie looked as if she were going to explode. "I have to tell you, promise you won't tell Pops, and promise not to be cross or say I'm too young or do anything whatsoever to spoil this. Yes?"

Kate looked indulgently at her young friend. "Go on, tell me, I won't say anything."

Cassie proceeded to tell Kate about David's kiss, the ensuing passion, all in graphic detail, until Kate begged to be spared the intimate details. Cassie was positively glowing as she regaled Kate with the early morning exploits and how she and David had declared their undying love for each other.

Kate was alternating between feeling pleased at her friend's obvious pleasure and trying to repress the feelings of alarm that were rising within her. There was something wrong, something horribly wrong but she didn't know what. She had had these feelings more and more every time she saw Cassie and David together but she didn't know why. He was such a nice man, they were so obviously close; with an affinity between them which seemed to have occurred in such a remarkably short space of time. Yet Kate remained troubled.

"Are you listening?" demanded Cassie.

"Sorry Cassie," replied Kate. "Of course I am, I was just mentally editing out the X-rated stuff!"

The answer seemed to satisfy, Cassie who continued. "I do feel badly, though. Aunt Lydia came in; nearly had a seizure, well actually worse than that, she had one of her angina attacks and I do feel dreadful about it, I really do. That's where I was just now, I was going to see her and apologise but she was asleep. Mind you," added Cassie after a moment of thought, "I'm not sure what I was going to be apologising for. I'm not ashamed of what I did," she said defiantly.

"Why don't you let the dust settle? Give your aunt some time to reflect – who knows, she may even come round to the idea," said Kate gently.

"I don't care if she doesn't," responded Cassie. "It's my life and I can do with it what I will. So there!" she added petulantly.

"Tremendously grown-up Cassie, that's the way to win her round!" said Kate sarcastically. "You don't want to fall out with her, you know you don't."

"As usual, I will bow to your better judgement," replied Cassie. "I'll go off to the studio. Oh, by the way, you can't come in this morning, okay?"

"Interesting," smiled Kate. "What are you up to?"

"You'll see soon enough. Promise?" asked Cassie.

"I promise," said Kate. "Are you not having any breakfast first?"

"No, not hungry now," said Cassie. "See you later."

Kate was about to go to the kitchen but decided to see if Lydia was all right. She knocked on Lydia's bedroom door and said, "It's me Lydia, Kate. May I come in?"

There was a quiet response. "Yes, come in."

"Are you on your own?" asked Lydia.

Kate nodded and moved over to sit on the bed. Lydia looked pale and, Kate thought, troubled. "How are you feeling? I've just seen Cassie and she said you'd had an angina attack. Can I get you anything?

"No, I'm fine now," Lydia looked at Kate. "Thank you for coming up."

Kate thought she would give Lydia the chance to talk if she wished so broached the subject of the events in the kitchen.

"Cassie came up to see you to apologise. I believe you stumbled upon she and David. She feels she caused your attack." Kate tried to gauge Lydia's response but her face gave nothing away. "You were asleep though," continued Kate.

"I wasn't actually. I just couldn't speak to Cassie at that moment," said Lydia.

She looked at Kate. Although Kate was much younger than Lydia there had always been empathy between them and Kate had often acted as buffer between Lydia and Cassie when Cassie's exuberance had sorely tested her aunt. She put her hand on top of Kate's.

"I need your help Kate, but by telling you I will be breaking a confidence. I suspect, however, that when Charles knows I've told you he will, in some way, be relieved." Lydia smiled at Kate. "He has always relied on your good sense, goodness me; we all have."

Kate was trying to follow what Lydia was saying but failing. "Lydia, you know I am happy to try and help, but are you sure you should be telling me. If it's about Cassie, I'm sure everything will sort itself out. David is going back to the States soon so it may be a short lived romance."

"It mustn't be any romance at all," said Lydia with alarm. "What do you think of David? Everything about him, his looks, anything at all." She looked at Kate expectantly.

"Well," replied Kate. "I'm not really sure what you mean. I don't really know him, I've only met him a few times but I like him very much. He seems a very pleasant man, obviously fond of not only Cassie, but I thought also you and Charles. There is something, I can't put my finger on it so it's just a hunch I suppose, but I feel a little uneasy about he and Cassie. I don't know why. The thing is," said Kate, faltering a little as she was unsure what she was trying to convey. "I know this is crazy but I think I'm uneasy because they look, well they look sort of alike. Weird I know, but I just think they do and to be honest, I find it a little unnerving." Kate looked at Lydia and shrugged her shoulders. "Told you it was crazy."

Lydia looked intently at Kate. "As ever, so perceptive, so very perceptive." She looked away from Kate. Her eyes had filled with tears and she struggled for control. "Oh Kate, it's dreadful, worse than that, it's **the** most horrendous situation."

Looking over at the door Lydia asked, "Is the door properly shut?" Kate nodded.

"I only found out about this after David had arrived unexpectedly that evening. Do you remember? He came to see Lizzie, hadn't realised she was dead," Lydia stopped. "I'm not making any sense, am I?"

Kate patted Lydia's hand. "Take your time. But you're right, you aren't making any sense," she said, smiling at her.

Lydia smiled back weakly. "Here goes then. Oh, one thing, Lizzie had always been honest about David to Charles, so David wasn't a total surprise. They had lived together in some commune, can't remember where, but not far because she used to cycle here when she worked on the book with Charles. Do you remember?"

"Not really," said Kate. "Remember I didn't know Lizzie back then. I only knew her after she and Charles were married."

"Of course," said Lydia. "I'm getting all muddled again. Right, back to what I was trying to tell you. David's arrival was the same day that Charles had been to Peter's to get the results and knew he had cancer. A ghastly day: truly ghastly. I wasn't here so it was just Charles and David. Cassie had been out and came in late so didn't really have a chance to meet him properly. However, Charles, like you, felt there was something familiar about David – his eyes actually – and felt this feeling of foreboding I suppose you'd call it. Anyway, after David left the next morning, Charles went up to the attic where there were a couple of trunks with Lizzie's things. Apparently after she died he'd put her clothes away in the trunk and there was also a sketchpad and some letters. He hadn't looked at any of the letters at that time; felt it was an intrusion."

"Typical!" said Kate.

"Well, this time he did look at the letters. There were a few from David and then, and this is quite odd, about ten letters written to David but never sent. Going off at a tangent for the moment," said Lydia. "May I ask you something?"

"Of course," responded Kate.

"Did you not think that Cassie's birth was rather quick considering when they had been married?" asked Lydia.

"Well, to be honest, no," replied Kate. "I don't think I've known anyone who is entitled to wear white on their wedding day!" smiled Kate. "No one would have given that a thought."

"Quite," said Lydia. "Changed days, such changed days since my youth. I digress again. Well," continued Lydia, "What Charles discovered in the letters was... oh Kate," said Lydia in anguish. "Charles isn't Cassie's father, David is!"

"What?" Kate could not believe what she had heard and moments passed before she could speak. "Oh poor Charles, how awful for him to find out like that." Realisation then struck Kate. "Oh God, what you're saying... this is truly a nightmare. Cassie and David – oh Lydia, no wonder you had an attack." Kate was trying to assimilate all the facts. Her heart went out to Charles; what must he have felt on reading that? She looked at Lydia and quietly said, "Thank goodness you did stumble across them. What if you hadn't, what if they had become lovers?" Kate felt herself shiver at that thought. "God that doesn't even bear thinking about."

Lydia nodded her head in agreement. "The last letter Lizzie wrote is lovely. Charles read it to me and it expurgates any feelings he had against her. In it she says to David that she realises she always thinks of the baby as being Charles's and also concludes that she has been happier with Charles than she has ever been before. It was lovely," said Lydia, with tears in her eyes.

Kate wiped away the tears that had welled up in her own eyes. "Thank goodness Charles has that letter," said Kate.

Lydia nodded in agreement. "I said to David that it was imperative I spoke to him. He will be expecting to hear from me, but I don't know what to do. I also don't know whether to tell Charles what has happened, I have no idea what to do for the best."

"Don't you think David has to hear this from Charles," said Kate.

"Yes, yes I do," said Lydia, "And under normal circumstances, well as normal as these can be, I would certainly agree with you but the strain Charles is under," she tailed off. "He's having to cope with such a lot."

Kate looked at Lydia and said quietly, "There is one person whom we haven't mentioned."

"Oh Kate I know, of course I've thought of that," said Lydia. "What on earth is Cassie going to be told? I have no idea, no idea at all. This is unbearable, simply unbearable. But," hesitated Lydia, "does she have to know, I wonder?"

"Who actually know?" asked Kate.

"You, Peter, Charles and myself: just the four of us," said Lydia. "David, he has to know. I am afraid it would possibly be up to David to decide if Cassie finds out. Don't you think?"

"I'm not sure," said Kate, mulling this over. "If Cassie ever found out inadvertently I cannot even begin to imagine how she would react. Can you?"

Lydia shook her head. "You have to tell Charles," said Kate.

Lydia nodded. "Time to get up and face the day I think." Lydia threw back the bedclothes. "As ever, you are right, of course you are. I just needed someone to tell me that. Kate," said Lydia, hugging her. "I have no idea, none whatsoever, what I would do without you. Thank you."

"Charles has to see David quickly, today even, because David will be wondering what's going on and can you imagine how Cassie will be feeling? She'll want to see him," said Kate. "How can we keep Cassie away?" Kate looked out of the window hoping for inspiration. "I know. It's not great, but it will have to do. I'll take the children to the pictures and ask Cassie if she'll come and give me a hand with them and then after the pictures we'll have a pizza. The children will be thrilled. Amazed, but thrilled, and that would give Charles about three hours with David. What do you think? I'm afraid it's all I can come up with."

"I can't come up with anything better. It will have to do. I'll go and tell Charles and then phone David and just hope he'll manage to come over. What time will you leave?"

"Before you phone David, let me quickly check that Cassie will agree to this. I'll meet you in the dining room," said Kate and headed off to find Cassie.

Although Kate was trying to remain composed in front of Lydia, her mind was reeling and in her heart of hearts she very much hoped that Cassie would never find out, for she had no idea what that knowledge would do to her. An unbearable thought Kate decided, and headed off to the studio.

"Cassie!" said Kate brightly. "I know I'm not allowed in but I need your help please. Can you come out?"

"Hi," replied Cassie. "You won't have to wait too long for your surprise. What can I do for you?"

Kate smiled at Cassie, "Are you due me any pay-back favours? I hope you are."

"Nope, can't think of any, bad luck," grinned Cassie. "However, as I am in a wonderful mood, ask away, for in this instance I may just be feeling benevolent!"

"How kind!" retorted Kate. "Do you fancy coming to the pictures by any chance?"

Cassie rolled her eyes. "Not especially. What's on?"

Kate had absolutely no idea what was on and for a moment was caught off guard, but quickly retrieved the situation.

"The children needless to say, want to go to different things, so they wanted you to have the casting vote so to speak."

"All right," said Cassie a little reluctantly. "Just say when and I'll be ready."

"Marvellous," said Kate who suddenly remembered that she now had to persuade the children they were wanting to go to the pictures. "See you later, about one-thirty."

Kate then ran back to the house. Lydia was in the dining room awaiting her return. Kate shut the door and, helping herself to coffee, asked Lydia, "Did you speak to Charles?"

"Yes. He agrees with you. He'll talk to David," said Lydia. "Cassie, have you spoken to her?

"Yes," said Kate. "Also, there is one teensy-weensy thing. Can you look after Ben this afternoon? I'm sorry about this but as I was suggesting the pictures I was quite forgetting that Ben as a toddler was, shall we say, a trifle young! Would you mind? It's just with Mum having such a bad cold I really can't stand the thought of any more colds in our household."

"It's the least I can do," replied Lydia. "What time are you going?"

"I said to Cassie one-thirty, so why don't you drive Cassie over to us and then I'll bring her back to ours afterwards and then that way we know where she is," said Kate.

"Will do," smiled Lydia gratefully. "And, thank you, Kate."

"I'd better dash and go and tell the children how much they want to go the pictures!"

As she left she bumped into Charles. "Ah Kate," he said looking around to make sure he wasn't being overheard. "I'm glad you know," he whispered.

Kate smiled at him fondly. He had aged such a lot in the last while and now, when he should be trying to fight his illness he had to cope with this. It wasn't fair. Not fair at all.

Charles smiled ruefully and continued. "Lydia told me what you think and I agree, sadly there seems to be no other way. It's a bloody mess though, that's for sure," and with a peck on her cheek he went into the dining room to join Lydia.

Chapter 16

David had been surprised to receive the phone call from Charles although Charles alluded to the fact Lydia instigated the call. David had an idea what this was about and smiled at the irony of the situation, for he suspected that Charles was going to read the riot act. David was unused to irate fathers but then he'd never before fallen for anyone half his age! He smiled; Cassie was a delight. She mesmerised him and he felt overwhelmed that she seemed to feel the same way for him.

He then realised that the feelings he was experiencing were probably the very same feelings that Charles had felt for Lizzie. A sudden and unexpected surge of jealousy reared within him at this thought.

Charles had been specific that he had to arrive after 1.45. For some reason this seemed important to Charles, so David adhered to this command, for command is what it felt. The clock showed 1.44 as his car swung into the drive. *Perfect timing,* he thought. He parked and went to the front door just as Charles appeared.

"Hello David, I saw you coming up the drive. Thank you for coming over," he said, indicating to David to go to his study. There was a lovely smell of coffee wafting from a tray on the table in the corner of the room. "I thought we'd have a coffee, care for a cup?"

David nodded. "Please, just black." He realised that Charles was as ill at ease with the situation as he was, so, attempting to allay his fears said, "I know why you've called me. I also know you must be concerned about Cassie but you have to know that I would never do anything to knowingly hurt her. She's wonderful, a credit to you. I love her Charles, I really do." David paused. "Charles, you have to believe that." Charles's face was expressionless. David was unnerved by this lack of response and decided on another tack. "By the same token I hope you will also remember that the age gap between Cassie and I, is no different from that of you and Lizzie."

Charles initially did not respond; he just looked at David with intense sadness in his eyes. As if ignoring David, Charles said, "David, what I am about to tell you will be one of the most difficult things I have ever done in my life. David felt the hairs on the back of his neck stand up.

"Please Charles," said David. "I know you disapprove, God I probably would if I was a father, I've no idea how I'd react, but give me a chance, please, just a chance."

"David, if I could say any differently I would, truly I would, but it's not what you think so please, don't interrupt and I'll try very hard to tell you." Charles indicated to David to sit down.

"When you arrived here that day, to see Lizzie, there was something about you that I have to say was familiar, but I couldn't think what on earth it was. I heard about you from Lizzie and of course knew about your going to the States and what have you."

Charles paused and took a sip of coffee. "After you left the next morning, I went to the attic where I had kept some of Lizzie's things; clothes and such like, but more importantly there were some letters which after she died I had put away without looking at."

"I think I'd have wanted to read them. I admire your restraint."

"Please David," chided Charles. "No interruptions."

"Sorry," apologised David.

"Anyway," continued Charles. "This time I did look at the letters. There were some from you which I confess to glancing at but, and more relevant to our discussion today, there were letters which Lizzie had written to you but had never sent." David furrowed his brow with surprise.

Charles stopped on the pretext of having another drink of coffee but in reality was trying to brace himself for the next sentence or so.

David looked at Charles expectantly as Charles opened his desk drawer and took out some envelopes and then, from the inside pocket of his jacket, took out another envelope.

"When you read these letters," said Charles, "You may be angry, hurt, bewildered, you may feel any number of other emotions, I do not know. But please do not tear them up in a fit of rage or whatever you may be feeling. I know I nearly did, for what Lizzie has written… God, this is impossible." Charles swallowed. "What Lizzie wrote is that… it is you who is Cassie's father, not I."

David stared at Charles as if mishearing. It couldn't be true for he thought he'd heard Charles say that he wasn't Cassie's father.

Charles looked at David, alarmed at his colour, for in an instant he was ashen. He looked as if he was going to faint. With concern Charles asked, "Can I get you something?" David mumbled something incoherently and leaping from his seat ran to the cloakroom where he vomited until his stomach heaved no more. He wiped his mouth and stared at his reflection in the mirror. 'He was Cassie's father.' David was shaking uncontrollably, covered in perspiration, he looked a wreck and repeated to his reflection, 'Cassie's father, I am Cassie's father.' It was too much to comprehend. His mind in turmoil he became aware of a knocking at the door.

"David, are you all right? Please open the door," said Charles.

David opened the door to confront Charles. David looked back at his reflection in the mirror and again at Charles. He couldn't decide which of them looked worse.

"Come back to the study," said Charles gently. Guiding David to the chair, he continued. "I know this has been something of a shock. I know how I felt when I read it but I've had a few weeks to try and get to grips with it. You can now understand my concern regards you and Cassie.

David just looked at Charles; the shaking was subsiding. "I gave up smoking about four years ago, I wish to God I hadn't. Why, why are you telling me this now?"

"David, you know why," said Charles patiently. "You and Cassie, you can't be intimate, that would be incest for God's sake."

"Of course, yes, sorry. Does she know, does Cassie know?" asked David. He had so many questions. "Why didn't Lizzie tell me. Why hide that from me?" Tears were spilling down his cheeks. "I would have taken care of her, I wouldn't have gone to the States. I would have got a proper job and looked after them both. Why did she not realise that?" he asked in a voice filled with hurt and pain. Charles was a blur in front of him. He wiped his eyes with the back of his hands. "You believe me, don't you?"

Charles nodded. "The letters, they may in some way help you understand. Shall I leave you to read them in private?"

David nodded. "Charles, would you mind, may I ask you for a brandy please?"

"Of course." Charles went to the decanter and poured a brandy for David. Leaving it on the desk in front of him he said, "I'll pop back in a little while. I'm so sorry David, so very sorry having to do this to you."

David sniffed as he fumbled in his pocket for his handkerchief. "This isn't easy for you either, I know that."

Closing the door quietly behind him, Charles left David with the letters and his thoughts.

After nearly an hour, Charles went back to the study. David was standing by the window, his glass of brandy seemingly untouched on the desk.

"May I come in?" asked Charles.

"Yes, yes of course," replied David. "I suppose you felt as I'm feeling right now. I feel I've gone ten rounds with Mohammed Ali."

"At least ten," responded Charles.

The two men looked at each other. Eventually David spoke. "You must have hated my turning up like that. I'm sorry."

"You weren't to know," said Charles. "I suspect you're feeling you're on an emotional roller-coaster. I know I did." Charles sat down. "David, I have no idea why Lizzie didn't tell you. I suspect it was because she didn't want you tied down when you had such an amazing chance. In the letter she says she didn't know she was pregnant until after you'd left. She was, I really do think, doing it for the most noble of reasons."

Charles bent his head and ran his hands through his hair. "I can't believe that Cassie is not mine, I really can't. I don't think I ever will and I also don't know if she should know. We have to, or perhaps rather *you* have to, decide whether to tell her."

David looked with incredulity at this suggestion. "I can't do that. Can I? Do you want me to?"

Charles replied, "I don't know what I want. I wish this situation had never arisen but maybe it's best it has."

David looked at Charles as if he were insane. "How do you make that out?"

"I know what you're thinking," said Charles. "But picture the scenario if we hadn't discovered the letters. After my death it would be the most natural thing for Cassie to have gone through her mother's things and she would have found the letters. Can you imagine how she would have felt?"

175

"Yes, I see what you mean," said David, still bewildered by the unfolding events.

"We have to decide what to do," continued Charles.

David looked at Charles. "You're such a decent man, such a thoroughly decent man. I read these letters and I wanted to hate you; that was after I hated Lizzie, but I can't; I can't hate you. We are the injured parties here; you, I and, most of all, Cassie."

"I agree about Cassie, but don't hate Lizzie, please don't ever hate Lizzie. She was young, she didn't know what to do for the best." He had tears in his eyes. "No hatred for her."

David smiled wistfully. "No, I didn't mean it. I could never hate her. The last letter to me," he looked at Charles with sadness and with a hint of regret, "That was probably true. She was happier with you. She had, at last, found happiness."

"Thank you David," said Charles, his voice cracking. "I appreciate that and yes, that letter means everything to me."

David took it from the pile and handed it back to Charles. "It means more to you than to me."

Charles looked at it, fingered it and, putting it back into his pocket, looked gratefully at David. "Thank you, thank you very much." It sounded stilted but he didn't know what else to say. "The others, would you care to have them?"

"Thank you," said David. "I would." He flicked through them. "I don't know what to do with them at the moment, but I'll take care of them. What do you want me to do Charles?"

"I don't know," said Charles. "I think you need time to reflect on what has happened. As you will have gathered Lydia knows, as do Kate and Peter. No others."

The two men sat in silence, each contemplating their own thoughts. Eventually, David spoke. "Charles, may I ask you how on earth you weren't suspicious about Lizzie's pregnancy. After I read the letters I did some calculations and you must have wondered, surely you did?"

"I can't remember," said Charles. "To be honest, I was in such a euphoric state that she could have had the gestation of an elephant I would have been none the wiser. Then, when Lizzie died, I was in a sort of vacuum, had no idea what I was doing, barely functioning. I even initially rejected Cassie, you know. I am ashamed to say it was about six weeks before I saw her. I thought Cassie would be better

176

off adopted but Kate put me straight on that," said Charles, smiling at the memory. "No, I can honestly say, I didn't put two and two together."

"Well," replied David, "You are not going to tell me that Lydia didn't know. That I can't believe."

"I asked her," replied Charles. "Lydia had apparently confronted Lizzie but Lizzie had obviously convinced her - or Lydia had wanted to be convinced – that the baby was mine. After Cassie was born Lydia did wonder, because of Cassie's size I think, but then with the turn of events, I suppose all logic went out the window."

"All right. The doctor, Peter, surely knew," said David.

"He wasn't here then," replied Charles. "He'd been a locum, only met Lizzie once, at our wedding I think, then he went off to finish his training and when he came back to take over the practice, Lizzie had died."

Charles looked at his watch. "I wanted to see you on your own without any interruptions from Cassie. She's off to the pictures with Kate and her family but," said Charles anxiously, "They will be back soon."

"Point taken, Charles," said David, rubbing his eyes. "I feel shattered, absolutely drained. I don't know what I'm doing, I don't even know what I'm thinking but I do know one thing and that is I'll have to go back to the States sooner rather than later and will have to give Cassie some reason. At the moment I can't think of her as my daughter." As soon as he said it he wished he hadn't, for Charles winced and the look that crossed his face was one of such sorrow, such distress. "Sorry Charles, I didn't mean to say that."

"This is too much to take in all at once," said Charles. "I don't know if I would have had the courage to tell you if the situation between you and Cassie had not occurred. I will confess though to initially having some romantic notion that it was meant. Here I was, dying, then you arrived and would take over the fatherly duties in one rather smooth transition."

"I somehow don't think Cassie would see it like that, do you?" said David.

"No, of course you're right. I mentioned that to Peter as well. He was of the same opinion," agreed Charles. "But Cassie has fallen in love with you, and it is she who is going to get hurt, no matter what happens."

"Between us," said David. "Let us try to make the hurt as minimal as possible."

David sighed, his head was spinning. "I'm not sure what I'm going to do; I really don't. I'll go back to the hotel and have a think." He took a sip of brandy. "I suspect it would be better if I don't return here. Wouldn't you agree?"

"I don't know. Are you not going to talk to Cassie first?" asked Charles expectantly.

"I haven't decided. I may write, or I may rather meet her away from here, I've no idea to be honest but I will let you know." David gave Charles a sort of half smile. "Ridiculous I know, but I'm going to miss my visits here. Not just Cassie, I mean everyone. I've only just met you all but I very much wish things could have been different. I really do." David sighed, "Lizzie was probably right though, I'd have made a useless father."

Pulling himself together David extended his hand. "I think its time I said good-bye." They shook hands.

"I'll miss you David. I'm truly sorry the way things have turned out," said Charles sadly.

"I wish you well with your treatment Charles and I hope that once things have settled I may come back one day and visit you all?"

"We'd like that," responded Charles.

"I'll see myself out; but there is one thing," Charles looked at David anxiously. "I've decided I won't tell Cassie; she'll never know from me, I promise," said David.

"Thank you David," said Charles, who felt a huge weight lift from his shoulders. He smiled at David. "I think I'm very relieved." He hesitated. "No, I **know**, I'm relieved."

At the study door David turned and looked at Charles. "You know something?" Charles shook his head. "Lizzie was lucky; she did marry the right man and at least had some months of happiness."

Charles stared at David's retreating figure, astounded by the last kindness of this statement, unable to respond. He watched David go to the front door and open it. Turning towards Charles, David gave a slight nod and, pulling the door behind him, left with what Charles felt was finality about the gesture.

Charles walked slowly, deep in thought, over to his study door. He shut it firmly, went back to his desk, sat down and wept.

David had no idea what to do or where to go. All that he had heard that afternoon was so incredible: so difficult to believe. One thing he did know he had to get away from Harrington.

Driving aimlessly round the countryside he finally arrived back at his hotel and informed them that he was checking out. He then telephoned the airline, the car hire firm and, lastly, his solicitors. He went to his room, packed, then sat down and tried to write to Cassie. The words, however, would not come, no matter how hard he tried. He decided he couldn't write when he was in the area, he had to leave and go and stay somewhere further afield. He checked out of the hotel, went to the car hire firm where, with a little regret, he returned the Lotus, and then took a taxi to a non-descript hotel some thirty miles away.

It was ghastly; dingy and the room smelt of stale smoke and cheap perfume, but all in all he decided it was just right, and fitted his mood perfectly. He went to reception and purchased a pack of five cigars and then went to the bar for some whisky.

Once safely ensconced in his room he set about trying to write to Cassie. He had absolutely no idea what to write. No reason to give why he had departed so quickly. He tried to open his mind to what he would say. He poured a drink and lit a cigar. The aroma filled the room. He loved the smell, he had forgotten just how much. The blank piece of paper beckoned and words started to form in his mind. He started writing:

> *Dear Cassie,*
>
> *I cannot begin to imagine what you must be feeling or thinking just now. I suppose you would be well within your rights to hate me. You probably do. You are also probably tempted to tear this letter into minute pieces – I wouldn't blame you. All I ask though is before you do that, you please read on, although at this stage I confess I'm not entirely sure what I'm about to say!!*
>
> *What has happened to me is that now, in the cold light of day, so to speak, I realise I would be grossly unfair to you if we were to pursue any relationship other than that of a deep friendship. My*

fervent wish is that some day we may achieve that. I do hope so. Let me try and explain why.

When I told you I loved you, I wasn't lying. I do, but I now realise not as a lover, more a doting uncle or whatever the equivalent would be. But, for just a little while, I was carried away. The portrait of your mother, which is remarkable, perhaps triggered these feelings, for at that time we had a common goal of trying to bring to life something we both wanted very badly. I suspect what was happening was that, in some bizarre way, you were like a reincarnation of Lizzie. In so many ways you're very like her and I suppose I was trying to recapture the memories of another time and have a second chance of happiness that, unknowingly, I had thrown away all those years ago.

Try to forgive me Cassie, and please do not blame Lydia. Your aunt was the only one whom I think understood what I was feeling. She realised I was having conflicting thoughts and feelings and was perceptive enough to suspect that what I thought I felt for you was in fact, intertwined with unresolved feelings for Lizzie. She was trying to save you from getting hurt – and she was right to do that.

For a little while I was happier than I have been for many years being with you all at The Hall. I will miss you, your father and aunt and 'the extended family' as your father calls the others, but perhaps one day you will allow me to come back into your lives. My thoughts will be with you and of course Charles during this worrying time. I will admit to you now, that I envy you and your family but for a short time, I felt I was lucky enough to be part of it.

Continued success with your work and every happiness for whatever the future may hold for you. Please Cassie, please try and find it in your heart to forgive me. I beg you.

Yours, with love,
David

David put down his pen and read the letter. He liked the 'doting uncle' bit, no mention of father figure; he'd been careful to avoid that. He read on. He hoped he had conveyed what he was feeling, more importantly he hoped he had convinced Cassie this was what he was feeling. He decided not to change it. He would never be satisfied with it. It had to go as it was.

He phoned reception and asked whether there was a delivery service who could take the letter today to Harrington. After some time, the reply was yes; a courier service would take the letter. Before he had time to change his mind he sealed the envelope, addressed it and awaited the arrival of the courier. It was guaranteed delivery within an hour. David looked at his watch, nearly seven; the family would be getting ready for dinner. He couldn't bear that thought and decided to close his mind to it by having another scotch. He poured a large one and gulped it down. It burnt his throat; he wished it would erase his mind. He lay on top of the bed, unsure what to do next.

Cassie and Lydia returned to The Hall at about six.

Cassie went looking for Benson. "Any calls for me when I was out?"

"No, sorry none. Did you have a good time?"

"To be perfectly honest, not exactly my thing," said Cassie. "Animated dragons and things, however the children seemed to enjoy it. Oh, please tell Mrs. Pearson I'm not hungry so I won't require dinner. I'll pop down and make my peace with her but I had to have a pizza; Kate insisted, but right at this moment it's lying fairly heavily on the tum! Is Pops in?"

"I think he's in the study, I was just going to see if he required anything," said Benson.

Charles heard Lydia and Cassie come back. He had had the presence of mind to return the coffee tray to the kitchen beforehand and had said to Benson and Mrs. Pearson that he would be grateful if Cassie was not made aware of David's visit. They may have been surprised at the request but would, he knew without question, say nothing.

"You look a bit peaky Pops, are you feeling all right?" asked Cassie with concern.

"Don't you fret, I'm just tired with a whole pile of paperwork, been at it all afternoon and you know how mind-bogglingly boring I find that!" he smiled at her. "Enjoy the pictures?"

Cassie grimaced. "Not exactly, not sure why I was there, but anyway, I've done my good deed for the day. I thought David might have phoned or called but Benson says there have been no messages."

Lydia arrived in the room just in time to hear that and to silently applaud her brother's performance.

"No doubt he's hectic, tying up loose ends with his Mum's things and what have you." Noticing Lydia in the doorway, Charles said, "Ah, Lydia, how was Ben? I suspect you are in need of a G&T."

Lydia smiled at him. "A large one, in fact two!"

"If you two are boozing again, I'll go and phone David," said Cassie running out. Lydia went and shut the door behind Cassie.

"You look whacked, how did it go?" Charles looked at her, "I am whacked, completely and utterly, but it went far better than I thought. He's a terribly nice man; fair and decent. He said he's going to miss us and I think he means it. I'm actually going to miss him."

Lydia looked at Charles and murmured, "Me too. What about Cassie? What is he going to do about that?"

"He promises not to tell her – ever," said Charles.

"And you believe him?" asked Lydia.

"Definitely, without question. As you can imagine he was stunned, nonplussed, poor guy had to run out to the cloakroom and throw-up. He looked a wreck – I hope he's all right. He's gone off, goodness knows where, and he's on his own thinking about the events of the afternoon. I don't envy him his solitude at this time." Charles smiled at Lydia. "I'm so lucky to have you, keeping an eye on things as ever."

"With everything happening so fast I don't suppose I considered that he'd have to leave immediately without first saying goodbye," mused Lydia. "I realise I will miss him, miss him dreadfully, considering how I was dreading him being here. It's ridiculous, but he just fitted in with everyone so tremendously well." Lydia looked into space. "I do so hope he'll be all right." Patting Charles's hand she continued. "Poor old you, what a time you've had." Charles raised an eyebrow. "Now, what about that large G&T."

"Good idea, let's go through to the drawing room. I've had enough of the study for today," said Charles.

As they crossed the hall Cassie was coming down the stairs. She looked at them and glared at Lydia. "Thanks, thanks a lot." Reaching the bottom of the stairs she went over to her aunt and inches from her face, and with venom in her voice said, "Well I'll find him, I will and there is absolutely nothing you can do to stop me."

"My dear," said Lydia, taking a step backwards preparing herself for what she felt was to be a verbal onslaught from her niece. "I've no idea to what you're referring."

"Really," said Cassie with anger consuming her. "David, as if you didn't know, as if you didn't bloody know, he's checked out of his hotel."

Lydia and Charles exchanged glances that did not go unnoticed by Cassie. Glaring at Charles she practically spat out the next words. "Don't feign surprise, it doesn't become you. Well, I love David and that is all that matters. I don't know what you have done to make him go away," and towards Lydia, "either of you."

She turned tail and went storming back upstairs, where the bedroom door was slammed to such effect Benson appeared. He looked enquiringly at Charles. "A little altercation, nothing to worry about. Lydia and I are just going to have a gin in the drawing room, there's no hurry for dinner; we may have a couple!" Benson just nodded.

With relief, Charles and Lydia went into the drawing room and shut the door. For a moment neither said anything; they hated what they were doing to Cassie, they would have done anything to protect her from this.

Breaking the silence, Charles looked at Lydia and said, "Ghastly, truly ghastly. I hate seeing her like this but we have to be strong."

"I know, but in the hall she looked as if she hated us." Lydia sat down as Charles prepared the drinks. "I wish I knew what David was going to say to her, I feel it would help in some way, but maybe I'm wrong, I don't know. Mind you, I don't feel I know anything just at the moment. Thank you," said Lydia, taking her glass. "I need this."

After dinner Lydia and Charles sat down in the library. "Should I go up, do you think?" asked Charles.

"Leave her at the moment," said Lydia. Both Lydia and Charles jumped when they heard the doorbell ring. "Who on earth is that?" asked Lydia and then with horror on her face she looked at Charles. "It can't be David, can it?"

"How on earth do I know?" asked Charles. "Act naturally, it's maybe – oh I don't know, just relax."

Charles got up and went into the hall just as Benson was closing the door. "Who was that?" asked Charles.

"Special courier service, for Cassie," said Benson. "Do you want to take it up?"

"No, it's all right, would you mind taking it?" asked Charles.

Charles went back into the drawing room. Lydia, looking at him expectantly, said, "Well?"

"Special courier service for Cassie," replied Charles. "I have a horrible sick feeling in the pit of my stomach. I wish I could do something, anything, to alleviate the hurt she is about to experience."

"Are you sure it will be from David?" asked Lydia.

"I would be 99% sure," said Charles grimly.

Up in her bedroom Cassie opened the letter. She had never seen David's writing but just knew it was from him. For some reason she had a feeling of apprehension. Why hadn't he rung? She looked at the letter; she had to open it but was loath to. Gathering herself together, she decided to take the bull by the horns, so to speak, and slit open the envelope. She sat down on the bed and started to read. Why was he behaving like this? Why David? Tears slowly slid down her cheeks as the realisation of what he was saying dawned on her.

She lost count of the number of times she re-read the letter. There was no address, no telephone number, no way at all she could communicate back to him. She suspected that he would leave for America soon, but how soon? She looked down at her bed, there were crumpled tissues all over the place. She took the least crumpled, wiped her eyes, blew her nose and looking through the telephone directory, looked for Heathrow airport.

She tried every airline going to America. They were initially reluctant to give out information regarding passengers but Cassie somehow managed to convince them of the life and death situation involved, without actually informing them what that was. They relented and checked their records for all passengers for the next two or three days but to no avail. There was definitely no Coleridge booked. Although she was well aware she was chancing her luck, she then asked them to look up his other name, Risi, but there was no luck there either.

She didn't know what to do next. Where was he? She knew he'd want to see her; this was a misunderstanding. It had to be. Once he saw her, he'd change his mind, she knew he would.

There was a knock at the door. "Go away, I don't want to see anyone."

"Cassie, it's me, Kate. May I come in?"

"I think I'd like to be on my own, Kate," replied Cassie.

Not one to be deterred, Kate persisted. "It's something to do with David, isn't it."

The door opened and a red-faced Cassie glowered at Kate. "You are so annoying, why can't you go when I ask? I just want to be alone."

"Ah, the Garbo routine," said Kate.

"What?" Cassie hadn't the first clue what Kate was talking about.

"Never mind," replied Kate. "I came over to see how Mum was and how Lydia was after her sterling efforts looking after Ben. She and your father are really worried about you. They hate seeing you hurt and upset. They said something about you receiving a letter or something," said Kate innocently.

Cassie looked at her. "There is no need for them to worry. There has been a misunderstanding that's all. David has been frightened off, temporarily."

Kate noticed the phone directory open at 'airports'. "Going away somewhere?"

"Might be, don't know yet," scowled Cassie.

"Anywhere special, with Christmas so near I mean? I'm surprised that's all." Kate smiled at Cassie. "Come on, let's see if we can sort this out. Do it for me? You know I hate falling outs!"

"There," said Cassie, thrusting David's letter at Kate. "Read it, you'll understand then." They sat down together on Cassie's bed.

"I don't want to pry," said Kate gently. "So I don't have to read this. But," Kate tentatively putting her arm around Cassie. "I do care about you and I hate seeing you hurting like this."

All Cassie's bravado evaporated at these words. "I was so happy Kate, really happy," sobbed Cassie. "We seemed so in tune, so as one. I didn't care about the age difference; look at Mum and Pops, they obviously didn't think it mattered, so why should it matter with David and I? Why?"

Kate cuddled her close. She understood Cassie's questions but she didn't really know how to reply. She decided she had better see David's letter. "I would like to read David's letter, that is if you really don't mind."

Cassie handed it to Kate and looked at her intently as she read the letter. Kate put it down.

"See," said Cassie. "Now you can understand my point, surely you can?"

"Oh Cassie, I'm sorry, I really am," said Kate.

Cassie at last smiled at Kate. "I knew you'd understand, I knew it. Sorry trying to keep you out, I'm so relieved you know what I'm talking about."

"Hold on a minute, Cassie," said Kate. "I didn't say that. No, I actually understand what David means."

Cassie looked dumfounded. "How can you? How? Traitor!" She practically spat the word out.

"Cassie, how would you like to always be second best? You'd like that, would you? I know you; you wouldn't. You never have been. When he realised what he had said or done for that matter, he was brave enough not to string you along and to be up-front and honest with you."

"Really brave!" responded Cassie. "So brave that he can't even come and speak to me face to face."

Poor David, thought Kate. *He didn't deserve this annihilation of his character.* She tried again. "Cassie, he was perhaps a little concerned that if he spoke to you face to face you would manage to twist him round your little finger," Kate smiled. "As you do to all of us. He, a mere man, may not have had the strength to fight you." Kate picked up the letter. "Look Cassie, read it, read it as David wants you to read it. He would always, always compare you with Lizzie – his first, and I suspect, only love. God almighty Cassie he even says in the letter that he felt you were some reincarnation of Lizzie. Would you want that? Would you honestly want that? I don't think so."

Cassie read the letter yet again. "Did she really have this affect on men?" asked Cassie.

"Not men; just the two she fell in love with," replied Kate. "And your father never married again, did he?" Kate looked anxiously at Cassie after she said that. She wondered if that was a bit below the belt, but Cassie just nodded, seemingly in agreement.

"I'm not very worldly wise am I?" asked Cassie. Kate hugged her again.

They sat in silence for a few minutes then Cassie turned to Kate, and with a slightly mischievous look on her face, said, "How come you're so knowledgeable about the ways of the world and men etc. etc.? Answer me that if you will?"

Kate blushed slightly. "I read a lot!!"

"You're blushing. The blush gives you away, not convincing, not convincing at all," replied Cassie, with the hint of a smile. "I'll find out your deadly secrets one day, just you see if I don't."

Kate laughed it off. "You'll be so disappointed; trust me you will."

Cassie suddenly looked serious again. "Kate, I do, or at least I am trying to understand what you are saying. I think I understand. I'll sort it out, really I will. But, I would like to see him again. I really loved his company. In his letter he did say he'd like us to be friends but he doesn't write his address." She looked at the open phone directory. "I was trying to find out if he was flying home. Can't find him though."

"David comes over as the type of man who means what he says," said Kate. "I'll bet you that soon, very soon, he will get in contact with you. It might be when he's back in the States, who knows, but I really think he will."

"How can you be so positive," asked Cassie.

"Just a hunch," smiled Kate. "Plus of course, the insight I have with all the reading I do!"

Cassie threw her pillow at Kate. "You really are exasperating at times. Also, so incredibly right all the time. It must become wearisome for you, always being right."

"Oh it is," smiled Kate. "It's a heavy burden to carry, but I try not to let it get me down!" Cassie rolled her eyes.

"Oh God, I've been horrendous to Pops and Aunt Lydia, simply bloody. Do you think they'll ever forgive me my tirade?" asked Cassie.

"I don't see why not, they always do," grinned Kate. "Feeling better?"

"A little," replied Cassie. "I'll sort myself out and then go down and make my peace – again!"

"I'd better go," said Kate. "Robert will be wondering where on earth I am. Good luck downstairs."

"Thanks for this," replied Cassie. "And for everything else."

In some ways, Cassie was still so young. She may believe what David had written and what Kate had said. Kate hoped so; she had to.

Cassie picked up David's letter again and read it as Kate had tried to convey, David wanted her to understand it. She supposed Kate was right, but just at this moment it didn't help to ease the deep hurt she felt – not yet.

Chapter 17

David had never felt so alone in all his life. All the radio stations were playing an endless stream of Christmas carols and all the television channels were only showing the 'feel-good' festive films; *White Christmas* or *It's a Wonderful Life*. Normally he enjoyed these films but right now all they did was remind him of what he was missing.

He wandered aimlessly around his apartment with a mug of coffee in his hand. He had been back for over three weeks and was as unsettled as the day he'd returned. He went out onto the balcony and gazed out across the ocean. Normally just doing that would restore his soul, inner peace, call it what you will; but not today.

He went back in and went to his studio. Work had to be finished on two portraits. They only required minor touches that normally he would do speedily and efficiently, but just now he couldn't trust himself to do even minor changes properly. He had to, he knew that, for he had been commissioned to do them and they were to be collected tomorrow – important clients should never be kept waiting. Important – a ridiculous word to describe someone, he thought – for, to him, their importance was only measured in terms of the amount of money they were willing to part with!

With that knowledge he decided he led an incredibly shallow existence. He had never felt as despondent as he did now. If only he hadn't gone back to find Lizzie; if only he hadn't fallen for Cassie; if only he hadn't so enjoyed the company of Charles, Lydia, Mrs. P. and all those at The Hall; if only, he hadn't been born! He felt that last thought was a little dramatic – even for him. He sighed; this wasn't doing him any good, but it was no use, his mind kept drifting back to Harrington.

He wondered what they were all doing. Would there be masses of preparations for Christmas or would it just be a quiet affair with only 'The Family'? If he closed his eyes he felt he could smell the

189

wondrous smells that he knew would be emanating from Mrs. Pearson's kitchen.

He felt hungry at the thought and went to his kitchen to see if there was any tempting morsel in his fridge. Sadly he was out of luck, for all that greeted him was a can of beer, some white wine, milk that had gone sour and some unmentionable looking sausage thing lurking at the back of the fridge. He shut the door quickly and decided to go out for a walk. Hopefully this would improve his mood and on the way home he would call in at the local shop and get some provisions.

Everywhere he walked he bumped into people laden with parcels, grinning inanely telling him, 'It gets worse each year doesn't it?' David would smile weakly and nod his head as if agreeing. He hadn't bought any presents; hadn't for that matter even sent cards. Scrooge and he seemed to be on a par this year. He normally rather liked Christmas; drinking and eating too much, partying with his friends, sometimes he even went to a church service to hear the Christmas message which he always hoped would restore his faith in humanity, then he'd sing a carol or two which always put him in the festive mood. Nothing would help this year. He knew that.

He walked for hours. Had Cassie forgiven him? Were they all relieved to see the back of him? He hoped that there might have been a slight twinge of regret at his leaving on their part, for he missed them. He missed them all.

He walked into a bar. Getting drunk wasn't going to help his mood but he needed a seat, so one little drink wouldn't do him any harm. He ordered a beer. The barman looked the chatty type so David paid for his drink and went over to a table and sat down. His thoughts inevitably returned to Cassie. He decided she would be fine. She had a back-up system of people who cared for her and with their help she would soon recover from her temporary aberration. Who did he have? No one. Whose fault was that? His own, he decided!

The expression 'crying into his beer' was in danger of becoming a reality so David finished his drink and with a nod to the barman left the bar and the temptation it afforded. He tried to lift his spirits from morose to feeling slightly down with little or no success. Morose is how he felt.

Arriving back at his apartment he fixed himself another drink and went out onto the balcony. It was still warm, even oppressive. He had hoped there would be a breeze from the water but there was none. He sat watching the lights of ships in the distance twinkling at him and wondered if he had been right in promising Charles he would never tell Cassie.

He remembered the look of relief on Charles's face when he promised he wouldn't and then the pain flitting across it when David referred to Cassie as **his** daughter. However David, couldn't think of her as his daughter. No matter how hard he had tried, he just couldn't.

When he had seen Cassie and Charles together they had so obviously a warm and close father and daughter relationship that he could never, and would never, do anything to destroy. He wondered if he should reiterate this to Charles. He smiled ruefully at that idea. Any excuse for making contact. He'd have to try better than that! Perhaps he'd call them in the New Year. That would be a more appropriate time he decided. He went back inside.

"Ah well, ho bloody ho and a merry Christmas to me," muttered David to himself as he poured himself yet another drink. "Drunken oblivion soon, very soon… I hope," he said gloomily as he flopped down on the sofa and awaited that state to descend upon him.

Cassie watched as Benson lent across the tree and put the star in its rightful place. This time it appeared straight, not the usual jaunty angle it normally adopted each year.

"Well done, it's straight. That's a first, it's looking good from here," smiled Cassie.

Benson gingerly climbed down the ladder, taking care not to knock the tree, and stepped back to admire his handiwork. "Fingers crossed it stays like that," he said. "Now, what next?"

"Holly, here, here, here and oh, over there," said Cassie, giving vague directions with her arms. "Wherever, just the usual."

Charles stood in the shadows, watching the ritual dressing of the Christmas tree. From there he watched Cassie, who even in her twenties, was as excited as ever, as she and Benson set about transforming the Great Hall.

Cassie had been four or five years old when she first saw Benson decorate the Great Hall and from then on had insisted this was her job as well and so now it was one of the traditions that no one else was allowed to intrude upon. Charles loved the traditions that had evolved over the years. He thought it looked even more splendid than normal but then remembered that each year he always thought it better than the last. He was so looking forward to Christmas and would do everything in his power to make it a happy and memorable occasion.

Increasingly of late, waves of exhaustion flooded over him. He had spoken to Dr. Parrott about this but the doctor had been encouraging, stressing that his last scan had shown no deterioration. He had, however, omitted to mention that neither had there been any improvement! Charles wasn't a fool. The mirror wasn't lying. He saw it in his own eyes and unless there was a miracle he felt it highly unlikely that he would be here for another Christmas.

In some bizarre way he had hoped that David would have been in touch. He didn't have his address or telephone number; he would have called if he had. It was now nearly a month since David's departure and to all intents and purposes Cassie had seemingly recovered from her short-lived love affair. She had been profuse in her apologies to her father and aunt and everything was, once again, sweetness and light. She had even explained to them what David had said; that she had, in some way, been a replacement for Lizzie but Cassie had tried to say it in such a discreet way so as not to cause Charles any hurt or offence. He had been rather touched by her attempts at diplomacy – normally not one of her strong points!

Charles knew that Cassie and Benson didn't like anyone to see their efforts until they had been completed, so he tiptoed back to his study. He looked at his watch; carol singers from the village would arrive in an hour or so to sing the obligatory three or four carols. They would sing, if not in tune, then certainly lustily, in anticipation of Mrs. Pearson's mince-pies which, if previous years were anything to go by, would be demolished in one fell swoop. To complete this fare, it was time for Charles to organise the mulled wine and cordials so that soon the wonderful smells of Christmas would permeate throughout the house and instantly put everyone in 'The Christmas mood'.

~~~~~

Cassie woke early. Popping a toe out from underneath the duvet she realised how cold it was and that the heating had yet to come on. She decided to stay where she was until the temperature improved. She looked at her clock it was 6.45 a.m. and it was Boxing Day. She always felt this day was such an anti-climax after the run up to Christmas.

Yesterday had been lovely and she smiled at the memory of her aunt's face when she had seen Cassie's present to her. It had so obviously been a painting but Lydia had ripped open the paper with fevered excitement and had roared with laughter when she saw the painting was of herself and Charles reclining on the sofa with the inevitable gin and tonic. She loved it and under no circumstances would she allow Cassie to paint out the drinks which had so concerned Cassie, for Lydia felt that Cassie had captured the two 'old soaks' perfectly! She had then spent some time wandering around the house, trying to decide where it should be hung.

Charles had also been somewhat taken aback with his present from Cassie. Firstly, he had thought the portrait presented to him a few weeks previously had been his early Christmas present so was not expecting anything and secondly, he had never imagined she would be able to better that present. However, much to the amazement of everyone, Cassie had painted a miniature of the portrait of Lizzie. She had never attempted this type of painting before and had been a little daunted at the prospect, but she couldn't think of anything else that would please her father more – and she was right, he had been thrilled. It would sit on his desk.

Cassie always slept with her curtains open and, looking out of the window, saw that it had started to snow. She felt a childish delight at this realisation. They would all be going over to Kate and Robert's for lunch and Cassie knew that at least four other people would be as delighted as she was about the snow. If the snow continued Cassie suspected that after lunch she would be involved in the making of a snowman and inevitably snowball fights would then ensue, so she made a mental note to take a change of clothing.

She continued looking out of the window, watching the spiralling snowflakes that tumbled out of the sky become larger and larger. For some reason this made her think about David. She wondered when he would have last seen snow. Cassie sank deeper into her pillow. She had hoped he would get in touch: she missed him, she missed him very much, but hadn't liked to voice this to the others. She had felt an affinity with David, she didn't know why; she supposed it was because of their art and more especially, the type of art in which they specialised. He had been such fun to be with, so easy to talk to. She let out a long sigh; that of course wasn't all. He had been so easy, so incredibly easy, to fall in love with. Thinking about David wasn't doing her any good, no good at all. She shook her head as if trying to banish him from her thoughts and decided she would give him until the beginning of the New Year and if he hadn't been in touch by then she would try to find him.

She looked at her clock – now nearly eight. She had been daydreaming for over an hour. *Ah well*, she thought, *At least the bedroom is warmer now*, and with that, got out of bed.

~~~~~

New Year at Harrington Hall had always been 'open house' and no amount of protesting from Lydia or Cassie was going to make Charles change this. He knew they were doing it out of concern for him but as long as he was able, this is what he'd do.

"Now ladies, I know you mean well, I really do, but I absolutely insist we will be having our usual New Year at The Hall. Do I make myself perfectly clear?"

"Charles," said Lydia in a voice filled with exasperation at her brother, "You need all your energy and strength for…" her voiced tailed off. She didn't know what to say, she was about to say, 'for what lies ahead' but felt that in his mood Charles could misinterpret this. Lydia glared at him. "You know what I mean Charles," and then quieter, even tenderly she added, "To fight the next batch of treatments."

Charles smiled at her. "My mind is made up and I'll worry about treatments another day. Right now, I'm looking forward to our party," said Charles defiantly and, looking at Cassie, he continued. "And before you feel the need to put your oar in, that is my final word. No, hold on, final word now. I promise I will rest as much as I can. I will even, if that would pacify you both, go to bed for a couple of hours before the festivities. Agreed?"

Lydia and Cassie looked at each other then at Charles and in unison said, "Agreed."

"Thank you," said Charles. "Now, just so you know what I'm up to, I'm off to see Benson." With that Charles quickly escaped before the ladies could say any more.

Cassie looked at the departing figure of her father. "How do you think Pops has been looking of late?"

Lydia looked at her niece and for a moment hesitated. She was going to say she thought Charles looked fine but that would be ridiculous and an insult to Cassie when it was patently obvious he wasn't. "I think he looks very tired. At the moment he looks as if a little bit of the stuffing has been knocked out of him." Cassie looked at her aunt with anxious eyes. Lydia continued. "But remember that although we have tried to have a fairly low key time, he's staying up later and on the go more than usual. I imagine that after the flow of people popping in and out have stopped, he'll look more like his old self. You'll see."

"Do you really believe that?" asked Cassie.

Lydia took Cassie's hand and squeezed it. "I'm trying to. I want to and I just keep on hoping as you do. That's all we can do."

"Sorry," said Cassie. "I'm trying not to think ahead but it was just a look I caught. It scared me."

"My dear girl, you are doing splendidly, but we must keep going for Charles and if he's exhausted by it or… or, whatever, it is what he wanted and that is the maxim we go by. Now," said Lydia straightening up, head erect. "Onwards and upwards, back into our Oscar award-winning mode. Yes?"

"Yes, you're absolutely right," said Cassie. "Let's make it the best New Year."

"Indeed we shall. Now what about you? What are your plans?"

"Just the usual; stay here to see in the New Year, then some of the crowd are coming over at about half twelve or so. I've said we should go on somewhere else so as not to exhaust Pops and so the plan is that we'll go to Sarah's and then finish up at John's. His Mum has, for the last few years, made masses of fabulous bacon rolls and so it's become a tradition that we end up there for breakfast. Should be good," said Cassie, who was now recovered from her temporary blip.

"Oh to be young again," said Lydia wistfully. "That sounds so good, especially the bacon bit. Nothing like it on a cold crisp night, it will be lovely."

"You are most welcome to come along. You know everyone, they'd be pleased to see you," said Cassie.

Lydia laughed, "Oh yes, they'd be thrilled to see some old codger, that is still the expression, codger?" asked Lydia.

"There is another," said Cassie smiling, "But codger is more suitable!"

Lydia looked questioningly but decided she'd better not pursue that. "It's very kind of you, but by the time you are eating your rolls, I will be thinking of getting up. Now, what do we have to do food wise for this evening I wonder? We'd better check with the boss." And off they went to see Mrs. Pearson!

"Shush everyone," said Charles, "Nearly time – five, four, three, two, one… Happy New Year to you all." The church bells pealed out the hour as they each wished each other a happy New Year.

Cassie went over to Charles and kissed him on the cheek. "Happy New Year Pops," she said, but cursed herself, for it came out in a slightly strangulated fashion.

Charles looked at her, he didn't trust his voice and just said, "And to you," hugging her tightly to him.

Cassie could feel his bones even through his jacket. Lydia watched and decided it was time to intervene. "Happy New Year to my favourite albeit my only, niece," she said brightly.

Cassie, with tears close to the surface, turned to her aunt with relief and hugged her. "Thank you," she whispered gratefully, "Happy New Year to you… to us all."

Lydia nodded, understanding what Cassie was feeling, for she also wondered what the year would hold for them. "More champagne please, little brother," said Lydia, handing out her glass. Just as Charles was replenishing her glass there was a loud knock at the door.

"Our first foot, hope it's someone tall, dark and handsome," said Charles as he opened the door. "Ah well, you'll have to do," he grinned as he ushered Peter and others in.

Peter, mindful of the Scottish ancestry on his mother's side, with due ceremony laid on the hall table the items he had brought. "Coal, for outer warmth; whisky, for inner warmth and shortbread

196

to soak up the former. A Happy New Year my friend." They shook hands and then, rather uncharacteristically, Peter put his arm round Charles and gave him a hug. "And may it be a good one," he added huskily.

Charles was surprised and for a moment taken aback for he saw that Peter's eyes were glistening but responded firmly, "Thank you and a Happy New Year to you."

It was now Rowena's turn to brighten the moment. "Charles, a happy New Year," she said giving him a kiss.

Taking her cue from Rowena, Cassie grabbed Peter. "Uncle Peter, a Happy New Year," and planted a kiss firmly on his lips.

"I like New Year, I really do, especially if I get to kiss lovely ladies like you Cassie," said Peter who had now recovered from his momentary lapse and was determined to be as bright and as full of bonhomie as all at The Hall seemed to be. Spying Lydia he went over. "Ah, my lucky night, another gorgeous girl for me," and kissed her twice for good measure. "Sorry about that hiatus at the door," he said quietly to her.

"Don't be," said Lydia equally quietly. "No one noticed. Fingers crossed though that this **will** be a good year."

Peter smiled back. "You bet! Right my good man," said Peter going over to Charles and propelling him towards the drinks table, "What have you to offer me?"

Within about an hour, Harrington Hall seemed to be filled with most of the village. Cassie and her friends thought this might be a good opportunity to leave for their next party.

"Pops!" said Cassie, "We're off now. We're going to Sarah's first then no idea where after that. See you," and she gave Charles a quick peck on the cheek.

With further byes to Charles from her friends, they left to go back up the drive. "Have a good time all of you," shouted Charles as he went to the door to wave them off.

By about 2.30 a.m. everyone from the village had left. Much to Charles's amazement, he didn't feel too tired; in fact, he felt quite good. He had enjoyed himself and he felt it was good for those in the village to see he was still at the helm so to speak. He also loved a good *crack* with some of the old timers and never tired of the stories they told: all in all a goodnight. Benson came out of the library, having just put out the lights. "Ah Benson, time to turn in don't you think? Where are the others?"

Benson smiled. "Cup of tea time. They are all in the kitchen. As people left the ladies started on the dishes. Nearly all finished."

"Good timing on my part then. Well let's join them and then bed, and a long, long lie," said Charles. "It was a good New Year though, don't you think?"

"One of the best," replied Benson. "Definitely one of the best."

Over in the States, David was full of indecision. "Heads I do, tails I don't," he said. "Damn, I'll do it again, out of three; heads I do, tails I don't, God I'm pathetic." David pocketed the dime. "I'm going to phone, I'm going to phone right now."

He looked at his watch, trying to calculate the time it would be in the UK. He realised that he was eight hours behind so reckoned it would be about 9.00 p.m. UK time. It was January the third so he thought everything in the UK would be back to normal by now and thought dinner at Harrington should be finished.

Taking a deep breath, he dialled the number and waited for it to connect. A woman's voice answered, not Cassie; Lydia.

"Lydia? Hi, it's me, David. I was just phoning to say Hi and a Happy New Year to you all. Is that okay?" There was a gasp then a pause that unnerved David. He repeated his greeting slowly. "Lydia, are you still there? It's David, a Happy New Year to you all."

"David, how lovely to hear from you. I'm sorry I couldn't hear you initially. A Happy New Year to you as well," replied Lydia with, David felt, genuine warmth in her voice.

David relaxed. It was going to be all right. "I just wanted to let you know I was thinking of you all and well, well actually I miss you all. How's Charles?"

"Oh a little tired after all the festivities, you know," replied Lydia a little guardedly, which David picked up on.

"He's there – I understand, and the others? Cassie – how is she?" asked David trying to sound casual.

"She's out with friends, David. She'll be sorry to have missed you," replied Lydia.

"Is she okay, Lydia? You know what I mean," said David.

"She seems all right now. You can imagine what she was like initially but your letter to her, it was beautifully done. I didn't read it but Kate did and she said you expressed everything very diplomatically and delicately. It must have been difficult for you, we do know that and we appreciated it. David, I'm sure you'll want a word with Charles." Without waiting for a reply, Lydia said, "take care."

"A Happy New Year to you. I am absolutely delighted you got in touch," said Charles. "Lydia's right, as ever," he said, smiling over to her. "We all miss you. David, would you give me your telephone number and address? I'd like to keep in touch and I think it might be something that Cassie would like. How would you feel about that?"

"There is nothing I'd like more Charles. I hope that, in time, Cassie and I can be good friends. Nothing more than that, I give you my word," said David.

"You gave me your word before you left. That was good enough for me and I have no reason to think you'd change it. Now, I've found a pen and paper so I'm all set, what's your telephone number?"

David duly gave it. He felt relieved, buoyant even, at having got in touch. They seemed genuinely pleased. "One thing Charles," said David. "I wondered if I might write to Cassie, just a friendly letter, the kind she could read out over breakfast. Just saying hello to everyone. Mrs. P. how is she? Tell her I miss her cooking very, very much. Stress that to her, won't you. Actually I thought I'd write to her as well and tell her myself, but please also tell her I phoned."

"I will David, I certainly will," said Charles. "I'm sorry Cassie isn't in. I'll give her your number but will also tell her you are going to write. Will I do that?"

"Yes, thanks, I'd be grateful if you did," replied David. He wanted to continue the call and ask about everyone in the hope that maybe, just maybe, Cassie might breeze in but thought the better of it. "Well Charles, I'd better be going. I have to finish a painting or two. No rest for the wicked and all that. Thank you for being so nice – both of you. I was a little nervous about this call; you two made it easier. Well I'd better go, bye."

"Bye," replied Charles who realised David had already hung up. He put the phone down and looked over to Lydia. "Well, I'm really glad he's been in touch. What about you? Are you pleased?"

"Yes, yes I am. I wonder what sort of Christmas and New Year he had? I thought he sounded, daft as this may seem, homesick; homesick for here. Hopefully he had a lovely time. Did I guess that he's wanting to write to Cassie?"

"Yes," said Charles. "He said the sort of letter she can read out over breakfast." Charles smiled. "He's a nice chap. He obviously wants to remain friends with us all and I hope he does. I really do. Here, before I lose it, can you jot down his number in your book and then Cassie can have this piece of paper to do with what she likes. How do you think she'll feel about him phoning?"

"No idea," responded Lydia. "It's sometimes a little tricky knowing what Cassie is really thinking. Remember when she was younger, she was like an open book; every mood in glorious technicolour for all to see but she has become a little more guarded now, although she doesn't always succeed as we well know."

"Quite," said Charles remembering the outburst about David of just a few weeks ago.

"I feel a bit whacked but I should sit up for her, shouldn't I?" asked Charles.

"No, you go to bed. There's a film I'm going to watch in ten minutes and if she's not in by the time it's finished, at about 11.30, then I'll leave a note."

"All right, thanks. Goodnight and sleep well." Charles was relieved to go up to bed. He was still recovering from the gastronomic excesses of the festive season. Back to bland and boring tomorrow, he decided.

Lydia sat up for another half hour after the film but Cassie was still not home so she decided to leave a note for her.

> *Cassie – hope you had a good time. While you were out, David called. He sounded well and was asking for you. He said he'd write but here is his number if you wish to phone. Sleep tight. Love, A.L.!*

Lydia hoped that would be all right and wouldn't upset Cassie. She had tried to keep it casual. It would have to do.

Cassie returned at about 2.00 a.m. She picked up the note Lydia had left on her pillow and her heart skipped a beat – David had called. Damn, she thought, but then decided she was glad she'd missed him for she could then speak to him when she felt ready. She felt ready now. She dialled the number.

"Hi – I'm sorry I can't take your call…" Cassie looked at the phone in disbelief; just when she'd plucked up the courage, he was out – God Damn him. She quickly decided to leave a message.

"Hello David, its me, Cassie. I'm sorry you're not there I just wanted to…" with that there was a beep and Cassie thought she'd been cut off when she heard David….. "Cassie, hi. Its me, sorry, don't hang up. How are you?"

"David, what's going on?" asked Cassie.

"Sorry I was working and wasn't going to answer then I heard your voice and dived to the phone," said David. "This is a lovely surprise. I didn't think you'd phone back."

"Why ever not?" asked Cassie, a slight edge in her voice which did not go unnoticed by David.

"Cassie I hate myself for having hurt you. I was behaving like some adolescent. I'm well aware of that, but I miss you… I miss our chats, the laughs we had… just being in your company. I hope… I really hope that you can forgive me and we can be good friends again."

He wished he could see her face to try and gauge what she was thinking. He continued anxiously. "I miss you all at Harrington. I had a chat with Lydia and your Dad and it was so good speaking to them, really nice. Did you all have a good Christmas and New Year? Oh Happy New Year by the way."

"The same to you David," replied Cassie. "Yes, we had a lovely time and Pops insisted on our usual New Year, with everyone arriving from the village. He coped well and loved talking to his old cronies. What about you David, did you have a good time?"

"Fairly quiet actually but fine, just fine," said David, lying through his teeth. The conversation was a little stilted but he didn't want to rush things. "Well this is your call so we shouldn't go on too long. I've written you a chatty nonsense letter; hope you'll like it."

"I'll look forward to it David. I had better go. I'll write back and will phone again. Would that be okay?" asked Cassie.

"You know it would," said David. "I look forward to it. Thanks for calling. Sleep well."

"Bye, David," replied Cassie. She put the phone down. She was relieved she had phoned. Tears pricked her eyes. It hadn't been the easiest of conversations and she wondered if she had sounded ill at ease, she didn't know. All she hoped was that one day the easy rapport they once had would come back. She so hoped it would!

Chapter 18

Charles awoke, surprised it was already light. He looked at his watch. It was 9.00 a.m. He was delighted. He hadn't slept so well in ages. It must be the new pills he'd been given. Whatever, he was full of a joie de vivre he hadn't felt in ages. He got up and looked out of the window. The snowdrops were beginning to emerge from their winter slumbers and it was a lovely bright crisp February morning. He decided it was going to be a good day.

He had plans for the day which had necessitated some subterfuge on his part to make absolutely sure no one would be around. Lydia had gone to visit her friend Beth for two days and Cassie was also away on a three-day course in London, so this was the perfect opportunity.

He had a quick breakfast, remembered to tell Mrs. Pearson he was going out for lunch then quickly departed before anyone could ask where he was going.

By midday Charles had accomplished nearly everything on his list.

He entered Pierre Gabriel's gallery. Pierre was talking to a customer, so Charles nodded an acknowledgement and indicated that he was in no hurry.

"Sorry about that, Charles," said Pierre as he returned from escorting his customer to the door.

"Not at all," replied Charles. "It gave me a chance to browse. I'm here on an errand, Pierre and I need your help."

"You know I will be more than delighted to assist in any way I can," smiled Pierre.

"Thank you," said Charles.

Pierre indicated for Charles to have a seat. "Would you like a coffee? I was about to have one."

"Mmm, that would nice," replied Charles. He got up and followed Pierre. "You have some amazing pictures Pierre, not all to my liking as you know, but, what's the expression you arty people use, interesting; that's it, you say interesting, when even you're not sure what on earth the painting is."

Pierre laughed. "You are *so* conservative Charles."

"That's as may be," grinned Charles. "But at least when you look at my pictures at The Hall you know what they are. I've heard you and Cassie use the most inventive adjectives when neither of you have the first clue what the painting is meant to be. The deeply worrying part is that the artist believes they are being praised. Astonishing, quite astonishing!"

Pierre handed Charles his coffee. "Have you quite finished being so disparaging?" laughed Pierre.

Charles wandered off to look at another picture and, shaking his head, said, "For the moment." He took a sip of coffee. "Nice coffee." Turning round he looked at Pierre. "Actually the reason I'm here is to buy a picture for Cassie. Firstly, she must not know I've been here. Secondly, I need to ask a favour of you."

Pierre looked at Charles expectantly. "Please, ask away."

"Would it be possible to keep it hidden here until," Charles hesitated, "this may sound a bit macabre, but could you keep it until after my funeral please?"

Pierre stared at Charles, a little unsure what to say. "Charles, I'm sorry, I thought you were in remission, I hadn't appreciated… of course I will but I…"

Charles interrupted, "Pierre, sorry, sorry saying it like that. You're correct, at the moment things seem reasonably okay. I'm just planning ahead, that's all. I want to give Cassie something as a way of trying to express my thanks, my love, you know… everything, and I thought of a picture because she adores art. One day she'll have loads of jewellery from Lydia but pictures are after all her first love. Can you help, Pierre?"

Yes, I think I can. There is one I know she definitely covets but, perhaps you should sit down for this, its £17,500." Pierre looked at Charles for his reaction.

Charles smiled, "I see. But she loves it, you're absolutely one hundred per cent definitely sure she does?"

Pierre nodded. "The first time she saw it she was in tears. I have never before seen her so moved by a painting. She'd gaze at it for hours if she could!"

"Where is it?" asked Charles.

"It's here," said Pierre. "But its on loan to me, so sadly is not mine to sell but I am sure I could get the price reduced. Come round and I'll let you see it."

Charles was a little surprised when he saw it. "It's not the normal type of painting she admires but, yes, I think I can see why she'd like it." Studying the work he asked, "Tell me, Pierre, is it worth it? It's a good deal of money. Tell me honestly what you think."

"The artist is called Patrick McCormick. His uncle you will have heard of, he was Henry McCormick; in fact I think you have one of his paintings at The Hall."

"Yes, you're quite right. This chap though is very different but if he does as well as his uncle, he'll be an excellent investment. Is it a sound investment? I'll be guided by you, Pierre," said Charles.

"I would stake my reputation on it. His work came to the notice of the art world about five years ago. It was pricey, even then, but sold quickly. Since then its value has gone up and up. You may not think so, but I think this is *under*valued. I could sell it for at least £25,000. In five years I predict it will have trebled in value."

"I'll have it," said Charles decisively. "And can you wrap it and keep it somewhere safe?"

"Certainly, let me call my colleague. Have a seat, I won't be long," said Pierre.

Pierre returned, smiling broadly. "I've a got a reduction; £15,000. All right?"

"More than all right," said Charles. "Many, many thanks. May I write a cheque to your personal account and then you pay your colleague? That way Cassie won't find out. I take it she sees the gallery accounts?"

"No problem. I didn't say who had bought the picture and Cassie won't find out. Now, let's go and wrap it and put it away safely for," added Pierre, "What is I hope, a very long, long time."

Charles smiled, "Thank you, I hope so too."

As Pierre started wrapping the picture Charles handed him an envelope. "Can you put this with the picture, please?"

"Certainly," said Pierre without any expression crossing his face.

Charles then wrote out the cheque and handed it to Pierre. Pierre looked at Charles. "This isn't right."

"It's perfectly right," said Charles. "And thank you."

"You're very kind, Charles, thank you, and now I will write a note to my lawyer just in case something should happen to me, and they will know to release the picture to Cassie," said Pierre.

"I hadn't thought of that, many thanks and good thinking," responded Charles. He looked at his watch; it was just after one. "Do you fancy closing for lunch. My treat, what do you say?"

"I'd like that very much," replied Pierre.

They went to the local fish restaurant across the square from the gallery. After giving their orders, Charles said, "I wonder if I might pick your brains again, Pierre? I'd like you to tell me about Cassie: what she's like at work, how good she is with the financial aspects, anything and everything and I want you to be honest. Think of me as a prospective employer, not a doting father."

If Pierre was a little surprised at the question, he didn't show it. "Well firstly, she seems to like the job and the customers sense that and respond to her enthusiasm. Anyone coming in who thought they *might* buy a picture inevitably *do* buy one." Charles smiled as Pierre continued. "She is much, much better at that than I am. Secondly, she is meticulous with the book-keeping and the business side of things. At the beginning she wasn't interested but in the last while or so has taken a greater interest. To be perfectly honest I wondered if she was thinking of having a gallery herself. I don't know. No, she is good, I can find no fault, no faults at all."

"Excellent, I'm delighted to hear it," said Charles. "The reason I ask is because Cassie is always so wrapped up in her painting that I didn't think she would have any business acumen. I'm relieved to hear that she has at least some, for I hope that she may have a little input into the running of the estate one day. Once again, this is between ourselves, so not a word please."

The waiter arrived with their lunch. "This smells wonderful and looks excellent," said Pierre and added, "You have my word Charles."

With gastric juices flowing, silence descended as both men began their meal.

After lunch they parted company. Charles drove back to The Hall feeling rather pleased with his morning's work. There was only one more thing to do: retrieve the box from the boot of the car without Benson seeing him. Charles decided to leave it in the car for the moment and have a reccé. First stop the kitchen, which is where everyone congregated, especially on a cold winter's day.

As Charles approached the kitchen wonderfully aromatic smells greeted him and at the kitchen table stood Mrs. Pearson chopping and slicing vegetables with vigour. "Ah, Mrs. Pearson. Something smells quite delicious!" Going over to the stove Charles lifted a pot lid and smiled at her. "Hopefully for tonight?" he asked enquiringly.

"Yes," replied Mrs. Pearson, "You have a choice as I'm making three lots of soup."

"You know I can't make that choice," said Charles with mock horror on his face. "You are being decidedly cruel – too, too cruel. There is therefore only one solution: I'll have to taste all three!"

Mrs. Pearson beamed at him. "Right you are, Master Charles." Mrs. Pearson was delighted that his appetite had returned although he was still far too thin so if he wished all three pots of soup, that was fine by her.

Charles then spied some baking cooling on a tray. "Jolly good, rock cakes; my favourite. Are they for anything special or can I dive in now?" asked Charles.

"They're for eating whenever," said Mrs. Pearson. "Do you fancy a cuppa to go with that?"

"Sounds good to me," replied Charles, "But don't let me interrupt you. I'll put the kettle on. Where's Benson, by the way?" asked Charles as casually as he could.

"Not sure, he said something about picking up some things from Ed over at Marshall's place. He said he'd be back, fourish or thereabouts," said Mrs. Pearson.

Waiting for the kettle to boil, Charles went over to the window. "Looks as if it might snow again; the sky has a heavy look about it."

"Dash!" continued Charles, "I think I've left my lights on. I'd better go and check, won't be a moment."

He went into the garage, retrieved the box from the boot and, without anyone seeing him, managed to get it upstairs and into his room. He was delighted that he had accomplished this manoeuvre without prying eyes. With a boyish sense of achievement he decided he deserved that tea, and off he went downstairs to join Mrs. Pearson.

Lydia arrived at the station with only minutes to spare. She looked at the board announcing the arrivals. Cassie's train was running twenty minutes late. *Typical*, she thought. She wandered over to the station buffet, contemplating whether she would have a cup of tea while she waited. She looked through the window just in time to see the assistant behind the counter blow her nose, then pocketing her handkerchief, serve the next customer his tea, without, Lydia noticed, any intervening hand-washing. Lydia decided against tea! She wandered back to the platform in time to hear the arrival of the London train being announced. She positioned herself at the entrance and watched the throng stream by. She then spied Cassie and waved.

"Hello," said Cassie. "What a journey, sorry we're a bit late. Have you been home yet?"

"No, I got held up coming back from Beth's so I came straight here. I arrived with only minutes to spare," replied Lydia as they walked to the car. "How was the course?"

"Wonderful, absolutely super. I wonder," asked Cassie as she got into the car. "Would it be possible to whizz into Pierre's just for a moment?"

"No problem," said Lydia who, with some difficulty, was trying to extricate herself from the parking space. "Bloody idiot, he's

207

practically in my boot." After much heaving and ho-ing she got the car out.

"Well done," smiled Cassie. "A nifty piece of manoeuvring! Are you okay? You look a little hot and bothered."

"I'm fine, just fine," said Lydia. "Now, off to Pierre's."

"Oh thank goodness, a space right outside. That was lucky," said a relieved Lydia as she pulled up outside the gallery.

"Won't be two ticks," said Cassie as she got out of the car.

"Hello. I wasn't expecting you until tomorrow. What was the course like?"

"Wonderful, absolutely wonderful. I'll tell you all about it tomorrow but I just wanted to give you this. As the saying goes, I saw this and thought of you," smiled Cassie.

Pierre took the package. "May I open it?" Cassie nodded. "This is intriguing, what can it be?" When he saw what was inside he gasped. "Oh Cassie, how kind, truly, this is too generous, it really is."

"Don't be daft. I was wandering past a second-hand bookshop, popped in, and it literally fell off the shelf. It was meant, obviously meant," said Cassie.

"I love it, I just love it. I really…" but Pierre's sentence came to an abrupt halt with an exclamation from Cassie.

"Where is it? Where's the McCormick? Have you moved it? Oh, please say you've moved it," said Cassie.

Pierre had rehearsed what he was going to say and so, wishing himself luck, said, "I'm really sorry Cassie. It was an Arab Sheik who came in. He saw it, loved it and bought it. I had to accept or I would have lost the sale. I'm really sorry Cassie, truly I am."

He hated lying to her because she looked so crestfallen. "I'll hunt around for another McCormick, I promise you," said Pierre.

"I'm being pathetic I know," said Cassie. "I just hoped it would be here for ages, for ever, if truth be known. I have a confession, actually. I hung it round the corner in the hope that people would miss it."

Pierre terribly wanted to hug her but gamely continued his charade. "I suspected that might be the reason for your choice of wall! But, sadly, that's the name of the game when you have a gallery. You have to sell if you get a good price."

"I know," said Cassie. "Sorry, I'm being selfish and pathetic. I'll see you tomorrow. Bye."

"Bye," said Pierre, "And many, many thanks for my book. I'll treasure it." Cassie just smiled weakly. "Good, I'm glad."

When Cassie got into the car, Lydia immediately sensed the change of mood. "What on earth's wrong?"

Cassie looked at her aunt. "Sorry, its just that Pierre had to sell a picture, a picture I adored. I even confessed to him that I'd hung it in the corner in the hope that people wouldn't notice it."

Lydia stifled a giggle. "Cassie, really, you are incorrigible."

"I know," said Cassie sadly. "It was rotten of me but I loved it, I really did."

"They'll be others," said Lydia, matter of factly. "Plenty of others."

Cassie looked at her aunt in disbelief. "She hadn't a clue, only Pierre really understood."

In ten minutes they had arrived at The Hall. It was dusk and Lydia was relieved to be home. Charles had heard the car and was at the door to greet them.

"Welcome back. I know it was only two or three days but this place is far too quiet without you both. I missed you," and he gave each lady a kiss.

"How was London?" asked Charles.

"It was good, really good," replied Cassie, but said it such a flat voice, Charles was concerned. "Are you all right?"

"I'm fine, Pops. I have a headache, that's all. The train was awful and I had to stand some of the way, the usual," said Cassie. "More importantly, how are you?"

"I feel pretty good. I've been doing some paperwork, so have been taking it easy. Just working away in the study," said Charles.

"I'm delighted to hear that," said Lydia.

"How was Beth?" asked Charles.

"Oh Aunt Lydia, I'm sorry. I didn't ask," said Cassie. "How is she?"

"Oh fine," replied Lydia. "I'll tell you her news at tea. Right now, I'd like to quickly change then have some tea and sit beside a nice warm fire. Any chance?"

"I'll go and tell Mrs. P," said Charles. "The study is nice and cosy, let's have tea there."

"I'll go and unpack as well," said Cassie. "I'll see you in a little while."

"What's wrong with her?" asked Charles with concern.

"Oh it's ridiculous," said Lydia. "We popped into Pierre's. She had a book for him – a present she'd picked up in some second-hand store – and when she came out of the gallery she had a face like thunder. Apparently the reason for this mood is that he's sold some picture that she, and I will now quote her, 'loved, positively adored'. No idea what it was but I told her to buck up and that there would be plenty of others."

"Ah," said Charles. "That was tactful!" Lydia just gave Charles a pitying look and shook her head. "Poor old Cassie," said Charles. Needless to say he was delighted at this news. Pierre had been correct; she did covet the painting. "One day, Cassie, one day," Charles thought to himself.

Charles looked at his watch. "Is half an hour long enough for you?" Lydia nodded. "I'll tell Mrs. P. to make tea at 4.15 then," said Charles as he went off to the kitchen.

Chapter 19

Charles looked at the clock. It was 9.00 a.m. He realised it must be about 1.00 a.m. in America and hoped David hadn't sat up especially to make the call. They now had a routine of fortnightly calls that Charles always enjoyed and suspected David did as well: this time David was phoning to wish him well for his clinic appointment. David and Cassie also now kept in regular contact with both letters and calls. Charles hoped David would pay them a visit in the not too distant future.

Time to get ready. Cassie was at work and Lydia was doing her stint in the charity shop. This was the first time Charles wasn't going under his own steam. He had asked Benson to take him as just recently he didn't have the confidence to drive having suffered increasing bouts of pain of such intensity that it literally took his breath away. Not an ideal situation in which to be driving. He decided that he had better speak to Dr. Parrott, hopefully would be able to alleviate this.

As they drove along the road Charles noticed the freshness and the greenness of the countryside. It had seemed a long and hard winter and spring had seemed only a few days before summer had taken its hold; it was so warm. Charles couldn't believe it was the end of April, with May in only two days time.

At the hospital Benson dropped Charles off. As Charles walked through the hospital doors he felt the usual knot in his stomach as he made his way along the, now familiar, corridor to the Oncology Department. He went for his scan and then to Dr. Parrott's office.

Julie, Dr. Parrott's secretary, greeted him warmly and offered him coffee. Normally he declined, but today he felt cold and thought it might be warming so gladly accepted her offer. He was just finishing his cup when Dr. Parrott arrived with the scan reports.

"Please, come through," said Dr. Parrott. There was never any preamble with the man so, he followed him into the office.

"How have you been feeling?" asked Dr. Parrott, indicating for him to have a seat.

"Not great, I'm getting quite a bit of pain which I was going to ask you about," replied Charles.

Dr. Parrott nodded. Looking at Charles he said, "Today's results are not as good as we would have hoped." Charles nodded. "The cancer has now spread to your liver and there is also bone involvement as well which may possibly explain the pain you are experiencing."

"That was quick," said Charles. Just three months ago the scan had seemed fine."

Dr. Parrott nodded. "I know, but sadly this can happen."

Charles thought for a moment. "Would I be correct in assuming that now that the liver and bones are involved we are talking about a finite time?"

Dr. Parrott looked, for a moment, disconcerted by Charles's directness. "I'm sorry, I think we are, although I never put on a time limit as I have been proved wrong too many times. How is your appetite?"

"Not great," replied Charles. "My housekeeper is a wonderful cook so I confess to finding that rather sad." Charles gave a slight smile. "Will you be able to give me anything for the pain and perhaps an appetite stimulant? That would please my cook very much, and also me."

"Yes, hopefully we will be able to resolve the pain situation speedily but unfortunately I'm not quite so confident about the appetite," said the doctor.

"I notice," said Charles. "You are not talking about any treatment."

Dr. Parrott hesitated for a moment, "I'm sorry but there would be no point in putting you through any more treatment when there would be no benefit."

"I had perhaps suspected but..." Charles paused briefly and swallowed quickly. "I suppose I had just hoped... I was feeling so good up until, well up until just a couple of weeks ago." He ran his hand through his hair and smiled briefly. "I think I was tempted to think a miracle had occurred. Stupid of me..." He looked at Dr. Parrott. "Thank you for your honesty."

Dr. Parrott sighed. "This is the part of my job that I hate, when we run out of options. But I never give up hope because one just never knows. As I said, I have been proved wrong on countless occasions and I hope this is one of these occasions." He gave Charles an encouraging smile. "Is there anything you'd like to ask? Would you like me to speak to your daughter? I would be happy to, although I know that you and Peter are close friends and I'm sure he is an enormous support." Charles nodded in agreement. "There is, however, something I think we should touch on and that is the hospice," he added quickly. "Purely because they are the best at pain relief. They truly are the experts. It's up to you. You may prefer Peter doing it."

Charles thought for a moment. "I think I'd like the backup of the hospice. Peter and I are such old friends that it might be easier for him if someone else were doping me with morphine or whatever you people use!"

"I'll arrange it then. In the meantime, here is a prescription to tide you over. Now I'd like you to make an appointment for July."

Charles raised an eyebrow. "Really? I admire your optimism." The doctor smiled weakly, as if apologetically. Standing up, they shook hands. "Thank you again for all you did. I'm very grateful."

"I'm sorry we can't do more," replied Dr. Parrott, opening the door.

"Goodbye Julie. Thank you for the chats and for the coffee," said Charles.

"Goodbye Lord Emerson," she replied.

Charles walked back along the corridor as fast as he could manage, which sadly, wasn't that speedily. Benson was waiting in the foyer.

"Is the car very far away?" asked Charles.

"No, I was lucky," replied Benson. "Just there."

"I've to go back in July," said Charles.

"Oh, that's good," said Benson smiling broadly. "That's certainly good news."

Charles didn't reply, just nodded and smiled. "I have a prescription. Can we stop off at the chemist?"

"Shall I go?" added Benson.

"If you would," said Charles, "Thank you."

Benson went into the chemist. There were two people in front of him. He had a quick look at the prescription. It read '*Morphine Sulphate Tablets – Continus 20mg, bd.*' Morphine – his stomach lurched. The chemist took the prescription and Benson sat down and waited. This wasn't good; he just knew it wasn't. He so wanted to ask the chemist what it meant but knew that what he really wanted was reassurance. Reassurance that he was over-reacting and that everything was all right. Looking out the window at Charles sitting in the car, with his grey, haunted features, Benson realised that was now, perhaps, a vain hope.

They drove back to the house in silence. Once home Charles, although tired, felt in need of a stroll. "I think I'll just have an amble around for a little while before lunch."

"Very well. Will you require the car again?"

"No, no thank you." Charles looked at Benson and smiled, a smile etched with weariness. Benson smiled back, compassion in his eyes.

"Thank you," said Charles. "Thank you for your understanding. As I think you gather, it seems possible that I may not be able to keep the July appointment!" Benson didn't say anything, just nodded. "I need to gather my thoughts before I see Cassie. I won't be too long," and with that Charles turned and walked slowly across the lawn towards his favourite haunt, the lakeside.

It took him fifteen minutes to reach the seat at the boat-house. It normally only took five! He sat down, relieved to have reached it and recovered his breath. In his jacket pocket he took out a small notebook and flipped it open. The list he had written had red ticks beside them indicating what he had accomplished. Everything was written in his usual meticulous way. However, there was one more thing to add to his list. '*Funeral – arrange!*'

Although he was not particularly religious, he still felt he should stipulate one or two things as he thought that would make things easier for Cassie and Lydia. He jotted down the titles of two hymns. They would do. He couldn't think of anything else for the moment so popped his notebook away again.

Unknown to him he was being observed. Kate, who had taken the opportunity to paint on this lovely sunny day, was further up the hill but had witnessed Charles make his slow and laboured way to the boathouse. She watched him for about ten minutes and then

214

saw the faint wisps of smoke. He'd lit a cigar. She decided to go down and join him. She bundled up her things and made her way down the hill, knowing that if he wanted solitude he would tell her.

"Hello Charles," said Kate as she approached him. "Tell me to go if you want peace."

Charles smiled, indicating for Kate to join him. "I'm always pleased to see you. You know that." He noticed her painting things. "It seems appropriate somehow."

"What does?" asked Kate.

Charles stared out over the lake. "Do you remember the first time we met? Well met properly. I saw you, didn't realise who you were, and went careering over the grass to give you a peace of my mind for trespassing."

Kate nodded and laughed. "I was actually terrified. You looked so fierce. I got up, totally flustered and things tumbled from my lap onto the ground. I was a little gauche then if I recall."

"Just a little," smiled Charles. He took Kate's hand. "But from that day we became the best of friends. Every crisis in my life, mostly concerning Cassie of course, you've been there. I don't think I can ever convey to you exactly what that has meant to me."

Kate put her arm through his. "It's mutual remember. You have always been there at every important moment in my life." She smiled up at him. Their eyes met and she realised what he was trying to say. The time she had been dreading for these past months was now becoming a certainty. Her stomach instantly tied itself in knots and her mouth went completely dry. She swallowed. "You were at the hospital today, weren't you?"

Charles nodded. "Yes," he squeezed her hand. "They have very kindly, and I felt all things considered, a little optimistically, given me an appointment for July! However, I suspect I won't require it."

Kate let out an involuntary gasp and nestled her head on his shoulder so that he would not see the sorrow that crossed her face. Neither of them said anything. After a few minutes Charles kissed the top of Kate's head, saying. "Come on, let's go back, its getting cold."

"Do you want me to walk back with you?" asked Kate.

"No, no need. You go back the short cut," said Charles. "I'll be fine."

"Right you are then," said Kate as matter of factly as she could as she bent to pick up her things. She looked at Charles trying to conceal the sadness she felt. With a light squeeze of his hand and a kiss on his cheek, she said a quick bye, and turned before he could see the tears flow unrelentingly down her cheeks.

Charles watched her go. "Dear Kate, dear, dear Kate."

Charles made his way back to the house. Unknown to him Lydia had returned a little earlier than anticipated from the charity shop. She had seen the car and had gone looking for Benson.

They met in the hall. "Ah, there you are." Benson followed her into the library and closed the door. "How did Charles get on?" asked Lydia. She looked at him intently.

"He has an appointment for July," said Benson, willing his demeanour not to give anything away to the ever-perceptive Lydia.

Lydia held his gaze. "That is not what I asked," she said quietly.

Benson looked at her and shook his head very slightly. "We stopped at the chemist – he has a prescription for morphine. Although you know, of course, that I should not be telling you that."

Lydia sat down. "I know. It's not being disloyal though. It's…" Lydia looked suddenly exhausted. "Oh God, I don't know. I certainly don't envy you the drive back from hospital. I really don't. What did Charles say?"

"Nothing," said Benson. "But he knows I am aware it's not good news. He's gone for a walk, down to the lake. He wanted a little stroll before lunch he said."

"Oh, what are we going to do? Every day I hoped," Lydia looked at Benson fondly and smiled sadly. "I know, so did you; we all did. I am trying, trying so hard to be strong for Charles, for Cassie, for me! I don't want to let him down." Lydia tried to blink away the tears that had pricked her eyes.

Benson looked out of the window. "He's coming back over the lawn," he said anxiously.

Lydia quickly wiped her eyes. "I won't say anything, I'll let it come from him. I'm glad I know. I cope better when I know, no matter how grim." Gathering herself together she said wearily, "Off you go; I'll pretend I'm just back." As Benson got to the door Lydia asked tentatively, "We can all keep going, for a little while longer, can't we?"

"Yes, you can count on all of us, you know that," he said. Lydia nodded. "I certainly do... and thank you, thank you for warning me. I needed to get my mind in gear so to speak."

Lydia went into the hall, trying to look as if she had just come home. She was going towards the study as Charles came through the door.

He seemed deep in thought and was a little startled to see her. "Lydia, you're back early."

"Yes, the next shift arrived on time for once so we got away sharply. I've just arrived. I was going to see if I had any mail. Where have you been?"

"I went for a walk, bumped into Kate. Guess where I went?" asked Charles.

"Gosh," replied Lydia, trying to look as if she were teasing. "I wonder, was it the boat-house by any chance?" Charles smiled and nodded.

Lydia looked at him. "You look whacked. Come and have a seat and tell me how you got on."

Charles sat down, wincing slightly as he did. Lydia pretended not to notice. "The news – it's not very good is it?"

"You could say that," replied Charles. "I have an appointment in July."

Lydia's eyes lit up expectantly. Even after her conversation with Benson she still had this fleeting hope.

"No Lydia, I'm sorry, I don't think I'll be around to keep it. He's given me something for the pain though – morphine. I have to take it twice a day but I think I can increase it or maybe I have to get Peter's say so, I can't remember. The other thing is that Parrott's going to arrange for me to have a chat with the folks at the hospice."

Lydia's head was spinning. Hospice? Benson hadn't mentioned hospice. *He can't know,* she decided. *Once you're in, that's that... finito,* she thought.

Charles continued, "I would go there for the day, perhaps overnight and they can regulate the drugs properly to minimise the pain. Experts in their field and all that."

"Oh," said Lydia with relief. "I always thought hospices were... well you know, you didn't come out again."

"A very old-fashioned thought, my dear," said Charles. "No, nowadays you can pop in and out. I have to say I'm quite relieved because it was the thought of pain, uncontrollable pain; that really frightened me. Do you know something?" asked Charles, running his hands through his hair. "The being dead bit is easy," he said wryly. "It's the dying bit that's scary."

He looked over at Lydia and realised he'd gone too far. Lydia's composure had deserted her. He got up and went over to her and held her in his arms. "That was a bit callous. Sorry, old girl, I'm truly sorry." She looked up at him and shook her head, trying to apologise but unable to speak.

After a few minutes, Lydia was back in control. She dried her eyes and they looked at each other and simultaneously and in unison said, "A gin and tonic is in order I think." Laughing, they hugged again and Lydia said, "I'll get them."

"Cheers," said Charles. "To be honest I'm not sure how much longer I'll be able to have these. The cancer is now in the liver and bone, which is why I've had no appetite and gone off my tipple." He took another hefty gulp. "Life's a bugger at times, a total bugger. The very time you'd like some solace from the bottle; you can't. Unfair, grossly unfair; so let's make hay while the sun shines. Come on, drink up."

After lunch Charles spoke to the others, which had seemed even more difficult than telling Lydia although they had all been stoic and tried to remain composed. He then went upstairs to lie down and have a nap before Cassie was due home. Lydia went to the drawing room but couldn't settle and paced about. She picked up her tapestry, worked on it for five minutes then put it down. She tried reading, no use; the crossword was no use either.

She decided to go to the kitchen; the others would be there and she needed company. "I hope I'm not intruding, I can't settle. May I join you?"

Benson pulled out a chair for her. "Of course."

Lydia sat down beside Mrs. Pearson and, smiling at her, patted her hand. "Charles enjoyed his lunch today. You know, he even asked the doctor if he could have an appetite stimulant because he hates not feeling hungry when there are all these lovely smells tempting him. He told the doctor what a wonderful cook you are."

Mrs. Pearson rummaged in her apron for her handkerchief and dabbed at her eyes. "That was kind, so kind."

"Would you like a cup of tea?" asked Margaret, trying to stop everyone descend into complete despair.

"Only if there's some left in the pot."

"No trouble," said Margaret, "I was going to make fresh. In times of crisis, what would we do without our tea?"

The afternoon passed reasonably quickly; each of them pleased to have had company. Lydia looked at her watch. It would soon be time for Cassie to come home. "Should I warn her, do you think?" asked Lydia anxiously. "Or is that unfair to Charles?" She looked at Benson. "I appreciated being forewarned. I might have been a complete basket case if you hadn't."

"Not you my dear," said Mrs. Pearson. "You're a marvel, you really are. We are all trying to follow your example."

"I have my moments when I'm not in control as well you know," said Lydia looking at Benson.

He smiled at her. "They've been few and far between. Cassie is like you; she's got your strength. It must be in the genes."

Hearing that took Lydia by surprise. Her mind flashed back to the day when Charles had told her about David. *Oh Benson, how wrong you are*, she thought.

He continued. "She'll cope. We'll all cope. We won't let him down," the last sentence said quietly but with determination.

"I know," said Lydia. She smiled. "The family have closed ranks, and we're a force to be reckoned with when we do. We'll manage, we'll all help each other." She sat thinking for a moment until she'd made a decision. "I'm going to warn her. I think it would be easier for Charles as well."

"I think you're right," said Margaret with Benson and Mrs. Pearson nodding in agreement.

As soon as Cassie walked into the drawing room she knew something was wrong. Her aunt was an excellent actress but Cassie knew all the tricks and couldn't be fooled.

She sat down beside her and taking a deep breath said, "Is there a problem? And is it a big problem?"

Lydia nodded but her voice was firm and in control. "The news isn't very good I'm afraid. It's in his liver and also the bone." Cassie held Lydia's gaze unflinchingly. "There is nothing more that can be done apart from making sure his pain is well controlled."

"I see," said Cassie quietly. She didn't feel surprised; she'd been half expecting it but had hoped she was wrong. She must be in control she thought. "Does Pops know you're telling me?"

"No, I don't think so, but he didn't say not to. I have no idea, to be perfectly honest," said Lydia. "I was forewarned by Benson and I was glad because I let your father down by collapsing in a heap so I cannot begin to imagine how I would have reacted had I no warning."

Cassie smiled fondly at her aunt. "Never ever have you let Pops down or, for that matter, me. Always, always remember that."

Lydia's eyes filled with tears for the second time that day and her voice lost some of the control of earlier. "Remember, the one thing, absolutely the one thing we don't do just now is 'nice'! Understood?"

Cassie smiled and kissed her aunt. "No more 'nice', matter of fact again, I promise." Cassie waited for her aunt to regain her composure. "Do the others know?"

"Yes," said Lydia, blowing her nose. Looking at her niece she was filled with admiration for her. In the months since Charles had been diagnosed with his cancer, Cassie had gone from someone who didn't have a care in the world, whom everyone had tried to protect from the harsh realities of life, to the confident, composed and poised woman who now faced Lydia.

Lydia suspected she wasn't the only one who had been oblivious to this transformation that had seemingly crept up unnoticed by everyone. Cassie had seemed to be just the same Cassie; full of bounce and vigour, flitting in and out but, an imperceptible change in her had definitely occurred. Cassie was about to endure one of the most appalling times of her life and yet Lydia knew that not only would she cope, but cope with a fortitude and dignity that would be an example to them all.

Lydia smiled, thinking how wrong Mrs. Pearson had been. It would be Cassie who will show them the way. Lydia could now relinquish the reins. Lydia looked at her niece. How proud she was of her. Cassie would undoubtedly be a worthy heir to Harrington Hall.

"I'm fine now, sorry about that," said Lydia.

Cassie smiled. "We'll try and do it in a rota system – 'falling about times' I mean."

"Absolutely, now I was…" but Lydia was interrupted by the doorbell. "I wonder who this can be?"

She heard Benson answer the door and Peter's voice saying he hoped he wasn't interrupting but was passing so thought he'd pop in. *Dear Peter*, thought Lydia, one didn't normally 'just pass' The Hall." Benson showed Peter into the drawing room.

"Hello girls, I thought I'd pop by and see how you were all coping. I heard from Graeme, Graeme Parrott. I'm so sorry about the news," said Peter. He noticed that on the surface at least, of the two of them Cassie seemed the more composed. He was a little surprised. "Is Charles upstairs?"

"Yes, I haven't seen him yet," said Cassie. "I've just got in and Aunt Lydia told me. May I go up and see if he's awake and then you follow?"

"Yes, off you go. I've finished surgery so I'm in no hurry," said Peter. He put his arm around Cassie and cuddled her to him. "How are you doing?"

"Okay," but she added quickly, "Aunt Lydia and I have a pact going."

"Oh yes, what kind of pact?" asked Peter.

"We don't do 'nice'. For the next little while, 'nice' is out; 'matter of fact' is in." For a brief moment she looked as if her composure was going but with admirable control she continued. "It's the only way we're going to cope." She paused. "You see that, don't you?"

Peter nodded. "Yes," he sighed, "I know exactly what you mean."

Cassie looked at him, realising how hard this was for him as well. His best friend was dying yet he had to be the strong one, in control at all times, supporting, not only his friend, but also everyone else.

Cassie looked at him. "We'll all help each other. You don't have to be the doctor all the time you know!"

"Okay, you have a deal," said Peter. He kissed her on the cheek. "You're quite a girl. Do you know that?"

Cassie gave a slight smile. "You didn't always say that. Sarah and I used to give you and Pops apoplexy at regular intervals. Remember?"

"I most certainly do," said Peter fondly. "Weekly intervals if I remember." He looked at her with tenderness. "Off you go, go up and see your Dad. I'll come up in a little while."

Cassie left them. Peter looked at Lydia. "Is it my imagination, or has Cassie changed in some way?"

"I don't think any of us noticed before," said Lydia. "It's been so subtle but yes, I don't know how to describe it, she seems suddenly grown-up. She's in control, she's the boss and do you know something Peter, I'm finding it rather nice; a relief of sorts. I think we always tried to protect her, possibly to make up for the fact she had no mother, but she's turned out surprisingly well considering the odd assortment of people she had looking after her. I'm rather proud of her."

"With every justification. And you, I am of course saying this in a most 'matter of fact' way," smiled Peter. "How are you?"

"I'm fine, really I am," replied Lydia. "Today, well it's just been such a blow. We always hoped, hoped so much for a miracle. I just reacted to the news. I'll be back up to full strength tomorrow. You wait and see."

"I have no doubt about that," said Peter gently. "The angina, is it stable with all this strain you're under? You haven't had a check-up for some time – I looked up your notes before I came over and it's over six months."

Lydia looked surprised. "I'm impressed by your efficiency," she said, teasing him. "You're quite right, I don't think I have been to the surgery since last September. Since then there has been Charles to think about. He took priority."

"Will you pop in and have a quick check next week. You've got to keep well. I personally could not cope with you also unwell," said Peter. "I want you around for a long, long time. Promise you'll come and see me?"

"I promise," said Lydia a little reluctantly. "I'm fine, really I am. It's just been the day."

Peter got up. "I'll nip upstairs." He bent down and kissed Lydia on the cheek. "Next week – or else!"

With that reminder to Lydia, Peter left the room and went upstairs. As he approached Charles's bedroom door, he took a deep breath, knocked, and went in.

Cassie was sitting on the bed, tears glistened in her eyes but she was coping. Charles, despite his nap, looked frail and vulnerable lying in bed. "Come in Peter, nice of you to call."

Peter went and sat down at the other side of the bed. He patted Charles hand. "Graeme phoned this afternoon and told me the results of the scan. I'm so sorry, so very sorry."

"Can't be helped," said Charles. "I think I got a bit longer than if I hadn't had the treatment. Don't you think?"

"Yes, definitely," said Peter. He was trying to be in his 'doctor' mode but finding it so difficult as he looked at his friend lying there.

"Graeme told me about the plan for the hospice," said Peter. "I phoned them and they'll see you on Wednesday, that will be when you are due your next lot of pills. This enables them to see how you coped with the 20mg of morphine. They may increase it, it just depends how you have felt. Be honest Charles, no heroics. If you need more pain relief just say."

Charles smiled at Peter. "I promise I will, I can guarantee there will be no, as you say, heroics."

"If, before Wednesday, you find that 20 mg is not enough, let me know and we'll sort it out. I brought you these as well," said Peter, handing Charles a small bottle. "You may feel a little sick – sometimes people do with morphine, so if you do, take one of these and that should do the trick. Is there anything you wish to ask me?"

Charles looked with concern at Peter. "I'm sure this must be a little difficult for you, but I'm so grateful and so relieved that it will be you looking after me. I feel in safe hands."

Peter wished the lump that was constricting his throat would disappear, for at that moment he could not trust himself to speak. He coughed, hoping that would alleviate the problem, but it didn't. All he could do was pat Charles's hand, smile weakly and mutter his thanks. He made pretence of looking for something in his bag as he tried to compose himself.

Charles was acutely aware of Peter's discomfort and decided to help by completely changing the subject. "I'm sure that tomorrow I'll feel better so, my friend, how do you fancy sharing the bottle of '45 Petrus with me?"

Peter looked at Charles speech yet again denied him, astounded at what he had just heard.

Charles continued. "I know I've been saving it – but for what? I can't think of anyone I'd rather share it with. I want to savour it while I can and I think sooner rather than later would be sensible. What do you say?"

Peter's eyes filled with tears which he tried to blink away as quickly as he could; his normal quick repartee had deserted him. He looked at Charles. "Are you sure? One bottle costs about £8,000, doesn't it?"

"Slightly more now, I suspect," said Charles quietly. Peter could only gulp and utter, "Oh God."

"Tomorrow then," said Charles. He looked at Cassie. "You don't mind do you? After all it's part of your inheritance?"

Cassie was slightly taken aback at that thought: inheritance. Everything was suddenly crowding in and becoming so final. She looked at Peter who was still grappling with the situation.

"I think it sounds obscene paying that for a bottle of wine. Now, a painting, that's a different story," she said, smiling. "But if it gives you and Uncle Peter pleasure to guzzle a bottle of wine, go ahead; I don't mind at all."

Charles and Peter looked at each other, then at Cassie, and together exclaimed, "Guzzle! You don't say 'guzzle' and Petrus in the same breath." They shook their heads in disbelief.

"Peasant, that's what you are my girl, a peasant!" laughed Peter.

Charles looked at them fondly. The tension had gone. Peter was back to his usual ebullient self.

Chapter 20

The Harrington Fayre was the highlight of the village calendar. Charles had always presented the prizes, although lately this had become quite an onerous task; as prizes were awarded for such feats as the tug of rope, egg and spoon race, the best marrow, the best rose, the list was endless; in fact most people in the village seemed to be awarded a prize of one sort or another.

Charles had insisted on attending and presenting the prizes as usual. He looked so ill but he was adamant so Cassie acquiesced but with the proviso that she would help with the prize-giving. Charles reluctantly agreed. To his irritation he had also to agree to being trundled around in a wheel-chair. However, this had not been the ordeal he had imagined as everyone had been very kind and solicitous and were obviously pleased to see him there.

On his return to The Hall, Charles, although tired, was delighted that he had managed to attend and felt a great sense of achievement.

"Well," said Charles. "I really didn't think I'd make that. Thoroughly enjoyed it, feel the better for it. Nice to see old Watkins there – he was telling me they didn't think he'd be around last Christmas and look at him! We compared notes on wheel-chairs. Mind you, I thought he looked worse than I do. It was a good day though. Made a nice change that we didn't have our usual down-pour!"

"Do you want to go upstairs?" asked Lydia.

"No, I'd like to stay here. In fact, I'd like to sit outside. Care to join me?"

"Love to. Stay in the chair and I'll whizz you out," said Lydia. "Hold on tight, right hand bend coming up."

"Good God, that actually felt more like a hand-brake turn," said Charles with mock horror. He looked around him. "This is lovely, I never tire of this view." He smiled at Lydia. "As if you didn't know."

"Do you fancy a little pre-prandial?" asked Lydia.

"If only," said Charles wistfully. "What about a flat tonic water, with a dash of morphine for me. If I add my elixir to the tonic it just might make it more palatable."

"Is the pain very bad?" asked Lydia with concern.

"Not bad," said Charles too quickly, and continued, "but you can make up for me by having a double gin in yours!"

"Sounds good to me," said Lydia. "Have you got your morphine in your pocket?"

"How do you think I got through the prize-giving? I kept having the odd swig," said Charles, as he reached into his pocket for the bottle. "Hip flask, no one knew. Benson's idea; brilliant." He handed the bottle to Lydia who noticed he had obviously required numerous 'swigs'.

"I tell you," said Charles. "I'll keep the bottle and then I can add it to the tonic as I need. Tell Mrs. Pearson and the others to grab a drink and come out. We haven't had a get-together in ages." With that, Kate came into view bounding across the grass.

"Sneaked in the back way," said Kate. "Hello, Lydia, Charles," Bending down, she kissed Charles on the cheek. "I came to see how you were feeling? I thought you were brilliant by the way. I'm very impressed although I hadn't remembered there were quite so many prizes!"

"Tell me about it," laughed Charles. "We are having a drinkie-poo; your Mum and the others as well. Care to join us?"

"Mmm, that sounds good. I'll go in and help. Lydia, G&T?" asked Kate.

"Please," replied Lydia, "And a flat tonic for Charles – so bring out a swizzle stick please."

The rest of the afternoon passed quickly, much of it talking about the Fayre and the people who had been there with Benson doing hilarious impersonations of some of the old worthies!

Kate looked at her watch. "Help, I'm in big trouble, I didn't realise the time. I'd better get back. This has been lovely, I'm so glad I gate-crashed!"

"It wouldn't have been the same without you," smiled Charles.

"Here, let me help," said Kate.

"Go!" said Cassie. "Get back to the family before Robert starts divorce proceedings."

"Well, bye everyone," said Kate as she went over to Charles. "I hope you sleep well; you should do with all this fresh air today." She smiled at him giving him a kiss on the cheek.

Charles took hold of her hand and held it tightly for a moment. He looked at her intently. "Goodbye Kate," he said quietly.

Kate looked at him. A strange feeling came over her – but the feeling passed as quickly as it had arrived. She smiled at him. "See you tomorrow."

She turned to go back across the lawn but had only walked about ten yards when something made her stop. She suddenly felt uneasy; a shiver ran through her. She turned round. Charles was watching her. Kate raised her hand and waved. He nodded and smiled at her. She waved one last time as she climbed over the wall. She looked back, but he had gone.

Charles's death took everyone by surprise at its suddenness. No one suspected it would be that day.

Not surprisingly, he had been exhausted after the Fayre and had forgone dinner, retiring early, but the full extent of the pain he had been suffering had been unknown to the others. He had been gulping his morphine down like lemonade which had given him the pleasantly euphoric feeling at the afternoon's impromptu party. He had enjoyed it so much though – a nice end to the day... or whatever the day may bring, Charles thought, philosophically.

He wanted relief from the pain but didn't want to leave Harrington Hall and die in the hospice. For some reason he couldn't bear that thought. He wanted to die there. Another wave of pain assaulted him as if grabbing at his insides and shredding them to a pulp. He twisted the sheet into a knot with a strength that belied his illness, as if to get some release, but to no avail.

Despite her father's protestations, Cassie could no longer bear to watch him in such obvious pain and telephoned Peter.

Peter materialised in what seemed to be moments. Cassie felt a huge weight lift from her shoulders – Uncle Peter was now in charge.

"Charles it's me, the pills and elixir are obviously not working too well so I'm going to give you a zap. Hold on... there we are," said Peter. "I've got something else here and this will really help. It's a pump, a morphine pump. I'll let the injection take effect first; then I'll fit the pump. Have a snooze first."

Charles grabbed Peter's arm. Peter bent to hear what he was trying to say. "No hospice, please no hospice, let me stay here Peter."

"I promise, Charles. I'm staying as well. Rest… and don't worry," said Peter kindly.

Peter looked over at Cassie. "You okay?" he asked quietly.

Cassie nodded and replied equally quietly, "Better now that you're here. Can you really stay?"

Peter nodded. "Absolutely." He indicated to Cassie to move outside for a moment.

"It's less worrying for Charles if we talk outside," said Peter as he closed the door slightly. "The last of the senses to go is the hearing. Cassie, do you understand that it may not be too long now." Cassie nodded. Peter continued. "I'm not sure how long. Do you want to go to bed? I'll call you when there is any change."

"No, I'm staying," said Cassie. Will I talk to him? What will I do?"

"Yes, talk," said Peter. "Hold his hand. Whatever feels right for you. If you wish, you can talk to me; your Dad may join in, who knows. He'll lapse in and out of consciousness for some time but he'll be aware of your presence. You're doing great. Are you ready to go back in?"

Cassie nodded. Peter patted her shoulder and they both went back in to the bedroom.

As Cassie sat down beside the bed and took Charles's hand he stirred and smiled at her. "Sorry, dropped off, makes you feel sleepy you know, its very pleasant this stuff, very pleasant indeed."

"Charles I'm going to fix the up the pump now," said Peter.

"Sounds good to me," said Charles drowsily. "No more pain, it's a lovely feeling, no more pain."

The night continued with Charles drifting in and out of consciousness with his periods of lucidity becoming but brief snatches. Lydia popped in and out throughout the night with coffee and sandwiches for Cassie and Peter. When she had something to do, she coped. She was so glad of the excuse not to sit at the bedside. She didn't know if she could do that – just sit and wait for the inevitable.

The inevitable eventually came. Charles died at 7.10 a.m.

~~~~~

"I can't believe he's done this. He's organised his own funeral. Typical isn't it." Despite her grief, Cassie could not help but smile. There had been a note to her that she had found on his desk, saying which hymns, readings etc. he would like. Everything was itemised. He wanted to be buried in the family plot beside the chapel and wanted a quiet and private funeral.

"I think that's wishful thinking, Pops," said Cassie out loud.

"Did you say something, dear?" asked Lydia.

"Pops, in his instructions, he writes he wants a quiet funeral. I don't think he realises that everyone in the village and more, want to be there. How can we solve this I wonder?" Cassie thought for a moment. "I know, what about this for a plan? Say no if you don't agree. The funeral in the village church; we'll get everyone in there. Then back here to the chapel for the private service with only the family oh, and Henry if he can manage. He was Pop's oldest friend, wasn't he?" asked Cassie.

"Yes," said Lydia. "From school-days but he's recently had triple bypass surgery so may not be able to come. We'll check though. I think that's a splendid idea. Good thinking. Well done."

There was a knock at the library door and Benson came in, followed by Reverend Matheson.

"My dear girl, how are you bearing up?" asked the vicar. Cassie gave a non-committal smile. They shook hands and he kissed her on the cheek and then went over to Lydia where he did the same.

Once seated Cassie asked if he would care for tea, coffee or perhaps a sherry. He seemed partial to sherry. As Cassie went over to the decanter to pour him one she wondered why sherry always seemed to be the preferred tipple of the clergy. She poured two and gave Lydia one as well.

They started on the proceedings. Cassie took charge and asked if it was permissible to deviate from Charles's instructions and have part of the service in the church followed by the chapel. The vicar didn't seem to think that would be a problem. Much to Cassie's amazement they accomplished the arrangements with speed and efficiency.

In the midst of this. Duncan Forbes, the undertaker, arrived. Cassie was pleased to see him as he had lived in Harrington all his life and knew the family. She told him about the arrangements for the chapel and burial in the grounds. He wrote it all down and then said they might like to think who they would wish as pallbearers. Cassie and Lydia looked at each other. They hadn't given this a thought. Cassie had a quick look at Charles's list. Neither had he, it seemed!

"We'll have to think," said Cassie. "We'd have to phone and make sure the men were agreeable."

"No problem," said Duncan. "Even on the day would be fine. You'll need six."

"I'm sure that won't be a problem," said Cassie.

"I'll go then," said Duncan. "Take care."

Lydia and Cassie looked at each other. So far so good – they were coping – just!

"Who are we going to ask?" asked Cassie. "Let's think. Firstly, Uncle Peter, Benson, Robert, Henry, once you've checked his by-pass will hold out," said Cassie. "Gosh, who else."

"You know that David is hoping to be here," said Lydia, a little hesitantly. "What do you feel about he being one?"

Cassie smiled, "Don't worry. I think Pops would be really touched he was coming over and yes, let's ask him. I would like that. Okay, one more. I wondered if we could ask Pierre. He was very fond of Pops and he's been so good to me." Cassie pondered for a moment. "Actually I don't know; is this something people like to be asked to do, be pallbearers? I'm not sure."

"I think it's considered a kind of honour," said Lydia. "Usually one only asks close friends or family so yes, let's say it's an honour shall we?"

Cassie raised an eyebrow. "If you say so! Well, we'd better start phoning people.

Lydia had been right. Everyone who had been asked seemed deeply touched and honoured to perform such a task.

The day before the funeral David was due to arrive. At Cassie's insistence she went to collect him. She wanted time on her own with him.

She scanned the arrivals board. David's plane was due in on time. She watched for his face amongst the mass of people who emerged through International Arrivals. Spotting him she shouted his name. He looked around and saw her. Smiling, he waved.

They met and he enveloped her in his arms. "Oh Cassie, I was so, so sorry about Charles." Mindful of their relationship, he only kissed her on both cheeks and then hugged her again.

"There is a rule we are having at the moment," said Cassie breaking away from his embrace. We don't have *nice* at the moment, 'matter of fact', is the name of the game. I have to be in control for tomorrow. I don't care what happens after that, but tomorrow I can't let him down, I can't let Pops down." Her voice was strong, only the tear that escaped gave her away.

"You won't," said David. He put his arm around her shoulder as they walked out of the airport. "How is everyone else?"

"Inwardly we are all wrecks but outwardly we are all playing our parts, and if I may say, playing them magnificently," said Cassie.

"Can I speak about Charles or would you rather I didn't. I promise, I'll play by your rules. Whatever you say," said David.

"Yes, please speak about him, especially funny things. Nothing too sentimental at the moment." Cassie looked at him. "I'm pleased you're here. I really am. For some reason it wouldn't have seemed right if you hadn't been, so thank you."

"I just wish I'd got over earlier," said David with regret.

"I know. But you're here now. Now," said Cassie twinkling at him. "How are you about coping with women drivers? You all set?"

David did an exaggerated gulp. "Ready as I'll ever be!"

By the time they reached Harrington the easy rapport they once had was re-established.

David arrived at The Hall and was greeted like the proverbial Prodigal son. He was quite overwhelmed by their welcome. He was trying very hard to maintain the stiff upper lip that all at The Hall seemed to be maintaining.

After he had unpacked, he went downstairs to the kitchen. "Mrs. Pearson," he said, kissing her on the cheek for the second time that day. "You have no idea how often I have dreamt of these delicious smells." He looked at her. She appeared to have shrunk; not looking at all like the formidable lady he had met all those months ago. The strain had taken its toll on her. He gave her a hug that took her completely by surprise.

"What on earth was that for?" she asked, feeling a little flustered.

"Because I missed you, that's why," said David, smiling at her. Mrs. Pearson just shook her head in disbelief at such nonsense.

In the drawing room Cassie put down the phone. "We've a problem for tomorrow," she told Lydia and Kate who had popped over earlier. "That was Henry, his doctor says he can't come over for the funeral."

"Oh," said Lydia. "He'll be vexed about that. I'm sorry."

"The thing is," said Cassie, "We need another man as pallbearer, just when the arrangements seemed okay. Ah well. Thinking caps on again."

Kate stood up. "I have to go just now, I have to do my stint at the nursery but I'll have a think as well. I'll pop back after the children have had their tea. I'll let myself out."

"They don't need this extra hassle at this time," thought Kate. "She'd speak to Robert he might know of someone."

Kate arrived home still mulling over the problem... "So they are now one short," said Kate, who was telling Robert about the problem of the pallbearer. "Who on earth can we get at this short notice? Was there anyone you know whom Charles was close to on the estate?"

"I can't think," said Robert. "You know what he was like Kate. The *Family* was all he seemed to need, but I'll try. I really will. You know something else? It has to be someone reasonably tall, the rest of us are, so it has to be someone vaguely the same height or else it looks a shambles and perhaps even a recipe for disaster!" Kate looked at Robert with horror. She hadn't thought of that.

A voice from the corner of the room spoke. "I could do it if you like."

Kate and Robert looked at their son with amazement. Kate went over to him. "Oh Charlie that's kind of you, it really is but you've never been to a funeral and this one... this one... is," Kate couldn't finish.

Robert tried to help out. "Son, it's going to be a big enough ordeal for you tomorrow. I didn't go to my first funeral until I was eighteen; it's not something that's very easy to cope with, and especially being a pallbearer."

Charlie had tears in his eyes. "Please I want to..." he begged, "I loved him and I want to do it. I'm tall, that's what you said; you needed someone tall. I'd be good, really I would. Please... please let me." He was angry that they wouldn't take him seriously. He tried again, his voiced raised. "Uncle Charles was the only one who ever let me do anything. He was the only one. He took me fishing, shooting and climbing to places you'd never let me go. But I never got hurt, never, so there. He trusted me. Uncle Charles would let me, he'd maybe even want me to do it for him." Realising what he had just said he burst into tears and ran from the room.

Kate and Robert looked at each other and shrugged. Charlie was perhaps right, why couldn't he do it? Kate went upstairs where he was lying on his bed, sobbing his heart out. She sat down beside him.

He looked up at her with his tear-stained face and gruffly said, "I miss him too you know. I wouldn't let him down, I wouldn't."

Kate looked at him, his earnest face begging her to agree. She relented. "I know you wouldn't. Let me ask Cassie first." She ruffled his hair with affection and went back downstairs.

"Is he okay?" asked Robert.

"As well as we all are. I'm going to The Hall. I'll ask Cassie what she thinks," said Kate.

Kate arrived at The Hall, and walked in just as Cassie was coming out of Charles's study. "Any luck?"

"No, I was looking through some of his things in the vain hope of finding someone, but no," said Cassie. "Have you any ideas?"

"Well yes," said Kate. "Well actually not my idea, Charlie's."

"Well he and Pops were so close, so yes, he'd possibly know. Who does he think?" asked Cassie.

Kate looked at Cassie. "Are you ready for this? Himself. He wants to be a pallbearer."

Cassie looked wide-eyed with surprise at this suggestion. "What do you think? Don't you think he's too young? Tomorrow is going to be horrendous, is he sure?"

"He was really upset. He said how much he loved Charles and misses him. He'd been listening to our conversation. Robert mentioned that the person we got would have to be reasonably tall to match the others."

"I wouldn't have thought of that at all," said Cassie, with surprise. "Well certainly Charlie fits the bill. The ridiculous thing is that Pops would be so touched by him wanting to do this… Yes, let him. I'll come over and speak to him."

By the time Cassie arrived at Kate's, Charlie was composed. "Your Mum tells me you'd like to help tomorrow." Charlie nodded. Cassie continued. "Charlie I'm sorry I hadn't thought of asking you before; I thought you were too young." Charlie's face fell. "But you're right." She smiled at him. "I can't think of anyone that Pops would have liked more than you; his right hand man. I would be grateful if you would do it."

Charlie swallowed; he wasn't going to cry again. "I won't let you down Cassie, I promise."

"I know you won't. You're a special chap, you really are. Thank you." Tears welled in his eyes again. "Shall I kiss you as a token of my thanks?" asked Cassie, trying to lighten the moment.

Charlie sniffed. "No way!" he exclaimed as he stepped back out of harms way!

"Well thank you anyway". She stood up and, looking at Kate, tried a weak smile. "See you… see you tomorrow.

As the funeral cars made their slow procession up the main street to the church, Cassie gazed out of the window, oblivious to the others in the car, trying to keep her emotions in check. With surprise she noticed that all the shops seemed to be closed. She suddenly realised what that meant and tears, already close to the surface, welled up. This gesture by the shopkeepers was nearly her undoing. She hadn't expected that. She blinked furiously to stop them escaping and with relief, succeeded.

They arrived at the gates of the church. Cars were unable to pass through; they had to walk up the path through the graveyard. People lined the path; some were in tears. Cassie helped Lydia out of the car. They looked at each other. They had not expected this reception. So much for Charles wanting a quiet funeral! Checking that everyone was ready Cassie and Lydia led the way, backs straight, heads held high as they made their way into the packed church.

The service was as Charles would have wanted; no elaborate fuss, no flowery sentiment, just an honest appraisal of a true and caring gentleman; of a life lived well in the service of his village and its people.

Cassie and Lydia stood outside the church and shook hands with all those who had come to pay their respects. Cassie knew she was sounding as if she were on automatic pilot saying, "Thank you for coming, how kind," etc. etc.

She had said this yet again as she shook hands with a tall, slim, youngish looking man. He looked at her and, smiling gently, said, "I was so sorry about your father, Cassie. He was a lovely man."

Cassie looked at him intently. She had no idea who he was yet he seemed to know her. "How kind," she found herself repeating for the hundredth time but was interrupted by him.

"You don't remember me, do you?" he asked.

Cassie looked him up and down. He was immaculately dressed in a dark grey suit, polished shoes, black tie, white shirt, short and well-cut hair. She really didn't know yet... yet there was something familiar, something in his eyes.

"I'll put you out of your misery," he said. Leaning forward he whispered, "It's me, Sputnik!"

Cassie gasped and looked him up and down again. "Really?" Lydia looked round, wondering who on earth Cassie was talking to. Cassie caught her attention. "You'll never believe who this is. Looking at him now, you'd never know," said an amazed Cassie.

Lydia extended her hand. "How do you do, young man, how kind of you to come."

Cassie said, "It's Sputnik. Do you remember?"

It was now Lydia's turn to look with some incredulity at the smart young man before her. She smiled. "I would have never guessed."

There was a queue beginning to form. Cassie whispered to Sputnik. "Please come back to The Hall. We'd like you there. It's just family and close friends so just follow the cars. Please say you will."

Sputnik looked at Lydia who nodded and whispered. "We'd like you to, please."

"I will then, thank you."

Cassie and Lydia eventually completed their handshaking. At last, they were able to leave and escort Charles on his journey home.

The funeral procession arrived at The Hall and stopped outside the chapel. The men who were to be pallbearers stepped out of the cars first. Cassie noticed that they seemed to know exactly where they were to go as if they had rehearsed. The lump in Cassie's throat threatened to choke her at the sight of Charlie, immaculate in his first suit, his face pale, but composed, and with not a hair out of place. Cassie was bursting with pride at the exemplary way in which he was carrying out his task; she couldn't even begin to imagine how Kate must be feeling and didn't dare look!

The time in the chapel was really to adhere to Charles's wishes and was also a time for quiet reflection for the family and close friends. The vicar read two passages from the bible, one chosen by Charles, the other by Lydia. Then he looked at David and nodded. David returned the nod, stood up and moved to the side of Charles's coffin. He coughed nervously, now regretting that he had agreed to speak. He had decided to read a poem – firstly because he liked it and thought it appropriate, and secondly because it was short! He looked at the strained faces of Cassie and Lydia who tried to smile their encouragement to him. He gave a strained smile back and then started to speak in as firm a voice as he could manage:

"Cassie asked me if I would care to say a few words today. I was honoured to have been asked, but have decided to read a poem instead. The poet, Anna Letita Barbauld, died in 1825 but the sentiment she expresses is how I feel and I hope you will agree, is appropriate for the occasion." He took a card from his pocket and started to read.

Life! I know not what thou art,
But know that you and I must part;
And when, or how, or where we met.

His voice cracked and his eyes blurred with tears, the next few lines he said from memory. He looked at Cassie who, smiling through her own tears, seemed to will him to continue. He struggled to regain control and taking a deep breath finished the final verse in a firm and controlled voice:

Tis hard to part when friends are dear -
Perhaps 'twill cost a sigh, a tear;
– Then steal away, give little warning,
– Choose thine own time;
And say not Goodnight – but in some brighter clime
Bid me Good Morning.

With relief, he finished the poem and, giving Cassie a slight smile, returned to his seat where he surreptitiously wiped away a tear.

The vicar finished the service with a prayer and a blessing. The men then took their places again and moved Charles from the chapel to his final resting place – on the hill, overlooking the lake, next to his beloved Lizzie.

Chapter 21

Sputnik had waited at the house, feeling it would have been an intrusion to go to the chapel and the family graveyard. He walked round the side of the house and surveyed the land around him. It really was quite magnificent.

He wondered who would now run the estate. Remembering Cassie from her youth he didn't think it was exactly her scene but who knows, she may have changed; she certainly looked different. He had watched her in the church and as she spoke to people outside. She looked poised and dare he say it, sophisticated. He smiled; she was quite unrecognisable from before. He caught sight of himself in the reflection of the window and smiled ruefully; she wasn't the only one who had changed! Hearing the cars return he went round to the front. Cassie emerged from the car so he walked over to her and, putting an arm around her shoulders, kissed her gently on the cheek.

"Where did you get to?" she asked.

"Didn't want to intrude," he replied as they went inside. He recognised a few of them but there were others whom he'd never met before.

Cassie took him by the hand and was about to introduce him to Rowena and Peter but stopped. "I can't introduce you as 'Sputnik'. What's your proper name?" she asked.

He gave a slightly sheepish smile and said, "James, actually the full whack is – James Edward Fitzroy Montague-Smyth, Viscount if you must know!"

Cassie looked at him and then, to her embarrassment, let out a guffaw which she quickly tried to stifle. "I'm sorry," she said, trying desperately not to giggle. "It's not your name, really it's not, its reaction of the day, relief." But it was no good; she laughed again.

"Have you quite finished?" asked James, trying to look hurt.

Cassie nodded. "You are such a fraud," she laughed. "Why the deception at art school? Why didn't you tell us?"

"Don't know really," he answered. "I felt a bit of a prat to be honest. However, that's what I'm called. Okay, have you finished with the hysterics?"

"Yes," said Cassie apologetically. "That was quite rotten and totally uncalled for. Allow me to introduce you... Lord Montague-Smyth." Her eyes twinkled at him.

"Ha, bloody ha!" he replied under his breath.

David looked round at the others. They were all trying so hard to keep going but their faces were beginning to betray the strain. His eye caught Charlie who was leaning against the wall wolfing down the food. He picked up a plate and went over to him. "Hi, how are you doing?"

Charlie looked at him and nodded. "Okay."

"You did well today, really well." Charlie just looked at him and nodded. "Your Dad tells me you are something of an expert fisherman. Would you take a complete idiot out to have a try? I'm talking about me in, case you didn't know. I've never fished," smiled David.

"If you like," replied Charlie casually.

"Thanks that would be good. We can arrange something sometime soon," said David who, beginning to run out of things to speak about, was relieved that Cassie had come over.

"Charlie and I were thinking about going fishing," said David.

"That would be good," said Cassie. Smiling at Charlie she said to David, "Watch though, this guy here is an expert: once caught a fifteen pound salmon with Pops."

David went 'Phew!' as if deeply impressed, and then rather spoilt the moment by asking if that was big.

Cassie and Charlie looked at each other and raised their eyebrows at him in disbelief.

"I think I'll go and get another sandwich," said David hurriedly.

Cassie watched him go. "Don't mind David. He's an artist and not used to the ways of the country."

"You're telling me," replied Charlie with undisguised disgust.

"Thanks for today," said Cassie. "I was **so** proud of you, so would Pops have been." Charlie just nodded. "One thing that did impress me," said Cassie teasingly. "Never in my entire life have I ever seen you with polished shoes. Today was a first," she smiled at him.

"You can always tell a gentleman by his shoes," said Charlie with authority. Cassie looked at him with surprise. He continued. "They may be old, but if they're polished then he's a true gentleman."

Cassie nodded and could only agree. "Yes, yes indeed you are absolutely right."

Charlie looked at her. "I know I am," he said emphatically. "Uncle Charles said so and he always had polished shoes."

They looked at each other. Their emotions, which had been so tightly controlled, now suddenly evaporated. Charlie bent his head, embarrassed. Cassie pulled him towards her and with an arm around his shoulder moved them away to a more private place.

After a few minutes he had recovered his composure. "Hoi Cassie, you're dripping tears on my head."

Cassie sniffed and released him from their cuddle. "Sorry," she said as she wiped her eyes. Smiling through her tears she asked, "Perhaps you'd like me to blow dry your hair for you?"

He just looked at her and shuffled with embarrassment, wishing his tears had never happened. "As if!"

He continued looking at the floor. "Sorry I was pathetic then."

Cassie pulled his head up to look at her. "Never think that was pathetic. Tears are fine for both males and females. Today has been the pits, the absolute pits and considering what we both felt for Pops I think we've both done brilliantly, so there."

Charlie wiped his eyes with the back of his hand and smiled weakly at Cassie. "You know something?" Cassie shook her head. "You are sometimes weird, decidedly weird but... you're also pretty cool!"

"Thanks," smiled Cassie. "Come on let's go back to the others. You okay?"

Charlie nodded. "Yup, what about you?"

"Yup as well," smiled Cassie.

They entered the room, both now composed. Robert smiled at them and went over. "Where have you two been?" he asked.

"We were in Pop's study, I've been showing Charlie the coin collection," said Cassie quickly.

Charlie looked, for a brief moment surprised at this lie, but didn't say anything.

"That must have been interesting," said Robert. Charlie just nodded.

"Indeed it must," said Lydia smiling at them aware that the collection was safely locked away upstairs!

Cassie looked at her aunt, daring her to say anything. Lydia looked at Charlie and, much to his amazement, she winked at him. He winked back, accompanying the wink with a conspiratorial grin!

"Let's go and find Mum," said Robert, oblivious to the hidden meaning of the moment. Charlie went off with his father, much relieved at being able to escape.

"I'd better go and make sure Sputnik… James is all right," said Cassie correcting herself. "I see he's talking to Pierre."

"Oh he's fine," said Lydia. "He and David have been chatting away non stop about art and now he's off chatting to Pierre."

"What about the others?" asked Cassie.

"Everyone's doing fine," said Lydia. "Relax, my dear. Everything has gone splendidly."

Cassie nodded. "Yes, yes it has."

Peter came over to her and put an arm around her shoulder. "We'll go now." He looked at Cassie and smiled. "It's a strange thing to say I know, but you look lovely today, very elegant."

Cassie raised an eyebrow and smiled. "Thanks."

"He'd be proud, so very proud of you," said Peter as he kissed Cassie on her forehead.

"Come on, you," said Rowena, quickly retrieving Peter in case he upset Cassie. "Time to go home. Cassie, I'll call tomorrow after the lawyer has been. He should be away by lunchtime shouldn't he?"

"I've no idea," replied Cassie. "I don't know what is involved, to be perfectly honest. Will you not be here tomorrow Uncle Peter? I thought you were an executor?"

"I am," he replied, "but I don't actually have to be at the reading of the Will. Anyway, I have surgery until eleven-thirty but I'm going to get Tony to see the last few patients and he'll do the calls so I'll be over as soon as I can."

"Okay. Actually," she pondered for a moment, "I have just realised that this may be trickier than I thought. I'm sure Pops said there has to be a male heir. Is that correct?"

Peter nodded, "Yes, so I believe."

"There always has been. I'm the first female." Cassie paused, "I wish I'd listened to Pops about all this but I wasn't particularly interested when he was telling me. I just vaguely remember Pops saying that he'd organise a group of people, like a Board of Harrington who would oversee the running of the estate. Would that be correct?"

"I think so," said Peter. "But we'll find out tomorrow. Who is the chap that's coming over?"

"It's Alan Napier from Keithly, Napier and Sharp. He's a friend of Kate and Robert's, so he must be all right," smiled Cassie.

"I know him," said Peter. He's a nice chap, a bit slow and deliberate but good. You'll be fine and I'll get over as soon as I can."

"Thanks Uncle Peter," said Cassie, giving him a kiss. "And… thanks for everything."

"No problem," replied Peter quickly. "Bye." Rowena smiled at Cassie and took Peter away.

Cassie went looking for Sputnik, whom she spotted still chatting to Pierre. "Ah, there you are. What are you two talking about?"

"James and I find we have quite a lot in common as regards our favourite artists," said Pierre. He continued. "However I must go now." He looked at Cassie with fondness. "I'll give you a call in a day or two. I hope tomorrow won't be too much of an ordeal."

"It shouldn't be, at least I hope not," replied Cassie. "Thank you for your help today," she said, giving him a kiss. "I'll be back on Monday."

"Whenever," said Pierre. "Take as long as you like."

Eventually there was only Sputnik left. "May I call you soon?" he asked.

"Yes, yes please," replied Cassie. "Thank you so much for coming and," Cassie felt a slight smile creep up her face. "Sorry for being so rotten about your name. I'm trying very hard to remember that it's James, really I am.

"Mmm," smiled Sputnik. "I believe you. Take care," he said, and with a final 'bye' and a kiss on the cheek, he left.

Cassie watched him go surprised at just how much she looked forward to seeing him again.

Chapter 22

"Good morning to all of you," smiled Alan Napier as he took a chair at the dining room table. Those whom he had not met before Robert introduced and then the formalities started.

"Firstly, I shall let you know of Lord Emerson's bequests," he said, whereupon he read out the names starting with Mrs. Pearson. Apart from her pension from the estate, she was also to receive a sum of money and would have accommodation at The Hall until her death. Tears coarsed down her cheeks. She was completely overwhelmed at such kindness. Benson and Margaret received similar kindness and, upon Benson's retirement, he and Margaret would move from The Hall into accommodation on the estate, in the cottage that had been Kate's childhood home. Kate smiled over at her mother who was looking as stunned as Mrs. Pearson. There were then legacies for Kate, Robert and their four children. It was now their turn to be overwhelmed.

Cassie and Lydia exchanged glances; they were both delighted with what Charles had done.

Mr. Napier then told them that Charles had changed a portion of his Will. Cassie thought this was strange and looked over at Lydia but her face showed no sign of surprise.

Mr. Napier then talked to Cassie directly. "As you may know your father wrote this section of his Will upon hearing of his illness. However, in February, February 26th to be precise, he asked that his initial instructions be amended."

Cassie sat stock-still, unsure of what was coming next. Mr. Napier continued. "As you know, the estate has always passed down the male line." Cassie nodded. "Your father, therefore, initially thought that the estate should be run by a Council, a Board, call it what you will, with a new Chairman elected from the Board every three years. This state of affairs would continue until such times as you had a son who, upon reaching the age of twenty-five, would then be considered as legal heir to the estate and would, as such, assume responsibility for Harrington."

"Yes, I vaguely remember him telling me that," said Cassie. "That is fine by me. Although," she added smiling slightly, "I'm not too sure what I can do about producing the heir part!"

"Ah," said Mr. Napier. "That has all changed." Cassie looked at him. He continued. "I confess that Lord Emerson had us all in a bit of a quandary at his idea but," he paused and smiled. "I am delighted to say, we have managed to accommodate his wishes."

Cassie listened to him as he burbled on, thinking why can't lawyers just get to the point. What on earth is he trying to say? But she did not let her face show even the slightest hint of exasperation; she just looked at him as if holding onto his every word and smiled encouragingly.

There was a knock at the door and Peter arrived. "My apologies, I was held up at surgery," he said.

"Not at all," said Mr. Napier, smiling acknowledgement at Peter. He opened another folder and, looking at Cassie, said, "Your father chose the following people to serve on the Board of Harrington Estate; people whom he felt would have the interests of the estate at heart but," he said stressing the word 'but', "and more importantly, your father felt, they had to be people who would have your best interests at heart."

Cassie swallowed; she was beginning to find this an ordeal she had not fully anticipated. She wondered what was coming next. He continued. "Here is the list, some of whom your father had spoken to and whom he hoped will agree to be on the Board of Harrington Estate. They are: Mr. George Benson, Dr. Peter Bartlett, Mrs. Rowena Bartlett, Mr. David Coleridge, Mrs. Katherine Grant, Mrs. Lydia Maitland, Mr. Pierre Gabriel and finally, as Executive Chairman, Mr. Robert Grant." Cassie nodded, surprised at hearing David's name.

"I am also included as the lawyer for the group. As you will no doubt appreciate, to have a quorum there will have to be at least five present, including the Chairman so I will now quote from what your father has said as regards the Chairman," said Mr. Napier. He read the amendment Charles had written. *After due consideration I have decided that the outmoded ruling of only a male inheriting Harrington Estate should now be abolished. I wish that my beloved daughter, Cassandra, be the overall Chairman, or Chairperson, if she feels particularly strongly about the use of that title.* Mr. Napier smiled across at Cassie and continued. *I hope she will accept what she may feel will be an onerous task, but I know that with her courage and strength of character she will be more than able to fulfil the position.* Cassie stared in front of her, trying to take this in.

"There is also a postscript from your father which I will now read. It says: *Cassie, please do not feel overwhelmed by this task. I promise you I did not take this decision lightly. I spoke to Pierre checking that you do have some business sense'.*" Mr. Napier paused and said, "In brackets your father wrote, *'(sorry for doing that!)'.*" Then he continued. *"'I am also sure this duty will not intrude too much on your time for your first love; your art – I would never wish for that to happen. I have spoken to Robert who will be your guide and the 'hands on' Chairman. Your role will be as mine was and if you remember, it is thanks to Robert that I had more than enough time for my writing'.*" Mr. Napier looked at Cassie. "Your father finishes by saying, *'Please accept Cassie, and do so with all my love, signed, Pops'.*"

Tears welled up in Cassie's eyes as she looked at Robert. He smiled and nodded his encouragement. She looked at Lydia, who also nodded and smiled.

Oblivious to these exchanges Mr. Napier continued. "Your father didn't realise that we had to practically re-write the whole constitution for Harrington Estate, it was quite a task, I can tell you."

But Cassie wasn't listening. Her father could not have given her anything she appreciated more, and that, was his trust. *I won't let you down Pops, I promise*, she thought.

Cassie gathered herself together and said. "Mr. Napier I will be happy to take over the Non-Executive Chairmanship of Harrington Estate." She looked at Robert who mouthed, "Well done girl," and grinned at her. She smiled at him and swallowed, hoping her voice would remain steady. "I hope I will be worthy of the trust my father has placed in me." She looked at 'the family' around the table who were all nodding, willing her to succeed. She continued, "But with the support of The Board and especially with Robert at the helm, I feel confident that Harrington Estate will remain a thriving and ,hopefully, flourishing business, giving continued work to those in the area, for a long time in the future."

Everyone around the table broke into spontaneous applause. Robert stood up and, looking at Cassie, said, "For a first statement of your Chairmanship that was pretty impressive, well done," and he went round and hugged her and whispered, "You'll be fine. You and I will be as good a team as your Dad and I were, I promise."

Cassie couldn't speak. She just looked at him and nodded her thanks.

Lydia decided Cassie needed a break and said, "Mr. Napier, if there is nothing more you require to do this morning I think we should perhaps adjourn for coffee."

"I have finished for the moment, thank you," he replied. "Alas, I have no time for coffee, perhaps another time." He gathered up his papers and, going over to Cassie, they shook hands. "Goodbye. I will be in touch soon with regards to finalising the new constitution. It should not take too long."

"Thank you, Mr. Napier. I look forward to hearing from you," replied Cassie. "Benson, can you show Mr. Napier out please."

"It will be my pleasure," replied Benson with a twinkle to Cassie.

Cassie caught his meaning and smiled, relieved that Benson had eased her tension for her mind was reeling. Everyone apart from Robert had taken Lydia's cue and followed her to the library for coffee.

"Robert, how long have you known about Pops ideas?" asked Cassie.

"He spoke to me in February when he was mulling it over. I agreed with him. It is right and proper that Harrington should come to you and who knows, one day, there may be a male to take over," smiled Robert.

"I'm going to kill that wife of yours for not warning me," said Cassie.

"She didn't know until today," replied Robert. "Your father told me not to tell anyone."

"What about you, Robert? You know I haven't a clue about the estate. Did your heart not sink when you heard Pops plans?" asked Cassie.

"No, and I am being honest, I promise. I thought the idea of a three yearly chairman was unsatisfactory. There has to be continuity of line – I'm a traditionalist remember," smiled Robert. "I love my job and your father always made me feel we were in partnership. We both had a vested interest in the estate. It's my livelihood." Robert paused and smiled. "Actually there is a certain someone who wants to step into my shoes as soon as he can."

"Pops would love that," smiled Cassie. "I take it we are talking about son number one."

Robert smiled. "Indeed we are."

"I can't think of anyone better," said Cassie. "Did Pops know?"

Robert nodded. "Yes, apparently on their walks your father and Charlie used to chat all the time about their plans for the estate."

Cassie smiled and then looked serious. "Robert, I will try very hard to do my best. You'll have to guide me but I hope that in time, we will work on the estate as you and Pops did; in partnership. I'll try to learn quickly, I really will," said Cassie earnestly.

"I know you will," replied Robert. "We'll be a fabulous partnership, just see if we're not. Now, I don't know about you, but I could certainly do with a coffee."

"Good idea," said a relieved Cassie, and she and Robert went to the library to join the others.

~~~~~

Cassie was in the study going through yet another box of her father's papers when David knocked and came in. "Stop that for a while, you look exhausted," he said. "Come and have some fresh air – let's go for a walk. It's a lovely evening."

"You're right, I'm bushed. My mind is still doing somersaults from this morning," said Cassie. She looked out of the window. "It looks nice. I don't think I'll need a jacket."

They wandered off down to the lakeside. Cassie always felt closer to her father there.

"How do you feel about being on the Board?" asked Cassie.

"Deeply touched actually," replied David. "Your Dad and I hadn't known each other that long, yet he was someone I respected and wished I could have known longer. I always enjoyed our phone-calls; we covered an amazing range of topics." He looked at Cassie. "You'll think I'm crazy again but by him putting me on the Board I felt I had become one of 'The Family' as he liked to call it." David looked out across the lake. "It's the first time in my life I have felt like that!"

247

Cassie looked at him. "Always feel that, David; one of the family. You know, I'm lucky, so lucky. I suppose I've always been a little spoilt but everyone on the Board is my family, Pops was right. And, he was right in asking you to join. I'm glad he did."

David smiled. "Thank you and I promise you I will always have your best interests at heart."

Cassie looked at David and smiled back. "Thanks," and then, kissing him on the cheek, added, "I think I knew that. Now don't take this the wrong way, will you?"

David groaned. "If I recall, I always land in hot water when you say something like this."

Cassie looked at David. "I'm glad you came over. I really am. You and Pops seemed close, even although you had only known each other a short time but I know he was fond of you, terribly fond. After you left the last time," Cassie blushed slightly at that recollection which David studiously ignored. "I eventually realised that I really thought of you as you had said in your letter, a favourite uncle, something like that. Would it be all right to think of you as that, an uncle type figure?"

David looked at her with, Cassie thought, a slightly strange expression on his face. Misreading it she tried to correct what she'd said, "When I say uncle, I mean young uncle," she laughed, "All right, very young uncle. Is that better?"

David laughed with relief. "Cassie, my dear girl, I will be honoured to be your favourite young uncle. But," he added, "let us always stress the young part!"

Cassie smiled at him. "Oh David, I love you to bits, I really do. I'm so glad we're back to normal, just like we were. And do you know something else? I bet Pops would be as well." She smiled at David. "Yes, I think he'd be thrilled."

"I love you as well, my brand new niece," he said, putting his arm around her shoulder. He looked at her fondly, "And I feel sure you are right, Cassie. Your Dad would be very pleased," David looked out across the lake and smiled ruefully. "Very pleased indeed!"

The next morning David watched from the window as Cassie drove off to work. He wondered what he would do with his day. He decided to make plans once he had been fortified by a 'Mrs. Pearson' breakfast.

On entering the dining room he saw that Lydia was already there. "Good morning, Lydia. Sleep well?" asked David.

"Not bad. Getting better," replied Lydia. "I've stopped taking Peter's pills. I don't think it's a good plan to be dependent upon pills."

David just nodded as he piled bacon, egg and sausages onto his plate. He sat down opposite her.

Lydia looked across at where Charles used to sit. "It's actually this time of day that I am finding the hardest. Charles and I used to plan our day at breakfast, sometimes doing things separately, sometimes together, but we usually knew what each other was up to. I rather miss that," said Lydia wistfully.

"To be honest I don't really know what that's like, I can only imagine," said David. "You wouldn't think so," he smiled. "But I'm not really a breakfast person!"

Lydia returned his smile. "Really!"

David eventually finished his breakfast and declared, "That was truly wonderful. I missed Mrs. Pearson's cooking so much when I left but I guess I'll have to get used to that again! However, I won't think about that at the moment. Lydia, how do you fancy doing something today? If you have plans, just say."

"No, I have nothing pressing," said Lydia. "I'd rather like that. What do you suggest?"

"Well," said David. "I rather fancy a mystery tour. We'll just jump in the car and decide as we go. How does that sound?"

"I'd love that," replied Lydia. "Perhaps we can find some quaint place and have a spot of lunch."

"Of course I'm really needing that," said David patting his midriff. "However, no doubt by lunchtime I'll be famished again! It must be the air here; undoubtedly the air!"

"Grab your things and I'll meet you at the car," said David.

Lydia got into the car and fastened her seatbelt. "I'm looking forward to this. This was a good idea of yours."

"Yes, so am I," smiled David. "Off we go." Looking at her he added, "And not too fast!"

They spent a pleasant couple of hours meandering along the back roads, stopping off at villages here and there.

"Time to look for quaint pub," said David. "I'm beginning to feel hungry."

In no time at all they found a lovely inn beside a river and stopped there. After their lunch they took their coffees out to the garden and sat and watched the ducks on the river. David leant back on the seat and stretched out his legs. "This is the life. I'm glad we did this."

"Me too," replied Lydia.

David looked at her. For the first time since Charles's death she had a little colour. Lydia caught his look. "What are your plans, David? Have you any?"

"Not sure," said David. "When I went back to the States I was so unsettled. I missed you all so much. I suppose I also had one or two things to think about!"

"How have you coped with that?" asked Lydia.

David smiled. "Cassie and I had a chat the other evening. She realises that she thinks of me as a favourite uncle, young uncle, I hasten to add. I apparently had mentioned that could be my role in my initial letter to her, but I'd forgotten."

"And you," said Lydia. "How do you feel about that?"

"Not sure, to be honest. I think relieved. Yes, relieved. In my heart of hearts I know I'm not father material and I promised Charles I would never say anything to her," David looked intently at Lydia. "And I never will."

Lydia nodded. "I know." Lydia watched David as he stared at the river, deep in thought. "Since you've come back, do you find that promise more difficult to keep than you had anticipated?"

David smiled. "Perceptive as ever, aren't you, Lydia?"

Lydia raised an eyebrow and gave a slight smile.

"But no, no I don't think so," replied David. "I will always – oh what's the expression people use – yes, I will always 'be there' for Cassie, should she need me. But the relationship she and Charles had was unique and I would never do anything to spoil that." David smiled at Lydia. "You're a good friend. You know you were quite scary when I first met you."

"I am ashamed of how I behaved," said Lydia, shaking her head at the memory.

"Sorry, I didn't mean to remind you of that. What I'm trying to say is I just cannot imagine not having you as my friend, as my confidant, because you certainly have been that." He turned round and faced her. "I don't want to go back. I am so lonely there, possibly I always had been but I had been so wrapped up in my work that I didn't notice. Until I came here I hadn't realised there was an alternative. But now… I can't face the thought. Pathetic isn't it? A grown man whingeing on like this… What am I going to do?"

Lydia realised that David wasn't really expecting a reply so sat quietly as he continued his monologue. "When I heard that Charles had wanted me on the Board of Harrington I cannot tell you what a thrill I got. Cassie even said I was family now, part of 'The Family' that Charles always talked about. I got such a kick out of that, it means such a lot to me. Sorry, I'm rambling," said David apologetically.

"Don't apologise," said Lydia gently. "We missed you very much. Charles and I both remarked how you fitted into 'The Family' so perfectly. He wished things could have been different, we both did. The phone calls were a highlight for him, he really enjoyed the conversations you two had and he looked forward to them."

"Thank you, Lydia," said David taking her hand. "You're a special lady, you really are… Do you know something? I don't want to leave you either." He laughed. "I'm making a complete and utter idiot of myself. I know I am, but I'd miss you so much."

"You're not making an idiot of yourself and it's very flattering," smiled Lydia. "Why don't you have a look around the area at Harrington and see if there was anywhere that took your fancy. Go back home, away from us all here and have a long hard think."

David nodded, thinking about what Lydia was saying. "Its food for thought, it really is. Come on, I've bored you enough. Let's head back and Lydia…" Lydia looked round. "Thanks."

~~~~~

Pierre looked up when he heard the door. "Cassie!" he exclaimed. "I really didn't expect you in today." He went over and gave her a hug. "How are you?"

"Okay I suppose, not sure to be honest. I think I'm still expecting to wake up and find this has been some awful nightmare. Unfortunately as each day goes by I realise it's not, and this is for real," replied Cassie.

Taking off her jacket she asked, "Shall I make some coffee?"

251

"Mmm that would be nice," replied Pierre. "I'm not quite organised as yet."

They sat with their coffees as Pierre went through the mail. Cassie looked at him. He was such a kind man. She was glad Pops had wanted him on the Board.

"Pierre?" asked Cassie. "What do you feel about being on the Board of Harrington Estate? I hope Pops didn't pressurise you or anything."

Pierre looked at her. "Your father would never pressurise anyone."

Cassie nodded. "You're absolutely right but how do you feel?" she persisted.

"I was taken aback when Mr. Napier told me," replied Pierre. "But I am honoured, yes, that is how I feel, honoured and I will do my best to serve the Board well."

"Pops liked you Pierre, he liked you very much," said Cassie. "I'm glad you're 'one of us' so to speak."

"That's a lovely thing to say Cassie, thank you," said Pierre. He looked at her wondering if this would be a suitable time to give her the painting that Charles had bought. He had left it out in his flat that morning in case she came to work. He decided to take the plunge. His instructions from Charles had been to give the painting after the funeral and he was sure Charles had not meant immediately thereafter. Today would be as good, or indeed as difficult a day, as any.

"Cassie!" said Pierre.

"Mmm," said Cassie absentmindedly, as she glanced at a new catalogue that had arrived in the morning's mail.

Pierre tried once again. "Cassie. I need to tell you something."

"Sorry," she replied. "I'm all ears!" Pierre was looking at her decidedly strangely. She wondered what was wrong.

"Here are the keys to my flat," said Pierre. "Go upstairs and in the sitting room is a parcel for you."

"Who is it from?" asked Cassie.

"All will be revealed," said Pierre mysteriously. "But open it upstairs."

"Okay," said Cassie wondering what on earth this could be.

She opened the door to Pierre's flat and walked into the sitting room. Standing against a table was a large parcel, wrapped in the gallery's wrapping paper. *Curious*, she thought as she bent down to inspect the parcel. She laid the parcel on the floor. It had to be a picture; that much she had decided. She carefully undid the tape and opened the wrapping.

She gasped, for instantly she knew who it was from, and what it was, but all she could do was stare in disbelief. She then buried her head in her hands and the pent up emotions erupted as grief overwhelmed her and the anguish of the last few weeks, that she had so valiantly struggled to control, finally dissolved as her tortured sobs wracked her body. "Oh Pops! I miss you. I miss you so much, so very, very much. Why did you have to die?" She rocked back and forth in distress till eventually her uncontrollable weeping subsided. She got up off the floor and went through to Pierre's bathroom and splashed cold water onto her face until it felt numb. She hoped her mind would as well! Drying her face she went back into the room and stared at the picture again.

It's glorious, she thought. "Oh Pops, you wonderful, wonderful man," she said out loud. "You could not have given me any picture that I could love more, you really couldn't." She smiled, for she suddenly realised he had obviously had help in this. "Thank you, Pierre," she also said.

She picked up the picture and, taking one off Pierre's wall, she replaced it with the McCormick. She stood back to view it properly, "I adore it. I positively adore it, thank you Pops, thank you, thank you, thank you."

She then noticed the envelope lying on the floor. She didn't know if she was strong enough for this. *I have to be*, she thought, and opened the envelope.

My dearest Cassie,

If you are reading this it means I am no longer here in body, but who knows, I may perhaps be here in spirit! I might even be watching over you – not all the time, I promise!! (My idea of a joke!).

I hope you like the painting. I wanted you to have something that I knew you'd love, (Pierre assures me you do) so this is a thank you for making my life so truly and utterly wonderful.

From the first moment I held you in my arms, I knew I was the luckiest man alive. I have been blessed to have had a daughter like you. I have enjoyed every aspect of your growing-up – well perhaps the teenage years were a little bit alien to me!

253

Cassie wiped away a tear and laughed, remembering the ructions she had caused on many occasions. She continued the letter:

> *But we survived them and I would not have missed them for the world. You have been a constant joy to me and this painting is my way of saying thank you for all the happy moments; all the happy years.*
>
> *I have so many treasured memories of our time together — too many to mention — but I have been filled with pride at your achievements, not only as an artist but, far more importantly, as a person. You are a very special lady whom your mother would have been as proud of as I am. In some ways you are like her, and my only regret for my own life is that she was not there to share with me the joy of watching you grow up.*
>
> *I shall close now but before I do, I wish you success in your art — you have a God-given talent (I think I said that before on one memorable evening) that you use to remarkable effect. Above all though, I wish you happiness, or at least an ability to achieve moments of happiness in whatever you do and with whomever you may share it. Lastly and more importantly, I hope you will have contentment that will sustain you throughout your life; a life which I hope is a healthy and fulfilling one.*
>
> *All my love for ever,*
> *Pops! xxx*

Through her tears Cassie noticed that there was a P.T.O. She turned the page and read:

> *P.S. I bought little thank you presents for 'The Family' which I hope they will all like. Cassie, our life has been enhanced by those who shared it with us so I do hope I was able to convey this sentiment in my presents to them, but please, you reiterate that for me. The presents are in a box at the back of the cupboard in my bedroom with a travelling rug covering it!*
>
> *Love,*
> *Pops! xxx*

Cassie felt exhausted and emotionally spent, but decided that perhaps she had needed that release for she felt better, well, a little bit better. She was intrigued to know what presents everyone was to receive. All she knew was the 'The Family' would be overwhelmed by this gesture.

She looked at the clock and realised she had been upstairs for nearly two hours. She folded up the letter; a letter she suspected would be read and re-read hundreds of times and put it in her pocket.

She put the wrapping back on the picture and took it downstairs. She hoped there would be no customers for she knew she looked awful.

Pierre heard her come in and went through. She put the picture down and went over to him. "Thank you, thank you for helping Pops."

Pierre held her close. "He was thrilled to have found something. He wanted it to be so special for you."

Cassie felt tears prick her eyes again. "It is, it is special. He could not have chosen anything I would have liked better."

She kissed Pierre on the cheek. "Let me go and tidy up, I look a wreck."

"No Cassie, you go home. You've had more than enough to cope with today. I'll see you whenever, off you go," said Pierre kindly.

"Thank you," said Cassie. "I think I'll take you up on that kind offer. I'll be in tomorrow."

"Here," said Pierre. "Let me give you a hand." Together they manoeuvred the picture into the car. "Bye, and drive carefully."

With a wave Cassie accelerated down the road but Pierre noted, with considerable more care than normal, with such precious cargo on board.

When Cassie arrived back home she found Sputnik there. "Hello, what are you doing here?"

"Popped by on the off chance, I didn't think you'd be at work. I was going to treat you to lunch," he replied. He looked at her with tenderness in his eyes. "Are you okay? You look a bit whacked. Anything I can do?"

"I am. Absolutely pooped if truth be known. It's been quite a morning. Let me tell you about it inside but first, can you help me with this please?" indicating the painting.

With ease, James lifted it from the car and took it into the house. "Where do you want it?"

"Can you bring it in here first; I'm using the study quite a bit, going through things of Pops and I'd like it beside me," said Cassie.

She looked at Sputnik. "Do you know, when I saw you just now my first thought was oh, there's James. Not, oh there's Sputnik. I'm into the way of James now. I'm quite pleased."

"I'm so pleased you're so pleased and, I confess, a little relieved," smiled James.

"I know I look a wreck but, and as if you didn't know, I've been having a crying stint."

James looked at her with concern. "You don't have to say anything. Have a lie down, anything you like. I just came over to see how you were."

"No, I want to tell you," said Cassie. She then proceeded to tell him about the morning, the picture and the letter. "And this is the picture. Are you ready for this?" She undid the wrapping and watched his reaction.

"Wow, Good God! What a man. Your Dad was quite something, he really was. You lucky thing," he said, smiling at her. "I love McCormick's work," said James, totally enthralled by what he was seeing. "I noticed you have a painting of his uncle's. In the drawing room, isn't it?"

"How observant," replied Cassie. They both stood in silence admiring the painting.

"I can't believe it myself. I look at it and can't believe it belongs to me. I had practically drooled over it at the gallery and when Pops had asked Pierre if there was anything he knew I liked, Pierre told him about this. I came back from a trip to London, a course or something, and popped into the gallery to find it gone. I absolutely threw a wobbly, thinking some swine had bought it. Pierre said it was an Arab Sheik which for Pierre was quite an inspirational story," smiled Cassie.

She looked at James. "I'm so pleased you were here when I arrived. You know how much this means to me, the others might not. Well David will and Kate, but none of the others. Thanks for being here. I think I might have found it difficult coming back with no one to share it with."

"I'm glad," smiled James. "How about some lunch? Do you fancy popping out, even for a sandwich if you aren't hungry?"

"Actually," smiled Cassie. "I'm famished, simply ravenous. Let me sort out this mess of a face and look more presentable. I'll try not to take too long," she said, as she ran out and up the stairs two at a time.

"You don't look a mess to me, you look gorgeous," said James quietly to himself.

Chapter 23

Cassie put down her cutlery and smiled across at James. "You would think I hadn't seen food in ages. That was yummy, really good. I don't think I've really tasted anything for a while which is why that was such a treat. Thanks, it was just what the doctor ordered."

"My pleasure," responded James, "It's really lovely seeing you again, although I'm sorry it is under these circumstances." Cassie nodded. "I can't think why we lost touch, so let's not again," said James. "Agreed?"

"Agreed," said Cassie. Now my next task is to find the box that Pops hid in his cupboard. I can't imagine what he's bought." Cassie stood up and pulled on her jacket. "However, I guess I'm about to find out." She looked at James and hesitated.

"What?" asked James.

Cassie looked at him with surprise. "What do you mean, what? How on earth did you know I was going to ask anything?"

James grinned. "Possibly the clue was your mouth opening and closing like some demented fish!"

"Highly amusing," smiled Cassie.

"Well," said Cassie. "What I was going to ask was, would you mind, and please, just say, in fact don't hesitate to say, if you did…"

James stood up and leaning against the wall gave an exaggerated yawn. "In your own time Cassie, preferably sometime before Bonfire Night!"

"Ouch," said James rubbing his arm where he had just been whacked. "That was actually quite sore, you've probably ruined my chances of becoming a world famous sculptor for ever."

Ignoring him Cassie continued. "What I am trying to say is…" James rolled his eyes. "I don't want to intrude on your time but would you come back to the house and help me with the box. Would you mind doing that?" she eventually asked.

"Of course, you dope! I'm happy to do that, I'm free all day," replied James and taking her hand they walked back to the car.

Cassie cast a surreptitious glance at James as they drove along. She decided he was rather handsome. She hadn't noticed before when he'd had long hair as it usually had been all over the place, although when he worked he had tied it back in an elastic band and let it trail down his back. Now, his well-cut hair emphasised his finely chiselled features and his attire was smart casual instead of the downright scruffy and unwashed look. She smiled to herself, much better, much much better.

They arrived back at The Hall to find that Lydia and David were still off gallivanting somewhere. *Jolly good*, thought Cassie. "That's exactly what Aunt Lydia needs just now."

Cassie went to the kitchen to find Mrs. Pearson preparing a salmon. "Hello, I'm back," said Cassie. "That looks good. Is it for tonight?"

"Yes," replied Mrs. Pearson. "Is your young man staying for dinner?" Cassie blushed at hearing James referred to as 'her young man'. Mrs. Pearson looked at her fondly. "Well, is he?"

"I hadn't actually thought," said Cassie, stammering a little. "But yes, I'll ask. I'll go and ask right now."

James was delighted to accept the invitation. Cassie went back to report to Mrs. Pearson. "Yes, James would be delighted to stay for dinner and thanks you for asking."

"I didn't ask him to stay, it's not my place," retorted Mrs. Pearson. "I just wanted to know how many for dinner." Cassie was getting decidedly flustered, much to Mrs. Pearson's amusement.

"Well he is, so its one extra," said Cassie aware that Mrs. Pearson seemed to be taking some pleasure at her discomfort.

Mrs. Pearson smiled at her. "He seems a very nice young man, very nice indeed."

Cassie grinned at her. "Stop pretending you haven't a clue who he is. He's Sputnik. You met him at the Graduation Lunch. You remember, I know you do, so don't go assuming things. He's a friend; a friend from art school that's all. Okay?"

"If you say so," replied Mrs. Pearson. "He's changed though hasn't he? Quite a lot if you ask me. I didn't recognise him at all. Handsome mind, very handsome. Nice clean cut boy now."

"Have you quite finished?" asked Cassie. Mrs. P. nodded and smiled.

Cassie remembered the box. "Let's all have dinner together, shall we? But only," she added. "If you promise to behave. No teasing him!"

"I'll set the table for us all. Do you want to check with your aunt first?" enquired Mrs. Pearson.

"No, that's all right, I think she'll agree," said Cassie. She put her arm around Mrs. P. and kissed her fondly. "You are the limit, you really are. See you later."

Mrs. Pearson watched Cassie go and, looking at the kitchen clock, decided she'd have time to make an extra special pudding for that evening!

Cassie walked into her father's room. She had been in and out lots of times but out of habit she still glanced over at the bed, wishing he was there, just waking up after having had a nap. Nonsense thoughts invade ones mind, she decided.

"It will be in this cupboard I should think," said Cassie, opening the door. She looked around and right at the back with a jumble of things on top she spied the corner of a rug. James helped her haul the box into the bedroom.

"Gosh it's quite heavy," he said straightening up. "I'm surprised he managed to carry it up here."

Cassie bent down and opened it up. On the top was a piece of paper with the names of Charlie, Robert, Peter and Benson, and beside their names Charles had written instructions with which gun or fishing tackle they were to get.

"Your father was a meticulous man," said James.

"Yes he was," said Cassie. "Look, there is a parcel for each of the others." Cassie took them out and laid them beside her.

Charlie, Kate and Robert and their other children, Mrs. Pearson, Benson, Pierre, Margaret, Lydia and David. Her father had forgotten no one.

Cassie looked anxiously at James. "How will I do this? I should ask Aunt Lydia, shouldn't I?"

"No," said James quietly. "Your father put you in charge. You're the boss now. It's up to you."

"You're right," said Cassie. "I have a feeling that one or two of them may react as I did this morning. They all loved Pops to…?" Cassie faltered and looked at James. "Sorry, I'm not very good at this, am I?"

"I think you're doing just fine," said James. "Come on, you were saying?"

Cassie looked him straight in the eye. "They all loved Pops to bits and have tried to be so brave, especially in front of me. I think that when they get their present they may wish to open it in private. That's what I was thinking."

James smiled. "Well done. See... you can do it."

"Next decision," said Cassie. "Presents before or after dinner. What do you think?"

"What do *you* think?" asked James.

"I think we should have an early dinner!" replied Cassie. "Oh, I don't know." She thought for a moment or two then decided. "How about I take over Kate and Robert's things and the others I'll distribute after dinner?"

"Good idea," smiled James.

"I'll go and collect the things for Charlie plus his parcel," she said as she retrieved it from the pile. "We'll pop the others in another box and take them over."

"You go on your own, Cassie. I'll wait here. I will be more than happy to have a wander round and look at the paintings. Or I could of course go to the kitchen and chat up my friend Mrs. Pearson," grinned James.

"Hmmm, whatever. Have fun. I won't be long," said Cassie.

Cassie arrived at Kate's to find only Emily at home. "Hello there, where is everyone?"

"Hello Cassie," replied Emily. "Mum's nipped to the village to take Hattie and Ben to the dentist, Dad's at work and Charlie is somewhere around... unfortunately."

Cassie smiled, "Little brother being a pain?"

"As always," groaned Emily. "You are *so* lucky being an only one, you really are."

"There are fors and against both. Sometimes I'd have liked someone to play with," said Cassie.

"Not him you wouldn't..." muttered Emily. "He's gross!"

"Right," said Cassie, thinking it was time to change the subject. "I have some presents here which Pops left for you all. I have no idea what they are but everyone has something," and she handed Emily her parcel.

"But Uncle Charles has already left us all money," said Emily. "Mum said we get it when we are twenty-one. Why are we getting something else?"

"I think this is something personal; something Pops chose himself, I don't know. I didn't know about this until today," said Cassie.

Emily looked at Cassie. "I thought he was great – I'm going to miss him."

Tears welled momentarily in Cassie's eyes which she quickly brushed away. "I thought he was great as well, and so am I."

Emily looked at her. "Will I open it now?"

"If you want," said Cassie. "I'll go if you'd like to be on your own."

"No, please stay, I want you to see what it is," said Emily as she carefully opened the wrapping.

"Look Cassie, look what he has bought me," said Emily, obviously thrilled. In the box was a Doulton figure. A lady with dark hair in a sapphire blue regency style gown.

Emily smiled. "I've always loved these, always, and Uncle Charles promised he'd buy me one for my eighteenth birthday." Her eyes filled with tears.

Cassie looked at the box. "Have a look at the name of the figure."

Emily carefully turned the figure upside down. "Oh Cassie, it's got my name, its called Emily." She said through her tears. "I so wish he wasn't dead, I really do."

Cassie went over and gently took the figurine from her, placing it out of harms way on the mantle-piece, and then hugged her.

"There's a card in the box," said Emily, wiping her eyes. She picked it up. "It's from Uncle Charles. Will I read it?" Cassie nodded. "It says: *As promised – your eighteenth birthday present. Sorry I can't be there and that your present is a little early! Lots of Love, Uncle Charles.* Emily stared at the card. "Oh Cassie, wasn't that lovely, imagine it, he remembered."

Cassie smiled and swallowed. "Yes, lovely," she agreed.

"What's lovely?" asked a voice from the door.

"Look Charlie, isn't it lovely? I got it from Uncle Charles," said Emily.

"Yeah, that's good, really nice," agreed Charlie.

"You actually like the figure?" asked Emily with surprise.

Charlie glared at his sister. "Of course I don't like the poxy figure thing. It's horrible, but its kind of Uncle Charles giving you something, that's what I meant, stupid!"

"It's you that's the stupid one," retorted Emily, "You're just..."

Cassie quickly interjected. "Come on you two, no fighting. There are presents for all of you." She looked in the box and brought out the parcel for Charlie and handed it to him. He just looked at it.

"Aren't you going to open it?" asked Emily.

"Not in front of you I'm not," growled Charlie as he turned to leave.

"Hold on a minute," said Cassie. "There's something else – it's Pops fishing tackle. Salmon tackle, his Hardy's."

Charlie just looked at Cassie wide-eyed at what she had just said. "That was his best, wasn't it?" asked Cassie. Charlie could only nod. Cassie knew he was struggling to keep his composure, especially in front of his sister. "Emily, look after these things while I get the stuff from the car for Charlie," said Cassie casually. "Come on Charlie." Charlie obediently followed, clutching his parcel, relieved to escape.

Cassie opened the hatchback. "Can you manoeuvre the rod and things out?" Charlie nodded and, handing Cassie his parcel, gently took them out.

"I can't believe he's given this to me. I was never allowed to use it before. He always said, 'one day, when you're older, when you can look after it', and I've got it now. He's given it to me now." His eyes filled with tears that, no matter how hard he tried, he couldn't blink away. He looked at Cassie smiling apologetically. "Sorry," he sniffed. "Thanks for getting me away from her," indicating to Emily who had been left in the kitchen."

Cassie felt so sorry for Charlie for he was the one who was closest to Charles. She tried to cheer him up. "I know how you're feeling. I cried solidly for two hours today. I bet you can't beat that!" she grinned.

Charlie smiled. He thought Cassie was great. Considering she was a girl and a grown-up she was great, really great. He wiped his eyes. "You're nuts sometimes!" He looked at the tackle. "Thank you for all this."

"It's nothing to do with me. I only found out today about the presents for everyone," said Cassie. "Pops obviously thought you were old enough now and there is no one else he would have wanted to give them to."

"What about you?" asked Charlie thoughtfully. "He was your Dad."

Cassie was touched by this kind thought and smiled at him. "Do you remember I once went fishing with you and Pops. I hated it; seeing the hook in its mouth and then I cried at how cruel you two were as you yanked it out the water and bashed it over the head. It was awful. You both just laughed and told me I could never go fishing with you two again. I wouldn't have anyway."

Charlie smiled as he recalled that day. "If you're sure?"

"Quite sure," smiled Cassie. "Come on, I'll help you put this away."

Once the tackle was sorted out they made their way back to the kitchen. "Do you know what's in the parcel, Cassie?" asked Charlie a little apprehensively.

"No idea." Cassie looked at him fondly. "Take a tip from me though; open it on your own." Charlie nodded – he thought that seemed an excellent idea.

Emily was still gazing adoringly at her figurine when Cassie and Charlie returned. She looked at her brother. "You've been crying? Cry baby!" she taunted

Charlie blushed slightly. "No I haven't… You have though, cry baby yourself."

"Actually," said Cassie quickly. "It was my fault. I managed to poke Charlie in the eye with the fishing rod." Charlie looked at Cassie, filled with admiration at the way lies, or he supposed they'd be called white lies, popped out of her mouth with no trouble at all. Cassie continued. "So of course his eyes just watered and watered and watered. Are they slightly better now?" asked Cassie, feigning concern.

"Not bad," said Charlie, screwing up one eye for effect. "This one, this one is worse but its getting better. Please don't worry."

"I'll try not to," replied Cassie sarcastically. "I'm much relieved to hear you're improving. Right, you two. Can I leave you on your own without killing each other?"

Charlie was still clutching his parcel. "I'm going out so I don't have to stay with HER!" he said, glaring at Emily.

"Whatever," sighed Cassie. "Emily, can you tell Mum I'll speak to her later?"

"Sure," replied Emily. "Cassie, thank you, thank you for bringing my present. I love it."

"I'm delighted you like it and so would Pops. He made a good choice that's for sure. See you later."

Charlie was waiting for her. "Thanks for the lie and I won't tell."

Cassie just shook her head, got into the car and, smiling at Charlie, drove off.

Charlie headed for his den. It was private and he was pretty sure no one knew about it. Only one person had been allowed there – Uncle Charles.

Looking round to make sure no one had followed him, Charlie went into the den. It was quite a cosy place because Uncle Charles, who initially hadn't been that keen to sit in the damp and grotty den, had brought things from The Hall to make it more habitable; a ground sheet, rug, cushions and things. Charlie loved it. He sat down and opened up his parcel. Inside were three separately wrapped presents. He opened the first one – it was a book on fishing. Charlie smiled, *Excellent*, he thought. This had been a book that Uncle Charles had called his 'Fishing Bible'. No fisherman should be without it. Charlie fingered it proudly. He couldn't believe it was his now. It would get damp in the den so he'd take it home and keep it safe. He laid it on the paper and opened the next parcel. Inside was a box with fishing flies. Some of them Charlie recognised as being the very best. He felt so lucky and so incredibly proud so have them.

He looked out of the den up towards the sky. "I'll take care of them, Uncle Charles. I promise," he shouted.

He went back in and opened the final present. This was weird he thought, for the parcel contained a padded envelope. He opened it and inside was a letter and his penknife. He'd forgotten about the knife. He looked at it and picking it up, flung it across the den. "You were meant to be lucky," he shouted angrily. "You were my lucky penknife and you haven't been; you haven't been lucky at all. I gave you to Uncle Charles to help him… and you didn't."

He got up and went outside and kicked the tree beside the entrance. He looked up at the sky again and with fury shouted, "Why did you die?" He stomped around, lashing out at anything in his path – branches, flowers, trees, leaves, anything within his radius. "I hate you! Do you hear me, Uncle Charles? I hate you for being dead. Why did you have to die?" Charlie asked, marching around and completely focused on venting his anger.

But his anger subsided as quickly as it had risen. "You were my best friend," he said quietly. "And it's not fair! It's just not fair!"

He lay face down on the grass, exhaustion taking over, and cried at the injustice of it all, trying to make sense of all that had happened. After a while he rolled over onto his back and looked up through the branches of the tree to the sky.

"Uncle Charles, I'm sorry, I don't hate you; you know that. I could never hate you. I love you and I miss you, really, really miss you."

Eventually Charlie got up and wiped his eyes and then his nose on his sleeve. He never had a handkerchief. Uncle Charles had always given him a row about that and then usually gave him his, which Charlie invariably lost. He smiled for the first time that afternoon. Cassie was right; there were plenty of good memories. He'd remember them; he'd remember them all.

He went back into the den, picked up his penknife and thrust it deeply into his pocket. It hadn't been entirely forgiven yet! He then saw the letter lying next to his book and picked it up and started to read:

> *My dear Charlie,*
>
> *I bet you thought I'd forget about your knife – Ha, didn't!*
> Charlie grinned and continued reading. *You are probably thinking it was 'a fat lot of use' – well you'd be wrong because it was and I'll tell you why. Having the treatments enabled me to live for possibly an extra six months or so which was great. But the downside was they sometimes made me feel sick and generally yuchy. When I felt cheesed off about all that, I'd get out your knife (which I always kept on me) and tried to fathom out what all the bits and pieces were for – still don't know! This would take my mind off what the docs were doing and then I'd think, 'Hey, I feel better now.' So it was lucky, because it helped me get through the treatments – it was like*

you were sending little thought waves, saying 'Hi, I'm thinking about you'.

I'm sorry I couldn't get better, it was no one's fault; sometimes these things just happen.

I hope you like the rod and remember to catch a whopper for me! I'll be really envious if you beat the fifteen pounder we once caught!

Lastly, thank you for all the good times we had, all the fun and Charlie, if I had ever had a son, I would have wanted him to be exactly like you (even the bit where you never had a hanky!!) Although tears were near the surface, Charlie laughed and continued reading. *You're the best. Thank you for your friendship – I couldn't have wished for a better or more special friend.*

Lots of Love,
Uncle Charles xxx

Charlie wiped his eyes. He'd keep his letter forever and so folded it carefully and put it inside his new book. He looked at his watch; he'd be in trouble. He was half an hour late for his tea. He gathered up his things and hurriedly headed home.

"Hello, we're home," shouted Kate. "Emily, Charlie, where are you?" A shout of "Hi" followed by the sound of an elephant charging down the stairs indicated that Emily had been in her room!

"Guess what," said an excited Emily. "Cassie came over this afternoon and brought us presents from Uncle Charles.

"Really!" replied a surprised Kate.

"Come and see what I've got," said Emily, excitedly hauling at Kate.

Kate duly followed. "I put it here in the display cabinet so it wouldn't get damaged by any grotty brothers or sister," said Emily, looking pointedly at Hattie and Ben.

"Yes, quite," said Kate taking it down from the shelf. "How lovely and how very kind. She's gorgeous."

"And that's not all," said Emily. "Look underneath, look at her name."

Kate turned it over and smiled at her daughter. "Typical Uncle Charles."

"And you've got something, we've all got something, even Ben and Hattie," continued Emily.

Hattie, upon hearing her name, "What have I got? I want to open mine now. I want a doll like yours," said Emily."

"I don't know what you've got and anyway, it's not a doll, idiot. You can't play with it," said Emily. "Come on," she said, taking her sister by the hand. "Let's have a look."

"My box now, please…" begged Hattie.

"Over on the table," said Kate. "It may be a figure like Emily's so be very, very careful."

Hattie gently opened her parcel. Kate was right. Charles had given Hattie a figure and she was delighted, thrilled to be the same as her sister. "It's gorgeous," she exclaimed.

"Look at its bottom," said Emily.

Hattie looked surprised but did as she was told. "It says my proper name, it says Harriet," she beamed. "I want to put it beside yours Emily. Can I?"

"Of course, I'll help," said Emily and off the girls went to the display cabinet.

Kate looked in the box. Her heart quickened when she saw a parcel for her. "Oh Charles, you've been so kind already. I don't know if I can cope with any more surprises." She then saw one for Robert and one for Ben.

"Come on Ben. Uncle Charles has something for you as well." She opened his parcel and in it was a toy tractor. Ben's eyes lit up. He knew exactly what to do with that and happily toddled off to play. There was a smaller box as well with a note attached from Charles. *Ben, these are for when you are older. Hopefully the fashion will not have changed too much by then, Lots of Love, Uncle Charles.* Kate opened it, inside were gold cufflinks with Ben's initials inscribed in italics. Kate smiled. *What a kind, lovely man.* She fingered her parcel but couldn't open it… not yet.

"Emily, where's Charlie?" ask Kate.

"Gone off – don't know where, but clutching his parcel from Uncle Charles. He also got a fishing rod which he seemed really excited about, in fact he nearly cried when he saw it," said Emily, delighted to impart this information.

"I hope you didn't tease him then," said Kate.

"No, of course not," said Emily with wide-eyed innocence. "I was just telling you, that's all."

Kate had just finished preparing the meal when Robert came home. "Good timing," said Kate. How's your day been?"

"Good. What about you? School holidays are always such a delight!" he grinned.

Kate proceeded to tell them about the trip to the dentist and then, before she had time to tell him about the presents, the girls hurtled into the room both trying to speak to him at once.

"One at a time," begged Robert. Emily spoke, glaring at Hattie not to interrupt, and told her father about the presents.

"Wasn't that kind of Uncle Charles," said Robert. "These are something to treasure for ever and with your names on them as well,"

"We're very lucky children," announced Hattie.

"Indeed you are," smiled Robert, wondering where he'd heard that saying before!

"There's a present for you as well," said Emily. "And for Mummy, but she hasn't opened hers yet."

Robert looked taken aback. "That was kind of Uncle Charles." He looked over at Kate whom he suspected was finding this a bit difficult. "Okay, why don't we have our meal first and then I'll open my present. I think that's a good idea."

"Come on everyone, hands washed," said Kate.

Robert put his arms around Kate and held her close. "How are you doing? Coping?"

"Only just," she replied. "Charlie is off somewhere; he got a parcel plus fishing tackle. Emily can't remember what it's called but said it was definitely special and Charlie was a little emotional about it."

"Poor chap," said Robert. "He really misses him. He was the son Charles never had…" Giving Kate a final hug he said, "Come on, let's eat, we won't wait for him, he'll be back in his own time."

Just as they were finishing their meal Charlie arrived back full of apologies and was somewhat surprised that his parents were totally understanding and told him not to worry, his meal was cold, so there was no problem.

"What did you get? Let me see what you got from Uncle Charles," demanded Hattie.

Charlie mumbled. "Later."

"Let him have his meal first," said Robert, trying to give Charlie some breathing space. "I'll open mine now."

There was a parcel and an envelope, Robert opened the envelope first. Charles had written:

> *Please accept the Browning Rifle as a token of my sincere thanks, firstly for your friendship and secondly for all your hard work on the estate. The success of the estate is entirely due to your efforts and I hope you and Cassie will have as fruitful a partnership as we had.*
>
> *With fondest regards,*
> *Charles*
>
> *P.S. I admit now, you were always the better shot! Enjoy!*
> *P.P.S. Remember to help yourself to any of the others if either Charlie or Ben wish to learn to shoot. The rest of the guns are for you, Benson and Peter: help yourselves!*
> *P.P.P.S. Hope you like the book – it was one of my favourites.'*

"Daddy, are you all right?" asked Emily. "You look strange."

"What?" replied Robert, "No I'm fine, really okay. It's just Uncle Charles has given me a truly magnificent present and I'm stunned." He looked at Kate. "He's been so generous to us already. It's hard to take it all in."

"I know," smiled Kate.

"Your turn now, Mummy," said Hattie excitedly.

Charlie quickly interjected. "Mum, I forgot to tell you. I'm sorry but Cassie wants you to go over as soon as possible. I forgot. She'd want you to go over right now." He emphasised the 'right now'.

Kate looked at him with surprise and then he winked at her, indicating her parcel. Robert caught the look between them and understood.

"You'd better dash then and not keep Cassie waiting," said Robert, practically manhandling her out of the door.

"Aww," said Hattie disappointedly. "That's not fair."

"I'll show you my presents if you like," said Charlie quickly. "But you must not touch, definitely not touch, promise?"

The girls both nodded but when they saw the presents they were very disappointed; typical boy things, and decided theirs were much better.

Kate walked to one of her favourite haunts which she had so often shared with Charles; the lakeside.

She sat down on the bench and looked out over the lake. She was so grateful to her son for allowing her to escape. Somehow he had instinctively known she would wish to be alone for this. She fingered the parcel again. It was lovely to have some peace and quiet, for this was the first time since Charles's death that she had time on her own.

She thought back to their last day; the day of the Fayre. She remembered how tightly he had held her hand and how his good-bye had been said with such a quiet intensity. It was as if he knew this would be their final parting. "Did you know?" she asked out loud.

She started to open the parcel. It was a box from Cavanagh Jewellers – even the box looked expensive. She felt a tightness grip her throat and her mouth go dry. There was card on top of the box. She opened it and started to read.

> *My dear Kate,*
>
> *I hope you will like the enclosed, for your present has been the most difficult for me to choose. Difficult, because it was impossible for me to find anything that would in any way adequately convey to you what our friendship has meant to me, for it has meant everything.*
>
> *I therefore hit on the idea of designing something myself – you and Cassie are not the only arty ones in the family you know!! And when you see it, I hope you will agree. I have incorporated your favourite flowers in the design which I thought was a rather novel touch and which hopefully you'll like. It can be worn as a brooch or as a pendant, hence the enclosed chain.*

Kate had to stop for a moment. Her vision was blurred and she wiped away the tears.

It is designed with all my love and all my thanks to you Kate, a wonderful lady, whom it has been my great fortune to have as my special and trusted friend.
Much love always,
Charles x

Kate opened the box, inside was a circular brooch with pale sapphires on gold stems, with the outer part of the brooch surrounded by diamonds. Kate smiled. Charles had succeeded. Instantly she had recognised 'forget-me-knots' which he had incorporated into the design. There was also a pair of pale sapphire earrings and the chain to complete the present. She sat and stared at the brooch. It was the loveliest brooch she had ever seen.

~~~~~

"That was delicious, Mrs. Pearson," said James. "Thank you very much indeed. I'm sorry I was a bit of a glutton, third helpings were a bit excessive, but that was a magnificent pudding. Fit for a king."

Mrs. Pearson glowed at the compliment. "You're very welcome young man, very welcome indeed. I'll give you a piece to take home with you. You need some flesh on you. You don't eat properly that's for sure."

"Not a feast like this," smiled James. "Thank you again."

Everyone was about to clear up when Cassie stood up. "Excuse me, everyone, excuse me." They all looked at her. Cassie looked at James and he smiled and nodded his encouragement.

"Today has been quite a traumatic day for me and I suspect it may well be a rather poignant day for you as well." She paused. "I'm not making sense, sorry. What I'm trying to say is that today I received a present from Pops that he'd left with Pierre. It's in the study if anyone wishes to see it. I'm thrilled with it – absolutely adore it." She beamed at them. "However, he also left a note for me and in the note he asked if I would distribute presents to each of you."

Everyone looked at each other, surprise registering on each face. "In the note he said I had to try and convey how all of you have enhanced our lives, mine and Pops, by your very presence at

The Hall. I suspect he was meaning my up-bringing which I grant you must have had its moments." They all smiled at Cassie.

"Many moments," smiled Benson. "Which we all loved being part of."

Cassie smiled struggling to continue. "Anyway, he wanted you to know how grateful he was and so the presents are in the library. Whenever you wish, please go through." They all looked at each other.

Trying to lighten the moment she said, "Well, as they say in the cartoons, 'that's all folks'."

"Come on everyone," said Lydia taking charge. "Let's go."

They all followed Lydia, and David came over to help Cassie and James clear the table. "David off you go; we can manage."

"No, its okay, I don't want to intrude."

Cassie looked at him and touched his arm. "Off you go; there's a present for you as well."

David looked at her, "Are you sure? But I..." he didn't complete his sentence. Oh Charles, what are you playing at?

"I think I'll go now if you don't mind," said James. "This should be private with just all of you. I'll give you a call tomorrow to see how you are. Would that be okay?"

"I'd like that," replied Cassie. "Thanks so much for today, for lunch, for listening, for... positively flirting with Mrs. P.," laughed Cassie.

"She's lovely," said James. "You all are." He smiled at Cassie and, kissing her on the cheek, said, "I'll see myself out. Through you go. Night and sleep tight."

"Night... and thanks," replied Cassie.

Cassie went into the library, assuming that everyone would have gone their separate ways, wishing to open the parcels in private, but not a bit of it. It was unexpectedly quiet, each with their own thoughts.

Cassie went over to Mrs. Pearson and put her arm round her. "What did he give you and do you like it?"

Mrs. Pearson nodded. "Look, he's given me pearls, real pearls, not like the things I wear." She looked at Cassie and smiled. "I used to wear. We talked about pearls once. He told me how you could tell real ones, you bite them – and I have – and they are!" She didn't know whether to be upset or thrilled. At the moment it was a

273

combination of both. "I told him that if I ever won money I'd buy myself real pearls. Fancy he remembered, just fancy." That thought was too much for her and tears trickled down her cheeks again.

Cassie wondered what everyone else had been given. Looking around they all seemed in the same state of emotion as Mrs. P.; even her aunt. She decided to leave them their own thoughts and quietly left the library and went outside.

It was a lovely warm summer's evening so Cassie decided to have a stroll. She'd been walking for about half an hour when in the distance she saw Kate, sitting on the bench at the top of the hill overlooking the lake. Cassie went to join her.

Kate, who was deep in thought reading her letter, jumped when suddenly aware of Cassie's presence.

"Sorry," said Cassie. "I didn't mean to give you a fright." She saw that Kate had been crying. "Just tell me to get lost if you want to be on your own."

Kate smiled. "No, please stay," and indicated to her to sit beside her.

Cassie noticed the box from the jewellers and smiled at Kate, "Pops?"

Kate nodded, not trusting herself to speak, as her eyes filled with tears again. Cassie squeezed Kate's hand, smiling with understanding for she knew how Kate was feeling. Kate handed Cassie the box. "Please, open it. They're lovely, so beautiful." Kate wiped her eyes again, "I'm completely overwhelmed by his generosity." She looked at Cassie. "He's been so kind to us already."

"Kate, he wanted to give us all something personal and you were his best friend – of course he wanted it to be special," said Cassie who had yet to open the box.

"No," said Kate. "You were."

Cassie smiled fondly at her friend. Kate, who had always been like her sister, always in control, now looked so vulnerable. "I was his daughter, he always confided in you. Any problems – I'll chat to Kate, that's what Pops always thought," smiled Cassie. "You two had a special relationship, you know that."

Kate nodded. "Mmm," she agreed. "But it worked both ways; he was always there when I needed him."

"We were lucky," decided Cassie. "Having Pops." Kate swallowed and nodded in agreement. "Now," said Cassie. "Before I join you in the 'falling about department', which I may add I have done quite enough of today, I will open your present." Cassie opened it and gasped when she saw the jewellery. She grinned at Kate. "He's been fab. Absolutely surpassed himself. They're lovely." She looked intently at the brooch and then at Kate. "I think I've seen drawings in his desk, similar to this brooch."

Kate nodded, her composure slowly recovering. "He designed it — in his letter he said we weren't the only arty ones in the family!"

Cassie laughed and hugged her friend. "You'll look gorgeous in them. We now need an excuse for you to dress up and do Pops proud."

"Thank you," said Kate. "Now, tell me, your present, I'm dying to know."

"A picture," said Cassie with a mischievous grin.

"I might have guessed," smiled Kate. "Well go on, don't keep me in suspense."

"The McCormick, the one Pierre had," smiled Cassie. "Can you believe it?"

Kate just stared at Cassie, speechless with delight for Cassie, "How wonderful, how utterly wonderful." She sighed. "We've been so lucky, so very lucky."

"Yes," agreed Cassie. "We certainly have."

Kate looked at her watch. "I'd better go back. They'll be wondering where I am."

"I think they'll guess," replied Cassie. "By the way, how's Charlie?"

Kate told Cassie about the presents everyone had been given and Charlie's insight into how Kate may feel upon opening her present and his lie enabling her to leave. Kate grinned at Cassie. "He was very convincing. I felt he must have had a very good teacher!"

"Really!" smiled Cassie.

They hugged again. "Thanks," said Kate. "I'm glad you came along. I was in danger of becoming, as you say, a complete basket case!"

"We'll try not to 'fall about' in tandem!" smiled Cassie. "Bye," and with a wave they both turned and went their separate ways back to their homes.

Chapter 24

"It's the next turning on the left," said Cassie, turning the map forty-five degrees. "No, sorry," she said as she looked behind her. "We've just passed it!"

"Excellent!" said David sarcastically as he looked for a place to stop and turn the car. "Map-reading is not exactly your thing, is it?"

"Not exactly," confessed Cassie. "Sorry!"

Eventually they reached their destination. "Well, what do you think?" asked David.

Cassie looked at him. "It needs quite a bit doing to it, don't you think? Look, there's a huge hole in the roof." She looked at David. "This house isn't for you, is it?"

"Nope, I don't think so but this is the tenth place we've looked at and I go back in three days." David was by now thoroughly despondent.

"Let's go to the pub and have lunch," suggested Cassie. "We can talk over the pros and cons again."

"Good plan," agreed David.

They got their meal and sat down at a table in the corner. "When I spoke to Lydia all this seemed so easy," said David as he had a mouthful of steak pie. "Mmm, this is really good." He continued. "My plan was to sell up and then come over and live happily ever after." He pondered, "I don't think I live in the real world sometimes."

"David, let's have a think. Before you came over last year you were perfectly happy with your lot, weren't you?" David nodded. "What happened?" asked Cassie.

"Good question, what happened," replied David. "Everything was fine I suppose, but then I didn't know what I'd been missing. That's what happened. I realised that all the years I had been in the States I had led a busy and, dare I say, successful life; knew loads of people, always on the go, but I didn't have anyone I could really talk to, no good friends. Oh, I had friends I'd play tennis with or have meals with, that sort of thing but it was all terribly superficial. I started thinking, you know the usual one, 'if I had a problem or some crisis at three in the morning who would I ask for help' – I couldn't think of anyone… that was a bit scary! I had never noticed that until I came here and met you all. In such a short space of time I felt closer to you and the others than to anyone else in my life and it was a rather nice feeling." He looked at Cassie. "You think I'm being pathetic, don't you?"

Cassie smiled gently at him. "No, I don't think you're being pathetic. "Tell me honestly, Cassie. Would you rather I'd stayed in the States?" asked David anxiously.

"No, heavens no," replied Cassie aghast that David should feel that. "Absolutely not, I love having you around. You know that, we all do. You've always fitted in so perfectly – it's as if you have always been around. No, please don't think that. But I don't want you regretting packing up lock, stock and barrel and coming over to a place you haven't stayed in for over twenty odd years."

"I'll go back and have another think. I'll give myself another month or so," agreed David. "But I'm pretty convinced its time to come home, so to speak."

"Okay," said Cassie. "And while you're back in the States we'll keep an eye out for something suitable, maybe even something wonderful, and you'll get a phone call saying 'get over here pronto'."

"Sounds good to me," said David.

"James is quite knowledgeable about buildings and technical aspects of that sort of thing so I'll inveigle him as well," smiled Cassie.

"You two seem to becoming quite close," said David with a twinkle in his eye.

Cassie blushed slightly, and said, "He's rather nice. I'm glad he got back in touch." She bent her head as if concentrating on her meal.

"Mmm," smiled David. Cassie looked up and twinkled back at him.

~~~~~

"I'm going to miss you so much," smiled David, eventually releasing Mrs. Pearson from a hug. "And thank you so much for the goodies which I'll hopefully smuggle in with no trouble. If they discover them I won't get on the plane until I've demolished the lot."

"You take care," replied Mrs. Pearson. "And remember now, I don't want you all skin and bones when I see you next time."

"I'll try not to be," smiled David. "But you are an impossible act to follow!" He turned and gave Margaret a hug and shook hands with Benson.

Waiting in the drive were Lydia, Kate and Charlie. "Sorry I was such a prat when you took me fishing," said David to Charlie. "Were you able to fix the line I got caught in the branches?"

Charlie smiled at him. "Yes, no problem. We can try again the next time you're here if you like."

"Are you sure?" Charlie nodded. "Thanks, I'd like that," smiled David as they shook hands.

"Thanks for coming to see me off," said David to Kate, kissing her on the cheek.

David then went over to Lydia and wrapped his arms around her. "Thanks, thanks for everything," he said quietly. He looked at her with tenderness in his eyes.

"And to you, for your support, for being here," she replied quietly. Their eyes met, both understanding what each was trying to convey. "I hate goodbyes," he whispered.

She nodded. "So do I."

Cassie waited at the car, looking at her aunt and David, realising they were finding this parting difficult. A special closeness had seemed to develop between them and Cassie although surprised, was also rather pleased.

"Come on David, we'd better be going. We don't want to be late," said Cassie. "I may have to break the speed limit if you don't get a move on!"

David gave Lydia one last kiss and, with a wave, got into the car where he turned and gave them all a look of pretend horror as Cassie started the car and hurtled him up the drive.

Within an hour they were nearly at the airport. "I'll just jump out when we get to the entrance," said David.

Cassie, who was concentrating on her driving didn't look at him, "Are you sure?"

"Yes, let's do it that way," replied David.

Nearing the airport there was an opportunity for Cassie to stop for a moment. She turned to him with tears in her eyes. "I hate goodbyes as well but I need a hug, I definitely need a hug."

David looked at her and smiling through his own tears kissed her tenderly on the forehead and hugged her tightly.

At the airport, David leapt out and retrieved his case from the back seat. He went round to Cassie's side.

She leant out of the window and looked up at him. "Thanks for coming, thank you so much," and then quickly she added, "See you soon. Yes?"

"You bet," responded David and with another kiss he turned and strode purposefully into the airport as Cassie drove off.

Chapter 25

"That was an unusually quick telephone call," smiled Lydia.

"He just wanted to let us know he's sold his apartment plus some of his furniture," said Cassie. "Seems to have got a good price, so as you can imagine, he's delighted. He sends his love and is counting the days."

"I can't believe David's been away for three, nearly four months," said Lydia. "Mind you, that might have something to do with his weekly phone calls!" she laughed. "Will the work on the cottage be finished by the time he comes over?"

"James is fairly confident that it will be finished in two weeks," replied Cassie. "Once the workmen leave, the painters can get going so, it should be at least habitable for his arrival."

"Good, I'm glad," smiled Lydia.

"You've really missed him," said Cassie. "You and David get on so well," Cassie laughed. "Considering your instant dislike of him, it's a miracle."

A strange look crossed Lydia's face. "Sorry," said Cassie. "I didn't mean to remind you. I'm just a little surprised, that's all. I mean, considering your start, it's amazing that you're now the mutual admiration society. Why is that, do you think?"

Lydia thought for a moment. "His word is his bond and that is a rare quality nowadays, practically non-existent. On top of that he is charming and fun, and that's a tremendously attractive combination," smiled Lydia.

"I suppose so," agreed Cassie.

"You should know," continued Lydia. "James has these qualities, don't you think?" She was trying desperately to get off what was in danger of becoming an in-depth study of David. She always became alarmed at these conversations in case Cassie would delve deeper.

Cassie smiled in response. "Yes, I agree. In fact the men in my life whom I admire, past and present, have very similar qualities. For

280

example David, now David has…" Just as Cassie was about to expatiate about his virtues, James arrived.

"Hello you two," he said, grinning from ear to ear. "I have come to boast. Guess what – I've sold The Dragon and… for a great price, better than great, amazing."

"Well done you," exclaimed Cassie with delight. "That is cause for celebration."

"How right you are and it's my treat. I'd like to take you all out, also Kate and Robert, and Pierre of course," said James excitedly. "He was marvellous, Pierre I mean, he put in a good word for me. And…" smiled James. "I've been commissioned to do two other pieces."

Cassie jumped up and kissed him. "You are clever," she smiled.

"I'm thrilled," said James. "Perhaps that's just a tad obvious!"

"Just a little," laughed Lydia. "Congratulations, that's marvellous. Well I for one can hardly wait. Where are we going?"

"I thought of booking for Friday at 'Number Ten'," replied James.

"James, that's very pricey, considering how many you're inviting," said Lydia. "Why don't we go somewhere a little less expensive? You don't want to blow all your money."

"No, I can afford it, trust me I can," said James. "I'll just go and ask the others and see if they can take us. I'll try for 7.30 – 8.00ish. Okay?"

"Okay," they both said as James went in search of Mrs. Pearson and the others.

The evening was a huge success, with two of the ladies in the party resplendent in the jewels they had received from Charles. It was such a happy evening, marred by only one thing; his absence. *He would have loved this*, thought Cassie, as she smiled over to Kate who for the evening was wearing the piece as a pendant. *I wish you could see how fabulous Kate's looking Pops.* She then looked over at Mrs. P. who caught her eye and touched her pearls. Cassie smiled back. 'They're gorgeous' she mouthed to her. Mrs. Pearson nodded in agreement.

Chapter 26

"Imagine you, forgetting the something blue bit," said Cassie, handing Sarah a garter.

"And how typical of you remembering," smiled Sarah. She straightened up and looked at Cassie.

"You look beautiful, simply stunning," enthused Cassie. "Wait till Claude sees you," twinkled Cassie. "He'll..." but she quickly stopped herself.

"Cassie, really, it's my wedding day," said Sarah feigning shock.

"I didn't say anything!" replied Cassie innocently.

"No," grinned Sarah. "It wasn't what you said, it was what was going through your mind, that's what."

"Takes one to know one and all that," responded Cassie. She looked at Sarah. "Why did you have to marry a Frenchman? I'm going to miss you when you live in France, really miss you."

"Me too," replied Sarah. She blinked furiously. "Now don't make me cry. I'm having enough problems with Dad!"

"I'll keep an eye on Uncle Peter," smiled Cassie. Leaning forward she kissed her on the cheek. "Every happiness, Claude's a lovely guy and a lucky one. Okay, no more gooey bits. I'll go and tell your Mum you're ready. See you at the church."

Although some of Claude's relatives were unable to speak English, by the time the champagne and wine had been flowing for a little while, the 'entente cordial' was well and truly established. All too soon it was time for the bride and groom to depart.

"Cassie!" shouted Sarah.

Cassie looked round and with an automatic response, amid cheers from the guests, caught the bride's bouquet, which Sarah had so expertly thrown in her direction. Cassie blushed furiously and glowered at Sarah. "I'll get you for this," she mouthed. Sarah grinned back and waved.

James suddenly materialised from nowhere, "Well, well!" he said, amused at her discomfort.

"Hmm." Cassie felt a hand on her arm and turned to find Lydia smiling at her. "That was nice, wasn't it?"

"I felt a total idiot. I'll kill her when she gets back."

Lydia didn't say anything, she just smiled at Cassie and James. "Well, we're going back now. I'll take the bouquet and put it in water. No doubt you'll be staying on for a while."

"Thanks. We'll try and be quiet," said Cassie as she leant forward and kissed her aunt on the cheek. "Night, night."

"Goodnight dear. Goodnight James," said Lydia, going off in search of Benson and the others for her lift home.

Cassie woke to the sun streaming into her bedroom. She slowly stretched and then turned over, bumping slap bang into James. "What on earth are you still doing here?" she asked, panic welling in her.

James, befuddled by sleep, was trying desperately to get his thoughts together. "Ah," he smiled. "Good morning, sleep well?"

"Sssh, its nearly ten, everyone will be up," whispered Cassie.

"Quite!" grinned James shifting the sheets. He moved over to her side. "It's too late to move now, come on, it's Sunday; we don't have to go to work."

"Are you mad?" asked Cassie.

"Oh possibly," smiled James. Turning, he lay on his back looking at the ceiling as if in contemplative mood. "Mad with desire for you no doubt." He turned and looked at her again "Last night was wonderful, wasn't it?" he asked.

"James please, you have to go. You've got to. Please stop teasing," she pleaded.

"It's you whose teasing I think," said James. "Looking all gorgeous, inviting." He was interrupted by a knock at the door.

They looked at each other. Cassie in panic, James, feeling a giggle bubble rising. Cassie thought she was going to have a heart attack, although at that moment death seemed the only possible alternative to anything she could think of.

"Hide!" she whispered. There was another knock.

"Where?" he mouthed, grinning at her.

"She pointed to the bathroom, so James tiptoed in that direction, retrieving items of clothing as he went.

"Mmmm," said Cassie, trying to sound sleepy.

"It's only me," said Lydia. "May I come in? I've brought you tea. I made some for myself and thought you might like some as well."

Oh no, thought Cassie, who was out of bed like a whippet. "How kind, Aunt Lydia," replied Cassie. "Hold on... I'm just coming,"

There was a snigger from the bathroom. Cassie glared in that direction, quickly put on her dressing gown and, hoping that Lydia wouldn't hear her pounding heart, opened the door.

She tried to wedge herself so that Lydia wouldn't come in. "This is kind of you, I was just going to get some," she smiled, with what she hoped was a convincing smile. "Why don't we go along to your room and I'll tell you all about last night," said Cassie, trying to steer her aunt in that direction.

Lydia turned, but out of the corner of her eye she could have sworn she saw a grey waistcoat lying on the chair. "Oh super," said Lydia. "I'd love to hear what happened after we left." As they walked along the corridor towards her room Lydia, with mischief rising, asked innocently, "Do you think James would like some tea?"

The look on Cassie's face was confirmation, if confirmation was needed, that Lydia had been correct, in all probability there was a waistcoat in Cassie's room.

"I don't think so," stammered Cassie. "I'm sure he'd like a long lie, we were back quite late." And before Lydia could question her any further, Cassie regaled her with stories of the festivities that Lydia had missed.

Lydia wasn't really listening to what Cassie was saying. She had other things on her mind and, looking at her niece thought, *I suspect there will be no more morning teas from me again!*

After about half an hour Cassie went back to her room. James had gone.

She showered and got dressed and went along to his room. She knocked loudly, knowing that her aunt would hear and standing outside said, "Good morning James, I'm going down to breakfast. Would you care to join me?"

Lydia did hear and giggled and went out into the hall. "Perhaps he's already gone down for breakfast."

"Perhaps," replied Cassie. "Shall we go and join him?"

James was indeed in the dining room. "Good morning, ladies," he said. He got up and went over and kissed Lydia on the cheek and then kissed Cassie. "Did you both sleep well?" he asked solicitously. Both replied in the affirmative.

He held the seat for Lydia. "I slept like a top, like a top, it must have been all the champagne and wine yesterday. In fact I thought I'd slept in but I then heard you both talking in the corridor and realised we must have all wakened much about the same time." He beamed at the ladies.

Lydia looked at Cassie, who was glowering at James who ignoring her look, smiled back. *You are rotten James*, thought Lydia, but she was actually rather enjoying this performance.

"May I help you to anything, Lydia?" enquired James.

"Oh that's kind," she responded. "A little bacon and an egg please. I'm rather hungry this morning."

"With pleasure," he replied, and going over to the sideboard he dished up Lydia's breakfast. "I must say I was rather hungry this morning as well, I had two helpings, it must have been all the exercise I had last night!"

Cassie choked and spluttered coffee down her front. James looked over at her with concern on his face. "Are you all right, something go down the wrong way?"

"No, I'm fine," said Cassie, red in the face.

"They say…" continued James, straight-faced, 'that dancing is one of the best forms of exercise'."

"So I believe," replied Lydia, trying very hard to keep the smile from her face.

"Excuse me," said Cassie. "I must go and change my top. A coffee stain is well nigh impossible to get out!"

Cassie ran upstairs. *I'll kill him, I really will*, she thought. She changed and went back downstairs, where she overheard James tell her aunt about the evening and how gorgeous he thought Cassie had looked in her bridesmaid's dress. She heard her aunt agree. "You may be forgiven James, just maybe," smiled Cassie to herself.

James looked up as Cassie came in and smiled. "That was quick. I was just telling Lydia, I thought you looked gorgeous last night." He went over and kissed her, whispering, "Am I forgiven?" Cassie smiled and nodding, whispered, "Perhaps!"

"What are your plans for today, then?" asked Lydia.

"I have to go to David's house at some point and check the painter's work," replied James. "Care to come along?" he asked Lydia.

"No, you both go," said Lydia. "Yesterday was lovely but quite tiring so I'll be more than happy to read the papers and put my feet up."

After breakfast they went their separate ways, with Lydia pondering her new found knowledge about her niece. *Who knows,* she thought, *There might be another wedding in the offing!*

Chapter 27

David emerged through International Arrivals beaming as he saw Margaret and Benson waiting for him. "This is so good of you, I really appreciate it. He shook hands with Benson and hugged Margaret. "It's lovely to see you both, so good. How is everyone; Cassie, Lydia, Mrs. Pearson?" he grinned. "I'm so pleased to be here," and he hugged Margaret again. "I'll shut up, I really will. Please tell me how everyone is."

Margaret told him all the gossip of Harrington and about Sarah's wedding so that by the time she had finished, they were nearing The Hall.

"I'm not allowed to take you to the cottage until I get a call from Cassie," grinned Benson.

"Oh, right you are," replied David. "That's fine, I'll see Mrs. P., have a freshen up and await further instructions."

He glanced out of the window. It was a typical November day. Everything in the countryside looked bare; the trees had nearly shed all their leaves and the sun had given up any attempt at penetrating the grey clouds. He smiled. A typical British November day and he loved it, positively and utterly loved it. *I'm home*, he thought. "What a wonderful feeling!"

Lydia put down her tapestry. Her eyes nowadays needed a better light than a grey November day. She looked at her watch. David should be arriving soon. *Oh Charles*, she thought. *I do hope this isn't a mistake*. But she had no further time for her concerns; she heard the car and went out to greet him.

"David, how lovely to see you," said Lydia, hugging him.

"Lydia, you're looking as gorgeous as ever," replied David. His eyes looked tenderly at her. "I've missed you so much."

"Me too," smiled Lydia.

In the background David spied Mrs. Pearson. "Mrs. P," he said, going over to her with outstretched arms. "How I've missed you,

287

I've missed all these fabulous meals. It's wonderful to see you again."

"And you," replied Mrs. Pearson.

"What do you want to do?" asked Lydia. "Benson will have told you we have strict instructions not to let you go to the cottage until told," smiled Lydia.

"Indeed," replied David. "I believe I'm to stay here for a couple of days, so I'd be very grateful if I could have a quick shower and then I'd love, a cup of Mrs. Pearson's wonderful tea. I didn't even manage to get that right when I was back in the States," smiled David.

"Away with you. Tea coming up."

They were just finishing their tea when the phone rang. Lydia answered and smiled over at David. "Yes, he's here. Yes, will do." Lydia put the phone down. "As if you didn't know, your presence is now requested at your new home!"

"I can hardly wait," said David excitedly.

Although the cottage was within walking distance of The Hall, Benson drove David and Lydia over.

Cassie came running out when she saw the car. "David, how lovely to see you. I've missed you so much, my favourite young uncle!" She flung her arms around him.

David grinned. "Favourite niece, the feeling I can assure you is mutual."

She stepped back. "Well, here you are. 'Lakeside Cottage' – what do you think?"

David stood and gazed at his new abode. "It looks bigger than the pictures you sent over. Come on," he said, taking her hand. "Show me around."

James was doing one last minute adjustment as David and Cassie walked in. "James, hello," said David, shaking hands. "Cutting it a bit fine I see," They both laughed. "You have been a miracle worker. Brilliant, thank you for all the help, thank you so much." He gazed around him. "This is just beyond my wildest imaginings. I can't really take it all in, it's really great."

Cassie and James beamed at each other. They were rather pleased with their efforts and relieved that David seemed of the same opinion.

Cassie looked over at her aunt. "You are unusually quiet, what do you think?"

"I'm completely staggered," replied Lydia. "David, this used to be, what I thought of as a derelict cottage. Hadn't been used for, at least thirty years, and this man..." she pointed to James, "saw it and wondered why we were phaffing around the countryside looking for something for you when there was a perfectly good property here on the doorstep, so to speak. I thought he had gone stark staring mad. But by jove you were right, you're a clever lad," smiled Lydia.

James bowed to Lydia in mock acknowledgement of this praise. "David we compiled this album for you."

David quickly flicked through. "My God, I must look at these in more detail. But I was right; you are a miracle worker James. Thank you."

Looking at Cassie, he smiled. "It's your hand I see in the interior decor, Yes?"

"Yes," agreed Cassie. With of course input from Aunt Lydia and Kate as co-designers, and Margaret who did all the sewing etc." David was trying to take this in. He couldn't believe how kind everyone had been. "And," added Cassie as she opened a kitchen cupboard with a flourish, "in the tins are Mrs. P's contribution, also, in the freezer, enough meals for ages, absolute ages."

David didn't know if it was the jet-lag or what, but tears pricked his eyes. He tried to quickly wipe them away and smiled weakly at them all. "As you can see, I'm overwhelmed, completely overwhelmed. Thank you so much."

Trying to help him, Cassie brightly said, "We are, of course, expecting the house warming party soon, very soon."

David smiled. "I can move in." He looked at James. "When do you think?"

"We thought the paint fumes might get to you and have you as high as a kite, as at the moment every room stinks of the stuff, but in a couple of days it should be fine," replied James. "Your things from the States arrive in two days, so the timing is good."

"In two weeks," said David. "Give me two weeks and I'll have a party. Don't tell Mrs. P., but I've actually been practising some things!"

~~~~~

David looked at the table again. It was going to be a bit of a squash, but hopefully it would be fine, intimate, he'd call it! He worked out where everyone would sit and looked at the clock again. Another half hour before everyone arrived but everything was ready now. He panicked; this meant everything was ready too early!

The starter and pudding were cold; they weren't the problem. It was the main course, the chicken dish he thought he'd perfected but which tonight looked like God knows what. He'd tried to jazz up the sludge grey colour with carrots, which were an addition to the unappetising dull green of the broccoli and mange tout he was already having, but the carrots weren't crunchy. He knew there was an expression the cooks used, what was it, he then remembered, 'al dente', they sure as hell weren't al dente.

This is going to be horrendous, he thought. He poured a drink and went out onto the verandah. It was a cold night but it cleared his mind a little. The meal was going to be a disaster and there was not a bloody thing he could do about it. Maybe Mrs. P. could resurrect things or he could order takeaways. That's what he'd do. If the meal was inedible, he'd say to everyone they'd have a takeaway.

He looked around him. He loved his house. It was small, smaller than he was used to, but to him it was perfect. It had a studio, and there were two out-buildings which were in the process of being renovated and he looked out over the lake, courtesy of the verandah which James had incorporated into the design. *Clever chap*, he thought, *hold onto him Cassie.*

He finished his drink and then hit on what he thought was his best plan. Alcohol! Alcohol would do the trick. He'd pour drinks down everyone before the meal, pre-prandial whoppers and everyone would be so pie-eyed they wouldn't have a clue what they were eating and perhaps with a little auto-suggestion as they left, they might even think they'd had a lovely meal. Some hope, he decided. He contemplated another drink but this thought was interrupted by a smell, a smell of burning. "Oh no," he shouted as he hurtled inside.

He opened the oven and smoke billowed out. He quickly opened the window then looked inside the oven and hauled the casserole dish out. He couldn't decide whether to be sick or to cry. He decided on neither and bravely opened the lid. To his untrained eye it looked all right. "Thank you God," he uttered. He then looked deeper into the oven, and spied the culprit of the inferno – the garlic bread – which now resembled a cremated offering. His relief knew no bounds, the meal seemed fine; it was only the bread. "Again, thank you God," he said.

There was a knock at the door and there stood Benson, Margaret and Mrs. Pearson. "How lovely to see you all. Mrs. P., let me take your coat and then," he looked sheepishly at her but her sense of smell had not failed. He smiled and said, as casually as he could, "Would you mind popping into the kitchen with me for a moment?"

Margaret and Benson smiled at each other. David was looking a little hot and bothered. *Poor David*, they thought.

"George," he said to Benson. "Would you get Margaret and yourself a drink and we'll be back in just a second."

"Sorry about this," said David, hurriedly ushering Mrs. Pearson into the kitchen. "You're looking lovely by the way, so don't get messed up, but I need you to tell me if this is all right."

Mrs. Pearson secretly loved this. She was still needed and he looked like a panicked youngster. "Don't you fret, I'm sure everything's fine, now have you an apron?"

David looked wild-eyed. "Apron, God no, dish towels, they're no good, ordinary towel, no, have one of these," and he dived into a cupboard found a bath towel and wrapped it around Mrs. P. "There we are, perfect. You won't get a drop on your dress."

Mrs. Pearson surveyed the casserole. "It looks fine, nothing to worry about. Lower the temperature, that's all."

With relief, David hugged her. "You're wonderful. Thank you. I should have thought. Hold on, what can I have instead of the garlic bread?

"Let's make Melba toast, do you have bread?" asked Mrs. P.

"Bread I have," replied a relieved David. He felt exhausted and the evening hadn't even started.

Within what appeared to be seconds, Mrs. P. had a basket of delicious Melba toast set out on the table. "There we are, no problem," she smiled at him.

"You are, without a doubt, a saint. I worship at your feet," he grinned. "Let me relieve you of the bath towel and we'll join the others."

There was a knock at the door and there stood Lydia, Kate, Robert and Pierre. "Hello," said Lydia. "I hope we aren't too early?"

"Not a bit," said David, trying to look the relaxed host.

"James and Cassie are just following," said Kate, looking with amusement at the harassed David.

"Hello, here we are," said Cassie.

Much to David's relief, George helped with the drinks. Once everyone had a drink David said, "I'd like to say a few words. This meal was my attempt at a thank you which I have to say is back firing just ever so slightly." He smiled. "You'll know what I mean when you see it! But I just wanted to thank each and every one of you for all the help you gave with the house. I love my new home and you ladies have absolutely made it that; a home. Even down to the home cooking," he said, smiling at Mrs. P. Looking over at James he said, "What can I say about you? You are remarkable. Thank you."

James looked around everyone and stood up. "I would like to propose a toast to David. May you have many happy years in your new home."

They all raised their glasses and drank, David's health.

Lydia glanced over at the table at the door. David had not noticed the presents on it. "Some house warming presents," said Lydia.

As he opened each one, he felt overwhelmed by the kindness they had bestowed upon him. *He was a lucky, lucky man*, he thought.

"Thank you, thank you all so much. I love them." He stood up. "Now, the moment you've been dreading! May I ask you to come through to the dining room?"

Everyone sat down and David handed out the first course. Everyone tucked in, seemingly with relish, much to his relief. *Moment of truth time now*, he thought, as he went to fetch the main course.

"Do you need a hand?" asked Cassie.

"No thanks, I'm fine," replied David. Everything was piping hot but he quickly dished up everything before the vegetables became even more limp!

Once everyone had been given their plates Robert said, "A toast to the chef!"

"I think that's a little premature," smiled David. "You haven't tasted it yet."

"Why do you think I did it now!" laughed Robert.

"Aaw," grinned David, pretending to be hurt. His appetite had deserted him. He looked anxiously at Mrs. Pearson who smiled back.

"This is lovely," she said, looking at David, and then, to the assembled party, said, "David was a bit concerned about the vegetables being too soft for everyone's liking but I think they're just right. This 'al dente' rubbish can be too crunchy, far too crunchy. Much better for my teeth as well," laughed Mrs. Pearson.

David could have leapt the table and hugged her he was so grateful. Everyone agreed they were perfect.

"Everything looks so grey though," said David. "Yours never does," he said, looking forlornly at Mrs. Pearson.

"It may not look that great," said Lydia. "But it tastes lovely. Presentation will come, just you see. Practice makes perfect."

"I couldn't go through this again," said David weakly. "I really couldn't," he repeated more to himself, but everyone laughed.

After dinner Cassie and Kate insisted on doing the dishes which David gratefully accepted. After they had cleared up Cassie went out the back door and arrived back with a package. Kate looked at her in surprise as Cassie winked. "It's his house warming from me!" she whispered.

They went into the sitting room. David was profuse in his thanks to the ladies.

Cassie went back into the kitchen and came out with the parcel. David looked at her, a puzzled expression in his eyes.

"David, firstly I'd like to reiterate what James said and hope you will have many happy years here." David stood beside her and thanked her as he kissed her on the cheek. "Secondly, the people who are here tonight you may remember Pops always called, 'The Family'. Well, from the time you arrived at Harrington you seemed to fit in, you were just one of us, even passing muster with Mrs. P.!"

Everyone laughed and David tried to look composed as Cassie was speaking for he had no idea what on earth was coming next. He suspected the parcel was a painting but tried to concentrate on what Cassie was saying.

She was also causing alarm to two others; Lydia and Kate. Lydia gave Kate an anxious look, as if asking, what is going on? Kate shrugged her shoulders. She had no idea.

"Well, because of that, and I think Pops would have agreed, no, I'm sure he would have agreed, I'd like you to have this painting as a welcome to your new home."

David felt his heart racing. He looked at the others and sensed that no one had any idea what this was. He daren't look at Lydia. He tore at the paper. Before him was a portrait, a portrait of 'The Family'. It was exquisite. Charles sitting on the sofa with Lydia and Cassie on either side of him and all the other 'Family' surrounding them; Kate and Robert's children were in the foreground; Charlie fishing, Ben with his toy tractor, the girls reading. David was painted standing behind Cassie; one of them. David was completely choked. He hugged Cassie to him. "Thank you," he said, struggling to get the words out.

As Kate looked at the picture her stomach knotted with anxiety. She very much hoped it was her paranoia, but the similarity between Cassie and David seemed to jump out of the painting. She looked over at Lydia, wondering what she was thinking, but her face was an inscrutable mask. "I'm imagining it," she decided and tried to convince herself of that fact. She looked at Cassie and smiled. "It's wonderful!" she said.

Cassie felt his tears against her cheek. His back was towards the others for which he was truly grateful. Cassie looked up at him. "I was a bit twitchy painting something for you; I really was."

"I've no idea why," he smiled. He tried to regain control, quickly wiping his eyes before he turned round. Embarrassed, he smiled at them all. "Sorry about that, everyone." They all shook their heads with understanding, feeling a little choked themselves.

David looked at the painting again and then at Cassie. "I now know how Charles felt when you presented him with Lizzie's portrait! Completely and utterly overwhelmed! Thank you, thank you so very, very much."

"Can you hold it up, David?" asked Lydia, trying to alleviate his unease.

David held it up for everyone to see, glad of something to do. It was unanimous; everyone thought it was wonderful. Cassie as ever, had triumphed. It was a masterpiece.

Chapter 28

"Kate, what do you think? Should I ask her do you think?" asked David. "I don't know what to do for the best. Everyone could come here, not for food. I'd get caterers," he added quickly, noting the alarm on her face. "I saw that," he said, teasing her. "You were thinking back to the house warming."

"Not at all," smiled Kate. "Whatever gave you that idea! No, I'm just thinking. The Hall always had special celebrations at Christmas, even last year; carol singers, Mrs. P. baking her head off. I think Cassie would want to continue the tradition." She paused, thoughtful for a moment. "I tell you, why don't we wait for another week or so, that would take us to the eighteenth and we'll see if Cassie mentions it. Usually the decorations don't go up until the twenty-third. Cassie and George have always been in charge of them ever since she was little. No one else is allowed to intrude, even Charles wasn't."

Kate looked wistful. "It's going to be a peculiar Christmas without him. He loved it so much." She smiled. "He was like a little boy if it happened to snow, beside himself with delight. I…"

David looked at her. "You miss him very much!"

Kate nodded, tears pricking her eyes. "Sorry, this is silly," she said. "It's just the time of year and everything."

"Sorry, mentioning Christmas, I didn't mean to upset you," said David, with concern.

"No, its all right," said Kate, wiping her eyes. "I still have, as Cassie calls them, 'falling about' moments, although she and I try not to 'fall about' at the same time! Its just he was such an important person in all our lives. Irreplaceable. We were so lucky to have known him but he's left such a gap, such a huge gap."

"He was a lucky man to have you as his friend. I wish I'd known him longer," said David sadly.

"He was very fond of you," smiled Kate and, she added, "very grateful."

David shrugged and smiled. "Thank you… Now, back to business, I won't mention Christmas unless Cassie does until after the eighteenth. She and Lydia may want it low key. What about New Year, what happens then?"

"Normally a huge party at The Hall, everyone in the village attending," replied Kate. She looked sad again. "The first year is always the worst isn't it?"

"Definitely," agreed David.

~~~~~

"Are you sure?" asked Benson gently.

Cassie nodded. "Pops would want it," she said firmly, "So it's the usual preparations and on the twenty-third we decorate as normal. For the meal, just us and…" she smiled a little shyly, "I thought I'd invite James. I don't think he particularly wants to spend Christmas at home."

Benson smiled. "I'm sure he'd far rather be here, the Earl; he's a queer fellow, mad as a hatter some say! James will make a welcome addition, he's a very nice young man Cassie."

Cassie grinned. "I think so and I also agree about the Earl. The wrong son was born first, that's for sure, but then James might not have been able to pursue his sculpting if he had to run the estate."

"You manage," said Benson.

"Oh George, you are a poppet," laughed Cassie. "We both know that if it wasn't for Robert, the Harrington Estate would be a shambles. I don't have a clue, I'm trying, but I come out in a cold sweat when I think what might of happened if we hadn't had Robert." She shivered. "Too awful to even contemplate.

Now back to Christmas lunch, how many will that be; you, Margaret, Aunt Lydia, Mrs. P., Kate, Robert and the children, James, David and let's ask Pierre as well. How many is that? Thirteen, that's no good, oh, and me, what an idiot, fourteen."

The days sped past and the twenty-third duly dawned. The huge tree was erected in the Great Hall and Cassie and Benson started on the decorations. Once this task was completed they stood back to admire their handiwork. Looking around her she caught sight of Charles's portrait she had painted for his birthday all those years ago. He seemed to be smiling down at her.

"I'm finding this so difficult Pops, so very difficult," she said to herself.

Benson, aware of what she was feeling, went over to her and put his arm around her. She put her head against his shoulder and let the tears fall as he cuddled her in.

"He was always the first to view our work," cried Cassie.

"Yes and every year he said the same thing, do you remember?"

Cassie laughed through her tears. "Yes, yes he said, 'I think this is the best you two have done, better even than last year', and we'd always agree." She tried to wipe away the tears.

"He'd be so proud Cassie, so very proud, you know that, don't you?"

"Suppose," muttered Cassie. "I'm not doing very well today though," she sighed. "I'm trying to be strong but it's so hard, really hard." She looked at Benson and gave him a tear-filled smile. "We're all trying so hard – he'd be proud of us all." She wiped her eyes. "Thanks, I'm okay now."

"Right," said Benson, giving her a final hug. "Let's ask that aunt of yours if this is up to our usual standard." And off they went in search of Lydia.

Although some tears were shed on Christmas Day, they were of short duration, done in fond remembrance and with much laughter and reminiscing. All were agreed; it had been a surprisingly pleasant day.

However, the day Cassie was dreading was New Year's Eve. She had told the others to let the villagers know that they would be welcome, as normal, at The Hall, but this year the number who attended would be very much an unknown quantity. Normally the whole village descended upon them; this year some had said they were unsure of their plans – for fear of intruding, they confessed.

Midnight came and 'The Family' wished each other a fairly subdued New Year and then awaited the arrival of any visitors. At exactly 12.01 there was a knock at the door. Cassie answered and was greeted by the sight of Peter and most of the villagers standing behind him.

"Happy New Year," said Peter briskly and unemotionally. He'd been warned by Rowena not to make this evening any more difficult for Cassie than it already was, so had done as he was told. Rowena looked at him, nodded her approval and then she too greeted

Cassie. The others followed on behind, wishing Cassie and the family well.

One old timer, Alf, whom her father had so enjoyed chatting to, greeted Cassie. "It's grand this, business as usual at The Hall, your father would have been proud of you. He was a wonderful man, Lord Emerson, wonderful, but you're shaping up fine, just fine." He shook her warmly by the hand, wishing her a Happy New Year.

Cassie, touched by his sentiments, bent forward and kissed him on the cheek. "Thank you for that Alf, and a very happy New Year to you as well," she smiled.

Lydia looked at her niece with pride. David was watching her as well. He caught Lydia's eye, smiled and went over to her. "She's been a star tonight, she was dreading it and look at her."

He looked at Lydia, the strain of the last year had taken its toll and for the first time since he'd met her, he realised she was an old lady. "What about you, how are you doing?" he asked.

"I'm tired David, really quite tired," she replied with honesty, for there was never any point in lying to him, he always guessed. "I think the events of the last while are catching up on me." Then, as if pulling herself together, she said, "But I'm fine, too much gadding about at this time of year. I'll be glad when we're back to normal again."

David was doubtful about this. "What about going to see Peter next week. Have a sort of MOT!" He smiled at her. "Please!" He took her hand. "I want you well, you're my confidant, my chum, I need you well – and that's an order."

Lydia looked at him and shook her head. "I'll think about it."

"You may just need a tonic, be anaemic or something: promise me you'll go," pleaded David.

"Thank you, doctor," she said sarcastically. "Although I suppose I'd better, for you'll just nag if I don't."

"How right you are," replied David. "I'll give you till a week on Friday."

"You're impossible," glared Lydia, pretending to be angry.

"But lovely with it," grinned David, kissing her on the cheek.

By two-thirty in the morning, only 'The Family' were left and James, who was not quite yet considered a member. Although this was not particularly late by her usual New Year standards, Cassie felt physically and emotionally exhausted. She flopped into a chair in the kitchen where Kate and Margaret were finishing the dishes with the men putting away. "I'm totally and utterly shattered. What about you people? Are you not?"

"Not as bad as you I don't think," said Kate. "But remember you were the hostess tonight, so had the strain of that. But you were brilliant, quite, quite brilliant." She went over and gave Cassie a hug. "Well done!"

"Where's Aunt Lydia?" asked Cassie.

"Whacked, totally whacked," said Margaret. "She slipped up to bed at about one."

"I'll nip up and check she's all right," said Cassie, a little concerned for this was out of character. She went to her aunt's room and quietly opened it. Her aunt was sound asleep. "Sleep well," whispered Cassie and crept out again.

By the time she got downstairs those who were going home were putting on their coats, ready to brave the cold night. Cassie hugged each in turn. "Thank you all, I have no idea what I would do without you, no idea at all. I couldn't have coped with tonight if I hadn't had my back-up system!"

Kate smiled. "That's what families are for!"

"Absolutely," agreed Cassie. "See you tomorrow, have you got your torches?"

David put his on, positioning it under his chin to give an eerie appearance. "Scary or what?"

"Pathetic, actually," grinned Cassie. "Night!" she said laughing, shutting the door. She went into the Great Hall to check the lights were off. "Of course they'd be off you idiot," she said to herself. "Benson would have seen to that."

She looked up at her father's portrait staring down at her, "Well I did it, Pops, struggled a bit, but I did it. Next year I'll be better..." she smiled up at it. "Night night."

Chapter 29

Lydia was going to argue with Peter but his face was set firmly. "I have written requesting an appointment with a cardiologist and that is all I have to say," said Peter. "You are going if I have to drag you, kicking and screaming! Right?"

"I'm well past my three score years and ten," smiled Lydia sweetly to Peter. "I don't require all this medical interference, perhaps a change of pills would suffice."

"I don't care if you're one hundred and ten," replied an exasperated Peter. "Up until last year, you have been a fit lady, even with your angina. I blame myself in many ways because I put your tiredness down to the strain of Charles's illness and his death, a reaction to everything, but the tests are conclusive; there has been deterioration and I need help now with the management of your illness from the specialist."

Lydia knew when she was defeated. "Very well," she said, with a resigned tone in her voice. "How long is the waiting list?"

"I'm checking that. It seems to change with the wind, but I put urgent so if I haven't heard in a week, I'll phone," replied Peter.

"From what I've read in the papers about waiting lists and whatever, I feel you are a trifle optimistic," said Lydia.

"Maybe," agreed Peter. "There is of course an alternative; private, which you and Charles never approved of... but you would definitely be seen within a week."

"Charles always waited his turn, so shall I. If our workers have to wait, why should we jump the queue?" asked Lydia.

"In this area, it's not like that. You wouldn't be in the NHS hospital, you'd be seen and operated at Westpark..." He stopped and looked at Lydia, realisation dawning on him. "Is that why you and Charles didn't go private, because Lizzie died there?" he asked.

"Absurd I know, but that was certainly one of the reasons," agreed Lydia.

Peter shook his head. "For God's sake, Lydia, it's considered one of the finest private hospitals in the country. The chap I'm thinking about is world-renowned. So we're not pratting about for the sake of an absurd superstition."

"Do you talk to all your patients like that?" enquired Lydia with surprise.

"Only the ones who do *'prat about'*," grinned Peter.

"You really are the limit," smiled Lydia. She looked at Peter and shook her head. "Very well, I know you're suggesting it for the best. This chap you know, I'll go to him but by jove, be it on your conscience if I should snuff it whilst there!"

With relief, Peter smiled. "Thank you Lydia for that overwhelming vote of confidence, but I feel pretty secure in assuming you'll survive the visit!"

~~~~~

Lydia went through to the kitchen. "Right everyone, I'm off now," she said brightly to Mrs. Pearson, Margaret and Benson.

"All the best," they chorused. "We'll see you soon."

"Yes, bye," smiled Lydia.

Cassie was waiting in the hall. "All set?"

Lydia nodded. "As ready as I'll ever be, and thank you?"

Cassie looked at her aunt with surprise. "What for?"

"For priming them," replied Lydia. "They were so casual it was as if I was off for morning coffee somewhere."

"Sorry," smiled Cassie. "I thought the stiff upper lip approach was best."

"I absolutely agree," said Lydia. "And you will as well, yes?"

"Yes, I'll try, I'll try very hard," agreed Cassie. "Let me take your case and I'll put it in the boot."

They drove to Westpark Hospital, chatting away about anything and everything that was in no way connected with the topic of bypass surgery.

Lydia was shown to her room and left to settle in. "You know, I feel reasonably calm about someone hacking open my chest and doing goodness knows what with my heart," said Lydia. She looked at Cassie who was looking a little doubtful. "Truly I do." She didn't know if she was saying this to reassure Cassie or herself.

"I very much hope that there will be a little more finesse than 'hacking' into your chest," smiled Cassie.

"It was rather good having all the tests yesterday and be allowed home for the night. I suspect you don't get that with the NHS," smiled Lydia.

Cassie was about to comment when the nurse came in with Lydia's gown and attractive white socks, she would have to wear for the operation. "The trolley will be along in about an hour to take you to theatre," said the nurse.

"Thank you nurse. I'll manage into them myself," said Lydia. Looking at the attire she would wear, she added, "Most fetching, I'll wow them in theatre that's for sure," she smiled.

The nurse agreed she'd be a sensation. "I'll be back in a little while to give you your pre-med," she added.

"My dear, I'd like you to run along now, before my injection. It's likely to make me even more dopey!" smiled Lydia bravely. "No great send-off and don't worry, what will be will be; but I have every confidence in Mr. Peel, I really do. He does triple, quadruple, goodness knows how many other uples... every day. I'll be fine."

Cassie swallowed, trying to keep in firm control for her aunt. "I'll phone tonight and perhaps pop by, you'll be a bit groggy but I'd just stay for a moment, just to make sure you're behaving." She smiled as brightly as she could then bent down and kissed her on the cheek. "See you later!" And with a quick wave she left.

Once she reached the safety of car, the tears flowed. "Good luck, Aunt Lydia. Please get through this... you have to, you absolutely have to."

Once Cassie had regained her composure she drove back to The Hall and joined the others in the anxious wait for news of Lydia.

After nearly six excruciatingly long hours, the phone rang. They all looked at Cassie. She picked it up and as confidently as possible said, "Hello!"

"Hello, Peel here, Michael Peel. I'm phoning about Mrs. Maitland. Good news I'm delighted to say. She did splendidly..." he continued but Cassie didn't hear, her taut emotions seemed to explode, and much to the alarm of the others, she broke down. By her reaction they were convinced there was a problem, but Kate realised it was with relief and grabbed the phone to talk to Mr. Peel.

"Sorry," sobbed Cassie, her head in her hands.

Margaret put her arm round her shoulders. You'll be fine in a moment, its just reaction."

Kate came off the phone and sat down beside Cassie, who was now regaining her composure. "He did a triple bypass which apparently is quite common and so far so good," smiled Kate. He's confident that she'll make a good recovery. I asked if you can pop in for a brief moment and he said yes. So dry your eyes and I'll drive you over. All right?"

Cassie nodded. "Sorry, I don't know what happened there, the relief that she's all right I suppose." She smiled at everyone. "Ha, she got through it. Well done Aunt Lydia... well done."

Although she had been warned there would be tubes, wires and an assortment of machines surrounding her aunt, it did give her a momentary jolt when she walked into the ward, seeing her like that. However, the nurses looking after Lydia assured Cassie that her aunt was doing fine.

Lydia seemed to be asleep so she went over and gently squeezed her hand. "Well done," she said quietly. "You're going to be fine now. I've popped in for only a moment. See you tomorrow. Night, night." Cassie bent over and kissed her aunt on the cheek whereupon Lydia opened her eyes and smiled weakly. "Told you so!" she said, and then promptly fell asleep again. Cassie beamed at the nurse.

Much to the amazement of the staff, but not to 'The Family', Lydia's progress was astonishingly speedy. Although the staff had been kindness itself, Lydia wanted to go home, and wanted to soon. Mr. Peel informed Lydia that most patients of her age stayed in for at least another five to seven days. This information gave Lydia even greater incentive not to be classed with the other 'oldies' and so with continued persuasion, Mr. Peel eventually relented, and granted her wish; he discharged her.

Cassie went to collect her that afternoon, complete with wheelchair for occasional use at home until she was back to full strength. So with a final thanks and regal wave to all, Lydia was driven home.

As they approached The Hall Cassie said, "Now sit in the car until I get the chair organised."

Lydia looked at her with disdain. "If you think for one moment I will be using that contraption you can think again. You can take it back from whenst it came."

"You promised Mr. Peel you'd behave, and behave you will," replied Cassie equally as firmly.

David was in the drive awaiting their arrival. "How's my best girl?" he asked, opening the car door and giving Lydia a kiss.

"Already misbehaving," said Cassie quickly.

David looked in mock surprise. "I can't believe it, I really can't."

Before Lydia could say anything Cassie said, "She refuses to use the chair, and she promised Mr. Peel."

"I didn't exactly promise," said Lydia. "I may have misheard what I was agreeing to. I didn't realise everyone expected me to use it here," she said innocently.

David smiled. "Well, its just as well you have a knight, albeit without the shining armour, to carry you inside. Will you allow me to do that?"

"I can manage," insisted Lydia. David looked at her. "Very well," she agreed. "If you must."

"Your room or downstairs?" enquired David.

"Downstairs, certainly downstairs. I'm not the least bit tired," replied Lydia. Cassie raised her eyes heavenward and smiled at David.

Once she was safely ensconced, afternoon tea was served and Lydia held court, regaling them all with stories, some embellished, of her stay in hospital. By early evening she admitted defeat and allowed David to carry her upstairs to her room.

"My own bed, how lovely," said Lydia. "I so hoped I'd get back to it!"

David looked at her. "Did you have any doubts?"

Lydia smiled. "One or two, but here I am – here to live another day." She took his hand. "Thank you, I'm fine. Just a little tired but nothing like I felt before the operation. You were right and I'm grateful to you for your nagging."

"Goodnight Lydia, sleep well. I've missed you. See you tomorrow." He smiled and kissed her goodnight. "Ah, here's your nurse for the evening, Cassie, over to you."

"I just came up to see if you needed help with anything," smiled Cassie.

"Thank you, I'll be fine but please, stay and chat while I get ready for bed," said Lydia.

Lydia eventually was ready. "I don't think I'll read, I'm sure I'll sleep the minute my head hits the pillow." She looked at Cassie. "Thank you for everything and I'm sorry I caused you all this worry."

Cassie bent down to tuck her aunt in. "You're home now and that's all that matters. I missed you so much, we all did." Cassie laughed. "No one to keep us in check. But please, you have to promise not to overdo things. Do you promise?"

"All right," agreed Lydia reluctantly but the words slurred as sleep overcame her.

Cassie put out the light and quietly closed the door and went downstairs.

Chapter 30

"Now this is the phone number and the address and what else?" asked Cassie anxiously.

"Go, will you please go," said Lydia. "And please give them my kindest regards."

"I can't believe I'm actually going, actually going back to Florence, said Cassie. "Oh James, I hope you'll love the Lorenzo's as much as I do; they were so kind to me when I stayed with them."

"I'll adore them, positively adore them, that is if I ever get to meet them, because at this rate we're going to miss the plane," replied James sarcastically.

She kissed her aunt and with a last, "Behave!" James bundled her into the car and at speed, drove off.

"This will do her the power of good," smiled Lydia to Kate.

"Needless to say I'm green with envy," grinned Kate. "Florence and in the spring, before there are too many tourists elbowing you out the way, bliss. But you are absolutely right, she most certainly deserves this." Kate smiled at Lydia, "And who knows…"

Lydia returned her smile. "Who knows indeed!"

The two weeks that Cassie and James had been in Italy flew by and so it seemed that no sooner had everyone waved them off, it was time to await their return.

"Here they are," said Lydia excitedly.

Cassie leapt out of the car, brimming with happiness, as she hugged Lydia. "How are you, how have you been?"

"I've been fine, absolutely tippy-toppy as they say," smiled Lydia.

Cassie looked at her aunt with relief, for she did look well, really well. "You look good. All the Lorenzo's send their love and hope we'll bring you the next time. It was wonderful, a lovely holiday," enthused Cassie.

"I'm so glad," said Lydia, turning to give James a hug. "You're looking good, a nice golden tan, very handsome."

James just grinned then he looked at Cassie who nodded. Lydia was a little unsure what all these supposed meaningful looks were conveying.

"We've got pressies for you all, so I'll take the cases upstairs and get them and then perhaps we could all have a drink and we'll tell you all about it. Is Kate coming over?" asked Cassie.

"Yes," replied Lydia, looking at her watch. "Oneish I think."

Cassie looked at her watch. "Okay, I'll go and sort this lot out, then pressies in the drawing room when Kate arrives. James, why don't you keep Aunt Lydia company, I won't be a tick."

"What… oh yes, right you are," replied James a little hesitantly.

James and Lydia went through to the morning room. "Well James," smiled Lydia. "You and Cassie look as if you've had a wonderful holiday. She looks positively radiant."

James blushed ever so slightly. "We had a wonderful time, magical. Italy is breathtaking but actually, well…" he stammered. "I wonder if I might ask you something?"

"Of course you may, always feel you can talk to me," replied Lydia with concern.

"Oh," said James quickly. "It's nothing to worry about, well at least I hope you won't think its anything to worry about. I, its… well."

"Take your time James, whatever, I'm sure it will be fine," said Lydia, perplexed as to what on earth could be wrong.

James took a deep breath. "With Lord Emerson sadly dead, you are Cassie's next of kin," Lydia nodded, still puzzled. "Well," continued James. "In accordance with tradition, I wish to ask if I may have your permission to have Cassie's hand in marriage!" he said. The last bit coming out in a rush.

Realisation at what James just said suddenly hit Lydia. She beamed at him then promptly burst into tears.

He looked aghast and went over to her. "Oh Lydia, I'm sorry, are you all right? Can I get you anything?"

Lydia smiled through her tears. "Emotions," she sniffed, "They're not in such tight control after the operation. Blasted nuisance…" She dried her eyes and kissed him. "I am thrilled, you most definitely have my permission and I am so touched you asked. Thank you my dear." She looked at him, then her moment of euphoria suddenly changed. "I just wish dear Charles could have

307

been here, been the one you asked," said Lydia sadly. She shook her head. "However, we won't dwell on that. We'll think to the future."

She then laughed. "I now understand why Cassie suddenly felt the need to unpack the second she arrived. Oh, I want to hear every single detail." James swallowed and blushed.

Realising what she had just said, Lydia laughed. "Edited highlights," James smiled with relief. She took his hand. "You have made an old lady very happy, very happy indeed. Now, off you go and get that fiancée of yours."

James grinned at her. "Fiancée! My fiancée. Sounds good doesn't it?"

Lydia went through to the kitchen. "Benson, I think we should have champers to welcome the holiday makers. It's so lovely to have them home and Mrs. P., let's see how quickly we can rustle up a canapé or two."

"No problem," smiled Mrs. Pearson who set about the task. *I think something's afoot*, she thought, *that's for sure*. She'd never seen Cassie so happy and, looking at Lydia, she suspected it was good news.

Benson smiled at Lydia. "Four bottles or more? It feels like a celebration."

Lydia returned his knowing smile. "Let's have six to be on the safe side and can we get a message to Robert, do you think? I'd like him to welcome Cassie home."

"Oh I'm sure he'd want to," grinned Benson. "I'll contact him."

Lydia then picked up the phone. "David, Cassie and James have just arrived home and we thought we'd have champers to say welcome back. Can you come over?" David was delighted.

One more member of 'The Family', Pierre. Pierre thought Lydia sounded decidedly 'high' and wondered what the celebration was for, but any excuse he decided was good enough for him, and, as business was slack, he did as he was told, and shut up the gallery for the afternoon.

"Excellent," smiled Lydia.

She then went to find Cassie. Cassie was coming down the stairs, smiling from ear to ear. She'd never looked happier thought Lydia. They went into the study and Cassie shut the door. "You approve, then?" she asked.

Lydia kissed her warmly. "He's lovely and you make a perfect couple." Lydia felt the tears well up again and just hugged Cassie to her.

"I know we've only really been back together again for about ten months," said Cassie. Her face suddenly clouded. "Since Pops's funeral, I suppose…" She looked at Lydia, "I wish…" but didn't say anything more.

"I know," said Lydia. "I wish that as well." She squeezed her hand. "Perhaps he knows, he was such a cynic about all that, but it would be the price of him if he is smiling down at us from a great height. 'Heaven', call it what you will. I do hope he is."

Cassie smiled at that thought. "So do I. He liked James. I just wish he had known him as he is now. He'd be happy though, I know he would." Then her happiness of moments before returned, and she grinned at Lydia. "I'm crazy about James, I love everything about him," she laughed. "Don't dare tell him that though!"

Lydia laughed, delighting in her niece's happiness.

From a chain around her neck Cassie took off a ring. "I kept it there in case anyone spied it before James spoke to you," said Lydia. She put it on her finger. "It was his Granny's. Isn't it gorgeous?"

"It's lovely, and fits perfectly. It was meant," said Lydia, "Certainly meant."

Lydia then told Cassie that she'd organised a little celebratory drinks party – just 'The Family'.

Cassie was delighted. The people who were so important in her life, she would now be able to tell all together. "I'll take the ring off at the moment," smiled Cassie as she slipped it back onto the chain. "Then I can show them all at once." She hugged her aunt again. "Thank you for this idea, it's wonderful. What time have you said?"

Looking at her watch Lydia said, "Now really, Kate should be here shortly."

Kate arrived at the backdoor and was surprised to see Robert coming towards her. "Hello, what are you doing here?"

"Summoned. Lydia phoned and said I had to welcome Cassie back!" said Robert a little disgruntled. "I could dispense with this, we've loads on but I thought it churlish to refuse. I could have seen Cassie tonight for heaven's sake, but I'll whizz in say, 'hello' and then whizz off again."

"Mmm," said Kate.

"What is that 'mmm' supposed to mean?" asked Robert.

Kate smiled at him. "I think something's up and I don't want you being Mr. Grumpy. I think…" Kate stopped herself. She had a self-satisfied look about her, "And I think I know!"

"Know what for goodness sake?" asked an exasperated Robert.

They arrived in the kitchen and upon spying trays of delectable looking canapés Kate smiled at him. "See!"

"No, I don't see," replied Robert.

"Men!" smiled Kate and she leant over and kissed him.

"Nice as that was, I still haven't a clue what you're talking about. I should be working!" growled Robert.

Mrs. Pearson came into the kitchen. "Hello you two. I've just two more trays to take through to the drawing room." She smiled at Kate. "I think something's up!"

Kate returned the smile. "So do I."

"God almighty, not you as well!" snarled Robert.

"That is quite enough blaspheming," said Mrs. Pearson sternly to Robert. "That's not like you."

"Ignore Mr. Grumpy," said Kate sweetly. "He's in a mood"

"I'm not in a mood," retorted Robert. With that, Benson came in. "George, thank goodness. Someone sensible. What on earth is going on?"

"Ah," grinned Benson. "Something's up that's for sure!"

Robert looked in disbelief at Benson. Everyone in the house was talking in riddles. He looked at his watch; five to one. "Right, let's go through," he said, taking Kate's arm trying to start the proceedings so he could leave soon.

"Well take the trays and make yourself useful," replied Kate.

At five past one everyone was assembled in the drawing room. Benson was distributing glasses of champagne, just as Cassie and James arrived, hand in hand.

"Sorry everyone," gushed Cassie. Benson handed them each a glass. James looked at Cassie and she smiled.

"Excuse me, everyone," said James a little hesitantly.

"Louder!" said Cassie.

"Excuse me!" said James. Everyone looked at him expectantly.

"I wonder if I might say a few words?" He took a drink of champagne, which he knew he shouldn't have done, but his mouth had gone completely dry. He looked at Cassie for reassurance. She smiled. Taking her hand, he tried again. "Ladies and Gentlemen," he sensed everyone's amusement; it sounded so formal but he didn't know how else to start. He continued. "Whilst on holiday in Florence I asked Cassie to marry me." He looked at Cassie and she squeezed his hand. "And I am thrilled, delighted," he grinned. "And completely beside myself with joy that she has agreed…" He looked at everyone. "That's all really," he spluttered.

Cassie kissed him and everyone cheered. Lydia then said, "Let's drink a toast to Cassie and James."

"Cassie and James." They all responded and then rushed over to offer their congratulations.

Kate grinned at Robert. "Told you!" she said triumphantly.

Robert smiled back. "It's lovely news but I do really have to get back!"

He went over to Cassie. "I'm delighted for you. I'm really sorry about this but I have to go back to work. Do you mind?"

"Oh Robert, I'm so pleased you were here even for just a quick glug. We'll have a proper dinner soon, so there will be no excuse for escaping then," smiled Cassie. She looked at him. "Is everything all right?"

"Fine," said Robert hoping he was sounding convincing. He hugged her again. "Every happiness." He turned to James and shook his hand warmly. "Sorry about this – having to dash. But I'm delighted for you both." He looked over at Cassie. "You have a gem there, you're a lucky man."

James smiled. "I know! Thank you."

Lydia went over to David who was standing back, surveying the scene, and quietly said, "I'm sorry I couldn't warn you. Are you okay?"

David smiled and put his arm around her. "Of course… I was just thinking ridiculously absurd thoughts, what might have beens! It just took me slightly by surprise, but no, I'm thrilled for her." He looked at Lydia. "You know that, don't you?" Lydia nodded. David continued. "If I'd scoured the earth, I couldn't have wished for a finer young man than James. I'm delighted, I really am…" He looked over at Cassie. "My turn to wish them well I think."

David put his arms around Cassie. "Favourite niece," he grinned. "Every happiness for a long and happy future together."

Witnessing this Lydia felt tears prick her eyes; this was so difficult for David, yet he was carrying it off with his usual aplomb.

"Oh thank you favourite young uncle," laughed Cassie, emphasising the young.

David turned to James. "You're a lucky man. Take care of her or else," he smiled. "You'll have me to answer to!"

James assured him that he would take the best of care.

The party eventually finished and it was time to clear up. With strict instructions to Lydia and Mrs. Pearson to rest, the others attended to the tidying.

"So," said Kate, as she and Cassie were putting away plates. "Have you thought when you'll get married?"

Cassie smiled. "No idea. Perhaps sometime next year. I'm still reeling a little from being engaged!"

"I'm so thrilled for you," said Kate, smiling at her. "He's lovely, and he fits in here so perfectly."

Cassie agreed. "I think he can now be considered one of 'The Family!'"

"Undoubtedly!" grinned Kate.

Cassie then looked serious. "Is everything okay here? Robert seemed a little preoccupied I thought."

"I've no idea, to be honest," replied Kate. "They've been exceptionally busy, but it's that time of year. I suppose it's also been one crisis after another and farming is a bit precarious at the moment, plus there was the problem with the forest."

"Yes," said Kate. "It's been horrendous of late. Pops always said that the bad luck on the estate came in spates and I guess we're having a spate. Hopefully we are now at the end of our bad luck."

"Fingers crossed," replied Kate. "I'm sorry I'm no help but Robert doesn't really talk about the problems at work."

"No, don't worry," said Cassie. "I'll have a word with him at our weekly pow-wow." She laughed. "He's really sweet. He comes along and tries to explain things in 'Noddy' terms in the vain hope that I'll understand. I'm getting better, but he must despair at times."

"You're actually wrong there," smiled Kate. "He has come home after one of your 'pow-wows', and said you are really getting the hang of things. He's actually very impressed at how quickly you're grasping things. But how unfair of him not to tell you. He's rotten. Wait till I see him."

"No," said Cassie quickly. "Don't say anything. If Robert should ever say anything then I'll know I'm doing okay. Don't prompt him; I'd rather he said it off his own bat. It would mean more to me."

"All right," agreed Kate. "I'd better be going. That was a lovely interlude, thank you, and I'm thrilled for you, so thrilled."

"I think that's the tenth time you've said that," laughed Cassie. "But thank you."

"See you later," smiled Kate. "Bye."

Everyone had gone their separate ways; David, Pierre and James and gone off to David's and everyone else was resting. Cassie decided to go for a walk. She wandered down by the lake and then up the hill behind the house, through the woods, to the graveyard. As she reached the hill she looked down and saw that Lydia was sitting on the bench beside Charles's grave. She seemed deep in thought. Cassie felt she was intruding but as she was trying to turn away quietly, Lydia looked up and beckoned her over.

"I thought you were supposed to be resting," said Cassie gently.

"I just fancied coming up here, it's so peaceful and I wanted to tidy the flowers; daffodils are so unattractive when they die," replied Lydia.

"I went down by the lake and through the woods," said Cassie. "It was lovely and it's so warm."

Lydia agreed. "Are you all right?" asked Cassie.

"Oh good heavens yes," said Lydia. "I often come up here, I chat to him if you must know." She looked at Cassie. "See, mad as a hatter!" Her eyes had a far away look, "I miss our chats…" then smiling at Cassie she added, "As you can imagine, they're a little one sided, but… well, as I said, completely mad!"

Cassie hugged her aunt. "I don't think you're mad. Lot's of people do. I confess I sometimes speak to his portrait." She grinned. "Do you think this madness is in our genes?"

A look flitted across Lydia's face, a look Cassie had seen before but couldn't quite place. "Is everything okay, are you feeling all right?"

"Yes my dear, quite well," replied Lydia.

"It's just you had a 'look', a sort of strange one," said Cassie with concern.

Lydia tried to laugh it off. "As you so rightly said, we're both mad!" She looked at Cassie. "I was just thinking into the future a little, about your wedding."

"Good grief," laughed Cassie. "We haven't a clue when that will be."

"No, I know," said Lydia. "But I was just wondering if you'd had any thoughts about bridesmaids and that sort of thing?"

Cassie's eyes lit up with excitement. "Well actually, I **was** thinking about these things on the plane home as a matter of fact. James had nodded off and was snoring away so I was planning the day. Do you want to hear?"

Lydia nodded.

"Well," continued Cassie, "I'd love if Sarah could be there, she'd be Matron of Honour, wouldn't she?"

"Yes, indeed she would," replied Lydia. "It would be lovely if she could be. You and she have been best friends since you were babies."

"Absolutely," agreed Cassie. "Then I thought I'd rather like Kate's girls to be bridesmaids or flower girls, whatever they'd be called and if it was next year, Ben as a page-boy."

Lydia's eyes flashed with alarm. "Ben! Are you sure? I'm now envisaging complete and utter havoc."

"He'd be fine," smiled Cassie. "I'm sure he'd behave. I'll bribe him! Then, I'd like Charlie to be an usher. What do you think?"

"You seem to have everything worked out," smiled Lydia. "What about James, who will he have as best man?"

"No idea," replied Cassie. "Hopefully not his brother, he's a bit weird, but James may feel he has to."

Lydia hesitated and looked down at the grave. Cassie caught her glance. "I don't know about who should give me away." Cassie felt tears well up. "Can you imagine what he'd have been like?"

Lydia smiled. "Yes, yes I can." She patted Cassie's hand. "As proud as punch. He would also have been a gibbering wreck."

Cassie smiled and wiped her eyes. "You're right." She sighed. "This is the tricky one. Actually I thought about Benson or Uncle Peter, they've known me the longest."

"Yes," said Lydia. "That's perfectly true. Although Peter and Benson have both been in the 'father of the bride' role."

"Benson?" asked Cassie.

"Yes," replied Lydia. "Do you not remember a couple of years ago, his niece, Anne, they went to Cornwall for her wedding and he gave her away."

"I'd forgotten," said Cassie.

"What about David?" asked Lydia as if the idea had just popped into her head; she so wanted Cassie to ask him.

Cassie beamed at her aunt. "That's a wonderful idea. You are clever. I don't know why I hadn't thought of him myself." She looked down at her father's grave. "You know, I think Pops would be pretty pleased about David giving me away, don't you?"

Lydia smiled. "Yes, yes I think he would."

Cassie looked at her aunt. "Let's keep this idea our secret at the moment. I'll ask him nearer the time. Hopefully he'll say yes, and thank you, brilliant idea."

"My pleasure," smiled Lydia. "Come on, let's go back, it's starting to get a little chilly." She looked at her watch. "Afternoon tea time, I think."

Chapter 31

Cassie noted Robert's grim expression as he entered the study. "Morning Robert," smiled Cassie.

"Morning," replied Robert. He took out the papers and laid them on the desk. Without any preamble he said, "Cassie, we have a slight problem."

"Slight?" questioned Cassie.

Robert looked at her. "More than slight then. I'm sorry landing you with this. Your father knew we were having financial problems but thought the estate could weather the storm so to speak. He asked me to try and keep this from you for a year, till you found your feet." Robert tried to smile at her. "I'm sorry Cassie, but I'm going to disobey Charles. We have had one thing after the other and we need to generate income from another source to try and keep things going. The accountants say that within two to three years things should be back on an even keel and that's what Charles was banking on." Robert sighed. "Unfortunately at this rate we will have to lay off some workers and will also have to increase the rents, hefty increases."

Cassie looked at him. "We can't do that."

Robert shook his head. "We have to Cassie. The rents are ridiculously low, but I've done some calculations and even if we raise the rents, we still don't have sufficient funds.

"I take it you wish to call a meeting of the Trustees," said Cassie.

"Yes," said Robert. "Sometime soon, very soon."

"Let's have a think. We won't raise the rents just now or lay off the workers at the moment," said Cassie.

Robert looked at her. "What are you up to Cassie?"

Cassie looked at him with her big violet eyes. "Nothing, Robert," she said innocently. "I just think we need to have breathing space. I'm just taking stock of what you've said."

"Mmm," replied Robert not at all convinced.

She and Robert then spent the rest of the morning pouring over the accounts and various options that Robert had drawn up. There was certainly a shortfall.

"Shall we meet on Friday?" asked Cassie. "Peter doesn't have a surgery in the afternoon so it's easier for him."

"Friday it is then," said Robert. He had no idea what Cassie was thinking but he was certain she was up to something. "I'll get these copied and let everyone have a look before then."

Robert put the papers away and looked at Cassie. "I'm sorry for doing this to you Cassie. I don't think Charles would be best pleased."

"Please don't worry, Robert," said Cassie, trying to alleviate his concerns. I'm not sure if he was exactly 'with it' in the last little while, he was on morphine remember, and so may not have fully grasped the implications of what was happening on the estate."

"That's kind of you," smiled Robert. "But to me he always seemed to have a grasp, but who knows. See you later."

Cassie gazed out of the window. She had to really think about this and where better to do that than her studio.

She was soon absorbed in her work. She was working on a piece she had been commissioned to do and was thoroughly enjoying herself.

She put down her brush and stood back to check what she'd done. Something outside caught her eye and she looked up; it was James at the door.

"Hi," smiled James as he came in. He went over and kissed her and then looked at the painting she was working on. "It's wonderful. They'll be ecstatic when they see it."

"I hope so," smiled Cassie. "Actually this is good timing on your part. Can we go for a walk? I need to talk."

"Problems?" enquired James.

Cassie nodded. "Yes!" she sighed. "Sadly quite big problems."

"Let's grab a sandwich and coffee and have a picnic at the lake," said James.

As they walked towards the lake Cassie told James what Robert had said. He listened intently.

"So that's it, in a nut shell," said Cassie grimly.

James looked at her. "Not quite all. I suspect there is something else you want to say. You have that look about you."

Cassie smiled at him. "Mr. Perceptive!" They sat down on the bench and opened their picnic.

"I wondered about this for a plan," said Cassie. James rolled his eyes. "Okay, fire away."

"Well," said Cassie, wiping a crumb from her mouth. "We need income for the estate and Robert has exhausted all possible avenues as regards cutting back, rent increases etc. etc. etc. *but*," she smiled, "we have four, no sorry, five assets, staring us in the face."

"Speaking in English would help enormously," said James sarcastically.

"All right, speaking in words of one syllable so that you may follow this," said Cassie equally sarcastically. "I'll try and explain." She looked at him intently. "David and I are primarily portrait painters, you are a sculptor, Kate – landscape and Pierre – well what Pierre doesn't know about the history of art and everything connected with art is not worth knowing." She looked at James. "Understanding so far?"

"So far fine," replied James. "Possibly because I knew what we all were! Have done for some time!"

Cassie looked at him with disdain. "Are you being deliberately obtuse?"

"Cassie," said James, totally exasperated. "I haven't a clue what you're talking about. So far all you've told me is what our occupations are!"

Cassie looked at him and suddenly laughed. "Sorry, you're quite right. I've worked it out in my head but I'm not conveying this awfully well, am I?"

"You could say that," smiled James.

Cassie looked at him with excitement. "We could run art master classes; here, at The Hall. We would charge people vast sums to come and receive the benefit of our wisdom and expertise and they could stay for say three to four days sampling the delights of a country estate. What do you think?"

She looked at James expectantly.

He was a little unsure of how to respond. "Cassie, firstly none of us are teachers. Secondly, you, David and I have all commissioned work to do for the foreseeable future; that is our livelihood. Are you asking us to do that on top of teaching?" Cassie felt completely deflated.

James sensed her disappointment. Gently, he continued. "Will the guests be beginners or gifted amateurs? How much would we charge? Where would they stay?"

"The 'where would they stay' bit is easy," replied Cassie. "Here at The Hall. We have six free bedrooms, all en-suite, they could be the guest bedrooms – and we could have more."

"You wouldn't mind sharing your home with a whole bunch of strangers then?" asked James. What about some of the wonderful things you have here. Would you trust people not to be, shall we say, light-fingered?"

"You're just putting millions of obstacles in the way," replied Cassie cuttingly. She was hurt that James wasn't filled with the same enthusiasm.

He put his arm around her. "I'm trying to be practical, that's all. What about staff? You can't expect Mrs. Pearson and the others to cope."

"I'd get help from the village, I'd employ some of the locals," replied Cassie.

"Oh I can see how that would generate income! Employ more people. Excellent plan," James sighed, amazed at what he was hearing. He thought this a ludicrous scheme.

Tears filled her eyes so James felt immediately contrite. "Cassie I'm sorry. It just seems such a completely *off the top of your head* idea. I don't think you've thought it through."

"Of course I haven't," replied Cassie, angrily standing up and facing him. "I only found out about all this, this morning. I'm just formulating plans for God's sake."

James stood up as well and tried to put his arm around her again but he was brushed aside.

Cassie stared out across the lake then, turning to him she spat out the words. "This is the first year I've been in charge and already I've totally and utterly cocked it up!"

James looked at her in disbelief. "God almighty Cassie. You only knew about this today. There is nothing you could have done." He grabbed her by the shoulders. "Look at me" She turned towards him. "This hasn't suddenly happened. It was happening even when your father was alive. It wasn't his fault. It isn't your fault. Do you understand – not your fault, it's the times, so many are in the same boat."

She wiped her eyes and, looking at James, said, "Look... look around you. Look all around you. This is Harrington Estate. I am responsible for this and for all the people that work here and do you know something? That scares me, it scares the hell out of me."

She suddenly looked exhausted and James held her close. "I'm sorry, truly I am but you can't shoulder the blame for this. It's not your fault. Things have been abysmal of late for estates, farms, everything to do with land, it seems. The accountants say that things will pick up in the next couple of years. Can we not tighten our belts? Even raise the rents a little?"

Cassie looked at him. "You're right," she agreed, resigned to the fact that James was making more sense than she was. "Perhaps we could explain to the tenants the position and that we'll have to increase their rents. They may not mind, well mind, too much!"

"Come on," said James. "I have to get back and do some work." They walked back to the house in silence.

"Sorry I was such a misery," said Cassie, giving James a kiss.

"I'm sorry I wasn't being supportive of your ideas," replied James. "Let's sit down later and look at it all sensibly."

"Okay," smiled Cassie. "That would be good. Don't work too hard. I'll see you later."

Cassie went back inside, deep in thought. She then had, what she thought, was a flash of inspiration. "Ha," she said and dumping her things in the hall, went through to the study where she shut the door and began work on the idea she was formulating from her newly found inspiration.

The day of the Extraordinary Meeting of Harrington Board arrived and everyone duly took their seats, awaiting the arrival of their chairman, Cassie.

"Sorry I was delayed," said Cassie. "I just wanted to photocopy some things for you." She smiled at them all. They, in turn, registered surprise at the vision before them. Cassie was in a skirt and jacket, giving the appearance of a well-groomed and competent business-woman, instead of the usual casual appearance she normally adopted. This had been part of her plan. They had to take her seriously and try to stop thinking of her as 'Little Cassie', hence the attire. She caught Kate's eye who winked at her. Cassie nearly grinned back but managed to stop herself and just gave a slight, but knowing smile.

Cassie looked over at Robert. "Robert perhaps you'd like to fill us in with recent events."

Robert stood up. "No doubt you've all read the papers I gave you at the beginning of the week. I'm sorry but nothing has improved since then so my projections are on course for being accurate." He looked around. "Any questions?" Various questions were asked which Robert answered as Cassie looked on. "I'm not sure what else we can do." There was a subdued murmur of agreement around the table as he sat down. They all looked at Cassie expectantly.

Cassie stood up and swallowed. *Here I go*, she thought. She went round everyone, passing out the papers she had photocopied.

"Since Robert told me of our problem I have given some thought to this," she started. "And I wonder if you would give consideration to this plan. It would involve us all having to sacrifice our time and would be extra work but, and I stress the word *but*, it may give us extra income and it would only be for a couple of years."

She then asked Kate and David what they felt about doing the occasional teaching. Although surprised, they both agreed they could manage that. Then she looked at Pierre. "Pierre, are you really thinking of retiring from the gallery?"

"Yes, I am," replied Pierre. "I've made a good living out of it and have been offered an excellent price. I confess, it's not been the same since you left." He smiled. "Why?"

Cassie smiled back. "I wondered if you'd join Kate, David and I with the teaching?"

"I'd be delighted," replied Pierre. "But exactly whom are we teaching?"

Cassie then explained her plan of residential art courses. David and Kate looked at each other, wondering if they'd agreed to something a little more time consuming than they'd expected.

Cassie caught their looks. "I can see anxiety mounting over there," she said smiling at them. "We wouldn't all be teaching at once. I would have thought two at a time for a couple of hours in the morning and afternoon, maybe less, maybe, on very rare occasions, more. At the moment it's a bit of an unknown quantity but before you get too anxious let me explain."

She then proceeded to tell them of the travel companies she had phoned both in the UK and abroad who specialised in residential art courses, to find out what the courses entailed and most importantly, the prices they charged. She had itemised about fifteen places and informed them, they were on page one of their handout. They duly turned to page one.

On page two was a breakdown of the prices of advertising, painting materials, tutors' fees, etc. She smiled at the newly appointed tutors. "Yes," she said. "You'd have a salary, albeit a small one – because if we do that, I can claim back from the tax man." She beamed at them all. She then told them about the rooms, how many guests they could have, the wages of the staff that would be employed to help. She had forgotten nothing.

Peter stood up and, looking at the others, he then smiled at Cassie as he picked up the handout. "A great deal of work has gone into this. I know we have to look at it in slightly more detail but from what you say, it seems a feasible proposition, it certainly does. Do you agree, Robert?"

Robert smiled broadly. "I most certainly do. It's a wonderful idea. It really may save the day. Well done Cassie."

Peter continued. "Cassie, Charles was right in placing his trust in you. You've done a first rate job." He looked fondly at Cassie thinking, was this confident lady in front of him, really the same little girl who got into all these scrapes and trouble with his daughter? He smiled. "Charles would be proud Cassie, so proud."

Cassie smiled. "Thank you, Uncle Peter," she said quietly and then sat down.

Robert turned to her, "Cassie why don't I take these to the accountants. Let them have a quick look."

Cassie looked surprised at this suggestion. "Do you not wish to discuss it all first? I mean I'm landing us all in it. Should we not at least have a think?"

David stood up. "Cassie we all have a vested interest in this estate. I am delighted to teach, something of course I always fancied!" He raised his eyebrows and grinned. "Seriously, we can work out the practicalities of doing classes, accommodation and such like. Let the accountants see the figures first. If they say it's a no-go, then it's back to the drawing board, but to me, it seems good." He looked over at Robert. "Do you think they could get back to us by next Friday?"

"We'll tell them they have to," said Robert forcefully.

"Right," said Cassie. "Meeting adjourned, and we'll meet next Friday at the same time. Thank you everyone."

They all looked at her and clapped. "Thank you Madame Chairman. A beautifully executed meeting," laughed Peter.

"Ha! Ha!" grinned Cassie, but she was secretly thrilled they had been so enthusiastic. All her hard work had perhaps, just perhaps, paid off. She could hardly wait to tell James.

They all went their separate ways but Lydia waited for Cassie. "Now I know why you've been burning the midnight oil," she smiled.

"I'm sorry I didn't have a chance to speak to you on your own, but I only finished it just before the meeting," said Cassie. "Come on, let's have tea in the study and we can go over this properly. I just sort of battered ideas in."

"These ideas were not, as you say, battered in. A great deal of thought went into your presentation," responded Lydia, with a knowing smile. "I know that today was quite a test for you and you passed, you most certainly did, and with flying colours."

"Thanks," said Cassie. "This is your home as well though and I am well aware that my proposals will cause disruption to you and the others but I have an idea should the proposals be accepted."

"Really?" asked Lydia.

"Yes, I thought we could block off the top corridor where our rooms are and put a door, a locked door, from say, just in front of the entrance to Pops room. That would at least give us all privacy. The morning room and study would be ours but we'd have to let guests use the drawing room and perhaps the library plus of course the dining room," said Cassie. She looked at Lydia anxiously. "So far, what are your thoughts?"

"Not bad," replied Lydia giving consideration to this idea. "Go on."

"We'd store our most valuable things, we'd provide dinner, bed and breakfast and a light lunch, sandwiches, that sort of thing. I really think we could charge a whopping amount for this. Anyone interested in art, and especially portraits, will have heard of D.F. Risi and I hope would be champing at the bit to have tuition from

David; a world-renowned painter. Also, the whole ambience of the place is another huge plus in our favour, don't you think?"

Lydia nodded. "The thought of total strangers tramping round the house fills me with horror, but the alternative is too ghastly to contemplate. You know, I had thought of opening the house and grounds to the public," she shuddered. "But then decided that was too horrendous an idea. I think it would be too invasive. Your way is much better, we can at least contain them and it would be far more lucrative – we hope!" Lydia then smiled. "You have jobs for everyone apart from me. Am I such an old useless fuddy-duddy?"

Cassie grinned. "No, not at all. I have the very thing for you and you won't have to move, you can just relax!" This intrigued Lydia. Cassie continued with as straight a face as she could manage. "People coming to learn how to paint portraits will naturally require sitters!!"

Lydia looked at her with alarm. "Fully clothed, I hope?"

"Most certainly," smiled Cassie.

"Splendid," smiled Lydia. "At least I'm down for something."

Cassie, who had been teasing, realised her aunt was serious and didn't want to be left out. "Good for you Aunt Lydia, thanks!" she said.

There was then a knock at the door and in came Mrs. Pearson, Margaret and Benson.

"Sorry for interrupting," said Benson. "May we have a word?"

"Come in, have a seat," smiled Cassie, wondering what on earth was about to transpire.

Benson looked at Cassie and smiled. "We were going over your proposals and have concerns."

"Right," said Cassie. "Fire away. These are just a sort of first draft of ideas, I'm open to suggestions."

Before Benson could speak, Mrs. Pearson interjected. "Well, this nonsense about employing kitchen staff for breakfasts and dinners: I've never heard such an absurd idea."

Cassie looked at her with surprise but before she could say anything Mrs. Pearson was off again.

"Look at the costings you've done for extra staff, throwing your money down the drain, and just at the time when we've to tighten our belts, ridiculous, no need for them, no need at all."

It suddenly dawned on Cassie what Mrs. Pearson was getting at. She got up and went round to her and hugged her. "Mrs. P., this is a lovely, lovely thought and kindness itself, but there is absolutely no way I am burdening you with extra work, a great deal of extra work, I may add."

"I've never been afraid of hard work, my girl," replied Mrs. Pearson indignantly.

"I am well aware of that Mrs. P. but..." she looked at her tenderly. "I want you around for a long, long time and I am not going to kill you with over-work." Mrs. P. gave an exaggerated 'tut', which Cassie ignored. "It's a small point, but I think a valid one, which happily you can't argue with, but you are now a **little** past retirement age. Women half your age might baulk at the idea of taking this on."

Mrs. Pearson was not to be dissuaded. "If you think I'm having all and sundry telling me what to do in my kitchen, then you can think again!" Her eyes filled with tears. "I'd manage, I would."

Cassie looked at Benson who shrugged his shoulders; he couldn't help.

She then had an idea which hoped would pacify Mrs. P. "Here's an idea which there is no compromise on," she said firmly. "How about we employ one or two girls to help with the cooking, waitressing duties and clearing up but you are the one who oversees the operation. You'd be in sole charge. But, and this is a firm but," said Cassie gently, "You will be directing operations from the kitchen chair! Would that meet with your approval?"

"It's better, but not right," sniffed Mrs. Pearson. "You're still wasting your money."

Cassie smiled. "There is an expression Mrs. P., 'you have to speculate to accumulate.' Have you heard that before?"

Mrs. Pearson shook her head. "No. What nonsense is that?"

"You know fine what it means," grinned Cassie. "Anyway you will be busy thinking up menus, which we'll have to discuss, so you'll have more than enough to do."

"That's more like it," smiled Mrs. Pearson. "Much more like it. I'll get busy with that straight away."

"Hold on," said Cassie. "Let's wait and hear if we have the go ahead from the accountant."

She looked at Benson and Margaret. "Right, now is there something bothering you two about the proposals?"

Benson smiled at Cassie. "Well actually we were going along the same lines as Mrs. Pearson. We don't need extra help in the house; let's try and save money. As David said, we all have a vested interest in the estate. We want to help, and help by trying to save money."

A lump developed in Cassie's throat as she looked at the three of them sitting before her. She was in danger of feeling completely overwhelmed by their kindness.

"Thank you," said Cassie. "I hate going on about age but I'll say what I said to Mrs. P., I will not be responsible for putting you all in an early grave. Selfish as this may sound, I need 'The Family' around me but I can assure you as you're so worried." She smiled at Benson. "That this *will* involve extra work for you, but I want you as Chief Delegator okay? If this takes off, I need someone at the helm to run the house, delegating to some youngsters from the village, not performing all the tasks yourself. But thank you for your kind gestures. I don't know what I'd do without you all, I really don't."

She looked at her watch; it was nearly five. "Oh to hell, lets all have a pre-prandial. We're not completely broke yet and we need something after today." She looked at Benson. "George, will you do the honours please."

"Hello, anyone home?" It was James, anxious to hear how Cassie had got on.

Benson got up and opened the study door. "In here."

James walked in, surveying the scene. "Here I was slogging away in my studio and I come back to find you all boozing, I don't know, some people have all the luck." He went over and kissed Cassie. He looked at her. "Are you all drowning your sorrows or celebrating?"

Cassie looked at the others. "Not sure, really. We just decided that it had been quite an afternoon and I for one, fancied a drink. Help yourself." She knew that James was itching to know what had gone on so tried to give him edited highlights of the meeting. Then she told him what the others had come in about.

He smiled at them all and then at Cassie. "Harrington Estate will never go under, not with people like you battling away, that's for sure!" He raised his glass. "To Harrington Estate and all who work on her!"

"Idiot!" Cassie smiled, but just the same, she joined the others in toasting the estate.

The week passed painfully slowly, or at least that's what everyone felt. By 11.00 a.m. on the Friday of the second meeting the accountants had still not been in touch. Robert was about to explode when, at 11.22 a.m., a Courier arrived from the accountants. He rushed to Cassie with it.

"Here's the accountant's verdict. I thought you should open it," he smiled nervously.

"Well, here goes," said Cassie as she opened the envelope with the paperknife. Robert was pacing up and down. "Robert, you'll wear out the carpet, and God knows, we may not be able to replace it!"

"If that's your attempt at humour, it stinks, as Ben would say!" grinned Robert. He got a chair and sat next to Cassie as she spread out the notes from the accountant.

"Robert, you understand this better than me. As they say in the trade, 'what's the bottom line'?" asked Cassie.

Robert was quickly scanning the pages. He looked at Cassie, then slowly a smile crossed his face. "It seems to be yes. Its feasible. They think your idea is good. Brilliant Cassie." He hugged her to him. "Quite, quite brilliant." He sank back into his chair. "The hard work begins now, with plenty of changes here."

Realisation dawned on Cassie. The only viable option was now reality, and life at Harrington would never be the same again. She looked at Robert. "There was no other option, was there?"

He shook his head. "No, your idea has, fingers crossed, saved the day." She looked suddenly apprehensive. "Cassie, its only for a couple of years, three or four at the most and it won't be a permanent, 365 days of the year commitment. Surely it will be seasonal? It can be as much or as little as you wish, or as the bank balance dictates, would perhaps be a fairer analysis," he said wryly.

"Right," said Cassie. "Let's go over this sensibly and have the facts right for the meeting." She looked at Robert. "There was something else, and you are of course right. The rents, they are a little unrealistic in today's world. What I thought I'd do is go round all the tenants personally and tell them of the increase. Do you think that would be fair?"

Robert nodded. "More than fair, not usual and not terribly business-like." He smiled. "Exactly what your father would have done! I'll have the increases worked out, then deduct a couple of pounds, from each of my original estimates. It saves you having to do it!"

Cassie looked at him and smiled. "Why do you think I'd do that?" she asked innocently.

"Because," Robert smiled. "That is what your father used to try and do! It makes my life easier if I do it for you, then I know what monies should be coming in and not the ones you and the tenant, agree upon!"

Cassie laughed. "Don't you ever wish you'd worked with more business-like people than Pops and me?"

"No," replied Robert. "I can't think of two better people to work for."

Cassie interrupted. "Not for Robert... with, work with!" Robert just smiled.

It was with mixed feelings that the Board of Harrington Estate heard the results of the accountant's deliberations, but all knew this is what had to be.

Cassie stood up and faced them all, again looking business-like in skirt and jacket. "I'm well aware of the mixed feelings we are all having. Personally, my stomach is in knots at the very thought of all this. However, to keep not only The Hall, but also the estate in good repair and working order, we need more income. Recent events have been out-with our control; we have had every farming catastrophe there is, then the flooding and possibly the final straw, the roof at the east wing needing repaired. All this happening at one time was too much for the estate to bear and, as you are well aware, costs have positively escalated. We'll come through this." She turned to her aunt. "Aunt Lydia, you call this something, the something spirit."

Lydia smiled. "The Dunkirk spirit!"

"Exactly," said Cassie. "We're having the Dunkirk spirit here and, who knows, we may even enjoy it!" She smiled at the sceptical faces. "Well we may, we just don't know!"

"Bravo!" smiled David proudly. "Fighting spirit, that's us." He looked at everyone and added, "As a new member of 'The Family', I feel proud to be part of this."

"Hear hear!" agreed Peter. "Cassie," he asked. "What can I do to help?" Rowena looked up at him. "And Rowena," he added.

"Oh don't you worry, smiled Cassie. "I suspect there will be loads for you to do."

Rowena looked at Cassie. "Who will you get to take the bookings and do the books?"

"Well," replied Cassie. "I was going to try and take the bookings myself and I hadn't thought about the books to be perfectly honest."

"Count me in then. I can do them," smiled Rowena. "I'd like to."

"Great," said Cassie.

"That still leaves me without a job," said Peter.

Cassie slowly smiled at him. "Not necessarily, Uncle Peter. You remember I said we'd have different art classes to suit all tastes. Well of course one of the classes would be life studies."

Peter nodded, a little unsure what they were. "That's more like it; I'm delighted to help out."

"Life studies," smiled Cassie, "are where the model is inevitably naked!"

Peter's eyes leapt out of their sockets. "You are joking, please tell me you are." He looked frantic as everyone started laughing. "Okay, anything other than that, something more pleasant… latrine duties perhaps, that will do nicely!!"

Cassie laughed. "We'll find something for you Uncle Peter, don't you fret," said Cassie.

"Now," said Cassie. "Back to more serious matters. We will require a business plan of sorts. I assume we have to get permission from the local council and what have you, if we are having paying guests."

Mr. Napier, the lawyer, who up until this moment had remained silent, indicated to Cassie he'd like to speak. "Alan, I think you can help us here," said Cassie.

By the end of the afternoon, the list of legal 'do's and don'ts' Alan Napier had drawn up were extensive, but as Cassie had reinforced to everyone, they were 'not insurmountable'.

The meeting closed at six with everyone's minds spinning.

"Phew, I'm whacked," said Cassie. "We've been at it for over four hours. It's unbelievable all the rules we have to adhere to. I'd no idea. However I'm not thinking about it any more tonight. I need a break; we all need a break! I'm going for a long soak in the bath, accompanied by a cool glass of Chardonnay!"

Everyone agreed a well earned break was richly deserved by all.

Chapter 32

Over the next couple of months Cassie's patience, not one of her strong points, was sorely tested by what she felt were archaic and pointless rules and regulations bound together in a melee of bureaucratic red tape.

Robert, although sympathetic to her frustration, was wise to the ways of bureaucracy and knew that the only way to win the officials round to their plans was by diplomacy peppered with a little flattery! Cassie, who could not abide this kowtowing, eventually realised Robert was right; this was the only way to get their ideas accepted, and so, with reluctance, she played the game.

The letter granting them permission eventually arrived. "Oh Robert do you think this is a good or a bad omen? It would have to arrive today, today of all days," said Cassie. "The first anniversary of Pops... not being... of his death!"

Robert looked at her and quickly said, "Good, definitely a good omen."

Cassie looked thoughtful. "I had wondered about having a little service in the chapel or something today, but then decided that was absurd; everyone remembers him in their own way. We don't need to go somewhere special; we all have our own places which are special."

"Mine are the moors," smiled Robert.

Cassie returned his smile. "We have a meeting this afternoon anyway so afterwards I think we should have a celebration. Champers to toast his memory, he'd approve of that, and to celebrate a new chapter in the history of the estate. What do you think?"

"Excellent idea, Madame Chairman," smiled Robert. "You can count me in."

"I'll go and tell Benson. Won't be a moment," said Cassie.

She went looking for Benson. "Ah, George, after the meeting this afternoon I wondered if we should perhaps have a little champagne?"

Benson seemed surprised. "Is there something to celebrate?"

"Well," said Cassie, pondering this for a moment. "I'm not sure celebrate is the word to use but yes, the council have given us the go-ahead, but keep that quiet till the meeting will you."

"Of course. How are you today?"

"Well we all have our own thoughts of this time last year, don't we?" said Cassie. Benson nodded. "In some ways this year seems to have raced by; so much has happened, in others it seems a long time ago. Sometimes I still can't believe it." She looked at Benson. "Be honest, do you think its bizarre, having champagne today, on the anniversary?"

"No, I don't," smiled Benson. "I can see why you're doing it. It sounds as if there is to be a new chapter, or era here at The Hall, we, toast the future."

"Yes," smiled Cassie. "That's it exactly and also it seems like fate that we know today, on the anniversary, so I want it to be a toast to Pops as well." She shrugged her shoulders. "You're right, it sounds bizarre. Will the others think it weird, do you think?"

"You're the boss," smiled Benson. "Your father would have done exactly the same; any excuse he'd have said."

Cassie smiled, "It's acknowledgement of the day, a toast to his memory, and because the future is a little terrifying I am trying to convince myself the letter arriving today is like a sign from above, from Pops saying, good luck to us." She looked at Benson and gave a half smile. "Straight jacket any time you like I'd have thought!"

"Its a sign, you're right," agreed Benson seriously.

"Good to see you're as cracked as I am," smiled Cassie. "Let's go for it, we'll only have a glass or two, not our usual booze up! Now, I'd better get back to Robert so I'll see you later. She went off to the study but turned and looked at Benson. "Thanks for pandering to my fanciful notions."

Benson smiled. "Not notions, it's a sign remember… we're agreed!" Cassie laughed as she went to join Robert.

Cassie started the meeting. "Good afternoon and thank you for all being here." She held up a letter. "This morning we got confirmation from the council that they accept our plans so, for

332

better or worse, we can go ahead." Everyone looked at each other. "I think we all feel the same," continued Cassie. "Mixed feelings; because for the next couple of years or maybe more, Harrington Hall is going to be different. I am trying very hard to think of this as a new chapter in the life of the estate and a positive one."

She smiled at them. "I'm sure we all know that today is the anniversary of Pops death." It was obvious by everyone's expressions that they were well aware of the fact. "Well, I have decided to think that the letter arriving today is an omen, a sign from above if you like," she smiled. "Of Pops blessing to us." Her voice cracked ever so slightly. "I think we've done the right thing, I hope we've done the right thing, we had no alternative," she added quietly, then sat down.

Lydia quickly stood up and, patting Cassie's hand, said, "We did have an alternative." Everyone looked surprised, something they hadn't thought of? "And that," continued Lydia, "was to go under! Harrington Estate to be taken over by goodness knows who and turned into goodness knows what. My girl, my dear girl," she smiled fondly. "Your idea has hopefully stopped that alternative, an alternative too ghastly to contemplate. We'll manage, we always do. Onwards and upwards, that's the motto. It has been said," said Lydia wryly, "that a challenge is so very good for a person." They all laughed, "I'm sure we'll find this a positively beneficial experience." She smiled gently at Cassie. "We will! We really will!"

Cassie was struggling a little on the composure front as she looked with gratitude at her aunt.

Peter noting this, stood up. "Well said, Lydia. And from a medical point of view, a challenge is very good for a person, so you're absolutely right." They all smiled as Peter continued. "In the last couple of months we've done much preparation, things just need a little fine tuning, so I don't think today our meeting should go on for too long."

Cassie smiled at Peter. "Thank you, Uncle Peter. I think you're right. Do you all agree?" Everyone nodded. "Some of you may think this a little peculiar but I thought today we should have a little champagne. Firstly to toast Pops memory, and secondly, to toast the future; the future of Harrington. If any of you would care to join me, it's all set up in the drawing room." She looked around at everyone. "Meeting closed." Everyone stood up and made a move towards the drawing room.

Cassie looked at Lydia. "Thank you for what you said. I was running out of steam a little there, thanks for stepping in."

"I meant it my dear. You've done splendidly, he really would be so very proud." Cassie looked a little unsure.

"He would hate what was happening to Harrington as much as we do; but it's just temporary, it will whizz by," said Cassie, trying to convince not only her aunt but also herself.

"The champagne, are you okay about that idea?" asked Cassie anxiously.

"Lovely idea. You know what your father and I were like," she smiled at Cassie. "That was more than obvious from the wonderful picture you did for me; Charles and I, any excuse to open the champers, you know that. It's so good you're following in the family tradition!" Cassie smiled. "Come on," said Lydia. "Let's go through and join the others."

Peter handed Cassie and Lydia a glass. "Do you want me to say a few words?" Cassie shook her head. "Thanks, Uncle Peter, but I'll try. Here goes!"

"Everyone!" said Cassie to catch their attention. "If you've all got a glass I'd like to try and say a few words." She took a deep breath. "I was going to try and make a speech but I don't think that's my best plan today!" She tried to smile. "Instead, I'd like to propose a toast to Pops, and to us all in our new 'challenge' and to the future of Harrington Estate, so please raise your glasses to Pops and Harrington Estate!"

"Charles and Harrington Estate!"

The next few weeks passed by in a blur of activity, with one of the first 'challenges' appearing fairly early on, at the interviews, more especially at the interviews for the kitchen staff!

Cassie sighed. "Mrs. P. you cannot, you simply cannot, use the term scullery maid. People are not called that now. They are called kitchen operatives. You are frightening them off and anyway, what was wrong with that last girl?"

Mrs Pearson hurrumphed. "Kitchen operatives, what nonsense. I'll tell you what was wrong with that one. Did you see her hands?"

"Yes," said Cassie relieved that she had noted them. "Yes I did and they were clean, fingernails spotless."

"Lily-white, that's what they were, lily-white," replied Mrs. Pearson. "No good at all."

"Why?" asked Cassie, grappling with why this was wrong. "Unless I'm very much mistaken, I thought clean was what we were aiming for!"

"Hadn't done a hard days work in her life. She'd have the vapours at the first sign of hard work, mark my words," said Mrs. Pearson emphatically.

What Cassie had thought would be relatively easy, was now proving a nightmare. "We're running out of people, they'll be no one left to interview. At this rate, we're going to have to trawl the next county, never mind the next village. Please Mrs. P.," Cassie begged, "Let's lower our expectations just a smidgen, perhaps even give them a trial period and lets, try very, very hard not to use the term scullery maid!"

"Lowering standards, that's what you're doing, more of this dumbing down rubbish. Standards **will be** maintained in my kitchen," stated Mrs. Pearson.

"Mrs. P." pleaded Cassie. "Of course I'm not doing that. I expect the highest standards to be maintained; of course I do, as they always have been. All I am saying is that if we find someone reasonably suitable, then you could train her up to your standards. If she fell short, then she's out, but we have to adapt to what is on offer."

Cassie then decided to sway her in another way. "Mrs. Pearson, some of these girls have not had the good fortune to know what standards are expected. They may have come from 'an anything goes' routine at home. But if they were here, you could show them the error of their ways and they in turn could pass that on to their children; it would have a cumulative effect. But for this to happen, they have to first be given a chance."

Inspirational, Cassie, she thought. She looked at Mrs. Pearson and smiled sweetly. "Don't you agree?"

Mrs. Pearson looked thoughtful. "Put that way, I see what you mean. All right, I'll try and be a little more tolerant, more understanding." She now understood about challenges. This would be hers; to teach someone the ways of the kitchen.

Cassie felt relief flood over her. "Thank you Mrs. Pearson, thank you. Now, shall we ask the next girl in?"

Eventually the kitchen staff were hired. I hope Aunt Lydia and George have had better luck than I did. She went through to the Morning Room where they were conducting their interviews.

They had just finished as well. Cassie overheard them laughing. "Well that went very smoothly, we're quite a team aren't we?" Lydia was saying to Benson.

Cassie walked in. "Hello you two, how did it go?"

"Fine," replied Lydia. "What about you, are you feeling all right my dear? You look rather pale."

"Pale… I'm surprised I survived!" She proceeded to tell them of her afternoon of interviews.

By the end of her story Lydia and Benson were helpless with laughter. "Sorry," said Lydia, wiping her eyes. "We shouldn't laugh, but…" Giggles erupted again.

"Thanks a lot," said Cassie, stretching out on the chair. "I need a large glass of wine. Who'd care to join me?"

"You and your aunt have it on your own," laughed Benson. "I'll go and make sure you get a breather from your interviewing partner! I'll bring back the wine." Looking at Lydia he asked, "G&T?"

"Mmm, please," said Lydia. "That sounds lovely."

The next morning Robert arrived with more bills for Cassie to see. "The builder's have sent in their bill, that's the last one. Thankfully."

Cassie looked at it and gulped. "Was this his estimate?" Robert nodded. "I'd forgotten," said Cassie. She went to the desk and took out a cheque book. "Don't give me a row, but we have to do this. It's just temporary and the estate can pay me back, but I don't want the estate account completely depleted."

Robert, although unhappy about this, reluctantly agreed. He and Cassie then continued the morning's work.

"Well," said Cassie. "In seven days, we'll have a rough idea if we have hit the right formula; three singles and one double have booked in. I think everything is in place now, isn't it?"

"Yes," agreed Robert. "The extension to David's workshop is finished and James's new studio will be finished tomorrow, Thursday at the latest. We've just got to finish boxing some of the more valuable items and I think we're all set. The girls from the village who are helping in the house seem willing and keen about this venture so fingers crossed they'll stay and be an asset."

"Hopefully we'll be saying the same about the kitchen staff!" said Cassie anxiously. "I suspect our turnover there might be a little higher!"

"Once they get to know her they'll be crazy about her," said Robert reassuringly. "I remember the first time I met Mrs. Pearson. She terrified the life out of me. I couldn't understand why Kate had her as a sort of surrogate Granny, but it wasn't long till I understood. She's marvellous and when she's your friend, it's for life."

Cassie smiled, agreeing totally with what he said, but she was still just a little bit nervous.

"Is there anything else you can think of?" asked Cassie. Robert couldn't think of anything. "I promise I'll try not to overwork Kate. I really will and please promise me that you'll tell me if you think the family plus all this is too much. You would say, wouldn't you?"

"Of course," replied Robert. "She's really looking forward to it, and anyway Ben's at nursery school every morning. Let's see how it goes but I'm sure it will be fine."

"Robert, I know I keep saying this," said Cassie. "But I have no idea, no idea at all, what I would have done without you. Not only have you had to keep an eye on me, but I'm now adding work to your already busy workload. You have to be honest as well. If it's getting too much, please say."

"Cassie," said Robert. "I would far rather have slightly more work than what was in danger of becoming a frightening reality, no work at all. We're all mucking in it's going to be fine. Just you see."

Cassie hadn't slept. She was petrified this venture would fail. A venture she had suggested; a venture she had poured her own money into. *It must succeed. It has to succeed*, she thought, trying to summon her own self confidence.

She got up, showered, dressed and went downstairs. It was only 6.00 a.m. so the house was quiet. She went into The Great Hall. One end of it had been cleared and easels were arranged in a semi-circle with painting materials on a nearby table. She hoped they wouldn't have to use here too much, only if the weather was inclement.

Cassie looked up at the portrait of Charles and said wearily, "Sorry Pops, couldn't think of another way. We'll get The Hall back to normal one day, you'll see, one day soon." She went over to the table and checked everything was laid out. "I've only done this at least fifty times. She looked up at Charles again. "Wish us luck, Pops. Loads of luck."

She then crossed the hall to check on the dining room when Margaret came out of there. They both laughed. "We're not worried about today at all, are we?" smiled Margaret. "I was just checking the dining room for tonight's dinner for at least the tenth time!"

Cassie smiled. "I've checked the painting materials for about that number of times as well! Where were you off to next?"

"Bedrooms," replied Margaret. "They've only been checked eight times!"

"Slacking I see," Cassie grinned. "Why don't we check them together and that can count as two, then they'll match the count in the dining room." They giggled and disappeared upstairs where they found everything in satisfactory order in all of the guest bedrooms, apart from the one last finishing touch; flowers, but they were to be picked later.

"This is going to be a long day I think," said Cassie. "Let's go and have breakfast or at least a coffee." They arrived in the kitchen to find Benson, Mrs. Pearson and Robert there.

"We're going to be exhausted by tonight," commented Cassie. "Today's the worst day, once we get through this, it will be plain sailing, don't you think?"

No one had time to reply for there was a knock at the door and in walked David. He looked at them all and smiled "Any more vacancies for the 'Insomniacs' Society'?"

Much to everyone's surprise the morning passed quickly and at two o'clock the first of the guests arrived. The guests initially seemed a little overwhelmed by their surroundings; they couldn't believe they were to be staying in a Stately Home. Cassie secretly thought this was no bad thing. *Be sure to tell your friends*, she thought, but she was charming, as were the others, and in no time the guests were put at their ease.

All the other guests had arrived by four and, after unpacking, were treated to a sumptuous afternoon tea in the drawing room. They were speechless with delight. Lydia was in her element as hostess; entertaining them with stories of The Hall. As the guests went out to admire the grounds, Benson was gratified to hear one guest comment that he'd have gladly paid double just to be in such lovely surroundings with such welcoming people. He dashed off to tell Cassie.

The three days passed smoothly and without any major hitches, with all at The Hall rising magnificently to the 'challenge'. David, as Cassie suspected, had been a huge hit; especially with the ladies. She watched with amusement as he flirted shamelessly with each one of them, regardless of their age; in fact the older they were, the safer he felt, and the more outrageous he became, much to the delight of the recipient.

James on the other hand, was taking his teaching very seriously and to his surprise, enjoyed it; especially if a pupil actually managed to sculpt something that had more than a passing resemblance to what it was meant to be.

All in all, the first guests had been a success. They left showering Cassie and the others with glowing compliments. Waving the guests off the premises 'The Family' then let out a whoop of joy. They'd done it. It was early days yet, but they'd done it. Three days' grace and then the next batch would arrive – time for a well earned breather.

When it was time to hand out the first wages to the new staff Cassie decided that she would do it, so she could try and gauge how they were coping with their new jobs.

Much to her amazement, but delight, they had thoroughly enjoyed their work. One of the kitchen staff even volunteered that Mrs. Pearson was adorable.

Cassie's face had obviously registered a moment's surprise, because the young girl laughed. "She's like my Grandma, that's my great, great granny," she said as way of explanation. "She looks fierce, and she's very strict, but really she's marshmallow, all soft and lovely."

Cassie smiled. "I think that's a wonderful description."

The young girl suddenly looked alarmed. "Don't tell her though; please don't tell her. She'll maybe kill me." Cassie assured her she wouldn't; it would be their secret.

The Board of Harrington Estate was delighted when, at their monthly meeting, Rowena was able to tell them that the finances from the master-classes were making a small profit. Although it was too soon to be able to forecast, she was cautiously optimistic that they were heading in the right direction. They had advertised in August for late September/October bookings, citing what an ideal time it would be to have the chance to paint the autumnal colours in beautiful surroundings. Although they had been tempted to increase the price they felt they should play safe and entice the guests in. This had paid dividends as all rooms were fully booked for the forthcoming weeks.

They were all relieved when the final guest had departed at the end of October. They would have The Hall back to themselves and although they had enjoyed it, they were exhausted.

Rowena, Robert and Cassie went over the books. "It looks promising for next year," said Rowena. "We already have bookings and won't have the kind of expenditure we had for this year. Cassie, I'm tempted to say, feel a little confident."

"It's been an exhausting few months, there are one or two things we'll do differently, but okay," she said, grinning at Rowena. "I'll try and feel a little confident."

She looked at them. "I'm a little concerned though. We're so tired, can we keep going at this pace from Easter right through?"

"It will be much easier," said Robert. "We know what we're doing now. Everything will be more automatic and also we don't have all the preparations to do, the buildings to renovate, everything's done. I really don't think it will be quite so exhausting."

"What about Aunt Lydia, Mrs. Pearson; they're both old ladies. I can't do this to them; have them working so hard," said Cassie. "If something happens to them, it will be my fault."

"Rubbish," replied Rowena. "They're both thriving on this; they love it, love the buzz. The Estate is their lives; they feel they are contributing, which of course they are, enormously. If, God forbid, either of them dropped down dead tomorrow, they would far rather go that way than sitting festering in a chair somewhere totally inactive." She smiled. "How many times have you tried to get Mrs. P. to retire?"

Cassie grinned. "I've lost count. You're right; I'll stop worrying. In some ways I also think Aunt Lydia's taken a fresh lease of life. After Pops died she lost her best friend, and was at a bit of a loss I felt, but now, I don't know, she seems to have a bit more oomph again."

"I agree," said Robert. "So we keep going with the same team and our tried and tested plan."

"Agreed," said Cassie. "I think everyone on the Board will be very impressed by the figures. I feel a celebration coming on? Can we afford it, Rowena?"

"Not too lavish," she smiled. "But yes, I think we can afford it."

"Let's have a sherry to celebrate," said Cassie, going over to the decanter. She handed them their glass. "Cheers, thanks, and here's to next year."

"Cheers! To next year," responded Rowena and Robert.

~~~~~

"This is nice," said James, stretched out in front of the fire. "Lovely food, delicious wine and the woman I love by my side. What more could a man want?"

"We don't seem to have done this for ages, " agreed Cassie, sipping her wine. "I love this sort of food, finger food, makes me feel quite decadent."

"I'm not sure you need that encouragement," grinned James as he helped himself to another drumstick.

Cassie just smiled at him in reply and took a bite from his chicken. "It's amazing to think that Christmas is just around the corner again. I can't believe it."

James cuddled her close. "We should think about wedding plans, shouldn't we?"

"Suppose so," agreed Cassie distractedly.

"Try not to be too overwhelmed with enthusiasm for the idea," said James, hurt by her indifferent response.

"What?" asked Cassie. "Sorry, I was miles away."

"Great! That makes it even worse," sighed James. "I was only asking about our wedding plans, that was all, a mere nothing really."

"Oh James, don't be like that," said Cassie. "I'm sorry, of course I'm enthusiastic. I was telling Aunt Lydia who the bridesmaids will be, the ushers, that sort of thing. I'm all organised really."

James's mood brightened upon hearing that she had at least given their wedding a passing thought. "So, tell me, who are you having?"

Cassie proceeded to tell him her ideas and then tentatively asked, "Who had you thought of having as your best man?"

James looked thoughtful for a moment. "I'd really like it to be Philip but I'm not sure. William might be a bit po-faced. I wouldn't care; we've never really got on, even as children, but he's my brother and so I feel duty bound to at least ask. If he does accept, and I'll be amazed if he does, Philip could be an usher. What do you think?"

"I think," pondered Cassie. "We should elope!"

"Sounds good to me," agreed James.

"I'd really like a quiet wedding, in the chapel would be lovely," said Cassie wistfully. "I suspect that's wishful thinking though. However we'll save money on the dress, my grandmother's dress is in the attic. Kate wore it for her wedding and I'm sure Margaret will be able to alter it for me."

"Is it a white dress?" asked James innocently.

Cassie grinned at him. "No, luckily its suitable, its ivory!!"

~~~~~

Christmas drew closer. "Are the children hyper about Christmas yet?" asked Cassie.

"Ben is, and has been since about October," grinned Robert. "Emily and Charlie are adopting the laid back approach and Hattie has festooned her bedroom with these ghastly paper chain things. She wants them in the sitting room as well but thankfully Kate's put her foot down. Unfortunately though, she has agreed to have them in the hall. Should be very tasteful!"

"Don't be such a misery," smiled Cassie. "That's what Christmas is all about, ghastly home-made things that the parents have to put up with. I remember I made a delightfully naff angel that of course had to go on the tree. Benson used to try and put it as high as he could and round the back, saying that angels were always high in the sky and were never seen. Needless to say I thought this was a piece of nonsense and demanded it be in its rightful place, prominent, at the front. As you say, very tasteful," grinned Cassie. She went over to a table to where there was a thermos of coffee.

"Coffee?" asked Cassie. "Please," replied Robert. "Reasonable news for a change," smiled Robert. He took out the papers which he explained in detail to Cassie.

"Thank God for that," Cassie smiled with relief as she finished reading them. "Are we able to give any Christmas bonuses? Everyone worked so hard to have the estate ready for our first guests."

"No wonder my hair's totally grey," said Robert nodding his head. "Just when I think the books are beginning to balance! However we can... as long as they are smallish ones!"

"I've written letters to everyone, thanking them for all their extra help this year. Perhaps they could go into their pay packets as well," said Cassie.

Robert shook his head but was smiling. "That's kind of you!"

"So why the grin?" asked Cassie, twinkling at him.

"No reason, no reason at all," replied Robert still smiling at her.

Chapter 33

The festive season seemed to finish as quickly as it had arrived. "There's something about getting back to normal," said Cassie.

"That's such an old person's thing to say," retorted James. "You're not going to become an old fuddy-duddy are you?"

Cassie, ignoring him, said, "I'm off to the studio. The Gibson's are collecting their portrait at eleven, but first I'll nip upstairs and see if Aunt Lydia's okay. This cold has knocked the stuffing out of her a bit. See you later."

James looked at her and trying to look hurt said, "Aawh," in a pathetic voice. "No bye-bye kiss? I really think you're going off me."

Cassie remedied the situation immediately. "That's better," smiled James. "That'll keep me going till lunchtime!"

Cassie returned his smile and went upstairs. She knocked and went in to Lydia's room. Lydia was lying with her eyes closed, but not sleeping, pale with dark circles under her eyes; she really didn't look well. She opened her eyes and smiled at Cassie. "I'm just going to the studio. Do you want anything before I go?"

"No, I'm fine thanks," smiled Lydia. "Just tired. I'll have a little nap before elevenses."

"I think I'll call the surgery. Perhaps Uncle Peter can come over and see you," said Cassie with concern.

"You will do no such thing," replied Lydia indignantly. "It's only the remnants of a cold. You're not wasting Peter's time. Right?"

"I just wanted…" but Cassie was interrupted by Lydia saying, "Do I make myself perfectly clear?"

"Perfectly," said Cassie, who knew there was no point in arguing with her.

"See you later," she smiled.

Cassie went downstairs and, grabbing a jacket, went outside. It was surprisingly mild for the middle of January. *It will soon be spring*, she thought, then she remembered, with spring came Easter, and with Easter, their next guests. She hated the thought of strangers invading her home again. *But needs must and all that*, she thought gloomily. However, on entering her studio, all these thoughts were immediately banished as she set to work on her next assignment.

After the Gibson's left Cassie went back to the house and upstairs to see Lydia. As she went along the hall she heard Lydia laughing and, on entering the room, saw David ensconced, regaling Lydia with obviously hilarious stories.

"Well, you look better," smiled Cassie to Lydia. "You're obviously just what the doctor ordered," she said, smiling at David.

"I've brought a magic potion," grinned David. "She's only had one spoonful and hey presto, a transformation already."

"What exactly is in this magic potion," enquired Cassie.

"Ah," said David mysteriously. "A secret, handed down through the generations."

"Any of your ancestors die at the stake?" asked Cassie.

"So cruel," replied David, looking hurt. "You've wounded me to the core. The ingredients of this wonderful concoction can only be known by one person at a time, and this was given to me by my old aunt Bess. Bless her soul."

"I see…" said Cassie. "May I have a look?"

David handed it to her and she uncorked the top and sniffed it. "Good God, David," she asked, spluttering, the smell caught the back of her throat. "Is that 100% proof ?"

"No, no," said David, shaking his head. "Nothing like that." He grinned at her. "Only 95%!"

"Ah well," grinned Cassie. "Obviously harmless."

"Whatever it is," said a voice from the bed. "I feel much, much better so the potion's staying here!"

"Sensible lady," observed David. "And so much brighter than your niece, who obviously knows nothing!"

He got up and, smiling at Lydia, said, "I'd better be going – work to do. I'll pop back later if I may."

"Delighted!" said Lydia, returning his smile. "But I don't want you catching my bugs."

"Don't you fret about that," smiled David, kissing her.

David caught Cassie's eye, indicating he'd like to speak to her. "Would you like a coffee or something?" asked Cassie.

"No, nothing for me," replied Lydia. "But stay for a moment and tell me about the Gibson's."

"I'll go and get a coffee for myself then and bring it back and chat," smiled Cassie as she and David left the bedroom.

When out of earshot, David turned anxiously to Cassie. "She looks hellish. Surely this is more than a lingering cold?"

"She won't let me call Uncle Peter," said Cassie with concern. "I've had to promise and I don't want to upset her."

"Well I haven't," stated David. "I'll phone."

"Oh David, thank you, I'd really feel so much happier if he saw her," said Cassie with relief. "But tell him he's here on a social call!"

"No problem," smiled David.

Peter played his part beautifully by pretending to ask them all for dinner. The surprise he registered upon hearing that Lydia was in bed was certainly worthy of an award! They hoped Lydia was hearing all this and that his acting debut had not gone unnoticed. He knocked on her door.

"Good afternoon," smiled Peter, sitting down on Lydia's bed. "I hear you haven't been feeling great."

Lydia glared at him. "She promised!" A puzzled expression crossed Peter's face. "Sorry, who promised what?"

"You know fine who I'm talking about, Cassie!" said Lydia continuing to glare at him. "She phoned you."

Peter's face then changed from studied bewilderment to one of dawning realisation. "No, no, I'm here on Rowena's instructions to ask if you'd all like to come for a meal on Saturday. I'm sorry, I didn't know you weren't 100%." Lydia stared at him to see if she could gauge if he was lying. He held her stare. She couldn't tell, she couldn't be absolutely sure. As she looked at him Peter was viewing her in his professional capacity, and was alarmed to see a tinge of blue at her lips.

"I should be better by Saturday, tell Rowena that would be lovely," smiled Lydia.

"While I'm here why don't I give you the once over," said Peter and before Lydia could interrupt he said, "I'll just nip out to the car and get my bag."

Peter returned and went upstairs to examine Lydia. "I think it might be a good idea to have a couple of tests at Westpark," said Peter.

"Don't be such an old fuss pot," replied Lydia. "I'm fine, it's a cold, that's all."

Peter sat down on the bed and took her hand. "I think you suspect its a bit more than a cold, don't you?"

"I want to stay here, I'm not going into hospital. You can't make me," she said defiantly.

"It's coming up for a year since your by-pass. What better time for a check-up?" smiled Peter.

"I want to die here. Not in some God forsaken hospital," snapped Lydia.

"God Almighty woman," said Peter with exasperation. "Who the hell said anything about dying. I just want you checked over. They have all the high-tech equipment. This," he said, holding up his stethoscope. "Can hardly compete!"

Lydia appeared to relent. "If you are 100% sure that I will not die in hospital, then I'll go."

"You really are an exasperating lady. I can't give that guarantee," sighed Peter. "Hells bells, I could walk out of this room, fall headlong down the stairs and kill myself, or drop dead from a coronary right here. And I have to say, at this moment with the frustration I'm feeling, the coronary is looking more of a certainty!"

"Very droll Peter," glared Lydia.

"Sadly, I meant it," retorted Peter.

It looked as if they had reached an impasse until Cassie came up with what she hoped was a suitable compromise, suggesting that Lydia could come home each evening after her tests. Lydia felt much happier at that idea. Peter, relieved that a solution had been reached, agreed to make the necessary arrangements.

"I'll see myself out," said Peter. "I'll phone you later." Looking at Lydia, he added, "You behave and take it easy. Do you promise?"

"Very well," agreed Lydia. Peter picked up his case and at the door turned. "See you later."

Lydia smiled. "Thank you for agreeing to the demands of a cantankerous old woman!" Peter shook his head, returned her smile, and left.

Cassie tucked her aunt in. "My dear, thank you for your excellent idea," smiled Lydia to Cassie. "I feel much happier about this plan."

"Jolly good," smiled Cassie. "I had to think of something though. You were giving Uncle Peter quite a hard time there."

"He thinks of me as a challenge," smiled Lydia. "He really likes it."

"If you say so," said Cassie. "Now, why don't you have a nap before dinner. Is there anything you'd like for your meal, some tempting morsel?"

"A little soup would be lovely," smiled Lydia. "I can't say I'm particularly hungry."

"I'll have my meal up here with you then," smiled Cassie.

"Oh, that would be nice," said Lydia. "Now off you go and do some work, and no more fussing. See you later."

"I hope you sleep," said Cassie and, bending down, she kissed Lydia on the cheek, put out the light and went back downstairs.

Cassie looked at her watch, it was nearly four and already dark, but she reckoned that she would get at least two more hours' work done. She wasn't enjoying this piece. It was for the General; a nice old chap who wanted to have his portrait painted, but unfortunately, painted upon his horse. Cassie had tried to explain that horses were not her specialty, in fact she was hopeless at them, but he was insistent, and wanted her to at least try. "This is my last attempt," she decided as she picked up her brush and tried again. Although the portrait of the General was her usual excellent high standard, she thought the horse was resembling something between a donkey and a camel. "This will not do," she said as she flung her brush down. She felt so frustrated. "Enough's, enough," she decided and with that proceeded to paint over the horse. I'll give him this at a knocked down price! She was intent on her work when she heard someone shouting her name. She looked up; it was Benson, running towards the studio.

A feeling of foreboding came over her. Her stomach contracted and she felt sick. Abandoning her work she rushed out of the studio.

"Quickly Cassie," said Benson breathlessly. "It's Lydia, hurry!"

Cassie raced passed him and taking the stairs three at a time, arrived in Lydia's room. Lydia was on the floor, being cradled in Margaret's arms. "Aunt Lydia! Its me, Cassie!" She flung herself onto the floor. "Let me help you back to bed." Shortly behind

Cassie, Benson arrived. "Call an ambulance, quickly," said Cassie frantically, but Margaret shook her head.

Cassie stared at her with disbelief as Lydia stirred and, opening her eyes, she looked up at Cassie. She stretched out her hand to Cassie and smiled, gasping out the words. "Cassie! ...no ambulance, got my wish though... Cass..." but she said no more. Her eyes closed and her arm went limp in Cassie's grasp.

"Aunt Lydia, please, please, you've got to hang on. Please..." she implored.

Margaret looked up at her husband for help. "Come Cassie," said Benson, gently. "She's gone."

Cassie shook her head. "She hasn't... she can't... Let's get her back to bed, she'll be fine, she'll be fine then, she really will. Please... please help me get her back into bed."

Benson bent down and helped Cassie pick Lydia up and place her in bed. Cassie straightened the sheets. "There you are Aunt Lydia. All neat and tidy again, just as you like."

Margaret and Benson looked frantically at each other. "Peter!" mouthed Margaret to Benson. He quietly left the room.

Margaret got a chair and placed it beside the bed. "Why don't you sit down Cassie. Sit with Lydia for a little while."

Cassie smiled at her. "Yes, I'll sit with her before dinner. She's only wanting soup tonight, just soup."

Margaret stood quietly awaiting Peter, hoping he would be quick.

Peter arrived, went over to Cassie and, touching her shoulder gently, said, "Hello Cassie, I've come to see Lydia."

"Thank goodness you're here, she had a turn, but we got her back to bed," said Cassie brightly. "She'll be fine now, now that you're here."

"I'll have a look at her now, shall I?" asked Peter tenderly. Cassie nodded in agreement. "Why don't you go with Margaret to your room and I'll come along in a moment."

"All right," agreed Cassie. She bent down over Lydia. "Uncle Peter's here now, I won't be long, I'm just going to my room."

"That's the way," said Margaret, guiding her out of the room and along the corridor to her room where she sat Cassie down at the window.

A few minutes later Peter came in and sat in a chair beside Cassie.

"What's wrong? You're looking very serious," said Cassie.

"I'm sorry," said Peter, taking her hands in his. "Lydia's not going to get better... she's at peace, she's dead, but I think you know that though, don't you?"

Cassie stared at him as if not comprehending what he was saying. After a few minutes she looked at Peter and slowly nodded. "I know... but I don't want to know, I don't want to believe it." She stood up and looked out of the window.

Peter stood behind her with his arm around her shoulder. "She got her wish. Just as she wanted, she died at home."

Cassie turned to Peter. "I think she knew... I think she knew she was going to die. Don't you?"

Peter shrugged his shoulders. "I'm not sure Cassie, not sure."

"I'll go along and see her again, excuse me for a moment," she said with a voice devoid of expression or any emotion.

"Do you want me to come along with you?" Cassie shook her head and left the room to go to Lydia.

"This isn't normal," said Margaret, wiping her eyes, "Not normal at all. What can we do?"

Peter looked at her, worry on his face. "We'll all keep an eye on her. Too much has happened to her too soon," he sighed. "Charles, the estate, now Lydia. Cassie's body's is, I suppose, reacting by saying, 'I don't want to acknowledge this is happening at the moment, so I won't'. Where's James? Any idea?"

"George is trying to contact him," said Margaret. She looked at her watch. "Why don't I phone Kate, the children will be home from school and she could come over."

"Yes," agreed Peter. "That's a good idea."

Margaret went away to phone her daughter and Peter went along to Lydia's room. He knocked and went in.

Cassie was dry eyed and apparently composed. "What have you put on the death certificate?"

"It was her heart, Cassie. I suspect what was happening in the last couple of days was a leakage from the by-pass but that's really just a guess," said Peter.

"I don't want her taken away or anything done to her. That won't have to happen, will it?"

"No, I'll get Tony to come along to certify the death as well, but no, there will be no investigations. Arrangements can be made when you feel up to it." Peter wondered how much she was taking in for she just nodded. There was a knock at the door. It was James.

He rushed over to Cassie's side. "I'm so, so sorry," he said, cuddling her to him. She stood rigid. He looked at Peter anxiously.

Peter stood in front of Cassie, willing her to make eye contact. "Cassie, do you think you should go downstairs now?" Cassie stared unblinkingly at him. He continued. "We should perhaps phone the undertaker."

Cassie eventually looked at him. "Yes, I'll do that." She released herself from James's arms and went over to Lydia and sat down again. Without looking at them she said, "Please go. I'll be down in a minute."

James was totally perplexed as to what was happening. Why was Cassie behaving like this? Peter nodded to James and indicated they should leave.

"Hang in there James," said Peter. "It's just the shock, she'll come out of this. We just have to handle her with care. All right?"

"I've never seen her like this, it frightens me. What can I do?" asked James.

Peter put his arm round the young man's shoulders. "Just be there, that's all she needs; you there." James nodded but his fears were not allayed.

Downstairs everyone awaited Cassie's return. They were all in a state of shock, firstly by Lydia's sudden death and secondly by Cassie's reaction. Peter was trying to reassure everyone but was finding it difficult, he had been so fond of Lydia, and was going to miss her terribly.

Eventually Cassie returned downstairs and, without acknowledgement, walked into the study, as if unaware of their presence. Mrs. Pearson took one look at her and promptly burst into tears again. James was desperate to follow her but Peter shook his head.

They heard her dial a number and speak. "Duncan? Hello it's Cassie, Cassie Emerson. I'm afraid I require your services… yes. It's Aunt Lydia, she died this afternoon."

They all looked at each other in disbelief, she sounded so cold and unfeeling, so matter-of-fact. They knew this wasn't how she was really feeling. "Can't you give her something," begged James. "Please Peter."

"Not a good idea at the moment," said Peter calmly, although he was as anxious as the others at what he was hearing.

Kate and Robert then arrived. Kate's composure when she saw the distraught faces of 'The Family' completely dissolved. She fumbled for a tissue. "I'm sorry, " she sniffed. "I can't believe this has happened, I really can't."

Peter went over to her and whispered to her about Cassie. She nodded then went through to the study, shutting the door behind her. Cassie stood up as she finished her call. "Oh Cassie, I'm so sorry, so very, very sorry," said Kate hugging her.

Cassie nodded, her eyes unblinking and her face like an alabaster mask. She stared at Kate, not returning the hug. "Duncan's coming over in half an hour. He's coming to take Aunt Lydia. Do you want to see her before then?"

Kate was surprised at the question. "No, it's all right, I'd like to remember her as I saw her yesterday, but thank you, thank you for asking." Kate didn't know what to say or do. "Can I get you anything?" she asked nervously.

"No thank you," replied Cassie. "I have things to do before Duncan comes." She smiled at Kate but not a smile that Kate had ever seen before. She was totally unnerved by Cassie's alien behaviour.

"Cassie please come and sit down, this has been a tremendous shock. It's so difficult to take all this in," smiled Kate. "I'm going to miss her very much… we all are."

Cassie nodded. "Yes, we all are." She looked at Kate and smiled her strange smile again. "You don't have to stay, I have things to do, so please, off you go back to the family. I'm fine, really I am."

Kate decided not to argue with Cassie. Kissing her on the cheek, she said she'd see her later and turned and left the study.

The others had all congregated in the kitchen. "Well!" said James. "What's happening, how is she?"

"She's not herself, that's for sure," said Kate as she flopped down in the chair. "She's been through so much… oh, Peter, is this the final straw? What is going on?"

Peter didn't have time to reply as the doorbell rang. Benson got up and went through to answer it followed by James. It was the undertaker. Benson asked him to wait in the hall and went to inform Cassie.

"Duncan!" smiled Cassie, extending her hand as she came out of the study. "How kind of you to come over so quickly. She's upstairs. Follow me." Duncan looked at Benson, surprise on his face.

"I can go up myself. There's no need for you as well," said Duncan kindly. "You wait in the study and I'll see you there."

Cassie, without question, did as she was told and went back to the study. James, who could stand this no longer followed her. "I want to be with you just now, just be with you, if you need me. I'm here," said James quietly.

"That's lovely," replied Cassie as she would to a stranger.

In the kitchen the atmosphere was as tense. "David, has anyone tried to get hold of him?" asked Kate to the others.

"I've been trying, but it's just his blasted answering machine," said Benson. "He was here at lunchtime, said he had to go back to work, so I assumed he was in the studio. I've no idea where he is, but I'll keep trying."

Duncan came downstairs and went to the study. He knocked and awaited a reply. James answered. He went in and, looking at Cassie, said, "We can take Mrs. Maitland now. Would you like us to do that?" Cassie nodded. "Yes… thank you."

"Please just stay here for the moment then," said Duncan.

James heard him open the front door and then heard another voice. Footsteps went upstairs and after about ten minutes, footsteps came downstairs with the sound of a trolley being wheeled across the floor. The front door opened and a car door opened and closed. Duncan came back in and went through to the study. "We'll go now, I'll come over tomorrow. What time would be convenient?"

"Any time," replied Cassie. "What about eleven?" suggested James.

"Eleven it is," said Duncan. "I'll see myself out." Cassie didn't reply, so, nodding to James, he quietly left the study.

Cassie looked at James. "I'm going to bed. I feel quite tired. Goodnight."

"Shall I come up with you?" Cassie looked at him. "No, I'd like to be on my own, goodnight," and with that she abruptly left.

James watched in despair as she slowly went upstairs. She didn't look back. Cassie went along the corridor to her bedroom. Her aunt's room was towards the end of the passage, and she noticed a light shining under the door. She went along to the room, was about to knock, but then remembered. She went in. The bed was empty. The quilt neatly folded; Lydia's glasses were on the bedside table, along with her wedding ring. Cassie stared at the table, then at the bed. Turning, she put out the light and left the room, closing the door quietly behind her.

She went to her room and experienced a surge of relief as she shut the door to the world. She undressed and went to bed. She lay looking up at the ceiling and watched the shadows from the trees blowing in the wind, dance above her. It had a strangely hypnotic effect, and despite her resistance, her eyes slowly closed and she fell asleep.

Chapter 34

Cassie awoke with a start, her heart pounding and perspiration trickling down her back. She'd been dreaming – something about Aunt Lydia but what was it? Sitting up she tried to shake the last vestiges of sleep from her mind. She was then aware of someone else in the room, in the corner, slumped in the bedroom chair. She peered at the outline – it was James.

"James, what on earth are you doing there?" exclaimed Cassie as she put on the light.

James also wakened with a start. "Cassie, sorry, I didn't mean to startle you," stammered James, trying to rouse himself. He looked at his watch; it was four in the morning. He went over to the bed and sat down. "How are you feeling?"

Cassie looked at James, his face so full of concern. "I had a dream, more of a nightmare really. It was about Aunt Lydia."

James nodded. "And?"

"And then I…" Cassie looked at him, horror registering on her face. "It wasn't a dream was it?"

"Oh, my love," said James as he hugged her to him, aware that this time she was allowing this. "I'm so sorry, so very sorry but it wasn't a dream. She died, Lydia died yesterday." He looked at Cassie's face, still no tears. He didn't know whether to continue; he was unsure whether what he had said had sunk in. "It was quick, she didn't suffer," he smiled gently. "She got her wish, she was at home."

"Why were you sitting on the chair?" asked Cassie, seemingly ignoring what he had just said.

"Because you went up to bed on your own, you wanted to be alone," said James. "But I was worried about you, so I thought I'd sit in the chair, make sure you were all right. We were all worried about you, it was a horrendous shock."

"Is that why you didn't come to bed?" James just nodded. "I just wanted to be near you, but I was trying not to intrude."

"Where is Aunt Lydia?" James was thrown by this question and looked blankly at her. "You know, Cassie. Duncan, the undertaker, came last night and took her to the Chapel of Rest or whatever it's called."

"I think I'll have another sleep, you go back to your room. I'll see you later," said Cassie.

"Are you sure?" Cassie nodded. "Quite sure."

James did as he was told and went along to his room. It hadn't been his room for some time but Cassie had obviously forgotten. He undressed and got into bed, debating whether he should phone Peter but tiredness overtook that decision and he drifted off to sleep.

Cassie lay for another hour or so then got up. Deciding to go for a walk, she dressed warmly, crept down the stairs, tiptoed into the kitchen and out by the back door. She took a sharp intake of breath as the coldness of the morning air assaulted her senses. Pulling her jacket tightly round her she wandered down to the lakeside. For a little while she sat on the bench staring at the water. The stars were still out, twinkling in the dark, crisp winter's morning. In the distance she thought she saw a light; there was a light, and it seemed to be coming from David's cottage. "I wonder if anyone told him about Lydia?" Pondering that question Cassie decided to walk over to his cottage.

Nearing the cottage she heard music blaring and there were lights on everywhere. She went round to the verandah and peered in, David appeared to be asleep, slumped on the sofa with an empty bottle of whisky by his side. She tried the door, it was open, so she went in calling out his name but he didn't hear. Going over to the stereo she turned off the music. The sudden quietness was all that was required to wake David from his stupor.

He blinked in the bright light, and, trying to shade his eyes from the glare, peered at his intruder. "Oh, it's you," he said with relief. As he tried to sit up he groaned. "Oh God, my head, I feel like shit! Sorry Cassie."

His memory slowly improved as consciousness fully returned. "I'm so, so sorry about Lydia." His eyes filled with tears. "I'm going to miss her so much, so very much." Cassie stood impassively before him, appearing unmoved by what he was saying.

David wiped his eyes and surveyed the scene around him. "Got a little drunk last night." He tried to smile but it came out as an inane grin. "More than obvious I suppose." He stood up, staggered, then steadying himself said, "Coffee, I think that's what's needed… perhaps with added aspirin." Facing Cassie he subjected her to the full force of his alcoholic breath, as he tried to hug her to him. She moved away in the pretence of tidying. "Sorry," he said, putting his hand over his mouth. "I'll go and tidy myself. I won't be a minute, you pop the kettle on."

David went through to the bathroom and looked in the mirror. It was going to be quite a challenge to try and rectify the mess that appeared before him. However, in a remarkably short space of time he returned shaved, showered and with breath minty fresh. "That smells good, thank you." He helped himself to a coffee and quickly swallowed two aspirins.

"My own fault, I just felt so sorry for myself, for my loss, selfish, really selfish." Cassie nodded, showing no emotion. He wondered what he could do. When Kate and Robert had come round last night and told him about Lydia, they were obviously upset by her death but their over-riding concern was Cassie and he could now see why. The three of them had spent an hour or so in a mixture of tears and laughter, just as Lydia would have wanted them to remember her. But after they left, the full force of what had happened hit David and he had tried to alleviate his grief through whisky. It hadn't worked.

"I need some fresh air, do you fancy a walk?" asked David.

"I walked over here," replied Cassie.

"Perfectly true," smiled David. "But not with such lovely company. Come on, let's have a little stroll." David didn't know what he was going to do, but hoped the air might clear his head. He could see how much she was hurting but right at this moment she would not, or could not, acknowledge that. David thought it was called delayed shock, or something like that, but all he knew was that her grief had to be released, and sooner rather than later.

They walked in silence for about five minutes and came to the seat, beneath the oak tree, overlooking the lake. "Here I go," he thought. He smiled at Cassie. "I can understand why Charles so loved the lake. I come down here nearly every day and its always different, there's always something new to see."

She returned his smile but all she said was, "Yes." David looked around him, the one person whom he wanted to speak to, who could help, was no longer there. Try as he might, he could not stop the tears falling and so let them. "Sorry, I just can't believe she's not here," he sniffed. "It must have been horrendous yesterday for you."

Again, all Cassie said was, "Yes."

David tried talking about Lydia, feeling a little cruel, as what he was really trying to do was get Cassie upset, but it wasn't working. "Come on, let's go back, I'm peckish, we can have breakfast." They walked back with David's arm lightly across her shoulder.

"You sit down and I'll rustle up a gourmet breakfast. Don't panic, my breakfasts are much better than my dinners," he laughed, but it was a hollow laugh. He busied himself in the kitchen, wondering what to say or do next. While he was waiting for the bacon to crisp as he liked it, he went back into the sitting room, and saw Cassie standing by the fire with a book in her hand; the book that Lydia had lent him only a few days previously. A first edition of *Wuthering Heights*; Charles's last present to her.

He went over to Cassie, was about to say something, when he noticed tears trickling down her cheeks splashing onto the cover of the book. He took the book from her and, pulling her into his arms, held her as, at last, her grief totally engulfed her.

Her tears eventually subsided and she tried to compose herself. "Sorry about that," said Cassie, wiping her eyes.

"Don't be," smiled David. "I'm very relieved," but his smile turned to alarm as the smell of bacon, burning bacon, permeated through to the sitting room. "God, the bacon," and he ran to the kitchen. He returned holding the grill pan. "What did I just say about breakfasts being better than my dinners?"

Cassie gave him a watery smile. "I like bacon bits," and she picked a piece from the smouldering pan and popped it into her mouth. "Yum!"

They sat down to bits of bacon, toast and coffee. "I think you should phone The Hall and let them know you're here, don't you think?" asked David.

Cassie looked at her watch it was nearly eight. "You're right, I…" Her eyes filled with tears. "I so wish this wasn't true… I've no idea how I'll manage without her, no idea at all." She wiped her eyes. "You know she was always the strong one, with Pops, the estate, everything, we all relied on her, maybe we relied on her too much."

David nodded. "I know I did." He gave a slight smile. "She was my best friend, she really was and my confidant. I'm going to miss all that. I loved everything about her, her humour, her sense of fun and adventure and perhaps most of all, her wise counsel, yes," he said thoughtfully, "she was a wise lady."

Cassie bent her head as tears started to fall again. David held her to him. "I'm so scared, David. I don't know if I can cope with all this on my own. Everything has happened too quickly: Pops, now Aunt Lydia. She was always there; I don't really know how to describe it, as my sort of safety net. Do you know what I mean?"

David nodded. "You're not on your own. You've got James and you and he will keep The Hall going, with the back-up of the older members of the team, and you have to agree." He tried to smile. "It's a fabulous team. Think of this as being your turn. You and James are the next generation; the new custodians of Harrington Hall and then you'll pass it onto your children. Charles and Lydia have shown you the way. You can do it. Look at what you've achieved already."

Cassie shook her head. "It was with her help I managed that. You know what I was like at some of the Board meetings, she was ready to leap in and help me out if she thought I wasn't coping, as I said, my safety net, always looking out for me."

David turned her head to face him. "There are plenty of us who want to be that safety net: let us Cassie. Charles and Lydia are irreplaceable but what an example they've given you. Remember we all look after each other and just because one member or even two members are not physically here, it doesn't mean that the family ceases to function. Does it?" Cassie shook her head.

"Now, off you go and phone and then I'll take you back to The Hall."

"I look a mess," decided Cassie catching a glimpse of herself in the mirror.

"The sight of you looking, as you say, a mess, will be an enormous relief to all of them, they were worried sick yesterday," said David. "Don't bother tidying too much, there's going to be a lot more tears shed today."

David was right. The moment Cassie walked through the door again, profuse in her apologies, the tears flowed again. They all sat in the kitchen, drinking copious amounts of tea and coffee and went through the details of the previous day. It had been Margaret who had heard Lydia fall and had run to her aid. When moments of sense prevailed, they knew that Lydia's death was as she would have wished, quick and at home, but at the moment, emotions were too raw to appreciate the blessing it undoubtedly was.

The relief that James was feeling at having Cassie back to normal was tempered by a slight jealousy of why he hadn't been the one she went to. David, who had sensed an imperceptible coolness in James, guessed what he was feeling and endeavoured to rectify the situation as soon as an opportunity arose. Eventually he and James were left on their own.

"How are you doing?" asked David.

"Fine," replied James curtly.

David continued. "It's a relief Cassie's back to normal, that's for sure. Thank goodness she saw the book." He was aware of James's puzzled expression but chose to ignore it. "If she hadn't..." he shuddered. "I don't know... this could have gone on for..." he pretended to think. "Well I suppose long enough."

James could contain himself no longer. "What book? What are you talking about?"

"Apparently she'd gone for an early morning walk, and in the distance saw my lights on, every light was apparently on," admitted David. "Well, very kindly, she came to investigate and found me lying on the sofa in a drunken heap, complete with empty whisky bottle and an absolute bugger of a hangover." He rubbed his head. "Still got a headache actually. Anyway Kate and Robert had been round last night and told me about Lydia, and also how Cassie was behaving. When I saw her I realised there was certainly something amiss. I didn't know what to do. I tried everything, absolutely everything to get her upset. Couldn't manage... so eventually decided upon breakfast, which, I may add, I managed to ruin. I burnt the bacon." James gave a slight smile at hearing this.

"I then went through to the kitchen to try and rectify this shambles and when I came back she was looking at a book Lydia had lent me, *Wuthering Heights*.

"Ah," remembered James. "Charles gave Lydia that."

"Indeed. It is a lovely book, but that, as they say, was exactly what the doctor ordered, for when I came back she was in floods of tears. Just seeing the book had perhaps triggered off thoughts of Lydia, then Charles, or a combination, I don't know. All I do know is thank God for that book," said David.

"Yes," agreed James. "Thanks David."

"Don't thank me," reiterated David. "None of us could get through to her, it was definitely the book!"

James looked a little embarrassed. "You'll think I'm pathetic, but do you know something?" David shook his head. "I was actually jealous, jealous that she broke down with you rather than me. Stupid wasn't it!"

David put his arm round James's shoulder. "Absurd!" he laughed, but was a little taken aback that at the same time, he was secretly rather pleased. *Now who's pathetic*, he wondered? "Let's see how she is. What time is the undertaker coming?"

"Eleven," said James.

"Good luck then," said David.

"Will you not be there as well?" asked James with alarm.

"No, it's not my place," replied David. "It's you she needs at a time like that"

James nodded, becoming aware of his responsibilities. "I've never arranged a funeral before."

David smiled at him and, patting him on his back, said, "You'll be fine."

To Cassie, the arranging of a funeral was sadly familiar, with Charles's still fresh in her memory. Duncan, however, guided her expertly through the arrangements. Unlike Charles, Lydia had left no instructions, but Duncan felt it should follow roughly the same form as Charles's; the village church then the chapel at home. Cassie questioned this, thinking there would be a smallish turnout, but Duncan assured her that Lydia, being a popular member of the community, would require a capacity of more than the thirty or so the chapel could hold.

He had been right. As Cassie arrived at the church she was grateful she had listened to him, the church was packed. She gave a slight smile, for she could visualise Lydia who, feigning surprise, would have been thrilled at the numbers who attended her funeral!

After the service the cortege drove back slowly through the village with the older men who lined the street, doffing their hats. Lydia would have thoroughly approved. After the chapel Lydia was laid to rest next to Charles.

The inevitable 'bun feast', as Lydia had always called these occasions, followed for family and close friends. The day eventually came to a close and for all at The Hall a new epoch in their history dawned.

Chapter 34

Cassie was aware of footsteps coming closer, they sounded as if they were coming from the woods. She peered and saw Charlie coming towards her. She tried to wipe her eyes but she was too late, he saw.

"Why do you always sit at the graves, Cassie?" asked Charlie. He wasn't really expecting an answer and continued. "Everyone is always crying. I've even seen David cry."

"We're just sad about Aunt Lydia. It's not the same without her, that's why," said Cassie sadly.

"I know… I miss her too, but why do you sit here? That's really weird."

"I feel close to both Aunt Lydia and Pops when I sit here, that's why," said Cassie.

Charlie looked at her intently, absentmindedly scuffing the front of his shoes on the gravel path. "Why?" he repeated. "They're dead. It's just a pile of bones and rotting skin down there."

"Don't be so unfeeling Charlie, that's an dreadful thing to say." Cassie started crying again.

Charlie was not to be deterred. "No it's not, its fact. I'm only saying what Aunt Lydia said, so there." He sat down beside Cassie. "She said that to me when I was sad about Uncle Charles. She explained that a person's body is like a car."

Cassie stared at Charlie, trying to follow what he was saying. "What on earth are you talking about," sniffed Cassie.

"If you listen I'll tell you. Aunt Lydia said that a body is like a car and when we die it's like the engine of a car has stopped. Yes?" Cassie nodded, more to pacify him than anything else. He continued. "If the engine is kaput in a car, its no use, agreed?" Cassie nodded again. "So we get rid of the car because it's not going to work without an engine, is it?" He smiled with a look of triumph, at his, or rather Lydia's, analogy.

He thought though that she still looked bewildered. "Don't be so dim Cassie. It's so obvious. What I'm saying is that Uncle Charles and Aunt Lydia aren't down there; that was just their shell, like the car. See?"

This time Cassie looked as if she understood for she smiled, for the first time in ages she smiled. "So," continued Charlie, warming to his theme. "You shouldn't be too sad, because they really are all around, like in things in the house and best of all, in our memories. You told me that when I was crying about Uncle Charles, that we had lots of good memories about him and you were right. Do you see now?" He sighed, unsure if he was getting through to her. "You know, you're a complete 'thicko' if you don't!"

The reply he got to that last sentence delighted him. She thumped him in the arm. For the first time in weeks, he was relieved to see her behave more like the old Cassie.

"Oh, I could hug you," smiled Cassie.

"No you can't... no way!" said Charlie, leaping out of the way. He grinned at her. "Are you feeling better?"

"Yes, much. You're right, I've been a bit of a prat," agreed Cassie.

"And no fun at all," added Charlie.

"And no fun at all," agreed Cassie. "You should tell David and the others what you've just said to me. It would help them."

"Dunno," said Charlie, embarrassed at the idea. "I can't talk to the others, the grown-ups I mean, like I can talk to you. You're not really like a grown-up very much of the time."

"Oh!" said Cassie, unsure if this was a compliment.

"That's good, really it is. My mates think you're cool, so it's okay," said Charlie. "But, if you want, you can tell the others if you like. That would be better."

"Okay," agreed Cassie. "I'll do that. I'll tell them it's your story." Charlie smiled. "And," added Cassie. "Thanks for the compliment."

"That's okay! I've got to go now, will you be all right?" Cassie nodded. "Bye then." He turned and started running back into the woods.

"Charlie!" Cassie shouted. He stopped and turned. "Thanks! Thanks a lot." He smiled back at her, and, with a wave, disappeared back into the woods.

Charlie's pep talk had the desired effect on Cassie. It jolted her out of her depression and in turn, the sombre mood that seemed to pervade the house was somehow lifted.

The next meeting of the Board was the first after Lydia's death and Cassie was determined to cope, and cope she did, but it was with a certain amount of relief that she closed that first meeting.

In six weeks their first lot of guests would arrive and it would be a steady stream until the end of October. Although this was hugely gratifying, the prospect of being invaded for a solid six months was just a little daunting. There was also the problem of finding a replacement for Lydia, for she had been the guide of Harrington Hall, enthralling the guests with her merry quips and hugely embellished stories of the previous incumbents of The Hall. *You're a difficult act to follow, Aunt Lydia*, thought Cassie.

Pierre hesitantly volunteered, modestly admitting that he knew much about not only The Hall and all its paintings, but also the surrounding area. Cassie was delighted. "Are you sure?" Pierre nodded. "That's such a relief. Pierre, that would be absolutely marvellous. Thank you."

"My pleasure," he smiled. "I think!"

"Well everyone, 'D' day one week from today. Are we all set?" asked Cassie. Everyone nodded. "Let's do Aunt Lydia proud then." Her eyes, for a moment, glistened. "Meeting closed," she added quickly."

Everyone went their separate ways but Robert stayed behind for a word.

"Do you not have work to do?" asked Cassie innocently.

"You know fine why I've stayed behind. Come on, we're going to the study."

The others were mingling in the hall as Robert marched Cassie through to the study. Everyone looked a bit surprised. "Do you think something's wrong?" asked Rowena. "Robert's looking quite stern."

"Not sure," replied Kate but she too, was aware of his expression and hoped another catastrophe hadn't befallen the estate.

As Robert closed the study door Cassie turned to face him. "Now Robert," she said sweetly. "Before you get all hot and bothered, I think I know what's troubling you, so let me explain."

"Well it had better be a brilliant explanation, that's all I can say," said Robert sternly.

"She would have wanted me to do it, you know she would. The estate was her life. She'd be thrilled," smiled Cassie.

"I won't let you do this," said Robert firmly. "I should have said something at the meeting but I wanted your explanation first. It had better be good though because I am not above holding another meeting… tonight even! The others would agree with me and you know that."

Cassie sighed. "I don't really have an explanation, but once the estate is back on its feet it can pay me back. It's just we're still sailing pretty close to the wind. I don't need the money. It just helps shore us up a bit."

"For God's sake Cassie, it was £200,000 and your legacy from Lydia. She'd be appalled," snapped Robert.

"She wouldn't and it's my legacy to do with what I will," retorted Cassie. "Please Robert, let's not fall out." She tried an angelic smile but he just glowered back at her.

"The reason you did this behind my back is because you knew I wouldn't sanction such a crazy thing," said Robert, pacing up and down the room.

"True, all true," said Cassie. "Now Robert, come and sit down, let's have coffee and speak of absurdities!"

"What? What the hell are you talking about now; absurdities?" glared Robert.

"The Chinese say it… except they have tea!" twinkled Cassie at him.

Robert shook his head and started to laugh. "You are the limit, the absolute limit and… stubborn, definitely stubborn."

"Pops would have done **exactly** the same," smiled Cassie.

"Possibly," agreed Robert, knowing when he was defeated. "Quite possibly."

The stream of guests arriving and departing throughout the season went smoothly, with only the occasional minor hitch to be sorted. The staff from the village had proved loyal and dependable and without exception, the kitchen staff completely besotted by Mrs. P.

Pierre had proved to be an excellent replacement for Lydia for not only could he talk about The Hall; he had in-depth knowledge of the many paintings. Cassie sometimes heard him use some of Lydia's expressions and stories, which Cassie found rather endearing.

Benson had placed a visitors' book in the hall by the door and as they left, the majority of guests had added their names, along with comments. The consensus seemed to be that a wonderful time had been had by each and every guest, with superlatives flowing throughout the pages and with many expressing a desire to return.

"A most satisfactory state of affairs," said Rowena, giving the report on the finances. "Our first full year, and it looks as if we are on course for a reasonable profit."

"Enough that we can stop this?" enquired Cassie hopefully.

"Not quite yet," replied Rowena. "Let's see how we do next year. I think though we could increase our tariffs a little, but I'll work that out in detail later." She grinned at Cassie. "And yes, a small celebration is in order!"

Cassie laughed. "You know me too well."

The months that followed sped by with Cassie, James and David given no respite from their busy schedules as they all had been commissioned to do more and more work.

"This is getting totally out of hand," said David. He was exhausted after having completed yet another piece and was watching Cassie put the finishing touches to one of hers. "I always said that when art became a chore it was time for me to give up and its getting close to that, perilously close." He was slumped in a chair in Cassie's studio, trying to summon up the energy to go home.

Cassie put down her brush and sat down beside him. "You do look whacked. This is my fault, all my fault."

David stroked her cheek. "How right you are, it's entirely your fault, I hope you feel suitably guilty."

"Well it is," countered Cassie. "If I wasn't working you so hard with the art classes from March till October, you'd have time to do your own work. I sometimes see your studio light on, way past midnight, so of course I feel responsible.

"Well you must be a contortionist to manage that feat from your bedroom window," he grinned. "Who else is burning the midnight oil then, tell me that?" He stretched and yawned.

"Anyway, of course it's not your fault. I do have the power of speech to use the word 'no'. It's greed on my part, that's all."

"What rubbish and you know it," smiled Cassie. "It's your magnetic personality that has everyone beating a path to your door. You're too nice that you can't say no, especially if it's a pretty lady! But I agree, we haven't had a break for, I can't remember when and God help us, it's soon going to be time to start the whole process again."

Cassie looked sad for a moment. "I can't believe its nearly two years since Aunt Lydia died."

"No," agreed David. "Neither can I and I still miss her like crazy."

Cassie nodded. "Me too."

"Changing the subject completely," said David. "How long is this engagement of yours going to be?"

Cassie looked at him. "Why? Has James been speaking to you?"

"Not directly," said David. "I suspect he's a little wary of talking about the wedding. I mean the last time he broached the subject you told him you didn't have time. That certainly must have given him that lovely, warm wanted feeling!"

Cassie looked immediately guilty. "He did say something then."

"No he didn't," replied David. "If you remember we were all together working and he mentioned it, testing the water I think to see your reaction."

"You think I'm being rotten, don't you?" asked Cassie.

David shook his head. "No, I don't. I know why you didn't want to before with Lydia and the guests and what have you, but it's over two years since you two got engaged. He'll be thinking you've gone off him."

Cassie looked horrified at this idea. "I love him; you know I do. Don't you?"

"It's not me you've got to tell. Have you told him lately?" asked David.

Cassie shook her head. "I don't think so, I can't remember. I've been so busy, we all have. I didn't think." Looking at David she smiled. "Thanks for putting me back on the right track. I'll tidy up here and then go to his studio. Now what can I do to rectify this?" David raised an eyebrow which caused Cassie to blush slightly. "David, really!" She thought for a moment. "I know, we can go away for a couple of nights, up to London or maybe not London but somewhere. What do you think?"

"You're getting there, good girl. Always keep the romance alive, Cassie," said David. "Take it as advice from one who knows, who sadly knows from experience." He stood up abruptly. "I'd better go, no rest for the wicked and all that." He grinned, trying not to let her see the sadness that came over him. "Have a good time!"

"Thank you," She kissed him on the cheek then giggled as she caught sight of her appearance in the mirror. "Perhaps something a little more seductive than this garb?"

"You look lovely as you are," he said, kissing her. "He won't care."

Cassie went over in her mind what she would say to James. She mustn't let him think David had prompted her.

"Hello!" she called as she entered his workshop. James, who was slumped in a chair dozing off, jumped.

"Sorry," said Cassie. "I didn't mean to give you a start. Knackered?"

James nodded. "So am I," agreed Cassie as she sat down on his lap. His smile was weary and she noticed fine lines etching the corners of his eyes. "You look as I feel," she said, as she cuddled him.

"This is a lovely surprise, to what do I owe this visit?" he asked.

"I miss you, that's all. We're working so hard that we hardly have any time for each other. I think if I paint for one more moment I'm going to scream. I wanted a break and I hoped you might as well," smiled Cassie.

James kissed her. "I feel revived already."

"I have a plan which has been going through my mind for a little while," said Cassie. "Just say if you think it's a no-go area."

"Okay," agreed James.

"I have about half a day to complete the painting I'm working on and the thought of starting another fills me with dread." She looked seriously at James. "I shouldn't feel like that. I love painting, it's just I'm so exhausted, we both are." She leant against his shoulder. "I think we need a break, so I have a proposition for you."

James moved so he looked directly at her. "You're propositioning me? You wanton hussy!" He hugged her to him and giggled. "Sounds great, tell me more!"

369

Cassie then told him her plan for them going away for a few days. His response was as she hoped. He was thrilled and unknown to her, relieved. For months he had wondered if she'd cooled to the idea of their marrying. At times she had seemed distant; disinterested in wedding plans and totally and utterly absorbed in her work and the estate, with little or no time for him. He now felt guilty for harbouring such thoughts; he must have imagined it, he decided.

Their break was a resounding success; not only had it recharged their batteries for work, it had reinforced the feelings they had for each other. Even a date for the wedding had been set. James's happiness knew no bounds and he set about his work with a renewed vigour.

Chapter 36

The day of their wedding dawned cold, but bright, and better than one dared hope for on the second of November. November would not have been Cassie's first choice as a month to get married but as there had been no let up with bookings for the art master classes, for which she had been eternally grateful, this was the earliest possible date. The service was to be held in Harrington Chapel, with only family and close friends and then, in the evening, a dance for all the others, including many of the tenants and old timers from the village.

The wedding was at 3.00 p.m. The hairdresser was coming at twelve-thirty, Cassie looked at her watch, it was only eight, she now wished she'd arranged the wedding for earlier; it looked as if it might be a long wait! She got up and hauled on her jeans, sweater and jacket and decided to go for a walk.

She started her walk as she so often did, at the lakeside, then up through the woods to the chapel. She unlocked the door and looked inside to view the flowers that had been arranged the night before. Margaret and the ladies of her floral art group had done a magnificent job. They were looking wonderful.

She looked down at what she was carrying and hoped that Margaret would not miss two of the cream coloured roses that were to be used for her bouquet. She closed the door of the chapel and went up to the graves and laid a flower on each grave. "One for you Pops, and one for you Aunt Lydia," said Cassie quietly. She sat down on the bench and stared at the graves. "I so wish you could have been here today. I'm going to miss you both so much."

Tears threatened and she swallowed, trying to gulp them away, deciding that coming up here today, today of all days, had perhaps not been one of her better ideas. She looked up at the wintry blue sky. "Who knows," she smiled. "Perhaps you're both watching." She laughed. "No doubt with champers in your hands." She stood up and taking a last look at the graves, said, "I hope so, I very much hope so."

Cassie started her walk back down the hill towards the house, unaware that she was being observed. She disappeared from sight and it was then that David emerged from the trees. He slowly walked over to the graves and sat down on the bench. "I don't know what she was saying, but I suspect it was much the same as I'm feeling." He sighed. "I wish you were both here today, I really do." He sat staring at nothing in particular for a few minutes and then slowly stood up.

Standing in front of Charles's grave he said, "I'll try not to let you down Charles. I'll be the proudest man there, that's for sure, and I have you to thank for that." David then crossed himself, something he hadn't done since a boy, but in some curious way it felt right to do it, completely and utterly right. He smiled and shook his head at the absurdity of that action and then started his journey back to his cottage.

By two in the afternoon the only person who appeared unruffled by the proceedings was Cassie. She was wandering about in her dressing gown, helping everyone else get dressed. Robert then arrived with Ben and Charlie.

"Robert's arrived with the boys, and he's wanting the hymn sheets to take over," said Margaret.

"I'll nip downstairs, I want to see how the men are looking," smiled Cassie. She ran downstairs in time to hear Ben inform his father he wasn't wearing these pooey clothes for any longer. He felt stupid. Before Robert could scold, Cassie interjected.

"Ben, aren't you looking handsome." she smiled. Then bending down, Cassie whispered in his ear. "You wriggle about in this outfit and say its pooey and we say 'bye-bye' new tractor don't we?" Ben glared at her. "However," she continued, "if we are especially well behaved and don't have even one teensy-weensy wriggle, we may get more than one tractor. Do you think you could manage perfect behaviour for two tractors?"

Ben nodded his head furiously up and down. "All day I'll be good Cassie, all day pomis!"

"Pomise? You're missing an 'r', Cassie grinned. Ben smiled back at her. "Tooth faiwy's been!"

"Ah," laughed Cassie. "So I see."

372

She then spied Charlie, resplendent in morning suit. "Good God!"

Charlie grinned, looking a combination of embarrassed and pleased. "You can call me Charlie as normal Cassie, no need for such formalities!"

"Ha, ha," smiled Cassie. "I can't believe the scruff bag of yesterday, can look so handsome today. Very debonair. Wait till the young ladies see you. You'll never be off the dance floor."

"Very funny," blushed Charlie.

Cassie looked at the three men before her. "You all look so handsome, thank you for looking so totally and utterly gorgeous."

Robert smiled. "Thank you and it is our pleasure."

Catching Ben looking her up and down, Cassie smiled at him. "Point taken Ben, I'm off to dress as well. Robert, the hymn sheets are in the study and Philip is already at the chapel, he was sorting the organist out. See you there. Come on Ben, you come with me to see your Mum and show her how handsome you're looking."

"Why? Don't want to… I go with Daddy," muttered Ben scowling.

Cassie bent down to him and whispered just one word. "Tractors!" Ben looked up at her and gave a toothy smile as he dutifully followed her upstairs.

At twenty to three Benson came upstairs, informing them that the two carriages had arrived and with that everyone finished getting ready and set off downstairs.

Before Kate left in the carriage there was someone she just had to have a quick word with. Entering the study she found David pouring over his speech for the hundredth time. He looked pale and anxious but undeniably handsome in his morning suit.

"You'll be fine, it's a lovely speech," smiled Kate. She knew David was finding this difficult, the surrogate father role. "Just to warn you she looks stunning, absolutely breathtaking." Her eyes suddenly filled with tears.

"Now Kate, think of the mascara," said David quickly. He took a handkerchief and gently wiped her eyes. "Excellent, not a blob in sight." He kissed her on the cheek. "Cassie isn't the only one who looks stunning today! You look gorgeous."

"Thank you," smiled Kate. She looked at David and squeezed his hand. "Charles was so right about you; he really was. You'll do her proud, you really will…" Then, before the atmosphere got too tense again, she turned quickly and went out to join the others. "See you at the church," she shouted.

David looked at his watch; nearly five to three. He felt incredibly nervous and so incredibly proud, both at the same time. He put his speech in his pocket and went out to the hall where he was just in time to see a vision of Cassie waft down the stairs towards him. He swallowed the lump in his throat and tried to blink away the tears at the same time, grateful that Kate had at least tried, although to some degree failed, to adequately describe how utterly exquisite Cassie looked.

He went forward and took Cassie's hand as she came down the last few steps. He looked into her eyes. "You look truly beautiful, exquisite." And he kissed her gently on the cheek. "Ready?"

Cassie seemed to hesitate and he noticed her eyes looking towards the Great Hall. David suspected he knew what she was thinking. He offered her his arm and instead of escorting her to the carriage took her through to stand before Charles's portrait. He stood back as Cassie looked up at Charles for a few minutes, deep in her own thoughts.

She then turned to David and smiled with gratitude at his understanding. "I'm ready now… Thank you, David." She then took his arm and he led her back through the hall to the waiting carriage at the door.

As the bride and groom emerged from the church after the ceremony, a great cheer went up from a crowd gathered outside. Cassie looked initially surprised and then beamed as she realised that most of the village seemed to have congregated outside the chapel. She gazed around her trying to convey her thanks to them and mouthed, 'see you later', for they would be attending the dance at The Hall in the evening. Photographs were taken and then she and James led the bridal party as they walked back to The Hall.

Much to his mother's relief Ben had behaved impeccably throughout the ceremony and the photographs, without so much as a 'wriggle' in sight! She had smiled at him as he followed the bridesmaids back up the aisle and mouthed, 'Good boy, well done'. Ben's response had been a wide toothless grin. He was surprised to find that he was rather enjoying the day.

The afternoon and the dance in the evening seemed to race by, and all too soon it was time for Cassie and James to leave on their short honeymoon.

Cassie went and said her goodbyes to 'The Family' in private. She and David hugged. "Every happiness, Cassie," smiled David. "James is a wonderful man, have a good life together."

Cassie looked up at David, tears glistening in her eyes. "Thank you David, for... oh you know, in the house before we left, at the church, everything."

He gently wiped a tear away. "Come on, no tears." He looked at her with tenderness. "I meant what I said in my speech; I couldn't have felt more proud today. Thank you for asking me to give you away. You'll never know how much it meant to me." David hugged her to him again and then lightening the moment, said, "Have a lovely honeymoon."

"Do you know where we're going?" asked Cassie. "James won't tell me, he's been very mysterious about it."

David grinned. "I'm sure wherever he has chosen, it will be wonderful! Enjoy, and I look forward to seeing you both when you get back."

Eventually all the farewells were said and Cassie and James got into the car, driving off to the accompanying sounds of cans tied to the back of the car scraping along the drive. Cassie caught Charlie's eye as they drove past. 'You'? She mouthed. He grinned back and nodded.

Their first night was spent in Claridges in London. "I thought, for old times sake," smiled James. "I remember the first time I was here, the graduation with you all. I thought it would be nice to come back."

"Oh it's lovely, so this is the surprise then?" asked Cassie. James continued to look mysterious.

The next morning James insisted they be ready to leave at seven. Cassie was still none the wiser. A car was waiting for them and drove them through what Cassie felt wasn't a particularly salubrious area of London. Eventually they arrived at Waterloo Station.

"Here we are," grinned James. "Lovely!" said Cassie, a little sarcastically. A porter then arrived and taking their cases asked them to follow him. They walked to the end of the station and then into sight stood the train bearing the name, The Orient Express!

Cassie looked at James in disbelief and then flung her arms around him. "Really? We're going on that train?"

James nodded and grinned. "My surprise. Do you like?"

The porter looked on with amusement as Cassie gave James her reply; a lingering kiss. "I like, I certainly do. It's wonderful. Thank you, thank you," she said excitedly.

James looked at the porter and smiled. "We're newlyweds!"

"Really Sir," he replied. "Who'd have guessed!" He smiled at them. "Every happiness to you both."

"Thank you," said James and discreetly gave him his tip. The porter looked down and noted, a rather generous tip."

"Thank **you**, Sir."

The train was everything and more that Cassie could have dreamt of and the destination – Venice.

After a sumptuous dinner, they went back to their carriage. "What a wonderful honeymoon. I'm so lucky," said Cassie, nestling against James. They lay looking out the carriage window as the lights of the towns and villages sped by. "I wonder what our future holds?"

"Who knows," smiled James. "Whatever, as long as it's with you, that's all that matters to me."

"Let's come back on this train for our silver anniversary," beamed Cassie.

"You think we'll last that long then, that's reassuring," smiled James.

"Till death us do part… remember?" said Cassie solemnly.

"I remember," said James. He leant forward and shutting the curtains, smiled knowingly at her. "Now what were you saying about a wonderful honeymoon?"

Chapter 37

Ten years later

"Happy Anniversary," smiled James. Cassie smiled back, "Mmm, and to you," she said sleepily.

"I have to go," said James.

"Go where?" asked Cassie, struggling to wake properly.

"The exhibition, dopey, it's next week. The lighting is going in today, so I have to oversee operations, remember?"

"What time will you be home? You'd better not be late."

"I promise, back by six at the latest," James leant over and kissed her. "Thanks for my pressie, I love it… Here's yours. Now I really have to dash."

Cassie looked at the beautifully wrapped box beside her. Earrings she decided and she was right, lovely pearl drop ear-rings. Exactly what she'd been hinting at for ages! She smiled, drop enough hints and he always came up trumps, although she always pretended to be completely amazed at how on earth he knew it was exactly what she had wanted!

She looked at the clock; quarter to seven, she had about half an hour before peace was shattered and the children would come hurtling into the bedroom.

She gave a long stretch. Her tenth wedding anniversary. She found it amazing that ten years had seemingly gone by in a twinkle of an eye. She'd been so lucky and she knew it. James was a wonderful husband and a patient, fun-loving father to his children. Their son, Christopher, was now eight. Surprisingly he had no talent whatsoever for art but was completely and utterly obsessed by all things mechanical and would happily follow Robert around the estate morning, noon and night if allowed. More like Pops, Cassie decided. Fiona on the other hand, was definitely talented and was equally happy trying to paint as she was trying to sculpt.

Cassie wondered what the future held in store for them and so wished her father and aunt had lived to see them. She smiled; perhaps they do. Continuing her reflective mood she thought back to the many changes that had occurred at The Hall in the intervening years.

George and Margaret, now retired, were living in the cottage which her father had promised them in his Will. They were, however, frequent visitors to their old home, and also provided an excellent baby-sitting service!

Despite Cassie's numerous attempts, Mrs. Pearson had never retired but remained in post until a stroke left her paralysed down one side. She was looked after by 'The Family' and remained at The Hall until her death a year later, aged ninety-four. As one of 'the family' Cassie had insisted that the only place for her to be buried was in the family graveyard. The inscription on her headstone gave her name with *'Mrs. P'.* written in brackets and underneath, *'A much loved friend'.* She had lived to see Cassie's children born, and to the amazement of all, had amassed a sum of money which enabled her to bequeath £2000 to each of Cassie's and Kate's children. She had also instructed that any residue was to go towards the estate. Her treasured pearls, she left to Margaret.

Mrs. Pearson's place had been taken by Helen, whom luckily Mrs. P. had thoroughly approved of. This was partly because she had been one of the kitchen staff initially hired when Cassie's art holidays had started all those years ago. Cassie remembered her as the young girl who had said she thought Mrs. P. to be like marshmallow. Helen had proved a willing pupil, and many of Mrs. P.'s secret recipes were now part of Helen's extensive repertoire. Her husband, Tom, was Benson's replacement and within a short space of time they had proved themselves to be welcome additions to The Hall. Cassie noted, with pleasure, that the relationship her children had with them reminded her of her own happy childhood. History seemed to be repeating itself and she was delighted.

Her time of quiet reflection was then interrupted by the arrival of the children. Cassie quickly looked at the clock; seven fifteen. She could set her watch by them. They always arrived exactly at quarter past.

"Happy anniversary," they chimed. Christopher's face fell. "Where's Daddy? We've got cards for both of you."

"That's kind, thank you," said Cassie who was now being smothered in kisses. "Daddy had to go to work really early so that he'd be home in time for the party. Do you want me to keep the cards till then?"

"No, no, no," said Fiona, jumping up and down with excitement. "Look at mine, I made it. Look at mine first."

Her brother looked at her with complete disdain. "You're pathetic. Why would Mummy want to see your grotty card first?

"It's not grotty," glared Fiona. "Anyway, you're the grotty one and your card is horrid."

"Hoi you two. No fighting," said Cassie. "It's a party day so we want to be big friends. Yes?"

Christopher muttered something under his breath that Cassie couldn't quite catch. "Sorry, what was that?"

"Nothing," said Christopher innocently. "I just said I'm looking forward to the party."

"That's a lie," shouted Fiona. "You said stink, I heard you say it."

"Well this has been a lovely peaceful start to the morning," sighed Cassie. "Off you go, go and get dressed but before you do it would be a lovely touch if you got washed first."

Christopher looked at his mother in amazement. He'd had a bath last night, he didn't need yet another wash. Astonishing what mothers sometimes wanted you to do. He ran out of the bedroom to get dressed, just in case she was going to inflict water on his body again!

Once breakfast had been completed Cassie drove them to school, and then went back to The Hall to help with the preparations for the evening.

James, as promised, was home before six. "Hi gang," he called out. "Hi Daddy," was the reply from, he thought, upstairs.

"In here," shouted Cassie. James went into the dining room where Cassie was putting the finishing touches to the floral displays.

"Nice!" he said as he kissed her. "I'm pooped. What a day. Do I have time for a long soak?"

"Nope," replied Cassie. "Quick shower!"

"Right you are," said James, knowing there was no point in arguing. He went into the kitchen. "Something is smelling gorgeous in here." He went over to the pots that were bubbling away and investigated their contents. "Helen, I'm starving. Any chance of a teensy-weensy bite?"

"Do you want a sandwich? Will that stave off the hunger pangs?"

"You are, as ever, a life saver," smiled James. Looking in the direction of the door he added, "Let's keep this to ourselves though!" Armed with his sandwich he went upstairs to shower.

The party had been a resounding success. Sarah and Claude's children had joined Fiona and Christopher and, much to the amazement of the parents, all the children had behaved beautifully, even handing round the canapés without any mishaps. The children were all staying at The Hall and Kate's youngest child, Ben, who was now nearly fifteen, had been bribed to look after them whilst the adults had their dinner.

Cassie looked around the table at her family and friends. *How lucky I am*, she thought, although she always had a tinge of sadness when it was time for Sarah and Claude to go back home. She wished they lived nearer. Peter and Rowena were going back with their daughter and family as Claude's parents were celebrating their ruby anniversary and had kindly extended an invitation to join them.

Peter always enjoyed his visits to France as it was a wonderful excuse to sample the many delights of the grape and he was additionally blessed by having a son-in-law who ran one of the best vineyards in Southern France. He could hardly wait; neither could James, for that matter. He'd placed his order with Claude for a case of '88 Leoville-Baton, which normally retailed at a vast sum but which Claude could get for a fraction of the cost, so he was very much looking forward to Peter's return with, hopefully, a full boot!

All too soon it was time for Sarah to return to France and Claude watched in amusement as the girls said their fond farewells. "See you at New Year," said Sarah tearfully.

Cassie nodded. "New Year, it's not far off." The family all got into the car. "Safe journey."

Cassie watched the cars disappear and then went into Peter and Rowena's house and locked up.

Chapter 38

What's that?" asked Cassie. She had just caught sight of a mark at the foot of Fiona's back so, deciding to investigate, lifted up her jumper. "How on earth did you get that bruise? It's an absolute whopper!"

"Don't know," replied Fiona trying to inspect it. "Probably got thumped, by him," she said, glaring at Christopher.

Cassie looked at him. "I did not," he said and answered with such surprise and indignation that Cassie did believe him. She could usually tell when he was lying! This time he didn't seem to be.

In the bath a few days later, Cassie noticed more bruises on Fiona's body. "Have you been bashing into things?

"No," answered Fiona, who was a little preoccupied with washing her doll's hair.

Over the next week Fiona complained of feeling tired, had headaches and generally wasn't feeling very well. Cassie looked up her book on childhood ailments but couldn't come up with anything specific. She decided to take her to the doctor. Although she wasn't very keen on this doctor, she accepted his offer of antibiotics and the explanation that there was a weird bug circulating the area.

Over the next couple of weeks Fiona was no better, in fact, worse. Cassie had taken her back to the doctor twice. He was not inspiring confidence. Dark circles had now developed under Fiona's eyes and she was permanently tired and happiest at home lying on the sofa watching TV. This was so unlike the normal Fiona that Cassie knew something was definitely wrong. She would not be fobbed off any longer.

"I will not have yet another dose of antibiotics. This is my fourth visit here and I know there is something wrong, something very wrong and I want, no I demand, a second opinion and will not leave until you arrange it." Cassie was at the end of her tether as she looked at her six-year old daughter, so lethargic, lying quietly in her arms.

"I think I am the best judge of what is wrong with your child," said the doctor. He smiled, a sneering, condescending smile. "I suggest you have a touch of the anxious mother syndrome."

Cassie glared at him. "God damn you," she said, standing up. "We'll see about that," and, snatching the prescription from him, went outside.

"I wish to see another doctor please," she said to Carol, the receptionist, whom she knew well.

"I'm so sorry, there is no one else, Dr. Whyte is the only one doing surgery."

Cassie's eyes filled with tears. "Please, there has to be someone else. He doesn't know Fiona, you know what she's normally like, she's ill, I'm sure she is."

The receptiontist was buzzed by Dr. Whyte. She indicated to Cassie to wait as she told the next patient to go through.

Speaking quietly she said to Cassie, "Dr. Bartlett's proper replacement will be here on Monday, he," indicating to Dr. Whyte, "is just a locum. He'll be away soon."

Cassie shook her head. "Monday… it's too far away. Look at her."

Carol nodded. "Hold on a moment."

Carol came back and beckoned Cassie to follow her into the nurses surgery. "This is Gill, I've told her you're not one of those over anxious mums, and she'd like to do some blood tests on Fiona." She squeezed Cassie's arm. "See you later."

Fiona lay in her mother's arms, totally uncomplaining and without so much as a murmur, as the nurse took, what seemed like bottles of blood. "What are you going to test for?" asked Cassie.

"A whole gamut of things," replied the nurse. "Don't worry, the results will be back in a day or two and I'll phone you. Hopefully Dr. Whyte needn't know."

"I'm tremendously grateful to you," said Cassie. "I really try not to be over anxious but she's normally full of action, always trying to keep up with her brother. This lethargy worries me."

The nurse smiled. "Well, let's hope we can alleviate the worries." She finished taking the last sample. "There we are, all done. You've been a brave little girl who most certainly deserves a lolly-pop."

Fiona just stared at it and gave a wan smile. "Thank you."

With profuse thanks to Carol, Cassie and Fiona left the surgery and drove home. David's car was in the drive.

He came to the door when he heard the car. "Hello, little one. How's my best girl?"

Fiona smiled weakly at him. "Hi Pappy."

David smiled back. He loved his role as honorary grandfather and was thrilled with the name they had been given him, but his heart was breaking as he looked at Fiona. With her titian-coloured hair, she was the spitting image of her grandmother, and was normally as equally feisty and high-spirited, but today she looked so unwell, so dreadfully unwell. "What did the doc say?" He tried to keep his voice as bright as he could.

"He's an ignorant, arrogant, self-opinionated," looking at Fiona Cassie continued, "You know what, he should be struck off. However the nurse was marvellous and she has taken blood to run tests."

David looked anxiously at Fiona. "Were you a very big brave girl?"

She nodded with her mother's violety-coloured eyes looking up at him.

"That probably deserves a special treat when you're feeling better. Yes?" Again Fiona nodded and tried to smile.

"Come on I think bed's the place for you, don't you," said Cassie. Fiona's eyes were starting to close as she nodded again.

"Is Christopher inside?" asked Cassie.

"Don't faint," smiled David as he helped her up the stairs. "Doing his homework."

Surprise registered on Cassie's face. "What did you bribe him with?"

David looked a little guilty. "Oh nothing really, I've got tickets for the match on Saturday, that's all!"

Cassie shook her head and smiled. "I see. Thanks for picking him up from school, that was kind."

"Is James back tomorrow?" asked David.

"No, hopefully tonight. Well at least he was going to try," replied Cassie. "He hopes to get the six o'clock flight."

"Does he need a lift?" Cassie shook her head as she undressed Fiona and got her into her nightie.

"Right, I'd better go back, phone me if he's not back and I can do the school run tomorrow, no problem at all," smiled David. "I rather like it, I love listening to their chats as we drive to school. One learns the most amazing things!" Fiona was now in bed. "Night night poppet, sleep tight and see you with an extra special treat tomorrow."

Fiona looked at him. "Promise Pappy?"

David licked his finger and made an imaginary cross. "Finger's crossed." Fiona smiled at him as she drifted off to sleep.

He and Cassie crept out of her bedroom quietly. As Cassie looked at David her eyes filled with tears. "I'm not being an over anxious mother, am I? You'd tell me if you thought so." David put his arm round her. "That doctor was ghastly. If it hadn't been for knowing Carol, you know, the receptionist," David nodded. "And her asking the nurse to take blood, I don't know what I'd have done. Oh I so wish Peter was here."

"When is he back from Sarah's?" asked David.

"The end of next week I think, it was the month they were away for, and so I'm just assuming but who knows, they may stay on. Carol said Peter's replacement arrives on Monday. I hope to God he's better than the Dr. Jekyll we have just now," said Cassie. "But I'll just swap doctors if I have to, go to the next village if needs must." She was saying this more to herself than David. "Now, I'd better go and check the homework."

"I'll go now, I'll see you tomorrow," David blew her a kiss as Cassie went into her son's room.

As David drove back home unease settled upon him. Fiona looked so ill. She hadn't been her normal self for the last few weeks. He was worried sick; everyone was worried, but Cassie, despite her insistence, kept being palmed off with platitudes. If anything happened to Fiona, David knew he would not be responsible for his actions towards that doctor. He tried to dismiss the notion from his mind but tears welled up in his eyes at the very thought, for he loved the children more than he loved life itself, so much so that he often felt overwhelmed at the intensity of his feelings for them.

When they had been born, David admitted to Kate that he had felt a tinge of jealousy when Charles, even although long since dead, had automatically been given the title of grandfather. But as the children had grown up, Christopher when aged about five, had the idea to christen David, Pappy. This was, he said, because he and Fiona didn't have any grandfathers like their friends and they thought David a suitable replacement. Needless to say he had been thrilled with their idea and accepted his title with pride.

The next two days dragged by but eventually the nurse telephoned and asked Cassie and James to come to the surgery that morning to see the doctor. Full of trepidation they set off.

Immediately, Cassie saw Dr. Whyte she knew something was wrong. He was oozing charm and was contrite to the point of obsequiousness. Cassie looked at him with cold contempt. "I would be grateful if you would get to the point and tell us what is wrong with our daughter."

"I am most dreadfully sorry. It appears your daughter's condition is suggestive of leukaemia." Cassie and James looked at each other, aghast at what they had just heard. Dr. Whyte continued speaking. "She will have to undergo further tests but I have arranged an appointment for her to be seen by the paediatrician. As luck would have it, today." He swallowed. "He's a very busy man, but I persuaded him."

James looked as if he was going to leap the desk and strangle him. Cassie held Dr. Whyte's gaze. "Please tell us the paediatrician's name and where we are to take Fiona." Dr. Whyte handed her an appointment card. Looking at James, Cassie stood up. Dr. Whyte attempted conversation again. "I'm most dreadfully sorry, really I am…" but Cassie had left.

James, white with rage, stood up and moved to inches from his face. "I will personally make sure you never ever put another family through what you have put mine through." Dr. Whyte's mouth opened and closed as if attempting to speak but no sound was forthcoming. James's eyes were black with fury. "You are not fit to practise medicine and I will do my damnest, my absolute damnest to ensure that you never do anything like this again. So help you if anything happens to my daughter, so help you." With that James turned, and left.

He ran across the car park to where Cassie was leaning against the car looking out over fields. They fell into each other's arms and wept.

"James, what are we going to do? Leukaemia, she could die, our little girl is going to die," cried Cassie.

"Cassie, look at me," said James. "Plenty of kids have leukaemia and they survive; there is loads they can do. Let's see what the paediatrician says, let's just wait till then." He wiped her tears. "Yes?"

She nodded. "We have to be strong for her, she mustn't see us upset."

James tried to smile. "You know there are things like bone marrow registers and all these things; the advances in medicine are incredible. We have to hope, we have to do that."

As they neared The Hall James pulled into a lay-by. "We have to look in control and be absolutely fine for her." After a few minutes, they felt suitably composed and so, after taking a couple of deep breaths, continued their drive to The Hall.

David was on baby-sitting duties again and had been reading Fiona a story. As he heard the car, he put down the book. "Mummy and Daddy are home. Shall we finish this later?" Fiona smiled at him. It was maybe his imagination but he felt she looked a little better. "Fingers crossed, little one," he said to himself. On seeing Cassie's face, however, he realised that his imagination had obviously been playing tricks.

"Hi, hi," smiled Cassie. "Have you been good for Pappy?"

"As ever," grinned David at Fiona. "She's my best girl." Fiona smiled at her mother and David.

"Well," said Cassie, who was willing herself to sound in control. "Daddy and I went to the doctor today and the doctor thinks he's found out what is wrong with you. This afternoon you, Daddy and I are going to see another doctor at the hospital. The doctor at the hospital is an expert so hopefully will have you feeling better very, very soon."

"I don't like the yuchy one, he's horrid," said Fiona.

Cassie held Fiona to her. "I agree, he's certainly yuchy, but the one in hospital, he sounds nice." Lifting Fiona up, Cassie said, "We'll go and get ready, shall we?"

Fiona yawned and nodded. "It would be nice to feel better; it really would."

Cassie carried her upstairs and David went to find James. James was slumped in the library with his head in his hands. "It's bloody, I can't understand why this is happening." He looked up at David tears in his eyes. "It's leukaemia, she could die from this. Why? Why Fiona for pity's sake?"

David sat on the arm of the chair and put his arm round James's shoulders. "You have to be strong, strong for Fiona," his voice broke. "And Cassie... all of them." He wiped a tear from his own face. "Come on James, Cassie's upstairs with Fiona getting her ready for the hospital."

James sniffed and wiped his tears. "You're right," he tried to smile. "I'll be strong. It's the only way."

James went upstairs to join Cassie and about ten minutes later they were ready.

"I'll pick Christopher up, take him for a burger, don't you worry about him, okay?" David looked down at Fiona. "See you later alligator." Fiona tried to smile back, "In a while... croc..." but it tailed off. He bent down and kissed her. "Bye."

Upon meeting the paediatrician, Dr. Campbell, Cassie and James felt suddenly better. He was a softly spoken man, with a slight Scottish accent, who exuded a quiet authority and confidence. He smiled warmly to them all and listened intently to Fiona's case history. Within a very short space of time he also had Fiona wrapped round his finger. They all felt they could trust the man and Fiona, after her examination by him, allowed herself to be led away by the nurse to play.

Dr. Campbell laid the facts before them which they did their best to follow but much to their relief he informed them he would have everything typed and they could read it over at their leisure and then ask questions when they had time to assimilate the facts. They were grateful to him for his consideration because their minds were a jumble of facts and figures that at the moment were making very little sense. Sadly though, before Fiona could get better she would have to endure treatments which would undoubtedly make her feel even worse than she was feeling now. More tests would have to be done and he advised that Fiona stay in hospital so that treatment could start as soon as possible. Cassie wanted to ask what Fiona's chances were, but could not bring herself to utter the words. The most frightening time of their lives was about to begin.

Over the next few months the routine for the family revolved around treatments at the hospital, check-ups, blood tests, and through it all Fiona was, for the most part, uncomplaining, apart from when her hair fell out.

She was miserable about this and nothing could be done to allay the distress this caused her until David arrived one day sporting a baseball cap which when he took it off showed him to be totally bald, not a single hair to be seen. Fiona, for a moment, had looked alarmed, but then had started to giggle and had wanted to try on his cap. He had then produced another cap from his pocket that said. 'No 1 Girl'. She wore it proudly, just as Pappy was wearing his and every so often the two of them would compare heads to see who had any hair reappearing. Much to Fiona's delight, she seemed to be winning.

After six months of this regime Dr. Campbell had cause for cautious optimism and decided that he didn't need to see Fiona for a while. She could go home. They were all elated by this news.

Cassie phoned David who upon hearing the news felt tears prick his eyes with relief. Christopher was at his side and looked with alarm thinking something was very wrong.

"Its good news Christopher, Fiona seems better. She's coming home." David grinned happily through his tears at Christopher.

"Oh," was all Christopher said. For to his embarrassment he felt tears spring to his eyes that he quickly tried to wipe away. "I'm actually quite pleased as well," he said gruffly.

David ruffled his hair and looked at him fondly. "I know, but its okay. I won't tell her!"

Christopher gave a sheepish grin, "We could do a banner or something; you know welcome back or something. We could string it across the door so she'll see it as they come up the drive!"

"Good plan," smiled David. "And balloons, she loves balloons.

Within a short space of time the hall had balloons tied to the banister going all the way up to her room and then the pièce de résistance, the huge banner draped across the door, with 'Welcome Home Fiona' and cartoon characters which David had quickly drawn. With minutes to spare, David and Tom managed to erect it before the car came into view.

It was James who spotted it first as Cassie and Fiona were seated in the back. Smiling at Fiona in the rear mirror he said, "Look, Fiona, look at the front door."

Fiona strained to see, then taking off her seatbelt, peered between the seats and beamed with delight at what she saw.

"Looks like Pappy's been up to his tricks," smiled Cassie.

The car stopped and David went forward holding out his arms as he picked Fiona up, "How's my number one girl?"

She answered by giving him a hug and a huge kiss. "Thank you Pappy, thank you for my surprise."

David gently put her down. "It wasn't my idea; it was this fellow's!"

Christopher was looking at the ground, shuffling his feet. He gave a half smile. "I thought you might like the surprise."

Fiona smiled with delight at her big brother, "I love it Christopher… you're the best brother."

Her smile then turned to amazement as Christopher leant over and gave her a quick kiss. "Actually I quite missed you! There's another surprise inside," he mumbled and with that he turned tail and went inside.

"Ta Ra!" He exclaimed as Fiona walked through the door.

Fiona let out a shriek of delight. "This is better than a party." She counted all the balloons, but got stuck after counting to number twenty-eight. Wanting no prompting she said. "There are lots." Everyone laughed.

David looked at them all, his family. It was at times like this he wished they knew. He decided they should be on their own. "I've got to be going," he smiled.

"Pappy stay," pleaded Fiona.

"No, I can't but I'll pop over tomorrow. Can I do that?" asked David. Fiona nodded. He kissed she and Cassie. "Bye," and looking over at Christopher he winked and mouthed 'well done'. Christopher winked back and mouthed, 'thanks'.

For nearly eight glorious months Fiona was in remission then, one day in the bath Cassie noticed a bruise. Her mouth went dry. *Please God, not again,* she thought.

The next morning Cassie phoned Dr. Campbell who arranged for Fiona to have more tests and the following day had the grim task of telling Cassie and James what they already suspected, the leukaemia had returned.

Cassie looked at him, her heart pounding. "There's something else, isn't there?"

Dr. Campbell leaned across the desk and as gently as possible broke the news that they had exhausted all possibilities for further chemotherapy. Cassie and James, their faces ashen at the news, just stared at him in disbelief.

Dr. Campbell waited for a moment to let this news sink in then continued. "I'm sorry but we are now going to have to look at the possibility of a bone marrow donor. Actually, I've already put the wheels in motion and contacted the bone marrow register," he tried to smile. "No stone will be left unturned."

"What about us?" asked James. "Would we not be the best chance – her parents?" His eyes lit up at this prospect. "Test me now, please do it."

"James," said Dr. Campbell kindly. "Of course we will. I also wondered if I might ask Christopher."

Cassie looked at him intently. "If he was a match, what happens; I mean what would happen to him?"

"Under general anaesthetic we'd take some of his bone marrow and although he'd feel a bit sore for a day or two, there should be no other side effects," Dr. Campbell looked at them both. "If we think of Christopher he'd have to be counselled so he'd know what to expect."

"He's a brave chap," smiled James anxiously. "I think he'd cope."

"I'm sure he would," smiled Dr. Campbell, getting up and sitting on the edge of his desk. "However, right at this moment, Fiona is the priority. She knows something is wrong so I think we should go and tell her. How do you feel about that?"

"Sick!" replied Cassie.

Dr. Campbell touched her shoulder. "I know, but let's try and think of this as a set-back, we've got to remain positive."

Cassie nodded. "I know." As if gathering herself together, she straightened up and, looking at James smiled. "Okay?" James nodded. "Off we go then."

Upon hearing that she may require more treatment, Fiona appeared resigned to her fate. James often wondered if this stoicism was lack of comprehension on the part of a six-year-old, but Cassie doubted that. On numerous occasions she had been amazed by Fiona's grasp of medical terminology and her apparent understanding of the treatments she underwent, even the consequences should they fail.

It was decided that Cassie would drive back home to collect the necessities for she and Fiona's stay in hospital. She would also break the news to Christopher.

David, who was on baby-sitting duties again, heard the car and went outside but his heart sank when he saw that Cassie was the sole occupant. She emerged from the car and fell straight into his arms. He held her tight, no words spoken, none needed and walked back to the house in silence.

"Where's Christopher?" asked Cassie.

"Ben came over for him, they've gone fishing." David looked into Cassie's eyes. "I thought it would be good for him, they'll be back about six."

Cassie nodded. "He'll enjoy that." She looked at her watch. "I'll have to get back though, I'm just here to collect some things." Her eyes filled with tears. "It's back, the leukaemia is back and we've only had eight bloody months of remission. Eight; and such a short time of normality."

David tried to keep himself in tight control. "She's a fighter." He tried to smile. "Takes after her Mum and Grandmother, she'll get through the next lot of chemo, you'll see."

Cassie looked at him and shook her head. "They can't give her anymore chemo… they've exhausted these options." She sank into a nearby chair and held her head in her hands. "She only has one more chance, just one, and if that doesn't…" She let out a sob. The thought of no more options was inconceivable to her.

David knelt beside her and held her to him. "I'm sorry, I don't understand," he said quietly.

Cassie's tear filled eyes held his gaze. "The only thing that may work, that may give her just one last chance, is a bone marrow transplant."

David was trying desperately to think clearly but his mind was in turmoil.

Eventually Cassie regained control. Looking at David she shrugged her shoulders as she wiped her eyes. "This isn't helping. Positive, that's what we've got to be. James and I will be tested, then Christopher and there's a bone marrow register, national and international, no stone will be unturned, so Dr. Campbell said, and surely… somewhere…" She shivered. "Someone will be a match. There has to be someone, there just has to be."

David nodded as if understanding but he was still trying to fully comprehend what Cassie was saying.

Oblivious to this she continued. "Relatives apparently are often the best match." Cassie grimaced. "Neither James or I have very many, have we?" She looked at her watch again. "I'll better get some things together and get back."

"What will I say to Christopher?" asked David. Cassie shook her head. "I don't know," she sighed. "He's quite perceptive and so it would be an insult to him if we kept the truth from him. Tell him that what we all suspected is sadly now reality. The leukaemia's back and she needs more treatment. That's all he needs to cope with at the moment. When I go back to the hospital James will come home. He may talk to Christopher about the tests for bone marrow donation but I don't know, I really don't know."

David put his arm around her. "Go up and get your things. Don't keep her waiting. I'll stay here as long as you like so tell James he doesn't have to rush back."

Cassie kissed David on the cheek. "You're always there when I need you…" she smiled. "When we all need you… Thanks."

David smiled and shooing her away said, "Off you go upstairs."

David went into the drawing room and looked out of the window, gazing unseeing at what was before him. He wished there was something, anything he could do. He heard Cassie running down the stairs and met her in the hall.

"Are you okay for driving back?" he asked with concern.

Cassie nodded. "Yes, I'm fine. Tell Christopher I'll call him later and that his Dad will be back soon." David nodded. "Why don't you come over and see Fiona tomorrow," added Cassie.

"Are you sure?" asked David.

Cassie smiled. "She always needs her Pappy. You always cheer her up."

David nodded again, trying not to let Cassie see the tears in his eyes. Too late – she had.

She kissed him on the cheek again. "They're so lucky having you, you're a wonderful grandfather to them; you really are."

Squeezing her arm he managed to say, "See you later, now go. Give her a big kiss fro…"

He couldn't say anymore and Cassie finished his sentence, "from Pappy. I will, you can be sure of that."

David helped her into the car and watched as she drove away. He wiped away the tears and, noting the time, saw he had about half an hour to get himself back in control before Helen and Tom arrived back from shopping and then Christopher who would be back by six.

David hoped that James would be home soon. He wanted time on his own to think about all that Cassie had said.

However, it was late by the time David returned home, his mind in turmoil. James had insisted he stay for a nightcap which then became three, or even four; he couldn't remember! Sense prevailed and he decided to go straight to bed; he would think more clearly after a good night's sleep. However, despite the amount of drink consumed, normal alcoholic induced slumbers were denied him. He got up and went out to the verandah and lit a cigar. The only thought going through his troubled mind was what Cassie had said; that the best chance for Fiona would be a bone marrow donation by a close relative.

For the first time since Charles had told him who Cassie's father really was, David now wished they had told Cassie the truth then, all those years ago. He shivered. He felt cold sitting on the verandah and decided to walk down to the lakeside. He reached the lake just as the moon came out from behind a cloud and threw its luminous light across the water. How on earth would Cassie react if she found out now, he wondered?

He took a last draw on his cigar. He couldn't even begin to imagine what she would feel. He tossed the cigar butt into the water and watched it bob about on the surface. He sighed. "What a mess... what a bloody mess."

David hadn't realised he had been walking around the estate for several hours until dawn finally emerged. He walked back to the cottage and immersed himself in a hot bath for a further hour or so until it seemed a reasonable time to officially start the day. Reasoning that he required fortification after his lengthy night-time walk, he set about cooking what Peter would deem an appallingly unhealthy breakfast of fried this, that and the other. It smelt delicious and David could barely contain himself from salivating in anticipation. Finally replete, he cleared up whilst he continued pondering the inexorable problem in the vain hope that a solution would be forthcoming. It wasn't. He needed Peter's medical advice but as Peter was away on one of his frequent sojourns to France and would not be returning until the following week, this was not an option.

He looked at the clock, it was nearly nine. A civilised time to phone Kate, as the children would be off to school and Robert would also have left. He picked up the phone and dialled her number. No answer. "Where the hell are you, Kate?" he demanded, glaring at the continually ringing phone. There was a knock at the door. "Kate!" he said with surprise. He smiled and, indicating the phone, said, "I'm phoning you, must be telepathy." He put the phone down.

"You're looking marvellous," said Kate.

"Why thank you. You're too kind. David grinned. "Do I detect a touch of sarcasm in your voice?"

"Just a smidgen." answered Kate. "Trouble sleeping?"

David nodded. "I've been prowling around the estate since about one this morning. Came back about six, soaked in the bath till it went cold then had a massive fry-up which, I have to confess, was absolutely and totally delicious. No doubt you're sorry to have missed out!" Kate smiled. "Coffee? I was just going to make some fresh, fancy some?"

"Mmm," replied Kate. "That would be lovely." They headed off to the kitchen. "So," asked Kate. "Why were you phoning? There's not even more bad news is there?"

David was piling spoonfuls of coffee into the cafetiere. "Stop," said Kate. "How many have you put in?"

David shrugged. "Not sure. I'll start again." With that, he tipped the coffee back into the jar and then measured out the usual four spoonfuls. "You know that the leukaemia is back." Kate nodded as he continued. "And you also know that chemo is not an option. Apparently her body wouldn't be able to take anymore." Kate nodded again. "Actually," continued David, "I was wondering if I should phone Peter, I really don't understand why Fiona can't have anymore, but anyway, her last chance..." David looked at Kate. "I can't believe I'm saying this in such a matter-of-fact way. I think its because the reality has not yet fully penetrated... I don't know. All I do know is that the doc says that a bone marrow transplant is the only option."

Kate's eyes filled with tears and she fumbled for a tissue. David stretched over to the paper towels and ripped one off for her. "Don't have anything as delicate as tissues, sorry."

Kate smiled weakly and wiped her eyes with the paper towel. "Robert and I are going to ask Dr. Campbell if we could be tested soon." Her eyes filled with tears again. "The children... they insist on being tested as well."

"Does Cassie know?"

"Not yet," said Kate. "We thought we'd just go straight to Dr. Campbell and be tested."

David looked intently at Kate. "You know that a close relative is likely to be the best bet." Kate again nodded. "I don't know what to do Kate. I have toyed with the idea of waiting to see if Cassie, James or Christopher were suitable and then, if the awful scenario of none of them being a match was the case, I'd speak to Dr. Campbell and ask to be tested. What I don't know, which is why I wanted to speak to Peter, is whether, if I were tested, would they be able to tell parentage by that? I've no idea, but I have this awful worry that some clown in the lab might go bowling along and say something inadvertently in front of Cassie."

He drained his coffee. "Another cup?" Kate declined.

"I see what you mean," she said. "I've no earthly idea, sorry." She looked at her empty cup. "May I change my mind? I would like another." David poured more coffee and she took a sip. "David you have to be tested."

"I know, Kate. Of course I will. I want to. You know I would do anything to save Fiona, just anything. All I want to know is if we got to that stage, and I was a match, how would that be explained? Should I tell Dr. Campbell my true relationship with Fiona? Would that help? I mean, he's bound by that oath thing that doctors take, what is it called again?"

"Hinno, hippo or something," said Kate. "Yes, Hippocratic oath, after Hippocrates, you know, the Greek physician."

"I'm deeply impressed," smiled David. "Well whatever, he wouldn't say anything to Cassie, would he?"

"I suppose not," agreed Kate.

David looked thoughtful for a moment or two then added, "This is certainly something Charles never considered. God, none of us did. Never in our wildest imaginings could we have foreseen this. When I was out for my nocturnal walk I wished we'd said something to Cassie at the time, all those years ago. We should have, but perhaps its just with hindsight, I'm saying this."

"I think so," replied Kate. "There would be no good time to tell Cassie. Way back then would have been as bad as now. If she has to know, I have no idea how she'll take it. I really don't and I've thought about this lots. I wondered if the older she is, the easier it would be to understand. Then I decided that even if she lived to be a hundred, it would still be lousy, hurtful, every emotion under the sun. I just don't know." Kate looked at David. "No help am I?"

David held her hand. "You're always a help. Always have been and I'm just so glad I have you to talk this over with. I really am."

Kate returned his smile. "Why don't we wait for Cassie and James's results."

"Good idea," agreed David. "I was thinking that myself, but its nice we're both in agreement."

~~~~~

"What time are the results due?" asked James as he paced the ward floor.

"James, sit down," said Cassie gently. "You marching up and down will do no good, no good at all."

Eventually the nurse came over and told Cassie and James that Dr. Campbell would see them now. Fiona was fast asleep and hopefully wouldn't notice their absence.

The moment they entered his office they knew the news was bad. "I'm sorry," he said. "Neither of you are a match, we're just waiting for Christopher's results. The first time they were run they were inconclusive. We're running them again just to be sure." He looked at his watch. "Should be through in about two hours." He looked at James. "Your brother sadly is not a match either."

James looked at him as if he hadn't heard. "Sorry did you say my brother?

Ian Campbell looked at James. "I'm sorry, I thought you knew," he looked at the notes in front of him. "Yes, it was Tuesday. He came in to be tested three days ago."

James looked stunned then, to his shame, felt tears prick his eyes which he tried to quickly wipe away. "Sorry Ian. Its just... I can't believe it... we've never been particularly close. I phoned him to tell him about Fiona, felt I should, but he didn't say anything. He didn't say anything either about being tested, he was his usual monosyllabic self. I can't believe it. Did he know if he had been a match what he'd have had to go through?"

Ian Campbell nodded. "Yes, we had a long chat. He was quite prepared. I telephoned him with his result and he was genuinely upset. We hadn't your results so were still hoping there would be a match. He wanted to try and help, he really did."

James nodded and looked at Cassie, still in disbelief. "That was kind of him." Cassie could only nod, for she was as taken aback as James.

There was a knock at the door and the nurse entered to say that Fiona had wakened. They stood up. "Just coming," said Cassie. She looked at Dr. Campbell. "We were her best chance, weren't we?"

He looked thoughtful for a moment. "I won't lie to you. Yes, next of kin is what we had hoped for but let's not give up hope. We're still searching for a match. You could even appeal in the media if you wished. That's been done before but let's wait, another few days. I promise I won't do anything that will compromise Fiona's chances."

Cassie looked at him. "We know that. This news was, what did you say once before, ah yes, a set back, we'll think of this as a set-back until we know differently. Yes?"

Ian Campbell put his arm around both she and James. "Yes. Definitely."

Cassie looked at James. "Ready?" He nodded and, taking her hand, they went along the corridor back to Fiona's ward.

James stayed for another couple of hours with Fiona, awaiting the results of Christopher's test. What had been inconclusive before was now definite, he also was not a match. James was dreading having to tell Christopher, for he knew how much his son had hoped he would be the one who would be suitable.

397

After James had arrived home and imparted the dreaded news, David made his excuses saying that James and his son should have time together. David then went back home and immediately phoned Dr. Campbell. To his surprise he was put through immediately. He told him he wished to be tested as soon as possible but was not prepared for the doctor's next question.

"How old are you?"

David sensed his age may be a problem and countered the question with, "Why? How old would you **not** wish me to be?"

Ian Campbell laughed. "No older than fifty."

David muttered under his breath but quickly recovered and laughed back. "Well that's lucky, certainly is. I'm just fifty. I won't be fifty-one for ages."

"I'm sorry," said Ian Campbell, "I know your age. Fiona told me. I can't remember why she did, but she did."

"All right," sighed David. "How old would the cut off point be for a close family member, father or grandfather?"

Ian Campbell sensed desperation in David's voice plus something else he couldn't quite place and so in a manner that was a little cagey said, "A year or two after fifty might be considered in extreme circumstances."

There was a long pause, so long that Ian thought they had been cut off. "Mr. Coleridge, are you still there?"

"What? Yes, I'm still here," replied David, quickly recovering. "Look, it's a little tricky speaking on the phone. Would you have some time when I may come and speak to you?"

"Of course," replied Ian. "Come to my office, tomorrow morning, first thing."

"Any chance of this evening, and…" David hesitated, "not in your office. I really don't want Cassie to know we have had this chat."

Ian Campbell replied, "Very well," he paused for a moment, "I know, come to the admin block of the hospital. It's a separate building from the wards and I have an office there. It's the red building, just as you come through the gates. Ask the janitor to direct you to my office. Would 7.00 p.m. be suitable?"

"It would," replied David. "I'm extremely grateful to you. I'll see you then."

As David drove to the hospital he was still unsure what he was going to say to Dr. Campbell. He arrived early, parked and went to the janitor's office. The janitor took him to the office where Dr. Campbell was already waiting. David quickly looked at his watch. "I'm terribly sorry, am I late?"

Dr. Campbell stood up and they shook hands. "No, I took the opportunity to catch up on paperwork, something I hate doing." He smiled. "You did me a favour asking to meet here. Well, Mr. Coleridge, what can I do for you?"

David shifted in his chair and at that moment decided to tell him the truth. "Please, call me David. Will you be honest with me?"

"I'll try," replied Ian Campbell.

"All right," said David, "What are Fiona's chances? Not the chances you may say to soften Cassie and James, but the chances that you truly believe."

Ian looked David straight in the eye. "Not great. In fact, I would have to say, if I was being honest, quite poor."

"Thank you for your honesty," said David. He returned the doctor's frank stare. "I am well aware there is a cut off point for people being accepted as donors and that my age," he smiled, ruefully. "Fifty-seven actually, is against me. But I have to beg you to test me."

David looked over at Ian, who wearing a puzzled expression, had started to shake his head. David quickly continued. "If Fiona's grandfather had been alive and he had been say, fifty-seven, would you have tested him?"

"Perhaps, maybe as an absolute last resort, but that is academic. Lord Emerson is dead. None of the family members have been a match," said Ian Campbell gently.

"Cassie must never know, no one must know, but I... I am Fiona's real grandfather," said David quietly.

Ian looked at him. "I know how fond you are of Fiona..." he didn't finish what he was going to say because for a second he thought David was trying to pull off a desperate last ditch attempt, but as he looked at the anguish on his face he realised that what he was saying was the truth. "It must be very difficult for you, keeping this secret."

David shrugged. "Not really. I only found out about sixteen or seventeen years ago. That's when I first met the family. I came over from the States to sort out my mother's estate and whilst here decided to look up an old friend, Cassie's mother. It was then I found out she had died in childbirth. I had gone to the States on a scholarship and didn't know Lizzie was pregnant. Soon after that she married Charles. I didn't know why she had, but I didn't come back to the UK until my mother died, twenty years later.

"When Charles met me he apparently thought Cassie and I looked vaguely similar, and something started nagging away at him – I suppose the timings of when he first knew Lizzie and when Cassie was born. I don't know but for whatever reason he looked through old letters of Lizzie's, which he had put away after she died, having never read them," David looked at Ian. "That was the type of man he was; a wonderful man. However I digress. When he did eventually read them, he knew that Cassie wasn't his daughter. It was there in black and white."

David stood up and went over to the window. "It gets better. I then thought I had fallen in love with Cassie, and she with me. It was a temporary aberration on both our parts. I think I was trying to recapture the moments I had had with her mother… anyway thankfully nothing happened, well no more than a rather passionate kiss because her aunt caught us. It was then, Charles decided he'd have to tell me.

"I went back to the States but returned just after Charles died. We had become quite close and I came over for his funeral. The relationship I have with Cassie is one of favourite uncle and niece and I feel so lucky that I have been able to become part of her family. I will do everything in my power not to hurt her, but if I were a match I could perhaps save Cassie's daughter… my grand-daughter, you have to at least try. I am begging you… please."

Ian Campbell sighed. "It goes against all the protocols, against all my medical knowledge." He looked at David's anxious face and relented. "Very well, we'll test you but you have to be aware that even if you are a match, it may not work."

"I know," said David wearily. "But at least everything will have been tried. I believe your expression is 'no stone will be unturned' and this way, that will be true."

He got up and paced the floor again. "What about Cassie? What will you tell her? Will the test show we are related? Would the lab staff know."

"You've really thought things through haven't you," said Ian. "Having you tested is the easy bit. But if you were a match you'd have to come in for two days to have the bone marrow extracted in theatre. How would you explain that?"

"God, I don't know, I'm not sure, but I'll worry about that later," said David. He looked at his watch. It was after eight. "I'm so sorry to have kept you so late. Do your own family ever see you?"

"Not often," admitted Ian. "But then if one of mine were ill I'd expect that doctor to try everything.

"Your patients are very lucky to have you," smiled David. "As are their relatives." Ian looked a little embarrassed and gave a shy smile. "When do I get tested?"

"Come in tomorrow, before you go and see Fiona. I'll tell the ward to expect you." They shook hands. "Don't worry, our conversation of this evening did not take place, I have a lousy memory anyway."

"Thanks Ian," smiled David as he opened the door. "I'll hear from you soon."

"Sure. Whether it's good or bad news."

David nodded as he closed the door behind him.

Chapter 39

To watch Fiona become weaker and weaker was heartbreaking for all concerned. Cassie and James were shadows of their former selves, both thinner, dark eyed and with strained haunted expressions on their faces. Every moment spent with Fiona was precious, every extra day a bonus; for they were now only too aware that time was running out. All they could do was be with her, they were powerless to do anything else.

Every time the phone rang, David's heart leapt, hoping it would be Ian. Eventually the wait was over. The phone rang. "David its Ian. We've got the results. Are you ready?"

"Yes," said David his heart now firmly in his mouth. "Tell me the worst."

"The first lot we have done show you to be a match," said Ian quietly.

David couldn't speak. Ian continued, "Now don't build up your hopes just quite yet. I need you to come in and get some more blood work done. Can you do that?"

David nodded. "Are you still there?" asked Ian.

David realised he hadn't uttered a sound. "Sorry, yes, I'm here. Where do you want me to go?"

"Meet me in the office in the red building, the admin one. Remember?" Ian could visualise David's reaction. "Can you come soon?"

"I'm on my way, ten minutes, give me just ten minutes," said David.

"David! Drive carefully." David agreed.

In just twelve minutes, David arrived at Ian's office and had more blood taken. "There we are," said Ian, filling the last bottle. "Later today we'll know for sure if you are absolutely and definitely compatible. Have you given any thought about what you're going to say to them if you are?"

"No," answered David. "Have you?" Ian shook his head.

"Do they have to know who the donor is?"

"No, I can say it's from the register. I don't have to be specific. I'm sure at the moment they wouldn't care. But how would you explain your absence?"

"A cold. I thought I'd say I couldn't come over because I thought I was getting a cold and didn't want to go near anyone. I'd remain in splendid isolation." David grinned at Ian. "Rather good, don't you think?"

Ian smiled back. "Not bad. I take it you've been practising your technique for 'voice afflicted by heavy cold'." David duly demonstrated. "Very convincing." Ian patted David's back. "I'll take these to the lab and then phone you later."

"I think I'll start my cold now, to be on the safe side, so call me at the cottage. I'll get someone to collect Christopher from school. Speak to you later and thanks," said David.

"Even if we get past the next hurdle, you know that we're a long way from the finishing line," said Ian, as he opened the door.

"I never took you for a racing man," smiled David.

Ian gave a wry smile. "I'm not, who has time!"

~~~~~

Ian's call came. "Can you come in?"

David could barely speak. "I'm a match, then?"

Ian agreed. "Yes, I'm delighted to say you are. If truth be known it's excellent but David you know that your age will maybe count against this taking. Be prepared for that."

"I know," said David. "But at least we will have tried. I can come in straight away and I can also have an anaesthetic whenever you like. Haven't had any food or drink since I came home." He looked at the clock. "Five hours ago, that should be okay, shouldn't it?"

Ian gave a slight laugh. "You're quite something. Yes, we can start right away then. I'll check that theatre is free. See you in a little while. You know where to go?"

"Yes, no problem. Bye." David hung up and then phoned Kate. He then picked up his overnight bag already packed and went outside and waited for Kate. He looked out over the lake. "I hope you're watching over us because we need all the help we can get for this one. Wish us luck Charles, by God wish us luck."

Kate, who normally was a fairly speedy driver, could not match David's record of twelve minutes to the hospital; they arrived in seventeen! She stopped at the back entrance to make sure they wouldn't bang into Cassie or James. "Good Luck, David. Fingers and everything crossed. I'll phone to see how you got on and when I can collect you tomorrow." She leant across and kissed him on the cheek. He gave her hand a quick squeeze and then hurriedly went to meet Ian.

David was whisked into theatre within the hour. He awoke, aware of someone doing something to his arm. He moved with effort and let out a groan.

"Hello, its all over," smiled the nurse. "I'm just checking your blood pressure and Dr. Campbell will be in to see you in a moment." The nurse put away the machine. "Do you need anything for pain?"

David tried to ease himself into a more comfortable position and winced. "I'm just a little achy, that's all. But thank you, I don't think I need anything." He smiled at the nurse. "Did everything go okay"

"As far as I know, yes, but Dr. Campbell will be in soon." She started to straighten David's sheets just as Ian arrived. The nurse looked at David. "I'll pop back later."

"Well, how do you feel?" asked Ian as he looked at David's charts.

"Feel a bit battered and bruised but not bad, pretty good in fact," smiled David. "More to the point how did it go from your point of view?"

"Its a waiting game now," sighed Ian. "We just have to hope. You can imagine how Cassie and James are feeling. They're all buoyed up. I hope…" He didn't finish the sentence.

David nodded. "I know what you're thinking, maybe we're giving them false hope. Perhaps we have but I'm still glad we've tried." He looked at Ian who looked absolutely exhausted. "It's nearly ten, you should get home."

"I'll have a last check at Fiona, then I'll push off and see you tomorrow. I hope you sleep well although I'd doubt it with all that goes on here," smiled Ian wearily.

404

As he reached the door David said, "I know I pressurised you into doing this but it was her last chance, she had to be given that."

Ian nodded. "She did, I know... and miracles, they can sometimes happen. Who knows. Goodnight."

David tried to settle down to sleep but his mind was along the corridor, wondering how Fiona was coping, how they were all coping. He was just drifting off to sleep when the nurse came in. He smiled. "No doubt you're here with a sleeping pill? You were nearly too late."

The nurse returned his smile. "You're wrong actually, a friend of yours phoned, Kate. She wondered how you were. I just popped in to tell you."

"That was kind," smiled David sleepily. "Very kind."

"Can I get you anything?" asked the nurse. The reply she got was a gentle snore. She leant across and put off his light. *I wish all my patients were like you*, she thought.

At seven the next morning, David woke feeling decidedly uncomfortable. He didn't care though, this was nothing compared to what Fiona was going through. "Good morning!" said a bright voice.

"God man, have you been home at all?" asked David.

Ian smiled. "Don't need much sleep. I popped in to see you but also to tell you I've seen Fiona and so far so good. She is, in the hospital jargon, comfortable. Now, what about you? How are you feeling? I expect a bit more uncomfortable than last night."

David agreed. "It's okay though, I expected this. I'm fine, really I am but I need to get home. Any chance?"

"I don't see why not," smiled Ian. "I imagine you'd discharge yourself anyway so we might as well do it properly!"

"I'll get a lift home from Kate. She'll be in mid-morning," said David. "Thanks for everything. Now all I need is to get back home without being seen by Cassie or James. What are they up to?"

"They don't venture far from Fiona's side. You should be okay," said Chris. "Go down the back stairs and along corridor four, you should be fine."

David phoned Kate to collect him. He was a little sore but had declined the offer of a wheelchair. He'd manage under his own steam and just wanted away from the place. It was with some relief that he emerged from the side entrance to find Kate's car immediately outside.

"Brilliant, Kate. I'm glad I didn't have to walk too much further. I feel about a hundred." He got into the car and leant across and kissed her. "Thanks for phoning last night, they said you had."

"Well, what did Dr. Campbell say?"

David crossed his fingers. "It's a waiting game. We won't know for a while so all we can do is hope, but at least we tried."

Kate helped David into the cottage. "Are you sure you're going to be all right?" she asked with concern.

With relief David sat down. "Yes, just seized up a bit. I've got a couple of painkillers to take. I'll be fine. Now off you go and thanks."

Kate looked at him anxiously. "Are you sure? I could stay."

"Kate! You've loads to do. I'll be fine. I'll phone you later, now go. Thanks again for my food parcel. It's much appreciated. I'll have another snooze and then tuck into it later." Kate was still looking a little sceptical that he would behave. "Scouts honour and all that. I'll be good. Snooze, then lie out on the sofa and watch TV. Promise." He held her hand. "Speak to you later. Now… buzz off." Kate laughed and did as she was told.

With effort he got out of the chair and went through to the kitchen. He took his painkillers then, as he had promised Kate, he went to have a snooze.

Cassie and James were sitting in their enclosed 'bubble' environment. Cassie looked at her daughter, she knew it was probably her imagination but in three days Fiona seemed to have more colour. She looked over at James, who was dozing in the chair. He had aged so much in the last year or so, deep lines crossed his forehead and the light feathery lines at his eyes were now replaced by deep furrows. She smiled slightly. *I still think you're gorgeous though*, she thought.

James, as if sensing he was being observed, stirred slightly. He opened his eyes and smiled at Cassie. "What are you looking at?"

"I was just thinking you're still rather gorgeous," answered Cassie.

James ran his hand over his face to feel the stubble. "Certainly I must be looking pretty hunky right at this moment." He moved his head around. "Don't let me fall asleep in the chair again, it knackers

406

my neck." He got up and looked at his daughter and then at Cassie. "Is it my imagination or do you think she's got more colour? I think she's looking a bit better."

Cassie took his hand. "I was looking at her just before you woke and I thought so. Maybe, just maybe," she said quietly.

James put his hands on her shoulders. "Fancy a massage?"

Cassie smiled up at him. "Normally I'd love one but right now, I'd love a shower." She sniffed at her armpit. "And a change of clothes." She looked at Fiona, "Do you think I could."

"Yes, good idea," smiled James. "A sweet smelling wife would make a delightful change, and who knows, Fiona may be awake again when you come back. I think I'll follow your example. Have we really been in the same clothes for three days?"

Cassie nodded. "Gross, as Christopher would say."

She stood up and kissed Fiona on the forehead. "Back soon." On leaving the inner door of the room, Cassie discarded the protective clothing they wore when entering Fiona's room. It was lovely to escape the claustrophobic atmosphere of the place. She had a word with the nurses and then made her way to the 'Parents' Room'.

She was walking along the corridor when she heard giggling from one of the rooms. "I know he's ancient, but he's gorgeous, lovely twinkling eyes."

Cassie smiled, wondering who they were talking about. She found herself slowing down to a stroll to hear who this gorgeous creature might be.

"His granddaughter is lucky, he did it for her and at his age. They don't normally do it over fifty and he's, I think he's fifty-six maybe even older, and giving bone marrow is no joke. He was pretty sore afterwards but didn't once complain, not like bay 2, bed 2." They groaned and then someone spoke again. "Brenda's nursing her and says that its only three days since they started but there is a slight improvement, she's a lovely little thing. I hope it works."

Cassie knew she should move but couldn't, she was rooted to the spot.

"He even has a romantic name." The conversation continued. "Coleridge, sounds like a poet doesn't it?"

407

Cassie felt herself become hot and bothered and thought she was going to faint. Steadying herself against the wall she continued listening.

The conversation resumed. "Aren't donors meant to be confidential?" asked someone.

"They are, but I saw the lab report when I was in Dr. Campbell's office. He'd been looking at the file and then got a crash bleep, he leapt up and the report was sticking out of the notes. I didn't intentionally peek." Cassie heard a door being shut. "But don't tell because if Sister finds out I've told, she'll string me up."

Another door closed and with every effort she possessed Cassie tried to walk along the remainder of the corridor before the nurses came out and saw her. With relief she arrived at the 'Parents' Room'. Thankfully it was deserted and she slumped into a chair. None of what she had just heard made sense. There must be some mistake. She'd ask Ian. Ridiculous nonsense, but still she wished she hadn't overheard their conversation.

After her shower and change of clothes Cassie felt much better. She decided she'd been over tired; her mind was playing tricks. She put a little make-up on and looked in the mirror – better, not much, but a little better. She picked up her bag and then made her way back to the ward.

James smiled as she came back into the room. "You look gorgeous. How do you feel?"

"Clean and ready to face the world again." Cassie was about to tell James what she overheard but then stopped herself. She smiled at him. "I can recommend the shower, trust me!"

He giggled. "I know, a bit pongy, see you in a little while." He left and Cassie sat back in her chair just looking at Fiona.

The days passed and there was a definite improvement. Ian, as ever, was extremely cautious but secretly was pleased with Fiona's progress and not a little surprised. He phoned David to tell him and also to tell him of Cassie's conversation with him. David listened intently.

"Sorry, putting you in that awkward position but well done for hopefully allaying her suspicion," said David. "I really am grateful to you for telling her it was a donor from the register, but knowing Cassie she'll still ask me. It's good to be forewarned." David hung up and tried to think what he'd say. After a while he phoned Kate who was appalled at the news.

"How did she find out?" asked Kate. "What happened to confidentiality for God's sake?"

"It wasn't Ian, he thinks it was when he got an emergency bleep or something whilst he was looking at the notes and he dashed off. When he came back he saw the lab report on my blood results poking out from the notes. It may have been like that when he left, who knows, all I know is that I've to be pretty convincing, but at least I have some time to think up something. How's this for an idea?" David then proceeded to tell Kate what his story would be. She was not entirely convinced it would work but agreed he had to give it a try.

The next few days for David were spent in a constant state of panic every time the phone rang or someone came to the door. Eventually the day he had been dreading arrived.

He opened the door to Cassie. "This is a lovely surprise, it's so good to see you." He gave her a hug, hoping she wouldn't feel his heart beating totally out of control. "How is she?"

Cassie's expression said it all and she beamed at him. "It's beyond their wildest hopes, they really think its working. Oh she's not out of the woods yet, but she's certainly in the right direction."

David hugged her again. "That's wonderful, truly, truly wonderful." He smiled. "Sadly we can't have champers at the moment, will a coffee do?"

"That would be lovely," smiled Cassie. "Its warm enough to sit out, shall I put a table on the verandah?"

"Good idea," shouted David from the kitchen. Taking a deep breath to steady his nerves he came out of the kitchen carrying a tray with coffee and biscuits and popped it on the awaiting table. He grinned at Cassie. "As we're outside I'll just nip in for something, won't be two ticks." He returned with a cigar and lighter. Cassie shook her head.

They chatted away for a little while which David realised was Cassie's way of lulling him into a false sense of security. Then she lunged. "Did you donate your bone marrow to Fiona?"

No subtleties there at all, thought David. *Keep calm.* he thought to himself.

He fixed his eyes upon her. "Yes. Yes I did."

He knew Cassie wasn't expecting that reply and was secretly pleased that his answer seemed to throw her off balance for a moment.

Her brow furrowed. "You did?" David nodded. She looked at him intently.

David wanted to pre-empt her next question which he knew would be the grandfather question so quickly before she had time to think, leant over and taking her hand said. "I have something dreadful to confess." Cassie's eyes penetrated his but beneath their glare, David noticed vulnerability. She was scared of what he would say.

"Are you ready for this?" Cassie nodded. "This has to be our secret, no one, and I mean no one, must know." Again Cassie nodded. David took a deep breath. "I was desperate and so I lied to Ian, I don't feel good about it, in fact in some ways I feel ashamed, but I would do it again with no hesitation at all."

Cassie had no idea what he was talking about. "What do you mean? I don't understand."

"I said to Ian I was Fiona's real grandfather so that I would be tested."

Cassie looked at David with incredulity. "You did what?"

"I couldn't think of anything else. He wouldn't test me, said I was too old, or rather the damned protocols say I am. So I asked him if there was some leeway with the age barrier if it was a family member. He said in extreme cases there was. This, my dear Cassie, was an extreme case. We had run out of options, you know that."

Letting go of Cassie's hand he stood up and looked out over the lake. He required a second or two to gather himself together again.

Turning, he looked at her. "I know it was low, underhand, any of these things. Ian is a wonderful man, a fabulous doctor. I know all that. But I had to try. We had to give Fiona one last chance. I don't know why I thought I'd be compatible, I just hoped, prayed perhaps... well maybe not pray exactly, I did chat to Charles and Lydia and said any help they could give would be much appreciated!"

He knew he was being flippant because Cassie had tears streaming down her face and he was unsure if that was a good or bad sign.

Cassie stood up and went over to him. She put her arms around him and said, "You are a wonderful man. Thank you for still having faith or whatever it was that kept you fighting for her. Wait till I tell James, he'll be overwhelmed, he really will." She stood back and looked at David. "Since you've arrived into my life you've been like my Guardian Angel."

"Hey, steady on," said David feeling guilt oozing from every pore. "That's a bit over the top, we're family, remember. We all help each other." He smiled at her. "I know you have to tell James but he really has to promise not to say anything to anyone. If any of the medical bods heard about this, Ian could be in deep, deep trouble." Cassie nodded. "And one last thing," David attempted to look a little embarrassed or coy as he felt this was a rather nice touch and one which he hoped would completely convince Cassie. "I lied to Ian about my age."

Cassie burst out laughing. "Really David, you are the limit. You are a one off but I wouldn't have you any other way. How old?"

"Just knocked a few years off." David managed to smile sheepishly. Cassie looked sceptical. "Really!" he added.

He put his arm around her. "Fiona's still got a long way to go yet. It's still one day at a time."

"I know," said Cassie thoughtfully. "Somehow I feel she'll be okay; with your bone marrow she's bound to be."

He shook his head but smiling said, "Daft logic but thank you, however I don't care whose bone marrow it is as long as she gets better. That's all that matters."

Cassie nodded. She looked at her watch. "I'd better be going. I just popped by to pick up some things but I had to find out what you'd been up to. You know I overheard a nurse say she'd seen your lab report and that you'd donated the bone marrow. I couldn't believe it. She said you were Fiona's grandfather." Cassie laughed. "They both fancied you like mad."

David grinned. "Excellent taste these nurses must have. What were their names, did you say?"

"They're young enough **to be** your granddaughters! Even knocking years off your age!" smiled Cassie.

David laughed at Cassie's supposed joke. "Very amusing." He helped her on with her jacket. "Hugs and kisses to my best girl. I can hardly wait to see her." He then looked serious. "Remember not a word, don't even talk to James in the hospital about this. I'd hate Ian to be hauled over the coals. He's been marvellous…"

As David opened the door he said casually, "Oh who did Ian say had been the donor?"

"Someone from the national register," laughed Cassie. "He's nearly as good a liar as you are!"

Not quite, thought David.

"Take care," he said. "Speak to you soon." He waved Cassie off and with huge relief shut the door.

He went over to the decanter to pour himself a whisky but he had to wait a moment – his hands were shaking too much.

After the shaking subsided, he poured himself a large whisky and then telephoned Kate.

The next few days flowed into weeks and the weeks flowed into months. Exactly one year after Fiona's bone marrow transplant she was still in remission. She was so full of mischief, it was sometimes difficult to remember how ill she had been. Cassie often watched her daughter and David together. Fiona had her Pappy firmly wrapped around her little finger.

When Fiona was eleven she was finally discharged from the hospital. That was a day for celebration at The Hall and the guest of honour was definitely Ian Campbell. He and his family had become close friends and were frequent visitors to The Hall.

"I'll probably be quite tiddly," admitted Cassie to Helen as they prepared numerous canapés for the party. "I can't remember the last time I had a drink." She laughed. "Mind you, Aunt Lydia used to say that champers never counted as a drink, not something as wonderful as champagne, which, unlike any other drink, was suitable for every possible occasion. In the old days we used to have it at the drop of a hat." There was a knock at the back door and in walked Margaret and George.

"Hello you two, a little early if I may say, but lovely to see you nevertheless." She leant forward and kissed them.

"We've come to see if we can help," said Margaret.

Cassie shook her head. "You know you're getting like Mrs. P., just like her. Why can't you relax and be a guest?"

George laughed. "Not in her nature, nor mine, I'm sorry. Does Tom need a hand with the wine or is it the usual?"

"It's the usual," smiled Cassie. "I was just telling Helen about the old days and Aunt Lydia. Do you remember?"

George laughed. "Any excuse for opening the champers she'd say." He smiled fondly at the memory. "Those were the days right enough." He looked around the kitchen at the trays of canapés. "Mind you, looking at the trays over there it takes me back to Mrs. P.'s day. You're just like her, Helen." Helen looked up, a little unsure whether this was good. He smiled at her, "That's the highest compliment I can pay you lass, really it is."

"Why don't you two go up and see the children, they've got something to show you," said Cassie. "Newly decorated bedrooms. Not exactly my taste or the taste of anyone who is over the age of twenty, but their choice because we promised, I'll warn you now, dark glasses may be required!"

The party was a resounding success. Fiona made her parents promise that on each anniversary of her bone marrow transplant she had to have as wonderful a party as this one. They were only too happy to oblige and each year faithfully kept their promise.

~~~~~

David and James surveyed the scene of the dance before them. "I can't stand the noise," said James.

"Old foggey!" retorted David. They looked at each other and retreated to the library.

"I just can't believe she's twenty-one," said James. "My little girl, twenty-one. We thought she'd want a disco, rave or whatever they're called now but no, she wanted her twenty-first at home with a mixture of everyone she knew young or old. I was secretly quite pleased." A look crossed his face. "It's hard to think we nearly lost her." He looked at David. "We could have."

David nodded. "But you didn't, so come on, its party time – go and show her what you're made of, shake a leg." James looked a little bewildered. "Perhaps that's not the expression. Whatever, go and dance with your daughter."

James laughed. "That should embarrass her nicely. But then that's what parents are for, making their offspring cringe!"

David got up and shut the library door behind him. The noise really was deafening.

He poured himself a drink and sat down in the leather chair. He looked around, remembering when he had first entered this room. He tried to calculate how long ago it was and decided it was over thirty years ago; such a long time ago. It was hard to believe how changed his life had been because of that first visit. He felt himself drifting off, and allowed himself to go down memory lane but just as this state was happily descending his thoughts were interrupted by someone entering the room. David jumped. "Sorry!" said a voice. "I was looking for the bathroom!"

David slowly got to his feet. "This way young man, I'll show you."

Chapter 40

David was vaguely aware of voices. He struggled to make sense of what was being said but for some reason felt a strange reluctance to try too hard. He was then aware of something at his mouth. He tried to lift his hand to remove it but he couldn't; his arm wouldn't move. He tried to speak, no sound came out. The calm pleasant feeling of moments before was now superseded by panic welling inside him. What was happening? He opened his eyes.

"Ah you're awake, I'm just going to wipe your mouth, bit of dribble here." He felt something at one side of his mouth. "There you are," continued the voice.

David tried to focus. The voice belonged to someone in uniform. His eyes cleared; it was a uniform, a nurse. "Where the hell was he?" He tried to speak, but again, no sound was forthcoming. He hoped he could convey in his eyes the panic he was feeling but the nurse was oblivious to such subtleties.

The voice spoke again. "The doctor will be along shortly, you have a nice sleep and you'll feel ever so much better."

Patronising irritating bitch, thought David. *I will not have a nice sleep. I want to know what's going on.* He watched as a blur of white shot backwards and forwards across the room. He tried to look round but he couldn't.

Another voice spoke. "This may be a little uncomfortable for a moment, but it will make you feel much, much better." The bedclothes were folded from the feet back. This increased David's panic. Then the voice put on rubber gloves and opened a pack.

Realisation dawned, *God Almighty. They're going to catheterise me. Please God… no.* He tried to shake his head in protest but that went unheeded. He then felt a searing pain ricochet throughout his entire body for what seemed hours but was only moments. Then it stopped.

The voice looked at him as she folded back the bedclothes. "There we are, that wasn't so bad now, was it?"

Speak for your bloody self, thought David. He tried desperately to think why he was here in hospital. His last recollection was of being at home, then blackness, nothing else. He heard a beeping noise. He wondered where that was coming from. He was then aware that there were wires protruding from above the bedclothes, the beeping must be from him he decided.

The voice came back again. "Here's a lovely surprise for you."

I think I'll be the judge of that, thought David with irritation, but his irritation was quickly dispelled when into view came Cassie followed by Fiona.

To his utmost shame he felt wetness flow down one side of his face.

Cassie took a tissue out of her pocket and gently wiped his eyes, both eyes. "We're here now," she said quietly. He looked at her with gratitude and more tears flowed. Sensing his distress Cassie leant forward. "You've had a stroke, you can't help the tears, so relax, concentrate on getting better and don't worry about them." David tried to speak his thanks.

Fiona then came into his vision. She bent down and kissed him. David tried to smile back. She looked so like her grandmother with her titian-coloured hair; she was beautiful, quite, quite stunning. He looked at her intently; the last time he had been in hospital was when he had donated his bone marrow. Looking at her now, one would never have guessed how close to death she had come.

The doctor eventually arrived. He looked about ten but had the social skills of someone much younger! He directed all his conversation to Cassie and Fiona. Cassie tried on numerous occasions to make him look in David's direction but to no avail. He continued to ignore his patient and proceeded to paint a prognosis that was decidedly pessimistic.

Guess I'm on the way out, thought David, *but I've had a good innings, so can't complain*. David didn't want to be a burden to anyone, but had always assumed he'd go out on 'a high', a quick heart attack, something like that; a dribbling incontinent wreck was not the picture he had envisaged. He wanted this young upstart to leave and was contemplating how he could engineer this when Cassie asked in an ice-cold voice.

"Has Mr. Coleridge's hearing been impaired?" The young doctor looked a little bemused by the question and started to open the case notes to see if anything had been written.

"Not to my knowledge, I can't see anything written down," he replied.

"The reason I ask," continued Cassie. "Is that you have conducted your entire dissertation as regards his stroke towards me. I wondered why. If his hearing is fine I suggest you speak to him. He may not be able to reply at the moment but I think it would be a courtesy not to treat Mr. Coleridge as some uncomprehending nonentity. It's these little things that make such a difference to a patient, don't you think?" She gave him a glacial smile.

The doctor looked fleetingly at David and nodded. "I'll come back later," he muttered.

Cassie looked at David and winked. "Now David, don't listen to that moronic doctor. He hasn't a clue, probably graduated yesterday. We take each day as it comes, that's what we do. Your speech will come back, you'll see and we'll look after you. The minute you can, you come home and then 'The Family' will leap into action."

David's eyes filled with tears again which Cassie gently wiped away. "Remember that's what families are for. Think how you've looked after us for all these years." Cassie looked in the direction of her daughter. David tried to nod, he knew what she was trying to convey. She continued. "Now its our turn."

"Mum's right," said Fiona. "You'll be back to normal in no time. We'll all help."

David looked at them both. Despite the situation he was in, he felt lucky, very, very lucky. He tried to mouth his thanks.

~~~~~

The phone rang at four in the morning. Cassie and James were away from home. Fiona woke instantly and answered. "I see. I'll be straight over." She replaced the receiver and quickly threw on some clothes. She phoned her brother. He was taking a party shooting on the moors and so had by now left the house. She hoped he would check his messages on his mobile. She reached the hospital in nine minutes and ran to the ward.

"I'm sorry," said the Staff Nurse. "He's had another stroke; we thought we should call."

"My parents are away, they'll be home about lunchtime. Should I phone them?" asked Fiona anxiously.

The nurse nodded. "It might be better if they got back a little earlier."

Fiona understood what the nurse was trying to say. "You don't think he's going to get better, do you?"

"I don't think so," said the nurse as gently as possible. "He's a bit agitated and I think would be pleased to see you. Do you feel all right about going in?" Fiona nodded; she was trying to remain composed.

"We've moved him to a side room, more privacy, I'll take you."

David's agitation stopped the moment he saw Fiona and he tried to smile. She bent down and kissed him. The nurse looked at Fiona and quietly asked if she wished to be on her own. Fiona did.

She sat beside him, her hand covering his, unaware that tears were trickling down her cheeks until one plopped onto her hand. She quickly wiped her eyes and gave a sad smile. "Trying to be big and brave…" she sniffed. "Not managing very well, am I?" She took a tissue out and wiped her own eyes and then David's. "Mum and Dad are away at the conference but they'll be back this morning. They were leaving early but I've left a message for them to come straight here." She tried to smile but failed miserably.

David croaked, trying to say something. She leant forward. "Try again Pappy, I can't quite get it."

David again struggled to speak. It was imperative he made her understand. He had to and, before Cassie arrived.

Fiona bent forward so her ear was nearly touching his mouth. He uttered something more. Fiona understood one or two words but nothing was making sense. "Letters, you have letters. You want them posted?"

He conveyed his desperation at his inability to make sense. "Try again Pappy, slowly. I'll get it, just go slowly."

He tried again. "You've got letters in the house." David gave a grunt. "Do you want them?" David gave a fierce grunt, frustration welling up inside him. Fiona was perplexed, what did he want? She listened again. "Ah," she said, triumphantly, "You want me to get rid of them. Is that what you want? David grunted again, trying to nod as well. Fiona sat up. "I think I've got it. You want me to find the letters and destroy them... destroy them? She asked.

Again David grunted and looked at the picture of Cassie on his locker. Fiona followed his gaze. "Destroy them before Mum finds them. Is that right?" David grunted again and sighed.

"Are they in the sitting room?" David became agitated again. Eventually Lizzie established where she thought they were. "You want me to get rid of them now, don't you?"

David closed his eyes then opened them, but he managed to convey that yes, that was exactly what he wanted her to do. "I'll go now, right now. I won't be long." She bent over and kissed him and started to walk away, then stopped and went back to the bed. She put her mouth to his ear. "I'll never tell Mum about them. I promise."

He indicated he wanted to say something else and she listened intently "Thank you," he uttered, the words sounding miraculously clear.

With a wave she dashed out of the room, told the nurse she had to do something for him and before further explanations were needed, left. She arrived at David's and hunted in his bedroom where she thought the letters were. Eventually she found the box and opened it. It was filled with letters. She was intrigued and was dying to look at them. She opened the box and quickly flicked through some; there were airmail letters addressed to Lizzie, her grandmother, from David. They must be love letters she decided, how delightfully romantic she thought. He'd kept them all those years and didn't want Cassie to find them because her grandmother had obviously ditched Pappy for Charles, her mother's beloved Pops. "I wonder if anyone will keep my letters?" thought Fiona. She suddenly jumped up, she couldn't waste time fantasising like this; she had to get back to Pappy. She took the letters out of the box and stuffed them into her bag, zipped it shut and raced back to the hospital. Looking at the clock, she saw it was just after seven. She wondered if her parents had arrived. Parking she ran to the ward.

"Your parents arrived about twenty minutes ago," said the nurse. "There's no change."

Cassie nodded, and entered the room. When he heard the door David opened his eyes trying to focus on who had come in. It was

Fiona. She smiled and nodded to him. Her parents looked up, their faces strained as they gave her a weak smile.

"Thank you for your call," said James, giving her a kiss. He squeezed her shoulder, trying to convey his support. Fiona then went over to her mother and put her arm round her.

Her parents were both looking at David but he had only eyes for Fiona. She smiled and mouthed, 'Its okay, they're safe. I've got them'.

The relief in his eyes was evident only to Fiona. He smiled as his eyes gently closed and he breathed what sounded like a contented sigh. Beside him the machine emitted a low humming noise. They all turned their eyes to the monitor and watched in disbelief as a continuous straight line flowed across the screen.

David's death was reported in the media and Cassie's grief was eased slightly by the sense of pride she felt upon reading the obituaries. They were universal in expressing their sentiments at the loss the world of art felt upon hearing of David's death.

They were all distraught at David's death but Fiona, especially. She'd momentarily forgotten about the letters but the following day discovered them, where she had hidden them, at the bottom of her capacious bag. She knew she had to find out what had been of such importance in the letters that had caused David such anguish. She went to her sanctuary, the attic: the place of sanctuary for countless generations of the young inhabitants at Harrington Hall. Each generation had left its mark on the place and Fiona, with her panache for interior design, was no exception. She settled down on a comfy old sofa that some years previously she had cajoled her brother into helping her lift up the stairs. She put the letters in date order but was surprised to see some letters appeared to have never been sent. She'd read them later she decided.

She read through the first lot of letters, saddened at how upset David had obviously been at her grandmother's rejection of him. She couldn't understand why her grandmother had done that. "Why couldn't you have waited for him?" she asked out loud. She then progressed onto the letters that hadn't been sent.

Realisation slowly dawned at what her grandmother had written. She felt her stomach tighten and the colour drained from her face. She read and re-read the letters and then carefully folding them returned them to their envelopes. She was trying very hard to make sense of what she had read and began to wish she had never looked at them.

Her mother had obviously no idea, no idea whatsover. Fiona now realised why David had been so distressed and so anxious to make her understand what he wanted her to do. She also knew her mother would be devastated by this news. News that her beloved Pops was not really her father. *She must never find out. Never. Who else knew or, knows, I wonder?* thought Fiona.

She pondered that thought for a while then suddenly the enormity of what she knew hit her with force and the tears started to flow. She couldn't even begin to imagine how David must have felt, knowing he had a daughter, then grandchildren, but never being able to say. "To me you were the best grandfather," she said. "I loved you to bits and I'm going to miss you so much, so very, very much."

She looked at the letters lying beside her. She could not bring herself to burn then. She had to think what to do with them, but sadly no bright ideas were forthcoming. *Think clearly you idiot*, she remonstrated with herself.

She went downstairs and, deciding fresh air would clear her head, she walked down to the lakeside. Eventually, after an hour or so and with clarity of thought, she made her decision.

Her appointment was for 7.00 p.m. Fiona had managed to leave the house without raising suspicions of where she was going. She arrived five minutes early and, checking that no one saw her, went in.

At exactly seven o'clock Fiona was ushered into the office of Mr. Sharp. She explained what she hoped to do and asked if he had any objections. He had none. He then asked her to follow him and led her to the Chapel of Rest where David was lying. Mr. Sharp said he would leave her for a few moments.

Fiona had never seen a dead body before, and so a little hesitantly, and with some degree of trepidation, went forward to the open coffin and looked in. Tears trickled down her face as she bent over and kissed David's ice-cold cheek.

Lifting the side of the coverlet, she placed all the letters she had tied neatly in a blue ribbon. "Goodbye Pappy. I do so hope I've done the right thing... I really do... but I didn't know what else to do with them."

She turned and went to the door. Mr. Sharp, followed by another man, came in and went over to the coffin and lifted the lid securing it in place. The coffin was then taken out to the waiting hearse for transport to the church where David would lie overnight.

The next day was dull and grey, as befitted the sombre mood. After the church service David was taken to the chapel at Harrington and then laid to rest in the family graveyard.

At Fiona's request, David was buried next to her grandmother.

Chapter 41

Epilogue – Twenty Years Later

"It's getting cold," said Fiona. "We should get back."

Kate nodded. "I know. I just wanted to be here today, on the anniversary, but you're right, it's getting chilly."

Fiona bent down and wrapped the rug firmly round Kate's legs, then released the brake on the wheelchair.

"Five more minutes Fiona, just five more minutes please."

Fiona put on the brake again and looked at Kate. She was now a frail old lady who found solace in sitting beside the graves. The graves of all 'The Family'. She had once said she had more of her family buried than she had alive and Fiona supposed she was right.

Fiona looked at the names on the gravestones of the many people she had heard of but had never met, starting with the head of this dynasty, Charles, then her grandmother, Lizzie and Aunt Lydia. She had a hazy recollection of Mrs. P. but had heard so many stories about her that she felt she knew her better than she really had. She looked at all the other names including Robert and he and Kate's daughter, Hattie, who had been killed in a car crash some years previously; then David's grave, her beloved Pappy. Fiona often wondered if Kate had known about David. Fiona looked over at Kate who immersed in her own thoughts, was oblivious to her gaze.

Lastly she looked at the freshly inscribed stone, the reason for their visit today. Tears pricked her eyes and she looked back at David's grave. "I kept my promise Pappy, she never knew. At least she never knew from me," she added.

It was the first anniversary of her mother's untimely death at seventy-three from cancer. Her father, inconsolable, could still not bear to visit the grave of his beloved Cassie and in truth, just longed for the day when he could join her. Fiona shivered. She bent down to Kate. "We should really go back."

Kate nodded and took hold of Fiona's hand. "She was a wonderful lady your mother. I miss her very much."

Fiona nodded in agreement. "Me too."

"And your grandfather…" added Kate. "A remarkable man, truly remarkable."

"Which one?" asked Fiona gently.

Kate's head shot back and her eyes met Fiona's. "What did you say?"

Fiona knelt down beside Kate. "You know what I said. Which one? I often wondered if you knew. I'm sorry, but for some reason I just had to know but saying it like that was unfair of me."

"Did your mother know? Did Cassie know?" asked Kate anxiously.

Fiona shook her head. "Never from me, I promised Pappy and I kept that promise. Do you think she knew?"

Kate looked over at Cassie's grave. "I don't think so because I think I would have known." Kate looked at Fiona. "Whether she should have known, I don't know, but what we did, all those years ago, we did for the best." Kate hesitated, unsure whether to say any more. "Did David tell you?"

"Not exactly," replied Fiona, "I actually read the letters."

Kate looked in horror at what Fiona had just said. "What possessed David to give you them? Were you not hurt or… oh I don't know, did you not feel betrayed or something. What **did** you feel?"

"When I read them I can't remember what emotions I felt, to be honest," said Fiona.

She then proceeded to tell Kate about the hospital ward and how David had struggled to make Fiona understand what he wanted her to do before her parents arrived. Fiona tried to smile reassuringly to Kate. "In some ways I thought it was quite romantic; a secret kept for all those years. I really can't remember feeling hurt or betrayed or anything. It was just fact, in black and white, and I suppose I just accepted it. Nothing else I could do was there?"

"I suppose not," agreed Kate. She shivered and for a moment looked deep in thought again. "Let's go back."

"Will you tell me about that time?" asked Fiona as she manoeuvred the chair. "I'd like to know."

"Yes, I'll tell you, you deserve that," agreed Kate.

They went back down the hill, past the chapel and through the grounds to the cottage where Kate now lived. She was fiercely independent and insisted on living on her own, which she did with a considerable degree of success, only occasionally being aided by the next generation of 'The Family' when they were allowed!

Kate then proceeded to tell Fiona of the revelations which had occurred at The Hall over fifty years ago. "David would have been about your age when he found out. He was a dashing looking chap. Mind you he was good looking until his dying day." She smiled fondly, remembering her friend. "I digress... I'll start when your grandfa..." Kate stopped herself. "When Charles found out."

Fiona listened, enthralled as the story unfolded. "So only the five of you knew; you, Pappy, Aunt Lydia and my gran..." she smiled at Kate. "When I found out, I then never knew what to call Charles. I think after what you have said I'll revert back to grandfather. David will always be Pappy." A sadness crept into her eyes. "I wish I could have spoken to him about it." She looked into the fire watching the glowing embers. "But he had you, thank goodness he had you."

"We all had each other," smiled Kate. She then looked pensive. "May I ask you something?"

"Certainly, fire away," replied Fiona without hesitation.

"What happened to the letters? Did you burn them?" Kate looked intently at Fiona.

"No," smiled Fiona. "For some reason I couldn't do that. The night before Pappy's funeral I took the letters to the chapel of rest. They're in beside him. The undertaker knew I was putting in something but didn't ask what. In front of me he then put the lid on the coffin, then a special seal to assure me it wouldn't be tampered with. I did check at the service that the seal was still there and it was." Fiona sighed. "I hope that wasn't wrong, I just thought that seemed the right thing to do!"

Kate patted Fiona's hand, "You're right, you are a romantic and absolutely, it was exactly the right thing to do." Looking at the clock on the mantelpiece Kate reached for her stick, stood up and went over to the drinks table. "Drinkie-poo time, I think. Care to join me?" Fiona nodded.

"As the truth is now out, there is one more thing I have to tell you. I probably shouldn't, but I'm going to." She handed Fiona her glass.

"I'm intrigued," smiled Fiona taking a sip.

Kate sat down again. "Remember when you were little and so desperately ill?" Fiona nodded. "Well, David, apart from being the one person who could cheer you up," Kate suddenly laughed. "Remember when he shaved his head?"

Fiona smiled. "I thought he was the greatest for doing that. Totally mad and completely wonderful."

"Well," Kate continued again. "He did something even more wonderful. It was he who donated his bone marrow for you."

Fiona stared at Kate as if unhearing, "But," she stammered, "I thought it was someone from the register, Mum always said that. Surely Pappy was too old?"

"He was," smiled Kate. "But a small thing like his age wasn't going to deter him. He told Ian that he really was your grandfather and so he just had to be tested. He was, of course, telling him the truth and Ian knew that this was your last chance so he had to try. He did and David was an excellent match. His age certainly was against him, but it worked… by some miracle it worked."

"How did Pappy explain that to Mum?" Fiona was finding this story even more difficult to comprehend than the previous one. "Wasn't she suspicious?"

Kate laughed. "He was masterful in this, he did a double bluff to her. Your mother had heard nurses say that David was the donor." Kate tutted. "Deeply impressive confidentiality!" She shook her head. "So your mother went to confront him but he told her that he had lied to Ian and said that he was your grandfather because he couldn't bear not being considered as a donor just because of his age. I confess to thinking when he practised his speech to me, that your mother would find this a little far-fetched, but he was obviously most convincing, for she never voiced any doubts because he made her promise not to tell a living soul in case Ian got into trouble. She didn't. Goodness me, your mother and I shared most secrets but not that one, certainly not that one!"

Fiona had tears in her eyes. "Thank you for telling me." She stared into space for a few moments contemplating all she had heard. "You know, I always felt especially close to Pappy, maybe that was why." She wiped her eyes and smiled. "Who knows."

She was about to stand up, then decided against it and sat down again. "I never told Christopher. I always wondered if I should have. After all, here he is, Lord Emerson, the so-called rightful heir to Harrington but he's not really. Is he?"

Kate shrugged her shoulders. "Remember what I said about your grandfather changing the Constitution. He knew your mother wasn't his own flesh and blood, but in his eyes she would always be his daughter, and as such, he considered her the rightful heir to Harrington, as her son now is."

Kate smiled across at Fiona. "I'm just an old lady whose advice you don't need but I think we should leave well alone. Christopher, even as a little boy, was born to the job. He loves it and I think we should take our secrets to the grave with us. That's what I think."

"I agree," nodded Fiona. "But I just wanted you to reassure me that my instinct had been right." She got up and kissed Kate on the cheek. "What a wonderful friend you were..." she smiled. "And... still are... To think you've kept that secret for over fifty years without breathing a word to anyone. In some ways that is amazing."

Kate looked at Cassie's daughter with fondness. "Perhaps you're right, but by the same token so have you." She smiled. "That's what 'family' is all about; looking after each other. Anyone looking at the graves beside the chapel would be surprised to see the assortment who lie there, but to me, each and every one was family and I feel so lucky and privileged to have been part of such a wonderful and caring group of people."

"Mum always said you were the lynchpin of 'The Family'," smiled Fiona.

"Really?" said Kate. "I'm surprised, I never thought of myself as that."

"I agree with her," smiled Fiona. "You're the one we've all gone to with our problems and Mum said you and my grandfather had a special relationship; that you were his confidant. Any problem he would say, 'I'll speak to Kate'."

Kate looked wistful as she fingered her brooch, the one she always wore, the one she got from Charles all those years ago. "It was mutual, remember." She suddenly laughed. "Mind you, it was usually some crisis regarding your mother that we talked about. She was quite something your mother, quite something." Tears pricked her eyes. "I still miss her so much, so very, very much." She looked at Fiona. "How selfish of me, she was your mother and I know how dreadfully you miss her, but it just doesn't seem right that she's away before me, not right at all."

Fiona patted Kate's hand. "Don't say that, Mum wouldn't think that. She'd probably say its because you still have to keep an eye on us all and how right she would be! Now, no more maudlin moments. Remember you have to keep going for at least another few years. Your 100th birthday party will be the highlight of The Hall."

Kate smiled. "I'll try." She looked at the clock. "Now, off you get home to that family of yours and I'll see you on Saturday for the party." Kate shook her head. "You know I find it amazing to think you have a daughter of eighteen. You don't look old enough." Fiona smiled her thanks.

"I've enjoyed our reminiscences, thank you," added Kate.

"So have I," replied Fiona. "And thank you for telling me about Pappy. I'm so glad you did. Lots of things make sense now, fit into place I suppose." Fiona picked up her things. "Can I get you anything before I go?"

"Nothing thank you, I can manage," smiled Kate. "Can you let yourself out?"

"Certainly," smiled Fiona. "Speak to you tomorrow. Bye."

Kate heard the front door shut. She shivered slightly; it was getting cold. She got up and drew the curtains. I think I'll have a little more inner warmth as well she decided and went to refill her glass. She placed another log on the fire and then settled down with another brandy.

It had been a strangely comforting afternoon she thought. She was glad Fiona knew everything, for Kate now felt that some burden had been lifted from her by having shared this long kept secret. Such memories: so many happy memories of times at The Hall. She took another sip of brandy, letting her mind drift further and further back to those early days.

She felt so tired, inexplicably tired, but the feeling was not an unpleasant one, for it was a tiredness associated with having accomplished something; something that had been on her mind for all those years. She continued gazing into the fire, deep in thought, nursing her glass.

Her eyes started to close and the glass dropped from her hand onto the carpet. She did not stir. Minutes later her eyes opened for a moment and she smiled. "Robert!" she exclaimed with delight.

That was the last word she uttered.

~~~~~

When Kate's son Charlie arrived later in the evening, he knew the moment he entered the room, that she was dead. He went over to where she sat, picking up the fallen glass and, placing it on the table beside her, he knelt before her.

He looked at his mother, tears welling up in his eyes. "You look so at peace..." he said quietly. "Even happy." He leant forward and kissed her gently on the cheek. *I wonder...* he thought, as he moved a piece of stray hair from her eyes. *I wonder why you were smiling?*

Charlie sat with his mother for a little while, reflecting on her life, holding her cold limp hand acutely aware of the contrast of the warmth of his own hands.

Eventually he slowly got to his feet. Wiping his eyes he looked down at his mother and found himself smiling. "No doubt... even as I speak, Cassie will have cracked opened the champers to welcome you. I hope so... I so very much hope so."